When careers tear lives apart,
despite the best intentions . . .

IRRESISTIBLE FORCES

Also by Danielle Steel

THE HOUSE	THE GIFT
TOXIC BACHELORS	ACCIDENT
MIRACLE	VANISHED
IMPOSSIBLE	MIXED BLESSINGS
ECHOES	JEWELS
SECOND CHANCE	NO GREATER LOVE
RANSOM	HEARTBEAT
SAFE HARBOUR	MESSAGE FROM NAM
JOHNNY ANGEL	DADDY
DATING GAME	STAR
ANSWERED PRAYERS	ZOYA
SUNSET IN ST. TROPEZ	KALEIDOSCOPE
THE COTTAGE	FINE THINGS
THE KISS	WANDERLUST
LEAP OF FAITH	SECRETS
LONE EAGLE	FAMILY ALBUM
JOURNEY	FULL CIRCLE
THE HOUSE ON HOPE STREET	CHANGES
THE WEDDING	THURSTON HOUSE
IRRESISTIBLE FORCES	CROSSINGS
GRANNY DAN	ONCE IN A LIFETIME
BITTERSWEET	A PERFECT STRANGER
MIRROR IMAGE	REMEMBRANCE
HIS BRIGHT LIGHT:	PALOMINO
The Story of Nick Traina	LOVE: POEMS
THE KLONE AND I	THE RING
THE LONG ROAD HOME	LOVING
THE GHOST	TO LOVE AGAIN
SPECIAL DELIVERY	SUMMER'S END
THE RANCH	SEASON OF PASSION
SILENT HONOR	THE PROMISE
MALICE	NOW AND FOREVER
FIVE DAYS IN PARIS	PASSION'S PROMISE
LIGHTNING	GOING HOME
WINGS	

DANIELLE STEEL

IRRESISTIBLE FORCES

A Dell Book

IRRESISTIBLE FORCES
A Dell Book

PUBLISHING HISTORY
Delacorte Press hardcover edition published November 1999
Dell mass market edition published November 2000
Dell mass market reissue / June 2006

Published by Bantam Dell
A Division of Random House, Inc.
New York, New York

This is a work of fiction. Names, characters, places, and incidents either are the product of the author's imagination or are used fictitiously. Any resemblance to actual persons, living or dead, events, or locales is entirely coincidental.

Library of Congress Catalog Card Number: 99025488

ISBN-13: 978-0-440-24346-5
ISBN-10: 0-440-24346-7

Printed in the United States of America
Published simultaneously in the United States and Canada

www.bantamdell.com

OPM   10 9 8 7 6 5 4 3 2 1

IRRESISTIBLE
FORCES

Chapter 1

IT WAS A brilliantly sunny day in New York, and the temperature had soared over the hundred mark long before noon. You could have fried an egg on the sidewalk. Kids were screaming, people were sitting on stoops and in doorways, and leaning against walls beneath tattered awnings. Both hydrants on the corner of 125th Street and Second Avenue had been opened, and water was cascading from them, as squealing children ran through it. There was an ankle-deep river running through the gutter. At four in the afternoon, it seemed as though half the neighborhood was standing around in the heat, talking and watching the kids.

And suddenly, at four ten, shots rang out in the noise of the talk and laughter and the sound of rushing water. They weren't an unfamiliar sound in that part of town, and everyone stopped as they heard them. People seemed to pause motionless for a moment, waiting for what would come next. They pulled back into doorways, shrank against walls, and two mothers ran forward into the geyser of water from one of the hydrants and grabbed their children. But before they could regain the safety of the doorway, another burst of shots rang out, this time louder and closer, and three young men ran into the midst of the crowd standing near the hydrant. They knocked over kids as they ran, and hit a young woman so hard she fell sprawling in the water, and suddenly there were screams as two cops appeared, running around the corner, in hot pursuit of the young men, guns drawn, bullets flying into the crowd.

It all happened so fast, no one had time to clear a path for them, or to warn each other, and in the distance there were already sirens. And over the distant wail of police cars approaching the scene, there was another round of gunshots, and this time one of the young men fell to the ground, bleeding from his shoulder, at the same time one of his companions wheeled and shot a police officer cleanly through the head, and suddenly a little girl screamed and fell to the ground in the fierce spray from the hydrant, and everyone nearby was shouting and running in all directions, as her mother ran to her from the doorway where she'd been watching in horror, as the child fell.

And an instant later, the chase was over. Two of the young men were lying facedown on the ground being handcuffed by a flock of policemen, an officer lay dead, and the third suspect was being tended to by paramedics. But only a few feet away, a child lay dying from the bullet that had hit her. It had passed cleanly through her chest, and she was bleeding profusely, as her mother knelt next to her, soaked by the continuing spray from the fire hydrant, and sobbing hysterically as she held her unconscious child in her arms, and the paramedics wrested the five-year-old girl from her. Within less than a minute, she was in an ambulance, and they pulled her mother in with her, still crying and dazed. It was a scene all of them had seen dozens of times before, if not hundreds, but one that only meant something when you knew the people at the core of the drama, the perpetrators, or the victims. The ones who got arrested, or those who got injured or killed.

There was a vast tangle of cars at the corner of 125th, as the ambulance tried to disengage from them, with siren screaming and lights flashing. And people stood on the street looking stunned by what had happened. A second ambulance took the injured suspect from the scene, and blue and white cars seemed to come from everywhere as they heard on the radio that an officer was down. People in the neighborhood knew what it would mean for them once word got out that he had been killed. Tempers would flare, and smoldering resentments would burst into flame. Worse yet, in the deadly heat, anything could happen. This was Harlem, it was August, life was tough, and a cop had been murdered.

And in the ambulance, as it sped downtown, Henrietta Washington clung to her child's hand, and watched in silent terror as the paramedics fought for her life. But for the moment, it didn't look like they were winning. The little girl was gray and still and her blood was everywhere, the floor, the sheets, her arms, the gurney, her mother's face and dress and hands. It looked like a slaughter. And for what? She was another casualty in the endless war between the cops and the bad guys, gang members, drug dealers, and narcs. She was a pawn in a game she knew nothing about, a tiny sacrifice among warriors whose goal was to destroy each other. Dinella Washington meant nothing to them, only to her friends and neighbors, her sisters, and her mother. She was the oldest of four children her mother had had between sixteen and twenty, but no matter how poor they were, nor how tough life was for them, or the neighborhood in which they fought to survive, her mother loved her.

"Is she gonna die?" Henrietta asked in a strangled voice, her huge eyes looking into those of a paramedic, and he didn't answer. He didn't know.

"We're doing what we can, ma'am." Henrietta Washington was twenty-one years old. She was a stereotype, a number, a statistic, but she was so much more than that. She was a woman, a girl, a mother. She wanted more than this for her kids. She wanted a job, wanted to work, wanted to be married to a good man one day, who loved and took care of her and her children. But she had never met a man like that. Her kids were all she had for the moment, and she had nothing to give them but her love.

She had a boyfriend who took her to dinner once in a while, with three kids of his own to support. He hadn't been able to find a job in six months, and drank too much when he took her out. There were no easy solutions for either of them, just welfare, an odd job from time to time, and a hand-to-mouth existence. Neither of them had finished high school, and they lived in a war zone. And the life they led, and where they lived it, was a death sentence for their children.

The ambulance screeched to a stop outside the hospital, and the paramedics raced out with Dinella on the gurney. She had an IV in her arm, an oxygen mask over her face, and all Henrietta knew was that she was still breathing, but barely. She ran into the emergency room after her, in her bloodstained dress, and she couldn't even get near her little girl. A dozen nurses and residents had closed around the child and were running down the hall with her to the trauma unit, as Henrietta followed, wanting to ask someone what was happening, what they were going to do. She wanted to know if Dinella would be all right. A thousand questions raced through her head as someone stuck a clipboard and pen in front of her face.

"Sign this!" the nurse said bluntly.

"What is it?" Henrietta looked panicked.

"We have to operate—fast—sign it!" Henrietta did as she was told, and a second later, she was standing alone in the hallway, watching other gurneys rush past, and nurses and doctors in hospital scrubs hurry toward operating rooms and other patients. She felt completely lost and terrified as she stood there and began to sob in total panic. And a nurse in green hospital pajamas came toward her and put an arm around her. She led her to a little cluster of chairs, sat her down, and crouched beside her to reassure her in a gentle voice.

"They're going to do everything they can for your daughter." But the nurse had already heard that the child was in very critical condition and not likely to survive.

"What are they going to do to her?"

"They're going to try and repair the wound and stop the bleeding. She lost a lot of blood before she got here." It was a massive understatement. Just looking at the condition the child's mother was in, they both knew how dire the situation was. Henrietta was covered with blood.

"They shot her . . . they just shot her. . . ." She didn't even know if it was the police or the men they'd been chasing who had done it. It didn't matter now. If Dinella died, what did it matter who had killed her? Good guys or bad.

As the two women held hands and Henrietta cried quietly with a look of despair, the nurse could hear the PA system paging Dr. Steven Whitman. He was second in command in the trauma unit, and one of the best men in trauma in New York, and she said as much to Henrietta. "If anyone can save her, he will. He's the best there is. You're lucky he's on call." But Henrietta didn't feel lucky. She had never felt lucky in her entire life. Her father had died when she was a child, gunned down in a street fight just like this one. Her mother had brought her and her sisters and brothers to New York, but their life here was no different. They had just taken their troubles from one place to another. But nothing much had changed. If anything, their life in New York was worse. They had moved to New York so their mother could find better work, but she hadn't. All they had found was the tough life they lived in Harlem, a life of poverty and no hope for a better tomorrow.

The nurse offered Henrietta some water or a cup of coffee, but she just shook her head and sat miserably in her chair, still crying and looking as terrified as she felt, as a huge wall clock ticked away the minutes. It was five minutes to five by then.

And at five o'clock sharp, Dr. Steven Whitman ex- ploded into the operating room, and was rapidly filled in by the resident who'd been in charge until he arrived. Steve Whitman was tall and powerful and intense, with short dark hair and eyes that looked like two black rocks in an angry face. It was his second gunshot wound of the afternoon, the previous one had died at two o'clock, a fifteen-year-old boy who had managed to shoot three rival gang members before they shot and eventually killed him. Steve had done everything he could to save him, but it was too late. At least Dinella Washington had a chance. Maybe. But according to the resident, it was a slim one. Her lung had been perforated, and the bullet had grazed her heart before it exited, and caused an extensive amount of damage. But even listening to the grim recital, Steve Whitman was not willing to give up hope yet.

Steve barked orders at them for an hour, as he fought to keep the child alive, and when they started losing her, he massaged her heart himself for more than ten minutes. He fought like a tiger to keep her going. But the deck was stacked against them. The damage had been too great, the child too small, the odds too slim, the evil forces more powerful than even his expertise or his scalpel. Dinella Washington died at 6:01 as Steve Whitman let out a long grim sigh. Without a word, he walked away from the operating table, and pulled his surgical mask off with a look of fury. He hated days like this, hated losing anyone, particularly a child who was nothing more than an innocent victim. He had even hated losing the boy who had shot three people before they killed him. He hated all of it. The uselessness of it. The waste. The despair. The pointless destruction of human life. And yet when he won, as he often did, it all seemed worthwhile, the long hours, the endless days that ran into even longer nights. He didn't care how long he stayed or how hard he worked as long as he won some of the time.

He threw away his surgical gloves, washed his hands, took off his cap, and looked in the mirror. What he saw was the fatigue of the last seventy-one hours he had spent on duty. He tried to work no more than forty-eight-hour shifts of being on call and on duty. It was a nice thought, but it rarely worked out that way. You couldn't exactly punch a time clock in the trauma unit. And he knew what he had to do now. He had to tell the child's mother. A muscle tensed in his jaw as he walked out of the surgical area, and headed toward where he knew the child's mother would be. He felt like the Angel of Death as he walked toward her, knowing that his was a face she would never forget, at a moment in time that would haunt her for the rest of her life. He remembered the child's name, as he did all of them for a time, and knew that he would be haunted as well. He would remember the case, the circumstance, the outcome, and wish it could have been different. As little as he knew his patients, he cared about them above all.

"Mrs. Washington?" he asked, after a nurse at the desk had pointed him in her direction, and she nodded, her eyes full of fear. "I'm Dr. Whitman." He had done this for a long time, too long he thought sometimes. It was all becoming too familiar. He knew he had to say it fast, in order not to hold out a hope he could no longer give her. "I've got bad news about your daughter." There was a sharp intake of breath as Henrietta saw his face, his eyes, and knew even before he said the words to her. "She died five minutes ago." He gently touched her arm as he said it, but she was unaware of his touch or even his compassion. All she had heard were his words . . . she died . . . she died. . . . "We did everything we could, but the bullet did too much damage both on entry and exit." He felt both foolish and cruel giving her those details. What difference did it make what the bullet had done and when? All that mattered was that it had killed her child. Another casualty in the hopeless war they lived. Another statistic. "I'm so sorry." She was clutching at him then, her eyes wild, fighting to breathe after the impact of the news he had just dealt her like a blow. It was as though he had hit her with a fist in her solar plexus. "Why don't you sit down for a minute?" She had stood up to hear the news as he approached her, and now she looked as though she were about to faint. Her eyes rolled, and he lowered her back into the chair, and signaled to a nurse to bring her a glass of water.

The nurse brought it quickly, and the child's mother couldn't drink. She made terrible, airless, strangled sounds as she tried to absorb what he had told her, and Steve Whitman felt as though he had been the killer, instead of the man with the gun. He would have liked to be the savior, and sometimes he was. There were wives and mothers and husbands who threw themselves around his neck with gratitude and relief, but not this time. He hated the losses so much. And too often, the deck was stacked against him.

He stayed with Henrietta Washington for as long as he could, and then left her to the nurses. He'd been paged again, for a fourteen-year-old who had fallen out of a second-story window. He was in surgery for four hours with her, and at ten thirty he walked out of the operating room, hoping he had saved her, and finally

made it to his office for the first time in hours. It was
the quiet part of the night for him, usually the really
bad cases didn't start to come in till after midnight. He
grabbed a cup of cold coffee off his desk, and two stale
Oreo cookies. He hadn't had time to eat since breakfast. He'd been on duty officially for forty-eight hours,
and had done another forty-eight as a favor to one of
his colleagues whose wife was in labor. He was long
overdue to go home, but hadn't been able to break
away until then. He had a stack of papers on his desk to
sign, and he knew that as soon as he did, he could go
home. There was already another doctor on duty to
take his place. And as he heaved a long sigh, he
reached for the phone. He knew Meredith would still
be up, or maybe even still at the office. He knew how
busy she'd been for the past few weeks, and he wasn't
sure if she'd still be in meetings, or if she'd finally gone
home.

The phone rang once, and she answered. Her voice
was as calm and cool as Meredith herself. They were a
good balance for each other. She had always matched
Steve's volcanic intensity with her own special brand of
silky smoothness. No matter how crazy things got, Meredith always seemed to stay calm in the heat of crisis.
She was quiet and elegant and cool. Her entire being
was a contrast to her husband.

"Hello?" She had suspected it would be Steve, but
she was in the midst of a huge deal, and it could have
been someone in her office calling her at that hour.
She had in fact gone home. Meredith Smith Whitman
was a partner in one of Wall Street's most respected
investment banking firms, and highly respected in her
field. She lived and breathed and ate the world of high

finance, just as Steve was totally engulfed by his work in trauma. And they each loved what they did. For each of them, it was an all-consuming passion.

"Hi, it's me." He sounded tired and sad, but relieved that she had answered.

"You sound beat," she said, sympathetic and concerned.

"I am." But he smiled as he heard her. "Just another day at the office. Or three of them actually."

It was Friday night, and he hadn't seen her since Tuesday morning. They had lived that way for years. They were used to it, and had long since learned how to work and live around it. She was all too familiar with his crazy two- and three-day shifts, the emergencies that dragged him back to work only hours after he finally got home. But they each had a healthy respect for the other's work. They had met and married when he was a resident and she was in grad school. It had been fourteen years, and sometimes, to Steve at least, it seemed more like weeks. He was still as crazy in love with her as he had been in the beginning, and theirs was a marriage that worked well for both of them, for a variety of reasons. They certainly didn't have time to get bored with each other, in fact they hardly had any time at all. And with their two all-consuming careers, they had never had the time or the inclination to have children, although they talked about it from time to time. It was an option neither of them had entirely ruled out yet.

"How's your big deal going?" he asked her. For the past two months she had been working on the prospectus for the initial public offering of a high-tech venture in Silicon Valley. They were going to take the company public and sell stock to people buying shares in the company. It was a hot deal for Meredith's firm, and fascinated her, although it wasn't as prestigious as some of the bond offerings they did. But Meredith was much more interested in the firms in Silicon Valley, and the opportunities they presented than their more traditional deals in Boston and New York.

"We're getting there," she said, sounding a little tired. She'd been at the office until midnight the night before. It was easy for her to do that when Steve was working. He knew she was going to lead the road show for the IPO, to tell potential investors about the company and encourage them to invest, in the next month, and she'd be gone for a couple of weeks. He was hoping they'd be able to spend some time together before that, and he was going to take time off to be with her on the Labor Day weekend. "I've almost finished the red herring." He knew the jargon, it was a term they all used for the prospectus, and it was called that because of the red caution-warnings required by the SEC along the outer edge of the prospectus. "When are you coming home, sweetheart?" she asked, stifling a yawn. She had just gotten home from the office, and it was nearly ten thirty.

"As soon as I sign some stuff they left for me. Have you eaten yet?" He was more interested in her than the forms he had to sign, as he sat sprawled in his office, staring at the papers on his desk.

"More or less. They threw me a sandwich a few hours ago, at the office."

"I'll make an omelette when I get home, or do you want me to pick something up?" Despite their heavy work schedules, Steve was usually the one who did the cooking, and he liked to brag that he cooked better than she did. And he obviously enjoyed it more. Meredith had never claimed to be particularly domestic. She'd rather eat a sandwich or a salad at her desk, than come home and whip up a four-course dinner. And he liked cooking a lot more than she ever had.

"An omelette would be great," she smiled, listening to him. Their time apart always made her miss him, even when she was busy. Theirs was an easy, comfortable relationship, and an attraction that had never dimmed, even in the fourteen years they'd been married. They were still passionately devoted to each other, despite their demanding careers and hectic lives.

"So what happened today?" She could always hear in his voice when things hadn't gone well. They knew each other better than most people did, and cared a lot about each other's victories and defeats.

"I lost two kids," he said, sounding depressed again. He couldn't help thinking of the young black woman who had lost her daughter five hours before, and how much he would have liked things to come out differently for her. But he was a doctor, not a magician. "A fifteen-year-old kid who got in a shoot-out against a rival gang. He managed to hit three of them before he went down, but they killed him. And a little girl a few hours ago. She was an innocent bystander in a shoot-out between three kids and the cops in Harlem. They shot her in the chest. We operated, but she didn't make it. I had to tell her mother, the poor woman was devastated. And after that, I operated on a fourteen-year-old who fell out a second-story window. She's in lousy shape, but I'm pretty sure she's going to make it." Meredith would have hated doing what Steve did, the constant agony of the patients he saw, the despair, the losses, the heartbreak. She knew all too well what it did to him, and she could hear the toll it had taken.

"Sounds like a miserable day, sweetheart . . . I'm sorry. Why don't you come home and relax? You need it." He hadn't been home in three days, and he sounded exhausted and disheartened.

"Yeah, I need a break. I'll be home in about twenty minutes. Don't go to bed till I get there." She smiled at the warning.

"There's no danger of that. I came home with a full briefcase."

"Well, park it somewhere when I get there, Mrs. Whitman. I want your full attention." He was dying to see her. Going home to Meredith was like being on another planet from his work and all the responsibilities he had there. She was a refuge for him, a breath of fresh air and normalcy and health, a safe haven from the brutality and violence he dealt with every day. And he could hardly wait to see her. He didn't want to come home and find her asleep or working.

"I promise you will have my full attention, Doctor. Just get your ass home." She grinned and he smiled, envisioning her, as beautiful and sensuous as ever.

"Pour yourself a glass of wine, Merrie, and I'll be there in a few minutes." He was always optimistic about time, but she knew that about him.

As it turned out, he walked in the door of their apartment nearly forty minutes later. The chief resident had needed a quick consultation with him before he left, about a broken hip and pelvis on a ninety-two-year-old woman, and the fourteen-year-old who'd fallen out the window had developed complications.

But Steve knew better than anyone that it was time for him to go home. He was beyond exhausted. He finished the paperwork on his desk, and signed out for the weekend. He didn't have to be back on duty at the trauma unit until Monday, and he could hardly wait to get out, he'd had it. Enough was enough. He was so tired by the time he left, he could hardly think straight.

He hailed a cab just outside the hospital and was home ten minutes later, and as he let himself into the apartment, he could hear soft music playing, and smell Meredith's perfume. It was like coming home to Heaven after three days in hell. His time with Meredith was what he lived for, but she knew he loved his work too, just as he knew how much she loved what she did.

"Merrie?" he called out to her, as he unlocked the door of the apartment, but there was no answer. She was standing in the shower when he found her, long and lanky, and blond and incredibly beautiful and graceful. She had modeled for extra money when she was in college. They had both gotten through school on scholarships. Both of them were only children, and both of them had lost their parents while they were in college. Hers in a car accident in the South of France on the first real vacation her parents had taken in twenty years, and his to cancer within six months of each other. For years now, they were not only husband and wife, but they were the only family each had, and as a result they meant everything to each other.

And as she saw him, she smiled broadly, turned off the shower, and grabbed a towel. Her shoulder-length blond hair dripped water on her breasts, and her green eyes were sexy and warm. She was as happy to see him as he was to see her when he kissed her and pulled her close to him soaking wet. He didn't care how wet she was, he just wanted to hold her.

"God, what you do to me when I come home like this . . . you make me wonder why I ever go to work."

"To save lives of course," she said as she put her arms around his neck and glued herself to him. She made him feel refreshed and alive again, better than a vacation or a night's sleep. He kissed her, and in spite of the grueling seventy-six hours he had just spent at the hospital, he was instantly aroused by her. She had a powerful effect on him, and had since the day they met.

"What do you want first? Me, or the omelette?" he asked with a boyish smile, and she looked at him with feigned consternation.

"That's a pretty tough choice. I was beginning to get hungry."

"Me too," he grinned. "Maybe the omelette first, and then I'll hop into the shower, and we can celebrate the fact that we're both here for the night. I was beginning to feel like they were never going to let me out. Thank God I'm off for the weekend. I can't believe we've actually got two days to spend together." But her eyes clouded as soon as he said it.

"I get the feeling you've forgotten I'm leaving for California on Sunday." She looked instantly apologetic. She hated leaving when he was off, it was so rare that they got a whole weekend together. As second in command in the trauma unit, it was pretty common for him to work weekends. And when he was off during the week, she had to be at the office. "I've got to go back out to meet with Callan Dow one last time before the road show. We're getting down to the wire, and I want to go over the prospectus one more time with him in California." She was meticulous about every detail.

"I know, don't worry about it. I forgot." He tried not to look disappointed, as he watched her towel-dry her hair, and then left her to go to the kitchen and cook them the omelette he had promised.

She joined him wearing a white cashmere bathrobe five minutes later. Her hair was still wet, her feet were bare, and he could glimpse that she was naked underneath the bathrobe.

"If you flash me, I'll burn the omelette," he warned, pouring the mixture into the pan with one hand, and then pouring himself a glass of white wine with the other. She didn't say anything, but he looked drained. There were dark circles under his eyes, and a worn look that came from three nights of no sleep. "It's good to be home," he said, turning to look at her with a tired smile and unconcealed admiration. "I missed you, Merrie."

"I missed you too," she said, putting her arms around him as she kissed him. And then she sat down on a high leather stool at their kitchen counter. Their apartment had a sleek New York look that seemed more Meredith's style than his. There was something very stylish about her, and everything about her exuded the aura of competence and success. Steven had the rumpled, disheveled look of a harried overworked doctor. It had been weeks since he'd had time to get a haircut and he hadn't shaved in two days. He looked younger than his forty-two years, and it was hard to tell in scrubs what he would look like dressed. He was wearing mismatched athletic socks, and a battered pair of clogs that were comfortable for him to work in. It was hard to imagine him in a blazer and gray flannels and a tie, although he looked terrific when he wore them. But most of the time when he wasn't working, he wore faded jeans and T-shirts. Most of the time, he was too tired to think about wearing much else.

"So what are we going to do tomorrow, other than sleep and make love and stay in bed until dinner?" he said, smiling at her mischievously as he set the omelette down in front of her on a plate on the granite counter. Their kitchen was all beige and white, and looked like a magazine layout.

"All of the above sounds good to me, except I have to drop by the office to pick up some papers. And then come home and read them. They're for the meeting in California," she said apologetically, with a look of regret.

"Can't you read them on the plane?" He looked disappointed as he devoured his half of the omelette.

"I'd have to fly to Tokyo to do it. I won't work longer than I have to, I promise."

"That sounds ominous," he smiled, as he poured them each another glass of wine. It felt great to be off duty. He had no responsibilities to anyone except his wife. He couldn't wait to get to bed and make love to her, and then sleep until noon the next day. "So tell me about work. How's your IPO coming?" He knew how much her work meant to her, and her eyes danced with excitement as she answered.

"It's going to be fantastic. I can hardly wait till the road show," she said, referring to the due diligence tour where they sold the opportunity to potential investors. "I just know this is going to go over big. I talked to

Dow this morning, and he's like a little kid waiting to hit a home run in the play-offs. He's a nice guy. I think you'd like him. He's built the company up from nothing, and he's deservedly proud of it, and now he's taking it public. It's like a dream come true for him. It's exciting showing him how it all works."

"Make sure that's all you show him," he admonished, pointing at her with his fork, as she leaned toward him and he could see one creamy white breast exposed within her bathrobe. She laughed at what he was saying.

"This is strictly business," she said confidently. For her, it always was.

"For you maybe. I just hope the guy is short, fat, and ugly and has a girlfriend who screws him blind. Sending you on the road with a guy is like waving fish at a porpoise . . . pretty damn tempting, sweetheart." He looked at her admiringly. It was impossible not to notice how spectacular looking she was, and he was sure the men she worked with weren't oblivious to it either. Better yet, she was smart, and fun to be with. And she had not only held his interest for fourteen years, but still aroused his passion. No matter how tired he was, he was always anxious to get her into bed, and she loved that about him.

"Believe me, all these guys think about is their business," she reassured him. "And Callan Dow is no different. This is his baby. His dream come true. The love of his life. He wouldn't notice if I looked like Godzilla. Besides," she smiled at her husband, "I love you. I don't care if he looks like Tom Cruise, you're the guy I'm in love with."

"Good." Steve looked pleased, and then glanced at

her with concern. "But now that you mention it, does he?"

"Does he what?" She looked baffled by the question. She was tired too.

"Look like Tom Cruise. Does he?"

"Of course not." She laughed, and then teased him a little. "More like Gary Cooper. Or Clark Gable."

"Very funny." It was true, but she didn't press the point, it was of no importance to her. "He'd just better look like Peter Lorre, or they can send some other partner on the road show with him. Besides, two weeks is too long, and I'll get too lonely. I hate it when you're gone that long."

"So do I," but that was not entirely true, and they both knew it. If the IPO was exciting enough, and she cared about the company, she loved it. She thoroughly enjoyed her business, and taking companies public. "Ten cities in two weeks is not exactly a vacation."

"You love it, and you know it." He finished his wine, and sat back to look at her admiringly. She looked relaxed and beautiful and sexy. And he felt in desperate need of a shave and a shower. He knew he looked a mess. But when he was at the hospital, how he looked was the last thing on his mind. It only mattered when he came home to her, and even then, sometimes he was too exhausted to get dressed.

"Sometimes I love the road shows. Not always. When they're good, they're a lot of fun, and a lot of work. It depends on the company. But this one's a good one. The stock is going to go through the roof." Steve knew they made high-tech medical diagnostic equipment, some of which the CEO, Callan Dow, had invented himself. Steve knew from Meredith that Callan Dow's father had been a small-town surgeon and had wanted his son to be a surgeon too. But instead, Callan had been fascinated by business and high-tech inventions, and had set up his company to make high-tech surgical instruments instead. Steven knew his products and had been impressed with them, but he wasn't particularly interested in the stock, no matter how impressive Meredith said the company was. Steve let Meredith handle all of their finances, after all it was what she did best. And he knew nothing about it.

She put the dishes in the dishwasher. Steve went to take a shower, and a few minutes later, she turned off the lights and met him in their bedroom. It was well after midnight, and they were both tired, and he found her in bed a few minutes later. He slipped into bed next to her, and she smiled as he took her in his arms and held her close. She could easily feel how much he wanted her, and it was entirely mutual. She kissed him, and then gave a soft moan as he began to caress her. And within minutes both the hospital, and her public offering were forgotten. All that mattered just then was the private world that they shared and thrived in.

Chapter 2

ON SATURDAY MORNING, when Steve woke up, Meredith had already left for the office. She thought she could get downtown and back before he woke up. But he was sitting in a towel, fresh from the shower, reading *The New York Times* when she walked back into the apartment in white slacks and a white T-shirt, carrying her briefcase.

"You don't look old enough to be an investment banker," he said with a smile when he saw her, and she set her briefcase down next to the couch. She looked happy and relaxed; the night before had been as good as it always was, maybe even better. Their sex life had always been four star, and they both enjoyed it, when they saw each other, which was always too rare. Sometimes she wondered if their erratic schedules kept the romance alive for them, and made them hungrier for each other than most couples were after fourteen years of marriage.

"How about going out to lunch?" It was still hot, but

he was longing to get out in the air, and go somewhere with her. "Tavern-on-the-Green?"

"That would be fun," she said, feeling only slightly guilty. She had to get her reading done, but she knew she could always do it later. She knew how much he needed relief and distraction after being on duty for three days. He needed a counterpoint to the misery he saw there, and he expected her to join him. She didn't have the heart to tell him that she needed to work.

He made a reservation and at noon they went out hand in hand, and were startled by how much hotter it had gotten. The heat of the New York summer was stifling, and it was so humid they could hardly breathe as they left the building.

They took a cab to the restaurant and enjoyed each other's company over lunch. She told him more about the offering she was working on, and he listened with interest. He liked hearing about what she did. It was her one and only passion for the moment, but he loved that about her. She was amazingly single-minded and relentlessly focused when she was working on something. It was part of why she was so good at what she did, that and the fact that she had extraordinarily good judgment. She was respected at her firm for it, although Meredith sometimes felt she didn't get the same opportunities the men did. She'd been a partner of the firm for the past four years, but more often than not, she did the lion's share of the work, and the truly creative things, and one of the male partners got the glory. It was something that had irked her for years, but it was also the nature of some of the firms on Wall Street. She worked for what was called a "white shoe" firm, where the men kept the control of the power in their exclusive little world. It was a very old guard way of doing business, and she knew it had its limitations for her. She had chosen to work in a man's world, and to conquer their mountaintops, and they didn't always thank her for it. In fact, she was going to the West Coast with one of the more senior male partners the next day, and she was annoyed that he had insisted on coming with her. At first, no one else had wanted to work on this deal with her, and now that they sensed how important it was going to be, they were trying to climb on the bandwagon with her. But at least Callan Dow knew she had championed his cause right from the beginning.

Meredith and Steve talked about some of his problems at the hospital over coffee. He had been the number-two man in the trauma unit for the last five years, and he was itching to run it. Harvey Lucas, the man in charge, threatened regularly to move on, but he seemed to be going nowhere. He'd been talking about moving to Boston for several years, but he just couldn't seem to tear himself away, and Steve's hands were tied until he did. He had to content himself with being the assistant head of the department. But it was the best trauma unit in the city and he had no desire to leave. And Lucas was a good friend to him.

After lunch, Steve and Meredith took a leisurely stroll through the park, listening to the steel bands and the jazz musicians, as they wandered past the model boat pond, and watched the children play. They still talked about having children from time to time, but the prospect seemed to get more remote to them every year. Lately, Steve had been talking about it a lot, but Meredith was still not yet ready to listen. And she wasn't sure she ever would be. At thirty-seven, she was beginning to think that there would never be room in their lives for children. They were both too busy with their careers. Meredith had always been afraid that a child would somehow come between them, rather than bring them closer, as Steve was so sure it would. The very thought of a baby made Meredith feel threatened. She didn't want to be torn between a baby and her job.

The heat was still deadly, and they were both tired when they got back to the apartment, and sprawled out on the couch side by side.

"How about a nice cool air-conditioned movie tonight, after I make us some dinner?" Steve looked happy and relaxed and like a different man than the one who had practically crawled into their apartment the night before after three and a half days on duty. All he had needed to revive him was some time with Meredith and a night's sleep. He already felt better and more alive.

"I can't go to the movies, Steve." She looked at him regretfully. "I have to pack, and I haven't even started my reading." She'd been out with him all afternoon.

"That's too bad," he said, looking disappointed, but he was used to it. She almost always brought work home from the office with her. "What time are you leaving?" he asked, as he sprawled out on the couch. He was wearing khaki pants and a blue shirt, and bare feet in loafers, and Meredith thought he looked unusually handsome. He would have looked better still with a tan, but he never had the time to get one. And his pale angular face somehow made his dark hair and eyes seem even darker and more intense.

"I'm on a noon flight," she explained. "I'll have to leave here around ten."

"There goes Sunday," he said, but there was nothing either of them could do about it. Business was business, and she had to see Callan Dow in California. Steve understood that.

He watched TV that night while she worked in the small den she used as an office. It was crammed with his medical books, and books she kept on recent rulings of the SEC, and an assortment of medical texts, finance books, and novels. Her computer was set up there, and Steve had one of his own, but seldom used it. In some ways, their interests were widely divergent, and always had been, and yet they were each intrigued by the other's field. But Steve always laughed about the fact that he knew virtually nothing about finance. She had a better grasp of what he did, and considerably more interest in it. But at the same time, he had a healthy respect for the fact that she earned a better living. She earned a big salary, which was something he knew he never would in his line of work. And she chafed at the fact that she didn't make more than she did, and felt she should have. But they had more than enough for their comfortable lifestyle. They had lived in the same apartment for the past five years, it was a co-op and Meredith had paid for it in full when she became a partner. Steve would have liked to contribute to it, but just plain couldn't. The disparity in their incomes had never been an issue between them, it was something they both understood and accepted. Unlike other couples, they never fought about money, just about whether or not to have kids.

She read until nearly midnight that night, and Steve was asleep in front of the TV when she finally finished. He had drunk half a bottle of wine, and was feeling relaxed and content. Meredith packed her suitcase before she woke him. It was one o'clock by then, and he was in a sound sleep when she kissed him, and he stirred.

"Let's go to bed, sweetheart. It's late. And I have to get up early tomorrow," she said softly. She knew he had called a friend that afternoon, and was going to play tennis with him after she left for the airport.

Steve followed her sleepily into the bedroom, and a few minutes later, they were in bed, with their arms comfortably wrapped around each other. And five minutes later, he was snoring. They both slept soundly until six A.M., when the phone rang. It was the hospital for him. Harvey Lucas, the head of the trauma unit, was in surgery with the chief resident and two other doctors, working on four victims of a head-on collision, and they needed Steve to come in. He could refuse if he wanted to, since he wasn't on call, but he knew from what they said that they needed someone there right away, and he didn't want to let them down. He never did. And with a glance at Meredith, he told them he'd be there as soon as he could. Two of the victims were children, one was a severe head injury, and the pediatric neurosurgeon was already on his way in. The parents were both in critical condition, and they weren't sure yet if the second child would make it. His neck was broken and they thought he had a spinal cord injury. He had been in a coma since they brought him in.

"I hate to leave before you," Steve said as he climbed into jeans and pulled on a clean white T-shirt.

He would change into scrubs in the hospital, and he slipped his bare feet into the clogs he wore at work.

"That's okay," she smiled sleepily at him, she was used to it, they both were. "I have to get up pretty soon anyway."

"So much for tennis, or a leisurely Sunday. I should be able to get back in a couple of hours." It was wishful thinking on his part, they both knew, and she'd be gone by then anyway. Meredith knew that once he was at the hospital, he'd stick around, and check on his other cases, and he probably wouldn't be home before midnight, if then. He might even stay overnight if there was enough for him to do, and he'd just go back on duty anyway the next morning. Although Meredith would be back Tuesday morning, he wouldn't be off duty till Wednesday, and she wouldn't see him till late that night.

"I'll call you from California." She wasn't even sure where she was staying. Callan Dow had said he'd make the arrangements for her.

"Just make sure Cary Grant, or Gary Cooper, or whoever the hell you said he looked like, doesn't sweep you off your feet while I'm saving lives." He smiled, but she could see a mildly worried look in his eyes. He was obviously concerned about Callan Dow.

"You don't need to worry," she said, as he sat on the edge of the bed next to her, and kissed her.

"I hope not." He gently touched her naked breast with his hand as they kissed again, and he looked at her with regret before he left. "I was hoping to make love to you before we both went back to the wars." But this was the story of their lives, and always had been, deferred hopes and canceled plans, postponements and promises and rain checks. They were used to it and most of the time it didn't upset them.

"Hold the thought. . . . I'll see you Wednesday night when I get back from the office. I'll try not to stay late." She knew he was coming off duty then.

"That's a date." He smiled at her, clipped his pager on his belt, and ruffled his hair with one hand rather than combing it. He had brushed his teeth, but didn't bother shaving. His was not a job that required him to look elegant or well groomed, and most of the time he didn't bother to try. He had more important things to think of. "Have a good trip," he said with a last wave from the doorway, and an instant later she heard the front door close, as she lay in their bed, thinking about him. He was exactly as he had been fourteen years before when they met and he was a resident. His whole life revolved around what he was doing, just as hers did. And as she lay there, she began thinking of the company she was going to be taking public, and everything she still had to do to assure that it would go smoothly.

She got up and brought a stack of papers back to bed with her, and read for two hours before she got up, and she was satisfied that she was nearly prepared for her meeting in California. She still had a few last questions to ask, and mostly she wanted to brief Callan Dow on what to expect when they went on the road. He had never taken a company public before, he was a novice at all this and he looked to her entirely for advice and information. In some ways, it made her feel both competent and important, and then for an instant, she felt a little guilty for it. She wondered sometimes if she enjoyed what she did because it made her feel powerful and independent. She loved what she did and the world of high finance she existed in. It was a world she had reveled in since the first moment she'd been in it, just as Steve was passionate about what he did. In some ways, they were so different, and yet they both loved their jobs, and knew they were doing something that mattered to people. Although Steve was saving lives, she was helping people achieve what they had worked so hard for years to accomplish, and that wasn't negligible either, although it was very different from what Steve did.

The phone rang while she was getting dressed, and it was Steve. He had just come out of surgery with the child with the broken neck, and the orthopod had said that he'd be fine eventually. He'd been very lucky, and Steve had assisted in the surgery and said he was going to hang around for a while. They had lost the mother shortly after he got there, and the older child was still in a coma. It was the usual drill, although every case that came along seemed like the most important one in his life, and she smiled as she listened to him. He was as excited about what he was doing as she was about going to California to go over the prospectus and the road show with Callan Dow.

"I'll miss you, Merrie," he said, and she smiled, thinking about him.

"Me too." She said and meant it, and he laughed when he heard her. He knew her better.

"Yeah, for about ten minutes. All you're going to be thinking about is your red herring and your book and your road show. I know you."

"Yeah, you do, don't you." While she was getting

dressed, she couldn't help thinking of what he'd said. He knew her as well as she knew him, their respective passions for their work, their goals, their weaknesses, their fears. Their total involvement in their work, which was why they had never had children. Where was the place for them, with him at the hospital for three days at a time, and her traveling all over the place for business? What would a baby get out of a life like theirs? Not much, she felt sure, which was why, so far at least, she had refused to have one. She was good at what she did, she was sure of that, and she was a lot less sure that she would be a good mother. Maybe later, which was what she always told Steve. But much later would be too late, and they both knew it. She wondered if she'd regret putting it off one day, but for the moment, she just couldn't see it. And as she put the rest of her papers back in her briefcase, and buttoned the jacket of her suit, she caught a glimpse of herself in the mirror. She looked as starched and impeccable as Steve had looked rumpled when he left the apartment at six that morning. He didn't have to look any better than that to stand around in the operating room or evaluate patients as they came in on the brink of death. All he had to do was be there and know what he was doing, and he didn't have to look good to do it. Meredith had to exude efficiency and competence and control in everything she did, and look the part, and she did, as she picked up her briefcase and left the apartment. She had her laptop and her cellular with her, and the final draft of the prospectus she'd been working on with the lawyers.

And as she headed for the airport in a cab, to meet Paul Black, the partner who would be traveling with

her, she glanced out the window at the New York sky-
line, thinking about how much she loved her life there.
There was, in fact, absolutely nothing she would have
changed about her existence. As far as Meredith was
concerned, it was perfect.

Chapter 3

MEREDITH WORKED ON her laptop for a while on the plane, and finished reading the material she had prepared for Callan. Paul Black, the partner she was traveling with, slept for most of the trip, and they chatted for the last half hour about the next morning's meeting. He was confident that she had laid all the groundwork properly, and as always, he was sure she would impress the client with everything she had organized for him.

Black had actually brought the client in, but Meredith's expertise in high-technology fields had led him to turn Callan Dow over to her. One thing they could always be sure of with Meredith was that they could be certain she knew what she was doing. He said as much to her on the flight but she was irritated by the fact that she thought he sounded condescending. She always half expected him to punctuate his sentences to her with "girlie." Paul Black was one of the senior partners of the firm, and he had never been one of Meredith's favorite people. She thought he spent most of his time boasting of his social connections and resting on his laurels, neither of which were pastimes Meredith indulged in. His original tie to Callan Dow had been a social one through one of his wife's brothers. But after landing him, like a giant fish, Black had done very little about it. It was Meredith who had done all the work so far in taking Dow Tech public.

The plane landed at three fifteen, and Callan Dow had a town car meet them at the airport. He had booked them into Rickie's in Palo Alto, which was close to his office. And once settled there, Paul Black left her to have dinner with friends in San Francisco. Wherever they went, he seemed to have connections, and he didn't invite Meredith to join him.

She was just as happy to stay at the hotel, and go over her material for her meeting with Dow again, and when the phone rang at eight o'clock, she was sure it would be Steven. Knowing him, he was probably still at the hospital, and she had left her phone number on his voice mail.

"Hi, sweetheart," she said as she answered the phone. No one else knew where to find her.

"Hi, sweetheart to you too." The voice on the other end was deep, and he was laughing when he answered. But it wasn't Steve, it was a voice she didn't recognize at first, and she was startled. "How was the flight?"

"Fine. Who is this?" For once, she was slightly off balance.

"It's Callan. I thought I'd make sure you were comfortable and you liked the hotel. Thanks for coming out. I'm looking forward to our meeting."

"So am I," she smiled in embarrassment, "I'm sorry . . . I thought you were my husband."

"I figured. Are we all set?"

"Just about. I want to show you the final draft of the red herring, and go over a few final details for the road show."

"I can hardly wait," he admitted to her. For all his expertise and sophistication and success in the business world, he sounded like a kid he was so excited. He had worked hard building his company, and the challenge of taking it public had been a long time coming. "When do we begin?"

"The Tuesday after Labor Day. Everything is pretty much set up, except for a few final details in Minneapolis and Edinburgh. The other cities are all pretty well locked in. I really think we're going to be oversubscribed. Everyone is excited about you, there's already been a lot of talk about it."

"I wish I'd done this sooner," he said in a voice that was an intriguingly low rumble. His voice was deep and in other circumstances she'd have called it sensuous, but all it sounded to her now was warm and friendly. She had enjoyed working with him all summer.

"I think the time is right now, Cal. If you'd done it sooner, you might not have been ready."

"Well, the time seems to be right now, Meredith. Although I'm still having trouble with my CFO. He's still fighting me about taking the company public. He believes I should have kept ownership myself," he said to her apologetically. He knew how hard she had worked on the public offering, and how little help she'd gotten from his CFO. He had resisted her every step of the way.

"That's a pretty old-fashioned point of view," she said, smiling. They both realized that it was going to be difficult traveling with Charlie, because of that, for two weeks.

"He's already complaining about the trip."

"Don't worry. We'll get him on the bandwagon tomorrow. I'll let Paul Black talk to him, he's about as conservative as they get, and even he's excited."

"Where is he now? I thought you two might be having dinner."

"Actually, he went to dinner with friends in San Francisco. I was going over the red herring one last time, and some notes for tomorrow."

"You work too hard. And are you telling me he left you all alone? Have you had dinner?"

"I had room service an hour ago, and I'm fine. Believe me, I brought plenty of work with me." She always did that. Meredith never went anywhere without her briefcase. Steven always teased her about it.

"What about breakfast tomorrow, Meredith? I thought maybe we should get together before you come to the office."

"That sounds fine. What about seven thirty here at the hotel? I saw a dining room when we checked in. I'll leave a message for Paul tonight, and we can all meet there tomorrow morning." She was all business, and anxious to get going, as he was. "Do you want to bring your CFO?" It seemed an appropriate question.

"Actually, I'd like some time with you without him. We can meet him at the office."

"Fine. I'll see you in the morning then."

"Don't work all night, Meredith. We'll have time to

get it all done tomorrow." He sounded almost fatherly as he said it. He was still a young man, but some fourteen years older than she was. He was fifty-one years old, and he barely looked older than her husband. Callan Dow was what everyone expected men to look like in California, healthy, energetic, suntanned, and good looking. But her only fascination with him was with his business. Nothing else about him intrigued her.

"See you tomorrow," she said, and after they hung up, she left a message for Paul on his voice mail and told him about the breakfast meeting in the morning. And after that, she took a shower and went to bed. She tried calling Steven again, but he didn't answer her page, and she assumed correctly that he was too busy with patients. And when he finally did return her call, she was sound asleep and he woke her. It was two o'clock in the morning in California.

"Hi, baby. . . . Did I wake you?"

"Of course not, Paul and I were just sitting here playing poker." Her voice was sleepy, but he was too wired to hear it.

"Really?"

"Yeah, sure . . . you know what a fun guy Paul is."

"Sorry . . . I didn't mean to wake you. It's five o'clock here, and I've been in surgery since midnight. I just got your message when I came out."

"How'd it go?" She yawned sleepily as she asked him.

"We won this one. For once. A drunk driver hit a seven-year-old and gave him a hell of a headache. But he's going to be fine, he's got a couple of broken legs, and his rib cage is a mess, but there's no permanent damage." One of his ribs had pierced his lung, but Steven had done some fancy footwork, and some very intricate repairs.

"What was he doing out at midnight?"

"Sitting on a hydrant. It's hot here."

"Did you ever go home?" she asked with another yawn, as she rolled over in bed and glanced at the clock. It was late, but she was glad to hear him.

"Nothing to go home to. I thought I'd just stay here and sleep. I've got to be back here anyway in three hours."

"You're the only human I know who works harder than I do, Steven Whitman."

"You taught me everything I know on that score. So how's it going? Did you see your client?"

"Not till breakfast tomorrow morning . . . or in a few hours, I guess. But I'm ready. I finished all my work on the plane. I spoke to him tonight, and he sounds pretty wound up." She was awake then, and couldn't help wondering if she'd get back to sleep again before morning. She had too much to think about now that Steve had gotten her going again.

"I guess I should let you get back to sleep. . . . I just wanted to tell you that I love you, and I miss you."

"I miss you too, Steve," she smiled into the darkness, holding the phone, thinking of him. "I'll be back before you know it."

"Yeah, and I'll be trapped here, like a rat in a cage, as usual. Do you ever think about how crazy our life is?" he inquired, staring into space at his end, thinking about her. They were both so goddamn busy. Sometimes far too much so, but he also knew that she enjoyed what she did, and so did he.

"I was mulling it over today when I left. I was thinking how impossible it would all be to juggle if we had kids. We could never lead the life we do now, Steve. I guess that's why we never had one."

"We could manage if we had to. Other people do, who're just as busy as we are." He sounded wistful as he said it.

"Name two," she said doubtfully, "name one for that matter. I can't think of anyone who lives like we do. You're never home, for days at a time, and I'm always on the road or in the office. What a great life for a kid. We'd have to wear name tags that said 'Mom' and 'Dad' so they'd recognize us when they finally saw us."

"I know, I know . . . you think we're not ready. I'm just afraid that by the time you think we are, I'll be too old to do it."

"You'll never be too old to 'do it.' " She laughed at him, but she knew he was serious about the subject, far more so than she was. She just wasn't ready to think about having children, and still wasn't sure she ever would be. She couldn't imagine fitting them into their already overburdened existence. And the idea had begun to appeal to her less and less over the years, although she hated to disappoint him. She knew how much having kids meant to him. And she hadn't closed the door on the subject permanently. But it was never something she was aching to do.

"We'll have to have a serious talk about this again one of these days, Merrie."

"Not until I take Dow Tech public," she said, sounding surprisingly alert. His talking about their having kids always made her defensive. But there was always some company she was taking public, some IPO that was the most important thing in her life at the moment, some company that needed her help, some deal she had to make, some road show she had to finish. In fourteen years, there had never been a right time for her to think about it, and he was beginning to think there never would be. And he had a real sense of loss when he thought that they might never have children. But he had always wanted children more than she did. He felt the lack of family more than she, she always said that he was all the family she ever needed.

"I'd better let you get some sleep, Merrie, or you'll be dead on your feet tomorrow." He knew she had a long day ahead of her, and she was taking the red-eye back to New York, and would be landing in New York at six A.M. Tuesday morning. And knowing her, she'd go home, shower and change, and be at her office by eight thirty.

"I'll call you tomorrow when I can," she promised, stifling a yawn, hoping she'd get a few hours' sleep before she had to get up at six thirty.

"Don't worry about it. I'll be here. You know where to find me."

"Thanks for calling," she said with another yawn. "G'night. . . . I love you." They hung up then, and it took her half an hour to get back to sleep, thinking about him, and then her meeting with Callan Dow in the morning. And it seemed like only minutes later when her alarm went off and woke her.

She got up and showered and dressed and did her hair in a neat French twist that seemed appropriate for her meeting. She had brought a dark blue linen suit with her, and she looked impeccable when she appeared in the dining room, in the suit, high heels, and pearl earrings, carrying her briefcase, at precisely seven thirty. And although she was unaware of it herself, she made a stunning impression. She looked more like a model posing as an executive, and several heads turned as she walked swiftly to the table where Paul Black was waiting. He had on a dark gray summer suit, a standard white shirt and conservative tie, and looked just like what he was, an investment banker from Wall Street.

"How was your dinner last night?" she asked him politely as she sat down, and ordered a cup of coffee.

"Very pleasant. It's a long drive to the city though. I came back later than I thought I would. You were smart to stay here." She didn't point out to him that he hadn't offered her an option, and went on to tell him about her call from Callan Dow the night before.

"He's very pleased about everything we've done to set up the trip."

"He should be. I think it's going to be a good one, from everything you've told me, Meredith. I think it's going to go very well for them."

"That's what I told him." But before she could say more, she saw Callan Dow standing in the dining room doorway and glancing around the room, looking for them. And he looked exactly as she had remembered. He was tall, well built, a handsome man with sandy hair, lively blue eyes, and an athletic air about him. He was almost too good looking, and although she knew he originally came from the East, he looked very California. He had a deep tan, and was wearing a blue shirt, a blue and yellow Hermès tie, and a well-cut khaki suit, with well-polished loafers. He looked like a *GQ* ad, and her description of him to Steve, as a Gary Cooper look-alike, seemed more apt than ever. He spotted them quickly and came over with a broad smile, and he shook hands with both of them with a look of pleasure.

"It's nice of you both to come out here," he said easily, taking a seat at the table, and a minute later they ordered breakfast. He ordered scrambled eggs and a bowl of fruit, and Meredith opted for toast and coffee. Paul was having eggs benedict and oatmeal.

They talked animatedly about the deal and his plans, and the due diligence tour, and Meredith calmed any fears he had, addressed all his latest concerns, and handed him the red herring, which he skimmed quickly while he drank his second cup of coffee.

"Looks like we're just about up and running."

"We'd better be. We start in Chicago two weeks from tomorrow." They had chosen to start the trip there because it was a less important city for them, and would give them a chance to get the kinks out of their presentation. From there, they were going to Minneapolis, and then on to L.A. and San Francisco. He was going to spend the weekend at home, while she flew back to New York. And on the Monday after that, they were going to meet in Boston, make their final presentation in New York, and then on to Europe. She had already set it up for the most part in Edinburgh, Geneva, London, and Paris. And then her job would be over. She hoped that the syndicate they would have formed would have dissolved, and his stock would be sold over the counter on the burgeoning electronics market. His eyes danced like a child's as they talked about it.

And as they chatted over the last of their breakfast, he commented again on the problems he was having with his chief financial officer, Charles McIntosh. He was still dragging his feet about taking the company public, and it was obviously a source of serious annoyance to Callan. Because of his objections to Callan's goals for the company, he was determined to cooperate as little as he could get away with.

"I've had a hell of a time convincing him we're doing the right thing. And I know he believes he's right when he tries to dissuade me. He's a good guy, and I've known him for years. He is incredibly loyal, but he's also unbelievably stubborn," Cal said, looking worried.

"He'd better get on the bandwagon before we start the road show," Meredith said with a look of concern. "It's going to worry people if he sounds like a dissenting voice, or looks as though he has reservations about it. People aren't going to understand that his objections are personal, and could misinterpret his position," she said firmly.

"Don't worry, Meredith, if he does that, it won't be a problem."

"Why not?" she asked with a look of surprise.

"Because I'll kill him," Callan Dow said with a rueful laugh. "We've worked together for years, and he's basically a grouch. He's just one of these people who's always heading upstream when everyone else is swimming downstream. He's a hell of a smart guy, but some of his ideas are back in the dark ages." Callan had such clear visions for his company. But he was younger than Charlie, and incredibly forward thinking.

"I'm not sure he's your greatest asset," Meredith said, smiling at him. She trusted Callan's judgment, and his ability to handle his people. He hadn't come this far by being a poor judge of horseflesh. And if he said he could control his CFO, she had to trust him on it.

"Actually, Meredith," he admitted to her as Paul Black signed their check, "I don't disagree with you, but that's another matter. For now at least, he'll be fine. I can't look too far into the future. He's been with me for a long time, and I'm hoping he'll come around on this one." Meredith nodded, and the three of them left the restaurant and walked out to the parking lot together. Callan had a car and driver waiting for him, to take the three of them to the office. And they chatted easily on the way about his company, his house nearby, and his three children. She had forgotten that he had kids, and was surprised when she heard him talk about them. It was evident from what he said that they lived with him, and she wondered where his wife had gone, if she had died or they were divorced. But it struck her as odd that a man as successful as he in the business world would be single-handedly bringing up his children. He had said that all three of them had been at his house at Lake Tahoe for the summer, and he had just brought them home with him for this business meeting, and they were going back for the weekend. He said he liked to keep them with him.

"I usually take the month of August off to be with them. But this summer, I seem to be commuting." There had been a lot to do at his end, and from what Meredith could see, so far, he had done all his homework. And she was even more impressed when they got to his office. Everything was impeccably prepared, and all the information she and Paul could possibly have wanted had been analyzed for them. As she had been before, Meredith was enormously impressed with his knowledge of technology, and the way he ran his business.

The only fly in the ointment, as the day went along without a hitch otherwise, was Charles McIntosh. He seemed to have a thousand unfounded objections to everything they were doing. What's more, he was highly suspicious of them, and even less pleased that the IPO was being handled by a woman, although he never actually came right out and said so. But he made it so plain to everyone that when he left the room finally, Callan Dow turned to her and apologized for him.

"I'm afraid Charlie is a dyed-in-the-wool chauvinist, Meredith, and there isn't a damn thing I can do about it." Cal actually looked embarrassed and she laughed it off graciously, although more than once he had seriously annoyed her.

"Don't worry, I'm used to it," she said quietly. "Paul isn't our most liberated partner either." In fact, the two had gone off together to continue their own conversation in Charlie's office, leaving Callan and Meredith alone to clean up the final details. Traveling with Charlie was going to be a real pain in the neck, she knew, but at least while Callan was around, she knew he wouldn't say anything too inappropriate about the company going public. She could see that he was mildly afraid of alienating Callan. But he certainly was no fun to be with, and could barely bring himself to endorse the project. "You'll have to keep control of him on the road show."

"Charlie will be all right," Cal said optimistically. "And the truth is he loves the company, and wants what's good for it, even if he doesn't agree with me. He's extremely loyal, even if he is painfully short-sighted."

"I'm surprised he let you do it at all."

"He had no choice," Callan said firmly, and she could sense in the way he said it that Callan wouldn't have tolerated anything less than Charlie's full support, and the CFO obviously knew that. "But I'm sorry if he's a thorn in your side."

"I've dealt with worse. I can handle a little chauvinism. He doesn't frighten me. I just don't want him giving people the wrong impression."

"He won't. I promise."

The four of them had lunch together in the conference room, and after that, Charlie offered to give Paul a tour, and ignored Meredith completely, which suited her to perfection. She was just as happy spending the rest of the afternoon with Callan, polishing up the risk factors for the red herring. And by the time the two older men returned, Meredith and Callan had done everything they needed, and it was nearly five thirty.

"What time is your flight?" Callan asked her with a look of concern. He hadn't even thought of it till then, they had worked straight through since lunchtime, but they had done everything they wanted to accomplish, and Meredith was extremely pleased with their meeting. There were no remaining unanswered questions. And even Charlie McIntosh seemed to have relaxed a little by the time she and Paul were ready to leave the office. Paul seemed to have won him over.

"We're on the red-eye," Meredith explained, glancing at her watch. They had several hours to kill, and didn't have to leave for the airport till eight thirty.

"What about an early dinner?" Callan Dow suggested, but Meredith didn't want to impose, or tie up more of his time than she had to.

"We'll be fine," she assured him. "Paul and I have plenty to talk about. We can have dinner at the hotel, and then leave for the airport."

"I'd much rather take you to dinner," he said, graciously including Paul in his invitation. Charlie McIntosh had left them by then, and had been barely civil to Meredith when he said good-bye to her. It was almost as though he were jealous of her, and her influence on Callan. He really did have a problem with her, and Callan seemed to be as aware of it as she was. Charlie blamed her for making it possible to take the company public. He had told Cal repeatedly that once they had stockholders, Cal would lose control of the company, and he saw that as a potential disaster for them. He overlooked entirely the enormous influx of money and opportunities that selling stock would bring them. And more than anything, Charlie saw Meredith as the source of all their potential future problems. And he was unrelentingly angry at her for it. He had long since chosen to forget that it was not Meredith's idea to take Dow Tech public, but Callan's.

"Do you like Chinese food?" Cal asked Meredith directly, and she nodded, still hesitating, but while she was trying to decline gracefully, Paul happily accepted, and the three of them left the office together to have dinner.

And as it turned out, it was a very pleasant evening. After working together since early that morning, the three of them felt completely at ease with each other. And even Paul relaxed and seemed less condescending than usual. And he told some very funny stories about old road shows. By the time Callan dropped them off at the hotel, the three of them felt like old friends, and Paul and Meredith were sorry to leave him.

"I'll see you in two weeks," Callan said with a broad grin as he shook her hand in the lobby before he left them.

"Call if you have any questions," she encouraged him, "or if you're worried about something."

"I'm probably too ignorant about all this to even know what to worry about." He laughed good-naturedly, and like Meredith, he looked as impeccable at eight o'clock that night as he had at seven thirty in the morning. They had that same kind of effortless style and impeccable neatness in common. With their blond hair and light eyes, and similar style, they looked almost like brother and sister. And he waved easily as he left them, and strode across the lobby to the car waiting for him outside. He had promised to send the car back in a few minutes to take them to the airport. He was going back to the office to pick up his Ferrari. Meredith had noticed it in the parking lot at Dow Tech that morning and wondered who it belonged to. It was bright red and convertible, and very striking.

"He's a nice guy," Paul Black said, sounding almost surprised as they went back up to their rooms to pick up their luggage. "You'll have a good time with him on the road show. He's got a great sense of humor."

"Yes, he does," she agreed easily, "and he knows

what he's doing, which is refreshing. And he's not afraid to admit it when he doesn't.'' Although she suspected he probably had a big ego in some ways, humility at the appropriate times was one of his strong suits, and it was more than a little unusual in his business.

"I think you'll do just fine with this, Meredith," Paul said, and they left each other to pick their bags up in their rooms and met in the lobby again half an hour later. She had called Steve, but he was unavailable as usual, and she left a message on his voice mail. And half an hour later, she and Paul were on their way to the airport.

The plane left on schedule, and she worked for a while, while Paul fell asleep beside her. And eventually, she turned off the light, put her papers away, and closed her eyes, and the next thing she knew they were landing at Kennedy and it was six o'clock in the morning. And just as Steven had predicted, she took a cab home, showered, and changed, and by eight thirty, she was at her desk, in her office, writing up notes from her meeting with Callan Dow, and working with the lawyers to put the finishing touches on the prospectus.

Steve called her at the office at noon, between surgeries, and he was pleased to know that she had returned safely.

"I like knowing you're back in town," he said with a relieved tone. "When I know you're that far away, I really miss you," but she couldn't help wondering what difference it really made, since they couldn't see each other anyway. Sometimes it felt as though she and Steve existed on different planets. His world seemed so far from hers and when she thought about it, it made her feel lonely. But she couldn't think about that now.

She had too much to do, taking Dow Tech public. She talked to Callan Dow later that afternoon, and he was ecstatic about their meeting the day before. He was flying high on the thrill of what they all knew was coming.

"It won't be long now," she encouraged him, feeling like a mother hen waiting for a chick to hatch. But the truth was that her clients and their companies were the children she had never had. They were her babies, and the only ones she wanted for the moment. She would never have said it to Steve, but she suspected that she didn't have to. He knew that, just as he knew everything about her.

And as she sat at her desk late that night, finishing her work on Dow Tech, she glanced out the window into the New York night, and thought about her husband. He was in the trauma unit somewhere, saving a life, or comforting a child, or reassuring a mother. It seemed like such noble work to her. And yet, for her in her heart of hearts, she still thought that what she did was more exciting. She loved everything about it. She thought of calling him then, but she knew she probably wouldn't get him anyway, so she didn't bother. She stayed at her desk until two A.M., and then with a satisfied smile, she left her office, locked her door, and went downstairs to hail a cab, carrying her briefcase. This was the only life she knew, everything she loved, and all that she wanted.

Chapter 4

IN THE NEXT two weeks, Steve and Meredith hardly saw each other. She was at her office until nearly midnight every night, working with her partners to set up the syndicate of other investment banking firms to underwrite the offering of Dow Tech to the public. A syndicate of nearly thirty investment banking firms was going to underwrite it. She spent hours talking to the analysts in her firm to make sure that they would support the stock in the beginning. And she spent an equal amount of time talking to the salesmen in her firm, to confirm that they were lining up the key institutions in the cities they'd be traveling to, and that they sent their people to see the road show. There were insurance companies, large universities, anyone with large funds to invest had to be made aware that they were coming. And of course she met with the firm's lawyers constantly to prepare everything for the SEC, to make sure that all their questions about Dow Tech were getting answered. In addition, she was thinking about the final number of shares to be sold, and the final price, although there were going to be ballpark figures in the prospectus, which was now well over a hundred pages. It was an unbelievable amount of work that required her constant attention, and she felt as though she were leaving halfway through the day when she went home every night after midnight.

Callan Dow was immensely impressed by what he heard whenever he spoke to her, and particularly so with the way she had turned the risk factor section of the prospectus into an almost positive treatise on the company's behalf, an art form she had carefully developed. In fact, he was delighted with everything she did, and couldn't believe his good fortune in working with her.

A week before the road show was to begin, the lawyers they used sent the final prospectus to the SEC for approval, and Callan was understandably nervous about it, but once again Meredith reassured him. She told him it was one of the best IPOs she'd ever worked on, and he didn't need to worry about it.

By the end of the last week, all the loose ends had been tied up, and she felt confident that they had thought of everything. The syndicate was set up, the analysts were pleased, the salesmen were as excited about Dow Tech as she and Callan were, and even the SEC wasn't giving them any trouble. The only thing she was worried about by the end of the week before the Labor Day weekend, was how little time she had spent with Steven, and she could tell from her phone calls with him that he was upset about it. But there was very little she could have done about it in the last two weeks. She had too many important details to attend to, to spend time with her husband.

"I feel like I'm married to an imaginary friend," he complained on Thursday night when he called her from work. She was still in the office at one A.M., and mercifully he had just come out of surgery himself and wasn't due to get off duty until noon on Friday. He had been at the hospital on and off since Tuesday morning. And he'd been called in four times for emergencies when he was on call over the weekend, so he couldn't complain too much that she was busy.

"I'm sorry," she said, sounding tired but pleased. She was thrilled that everything had gone so smoothly. It had been an unusually good deal for the firm, and one of the rare ones where no unexpected dragons reared their heads with surprise disasters at the last minute. "It's just been crazy for the past two weeks, but it's been worth it. I don't think we've ever been as well prepared for an offering as we have this time." She felt good not only about the validity of the company, but about the quality of its products. Even Steven had told her that the instruments they made were exceptionally good ones. Meredith had talked to him about it right from the beginning, and he had reassured her on that subject.

"If you have to work this weekend, Merrie, I'm going to kill you." And for once, he sounded as though he meant it.

"I swear I'm going to try to wrap up everything by noon tomorrow, and I'm all yours till Monday." She had promised herself and him that she would keep the

Labor Day weekend sacred for him. He deserved it. "You're not on call, are you, sweetheart?"

"No way. I don't care if half of New York bleeds to death or if a volcano erupts in Central Park, I'm off call, and I'm throwing my goddamn pager in the garbage can at noon tomorrow. I intend to spend the weekend in bed with you, if I have to handcuff you to the headboard."

"That sounds pretty kinky," she giggled as she listened to him, but she could hear that he was tired too. And when he finally came home at noon the next day, she was already there waiting for him. It was another one of those steamy humid days that everyone in New York expected at the end of August, and she was wandering around their living room in her underwear when he walked in, in wrinkled scrubs and a two-day-old beard he hadn't had time to attend to. It had been a hellish week for him, but as promised, he had walked out of the unit at noon, and when he saw his wife, he grinned, and tossed his pager on the kitchen counter.

"If that thing goes off in the next three days, I'm going to kill someone," he said as he helped himself to a beer and sprawled across the couch with a look of admiration at his wife's white satin bra and panties. "I hope this isn't a preview of what you're wearing on the road show. You might sell a lot of stock, but you could cause a riot."

She leaned over and kissed him, and he ran a practiced hand up her silky thigh, and then took another sip of the icy beer before setting it down on the coffee table. "God, I'm tired," he admitted. "Half of New York must have shot each other this week, and the other half fell on their asses and broke something. If I see another damaged body, I think I'm going to have a psychotic break." He smiled at her then, beginning to unwind from the pressures of three days straight at the trauma unit. "It's good to see you. I was beginning to wonder if we were still married. It's like being married to a flight attendant, every time I'm here you're not, and when you're home, I'm working. It gets a little old sometimes, doesn't it?"

"It does, but I just couldn't help it for the past two weeks. When I get back, everything will calm down again. I promise."

"Yeah, for about two minutes," he said, looking uncharacteristically weary, but he'd had roughly a total of six hours' sleep in the past seventy-two hours. She wondered how he did it. At least she got to come home at night, and get some rest, before rushing back to the office again the next morning. "I hope you don't have another IPO for at least another six months," he said, and she smiled.

"I'm not sure my partners would be too thrilled with that," she said, taking a sip of his beer and sitting down next to him on the couch. Even with the air conditioning on full blast, it was still warm in the apartment. It had been over a hundred degrees all week, and still in the nineties at midnight, and several times that week they'd had a brownout in her office, but she and her associates worked right through it. Only the hospitals were unaffected by it, as they had their own generators and couldn't afford to lose power, in the midst of surgeries, and with all their essential life-preserving equipment.

"What do you want to do this weekend?" he asked, looking at her lovingly, and running a hand gently over her pale blond hair. He was dead tired, but he couldn't help noticing that she looked sexy and pretty. She never looked like an investment banker to him, just a very beautiful woman. Her professional expertise was purely coincidental, and about as unimportant to Steven as her income. He was proud of her, but he had never cared about how much money she made. When he married her, when she was in business school at Columbia, she had been on a full scholarship, and didn't have a penny. And all the good fortune, and rich rewards that had come her way since seemed nice to him, but he wouldn't have cared if they'd been starving and living in a studio apartment somewhere on the Upper West Side, which they would have been, if they had been living on his wages. But the financial disparity between them had never been an issue to either of them. She made a huge salary, and had made some excellent investments over the years, but he regarded it as a bonus for them, and in truth, it was of no real importance to him.

"I'd love to go to a baseball game," she admitted with a grin. She was an avid baseball fan, when she had time, and so was he, but for once he was less than enthusiastic about the suggestion.

"In this heat? I love you, but I think you're crazy. How about a movie . . . after I spend the next twenty-four hours in bed with you. First things first, Mrs. Whitman." He smiled at her lasciviously and she laughed. He had a healthy appetite for her, even when he was dead tired. It was rare for him to be too worn out to have sex with her, except when he'd had a particularly depressing day at work and lost a patient. Only she knew how much he suffered when he lost them, particularly children.

"Actually, I was thinking of getting my packing out of the way this afternoon, so I won't have to bother with it all weekend. Why don't you relax, clean up, have a nap, and by the time you wake up, I'll be all finished."

"That's not a bad idea. I'm beat . . . but I'll only agree if you swear you won't sneak back to the office while I'm sleeping."

"I swear. They don't expect to see me for a full two weeks, *and* I just want to remind you that I'm coming home to be with you next weekend, after we finish San Francisco. Callan is going to spend the weekend with his kids, and I'm taking the red-eye on Friday night. I'll be home at six o'clock Saturday morning, and I'm here till we leave for Boston on Sunday."

"That's something at least. I guess I should be grateful for small favors."

"You know, you could meet me in London the following weekend, or Paris, when I finish the road show."

He looked momentarily intrigued as he thought about it and calculated briefly. "What weekend is that? Two weeks from now?" She nodded in answer. "Shit, I'm on call. Lucas has to be in Dallas for a meeting, and I'm in charge that weekend."

"Don't worry about it, I'll come home. We can go to Paris some other time." She leaned down to kiss him, and then wandered off to their bedroom to do her packing. And Steve headed for the bathroom and stood in the shower for nearly half an hour, to wash away the smell and the exhaustion and the sorrows of the trauma unit. And after that, he lay on their bed, relaxed and naked, and watched her moving quietly around the room to pack her bags, and within five minutes he was sound asleep, looking like the handsome man he was, as she stopped once or twice to smile, and watch him sleeping. As challenging as their lives and schedules were at times, they were still very much in love with each other, and she didn't overlook the fact that part of why their relationship worked so well was because he was so understanding and so patient. She knew that a lot of other men would have felt threatened by the demands her work put on her. But Steve never did, he was happy that she enjoyed what she did, and fulfilled by his own work. It was the perfect combination.

Meredith zipped her last bag shut just after four o'clock, and then sat down to read a magazine and relax, something she did too little of, but she had finished all her work, and even the endlessly revised red herring was complete now. Her briefcase sat next to her packed bags, and she had nothing to do for the next two and a half days except enjoy her husband. He was still sound asleep on their bed, and snoring softly when she heard an odd buzzing sound from the living room, and when she walked into the room to see what it was, she realized that it was his pager. She looked at it suspiciously for a long moment, like an animal that might attack if she got too close to it, but she also felt guilty on his behalf ignoring it. They knew he was off call and if they were paging him, she suspected it had to be important, maybe someone in dire straits needed an expertise that only Steve could offer. She walked slowly to where the pager lay, still on the kitchen counter, and glanced at the display. A flashing red light was going off on it, and the numbers 911 were repeated all across the screen. Whatever it was, there was no question that it was urgent. She picked it up, and stared at it, and then knew what she had to do. She was still holding it in her hand, when she walked softly back into their bedroom and ever so gently touched his shoulder. He stirred after only an instant, and smiled in his half sleep, and then reached out to find her breast with his hand. He was more than ready to make good on the promises he had made earlier, but with a frown, he heard the buzzing of his pager. He opened his eyes to look at her, and without a word, she handed it to him, and he saw the same numbers she had.

"Tell me I'm having a nightmare," he said, rolling over, and taking it from her. "Lucas is there this weekend, they don't need me." He groaned as he said it.

"Maybe you should call them," she said softly, sitting on the bed next to him. "Maybe he wants to consult with you about something important." He and Steve worked together very closely and had enormous respect and admiration for each other.

Steve sighed deeply as he sat up, and reached for the phone next to the bed, with an unhappy expression. "This better be good," he said, as he punched in the numbers and waited. As always, in his opinion, they took a little too long to answer, but they were understaffed and always busy. "Dr. Whitman here," he said tersely when they did. "I just got a 911 on my pager, with red lights. Tell me it was a mistake, Barbie," he said, recognizing the voice on the other end, and then for a long time he listened, and Meredith couldn't assess what he was hearing. His face looked blank for a long moment, and then he squeezed his eyes shut. "Shit. How many? And how many did we get?" He groaned audibly when she responded. "Where are you putting them? The garage? . . . are they crazy? What are we supposed to do with a hundred and eighty-seven criticals? It sounds like Gettysburg, for chrissake. . . . all right, all right. . . . I'll be there in ten minutes." He hung up the phone and looked at his wife mournfully. They had not only blown his night all to hell, but his weekend, and possibly his entire week. "You'd better turn on the news. Some fucking crazies tried to blow up the Empire State Building at four o'clock, just in time to get everyone still in their offices, and all the tourists. Nearly a hundred people were killed, over a thousand injured. They're sending us somewhere between two and three hundred critically injured people. They're splitting up the rest of the minor injuries between hospitals all over the city. I have seventy-five trauma beds available, and over a hundred people in the halls now, with paramedics, and another hundred coming in, in the next hour. They're calling in medical personnel from Long Island and New Jersey. There goes our weekend. I'm sorry, baby."

He looked like his best friend had died, but in fact a lot of people's best friends had died, and husbands and wives, and children. It sounded like the *Titanic*. Meredith flipped on the TV while he dressed and there were bulletins about it on every channel. There was a gaping hole in one side of the building, from what they could see, and so much smoke surrounding the building, from fires the bomb had caused and the explosion itself, that it looked like a volcano.

They both stood staring at it for a moment, and then the cameras panned to the snarl of ambulances and fire engines on the street below, people still being ushered from the building, some of them having crawled down a hundred flights of stairs in smoke and darkness, covered with blood and lacerations, and then there were some grisly shots of tarp-covered bodies. It was an abysmal example of what the human race was at times capable of, and what gave Steve his business. "How can anyone do something like that?" Meredith asked in a choked voice as Steve pulled the drawstring on his scrub pants, and stuck his bare feet into clogs. At least he had slept for two hours, and felt human again. It was going to be a long haul for him now, and they both knew it. "Can I do anything if I come with you?" She hated the thought of sitting at home, useless. And her heart ached at what they had just seen on the news bulletin.

"I don't think so, sweetheart. Volunteers aren't much help in a mess like this. The city will give us some civil defense people, and Barbie said something about sending us National Guard medical personnel from New Jersey. I'll call you when I get a minute." She knew it wouldn't be anytime soon, from what they had just seen on television.

He was dressed and gone in the next two minutes, and she sat down on their bed, staring at the TV in disbelief and horror, as they interviewed dozens of victims. She switched to another channel then, and it was even more gruesome. She couldn't begin to imagine what Steve would be seeing at work, especially if they were only sending them the critically injured. It reminded her, but much worse, of the 1995 bombing in Oklahoma.

And for the next twenty-four hours, she heard nothing from Steven. She stayed in the apartment, afraid to miss his call, if he had a free minute to call her, which he didn't. And she went over her materials for the trip again, for lack of anything better to do. He called her finally on Saturday, at midnight. It was thirty-one hours since he had walked out of their apartment. He said he hadn't sat down, slept, or eaten anything but potato chips and doughnuts since he'd last seen her. They had lost fifty-two of the nearly three hundred critically injured that had been sent to them, and the others were still in grave to critical condition. There had been some children, too, inevitably, and an entire day camp group among the tourists.

"Are you okay?" she asked him, sounding worried.

"I'm fine, babe. This is what I do for a living. I could have been a dermatologist if I wanted holidays and weekends. I'm just sorry not to be spending this particular weekend with you before you leave." But that was the way their life worked, and they both knew it. It was something she had long since accepted. "I don't think I'll get home before you go," he said, sounding apologetic.

"Don't worry about it. I'll see you next weekend."

"I'll probably be here till then. I'll call you later. I've got to go now." He was still doing surgeries, and they were still getting transfers from other hospitals that couldn't cope with the severity of the cases they'd gotten. He knew he'd be dealing with chaos for days, and when he called her again later that night, things hadn't improved much. And she didn't hear from him again after that until late Sunday morning. And by then, he sounded exhausted. He said he'd managed to sleep for a couple of hours the night before, but other than that, he hadn't slept since he left her. He was living on black coffee.

"You've got to get some sleep, Steve." She worried about him being too tired to make sense, or making poor decisions, but that never seemed to happen. He tried to keep his hours within a reasonable time frame most of the time, but in major emergencies all limits and guidelines went right out the window. And in a case like this, she knew he'd stay at the hospital as long as he had to. He seemed to be able to stay on his feet forever, and in truth, she knew he thrived on it. He didn't like what had happened to his patients to bring them to him, but once they were his, he gave them his all, and would have died for them. It was what made him so good at trauma. He had the stamina of a warhorse.

"I'm going to sleep for a couple of hours now," he promised her. "I'm scheduled for surgery again in a few hours. But Lucas is here, and he's covering for me." They were a great team, and Meredith was sure that they had saved countless lives since the explosion. Earlier that day, a group of militant lunatics had taken responsibility for it, but so far, none of the perpetrators had been apprehended. "I'll call you before you leave tomorrow."

It was hard to believe it was already nearly Monday. Even to her, her trip seemed mundane by comparison,

and so shockingly unimportant in the face of this tragedy that had claimed so many innocent people. "You'd
better get to the airport early tomorrow, sweetheart,"
he warned, "they're going to be tightening security
everywhere, and it may take you a while to check in." It
was a good reminder, and she made a mental note to
leave early, although she was only going to Chicago.

"I'll call you from the road, if I can get through to
you. Don't worry if you can't call me. I know you're
busy." He laughed at the word, *busy* didn't even begin
to touch it. You could still hardly walk through the halls
of the trauma unit. There were people on gurneys, on
stretchers the paramedics had left them on, some even
on mattresses on the floor. They were filled to the raf-
ters, and the whole trauma unit staff was exhausted.

"Thank God most of them are on IVs and we don't
have to feed them," he said ironically. The National
Guard had provided food trucks outside to feed the
staff, and the Red Cross had sent them a battalion of
volunteers trained on advanced first aid to help them.
"Have a good trip, Merrie . . . knock 'em dead in
Chicago!!"

"Thanks, sweetheart. Take care of yourself. Don't
get too worn out if you can help it."

"Yeah. . . . I thought I'd play some tennis tomorrow and catch a massage afterward . . . be a good
girl . . . don't wander around the road show in your
underwear . . . or that Dow guy. . . ." He still remembered the Gary Cooper comparison and didn't
love it, but he trusted her and knew she had always
been faithful to him. He just hated it when they didn't
have time together, and they hadn't in weeks now. He
was hoping to improve on that once his disaster and

her travels were over. "Maybe we can go away for a weekend."

"I'd love that."

He called her again just before she left for the airport on Monday afternoon, but he was between surgeries and had to get off the phone in a matter of seconds. And with that, she picked up her bags and her briefcase, and went downstairs to catch a cab to the airport. It was a zoo there. As Steve had predicted the day before, they had tightened security every step of the way, and it took her over an hour to check in for her flight to Chicago. She felt as though she were leaving a war zone. There were even armed security guards and soldiers at the airport carrying machine guns.

It was a relief to get on the plane finally, and to get off in the relative calm of O'Hare in Chicago. An hour later she was at her hotel, and when she checked, Callan Dow hadn't arrived yet. He called her from his own room half an hour later, and he sounded like a kid going to camp for the first time, a little scared and a lot excited.

"That's some city you live in," he said, without preamble. "I've been watching all that on the news since Friday. Christ, it's awful!"

"Yes, it is. My husband works at the principal trauma hospital in New York. They've had over three hundred critically injured patients transferred in since Friday."

"He must be a busy guy," Callan said admiringly.

"He is. I haven't seen him since then. It sounded terrible every time I talked to him. There are nearly two hundred fatalities now from the explosion. Anyway, how about you? All ready for the big show tomorrow?" They were starting with a breakfast meeting in the morning, where they would make their presentation to representatives of the institutions that were their potential investors. There would be a slide show, she would speak for a few minutes and introduce Callan Dow, who would then make a presentation, followed by one given by his CFO, Charlie McIntosh, who had come with him, and a brief time for questions and answers. And at lunchtime, they would start all over again and do it for another group of potential investors. She knew that by the end of the week, it would all be familiar to him, but for the moment, before it all began, she expected him to be nervous. This was the big moment they had all worked so hard for. And Meredith wasn't anxious at all. To her, it was a thrill seeing who was there, and orchestrating it all with infinite precision, particularly if they were well received, and the book was oversold, which meant they had far more orders for shares than they had shares to sell. Their goal was always to be oversubscribed, by having more orders than they could meet, which would ensure a strong price in the aftermarket, if there were not enough shares to go around. In that case a "green shoe" of five to ten percent more shares, would have to be added to what was previously available, which would add some more shares, but not enough to supply all the orders. It was highly desirable to leave potential investors hungry for more, which would be a real victory for Callan's firm and the underwriters. And she was hoping that in this case, that would happen.

"I hate to admit it," Callan said sheepishly, sounding boyish, "I think I'm a little jittery. I feel like a virgin."

"You won't for long," she laughed. "By the time we hit New York, you'll be a pro at this, and I guarantee you'll love it. It's addictive."

"If you say so."

She gave him the details of who would be there both at the breakfast and the lunch meetings the next day. And after lunch, they were flying to Minneapolis to do a dinner there, and breakfast again on Wednesday morning. And then, on to Los Angeles for another dinner, and a full day in L.A. on Thursday, and up to San Francisco after dinner, for yet another breakfast and lunch on Friday. He was going home then, and she was taking the red-eye back to New York, hopefully to see Steve for the weekend. She wouldn't have seen him for a week by then, and she was sure they would both be exhausted, but she wanted to be with him. But she had a lot of work to do in the meantime.

"I'm worn out just listening to our schedule," Callan said, sounding pleased about it. "If any of our flights are delayed, we may blow the whole deal," he said, sounding worried.

"I have backup arrangements for chartered jets in every city, if we need them. We'll see how it goes. But tomorrow is a quick hop from here to Minneapolis." She sounded in full control, as always. She had thought of everything. She was used to this, and to handling all the most minute details. She had even found out from his secretary what he liked to drink, and there was a bottle of his favorite Chardonnay and the makings of a Sapphire martini in his room at the hotel, which was a little touch that he appreciated when he looked around his suite. She was quite a woman. "You'd better get lots of rest tonight, so you're fresh for our first show tomorrow," she said, sounding like a house mother in a boys' school, and he laughed at her.

"Actually, I was hoping you'd have dinner with me. We can make it an early night, Meredith. But if I sit here by myself worrying about tomorrow, it'll drive me crazy." She seemed to hesitate for a long moment. She had spent a quiet weekend at home, without Steve, and dinner appealed to her.

"I'm not sure I should let you do that, but maybe if we make it early, Cal. I don't want you staying up late." He laughed again and promised to go to his room immediately after dinner.

"You sound like me with my kids. I'll be good. I promise. I'll just come back here and drink martinis till tomorrow morning."

"Oh great," Meredith laughed. "Maybe I should take those bottles away. I think we may have to just give you a sleeping pill and knock you out. You're going to be fine, you know. You're going to be very proud of Dow Tech when this is all over. We all will be."

"I'm just so grateful to you for everything you've done for me, Meredith. You've been incredible." He sounded sincere and very humble.

"No more so than anyone else in the firm, Cal," she said modestly. "There were a lot of people involved in this, and the analysts and the market makers have been very supportive, as have been my partners."

"Even the SEC has been pretty good to us," he said, sounding pleased. The prospectus had been very straightforward, and so far, they seemed to like it. "Anyway, let's go have dinner and celebrate. It's probably the last decent dinner we'll have all week." He'd already heard that road show meals were traditionally inedible and usually featured what was referred to as "rubber chicken." But he didn't really care what they'd be eating, he just wanted the presentations to go well. And in Meredith's capable hands, he was beginning to feel as optimistic as she did.

They agreed to meet in the lobby at seven thirty and he said he'd make a reservation at the Pump Room, which was actually one of Meredith's favorite places in Chicago. She had been there often, and loved it.

As promised, she met him promptly at seven thirty. He had arranged for a limo to take them to the restaurant, and it was waiting outside, and he looked as handsome and well dressed as he always did, with his healthy California suntan. He always looked more like an actor or a male model than a businessman to her, but she had worked with him for long enough that she no longer paid any attention to it. And what she liked best about him was his bright mind, quick wit, and easygoing sense of humor. She always had a good time when she was with him.

They chatted on the way to the restaurant, and were shown to a quiet corner table. And after they had ordered steaks and wine, he turned to her with a smile, and asked her a question she hadn't expected.

"So tell me about this Dr. Kildare you're married to, Meredith. Trauma work must be pretty intense, particularly after a disaster like this weekend. You mustn't see much of him."

"Sometimes I don't," she smiled, "but I'm pretty busy too. We're a good balance for each other."

"Have you been married for a long time?" He seemed to be intrigued about her, and she never talked about her personal life. All he knew of her was how she handled her professional dealings.

"Fourteen years. We got married when I was at Columbia, in business school." Their wine had arrived by then, and the waiter poured it for them.

"Do you have children?"

"Nope." She said it in a surprisingly firm tone, and he raised an eyebrow at the way she answered.

"That sounds like a resounding *nope*. I take it the idea doesn't appeal much." He was curious about her.

"Not at this point. Neither of us has time. I always thought we'd have them one day . . . but I just can't see when. I'm beginning to think it may never happen."

"Would that be a disappointment to you, if it didn't?" He seemed hungry to know more about her, but she was comfortable talking to him. And in the next two weeks, they were going to see a lot of each other. There didn't seem to be any harm in knowing more about each other.

"It wouldn't be a disappointment to me," she said honestly. "In some ways it would be a relief, not to worry about it, or have to figure out how and if we could do it, and still be fair to the kids and each other. But it would be a disappointment to my husband, if we didn't have children. He's been talking about it a lot lately."

"And you? Have you been talking about it too?" Cal pressed her.

She smiled in answer to his question. "I've been talking about your IPO, and your red herring, that's what I've been talking about."

"That says something, doesn't it?" He smiled at her.

"I just can't see the point of having kids when you're in the office till midnight most of the time, and sometimes two in the morning. And when things get crazy at work, Steve works sixty-eight to seventy-two-hour shifts, until there's a real emergency, and then he's gone for however long he has to be. Where are we supposed to fit kids into all that? On the occasional long weekend, or for a week in the summer? It wouldn't be fair to the kids. They deserve more than that from their parents. What about you? How do you manage it? You said you have three children, the last time I was in California."

"I do. Their mother was a lot like you. She's an entertainment attorney. She was working in L.A. when I met her. I was living down there too then. She didn't even want to get married. I talked her into marrying me, 'forced her' to, as she said later, and when I moved up to San Francisco to get involved in Silicon Valley years ago, she refused to come with me."

"And that was the end of it?" Meredith looked surprised that his wife had been so adamant about it. San Francisco didn't seem like a bad place to live, and she assumed there had to be entertainment lawyers there too, though maybe not of the magnitude of those in L.A. But Callan smiled as he answered her.

"No, that wasn't the end of it. She commuted. It was a crazy existence. We were never in the same city at the same time, and when we were, we were either annoyed about something, out of touch with each other, or exhausted. The only surprising part of it is that that was when we decided to have children. Maybe *decided* isn't the right word exactly. The first one was an accident, and the next two were a result of my convincing her that it wasn't fair to have an only child."

"I'm an only child," Meredith said with a look of amusement.

"So am I," Callan said, and didn't really surprise her. He had the kind of intensity and drive and urge to succeed typical of only children. "It's all right now, but I didn't think it was much fun as a kid. And I thought that as busy as we were, it would be better for them to have siblings."

"I'm surprised she went along with that theory."

"She was a good sport. She really tried for a while. We both wanted to make it work, but I guess I wasn't very realistic. She was never very maternal, and she was far more interested in business than in her children. She hired a nanny, and as soon as she had each of them, she headed back to L.A. on the next plane she could get on. She acted more like a visiting aunt when she came home on weekends, when she did, than their mother. And eventually, she came home less and less often. She said it was too noisy and too confusing. The truth is, I'd never say it to them, but the kids drove her crazy." It sounded sad to Meredith, and exactly what she didn't want to happen in her life. She wondered how they were now, and how high a price they had paid emotionally for their mother's bad behavior.

"Where is she now?"

"That's another story. What I didn't realize in the midst of all that was that she and her partner had been romantically involved for several years before we met, and for most of our marriage. We'd been married for seven years before she told me. And by then, we had three kids, and she wanted out. She gave me custody of the children without batting an eye, they closed their practice in L.A. a year later, and moved to London to open up an office there. We've been divorced for eight years, and she finally married him a few years ago, and I think they're very happy. Needless to say, they don't have children."

"Does she ever see the kids?"

"She flies over a couple of times a year for a few days, usually if one of her clients is making a movie in L.A., and then she comes up to see the kids. And she takes them to the South of France for a few weeks every summer." She sounded heartless to Meredith, and she couldn't help feeling sorry for his children.

"Do they hate her for it . . . or are they just heart-broken?"

"Neither one. I think they accept her as she is. They've never known anything different. And I'm around most of the time. I try not to work too late usually, and they can always call me at the office if they have a problem. My house is only about five minutes from the office. Weekends are sacred, and I take a month off to be with them in Tahoe every summer. It's worked out pretty well, though not exactly what I had in mind in the beginning. I thought we were going to have one of those perfect little families with a mommy and a daddy and a flock of little children. Instead, it's just me and the flock . . . or rather, the flock and I." He smiled at her. "We have a good time together, and they keep me pretty busy, mostly on weekends."

"I'm surprised you never remarried," Meredith said honestly. "It can't be easy bringing up three kids on your own."

"In some ways it's easier," he said with surprising candor. "You don't have to argue with anyone about how to bring them up. There are no battles over what's right or wrong or good for them. You get to make all your own decisions. We have a good relationship, and I think they respect me. And to be honest, I think Charlotte cured me. I've never been anxious to get into that kind of relationship again. There's something incredibly artificial and dishonest about marriage.'' Particularly if your wife spent the entire marriage sleeping with her business partner. But Meredith was careful not to say that. After all, they may have been friends, but he was still a client.

"You must have been pretty badly hurt when she told you the truth,'' Meredith said gently. "Were you surprised, or did you suspect it?"

"I never suspected it for a minute. I thought she was the most honest woman alive. And so did she. In fact, she was very proud of herself that he was the only 'other' man she had ever slept with while we were married. In her eyes, that was almost as good as being faithful. I didn't see it quite that way. I was pretty bitter about it for a long time.''

"And now?" Meredith asked, as they finished their first glass of wine and started on dinner. It had been an interesting conversation, and a surprising glimpse into the private man. It was a story that made her sorry for him. If Steve ever had an affair, she knew she would have been heartbroken. In Steve's case, she knew he never would. But Callan's wife sounded like a different breed completely. "Do you think you're still bitter about it?"

"Bitter? No, not now. I still get angry about it sometimes when I think about it. It wasn't exactly fair play, but that's the way it works sometimes. I'm just not inclined to do anything as foolish as that again. I don't need to put my head on the chopping block and offer someone the opportunity to knock it off, or rip my heart out. Marriage can be kind of a tough playing field at times, kind of like the Colosseum. I just don't have the urge anymore, to offer myself up to the lions." The images he used were strong, and so was the picture he painted with them. He had been betrayed by the one woman he had loved and trusted, the mother of his children, and it was obvious that he had never forgiven her for it, or entirely recovered from it either. And Meredith wasn't sure she blamed him.

"How old are your kids now?"

He smiled as soon as she asked the question. It was easy to see that he was crazy about them. "Mary Ellen is fourteen, not an easy age, I might add. She thought I was great until about a year ago, according to her my IQ has been slipping ever since then. She thinks I'm senile. Julie is twelve, and still thinks I'm okay, but she's starting to slip into that same red zone. In another year I'll be heading downhill with her pretty quickly. And Andrew is nine. By some miracle, he still thinks I'm terrific. I hope you meet them sometime, Merrie." Without prompting, he had adopted the same nickname Steve used, but she didn't mind it.

"I hope I do too. They sound like nice kids." But she couldn't help wondering how hard it was for them not having a mother figure around, particularly for girls going into their teens. She couldn't imagine that it was easy for them, or for Cal either. And it was a very intriguing story. He was a man of many faces, and it was interesting knowing something more about him. She didn't want to ask, but she wondered if he had a girl-friend, or if he was one of those men who, once bruised, was satisfied to have a chorus line of temporary companions, maybe even one at a time, to be disposed of any time they got too close to him. He didn't sound like a man who was willing to entertain the idea of commitment, not after what he'd experienced the first time, and in a way, she felt sorry for him.

But he surprised her with his next question. "Why do you think you don't want kids, Meredith? You're missing out on a wonderful experience, but people who don't have them don't know that."

"I've never had time to have a baby. I'm just too busy. It wouldn't be fair to my children. I don't want to do what your wife did, hire a nanny, and rush back to my office. I think children deserve to have full-time mothers, and to be honest, I think I'd hate that. I have too much fun doing what I'm doing."

"Do you really think it's that, or is it more a statement about your level of commitment to your husband?" She was stunned when he asked her the question, and she was quick to shake her head when she answered.

"I think Steve and I are about as committed to each other as two people can get. That's never been the issue between us. It's really entirely career-related."

"That's what Charlotte said when I first suggested we have kids. But the truth was something very different. She was in love with another man, who had never wanted to marry her. And I don't think she was as sure of her feelings about me as she thought she should be. I think when a woman really trusts a man, she wants to have his children. Maybe you're not as sure of Dr. Kildare as you think you are, Meredith, or your feelings for him." It was a shocking theory, and she didn't even like hearing it. There was certainly no truth in it for them, whether or not Callan Dow believed her.

"I promise you, it's not that in our case. We're very much in love with each other. Maybe I'm just one of those women who don't need to have children, and I'm smart enough to know it. I probably wouldn't be a very good mother. But it has nothing to do with a lack of commitment to my husband."

"I'm not sure I believe you, Meredith. You may think you're committed to him, but I think it's only natural if you truly trusted the relationship, you'd want to have his children." Just listening to him say it to her suddenly annoyed her.

"That is utterly ridiculous, Cal, and you know it. I can't believe you actually think something as chauvinistic as that. You've got to tell me you're joking."

"I'm not. You don't have to admit it to me. But think about it when you're alone tonight. Why is it that you really don't want his children?"

"Because I've spent the last twelve years doing exactly what I'm doing for you, organizing syndicates, writing red herrings with the legal staff, and taking clients on road shows. Just how much time do you think I'd have for my children?"

"As much as you wanted to. Your clients are no substitute for a baby in your arms, Meredith. We all come and go, a child is forever. But maybe your marriage isn't." At a glance, he saw then that he'd offended her, and with a kindly look, he changed the subject. And for the next two hours they talked about his IPO and the road show. But in spite of the assurances she'd given him, he had nonetheless managed to unnerve her. And when she went back to her room at the hotel, shortly after ten o'clock, she was still thinking about it. What he had said was ridiculous. She had the kind of valid reasons women used all the time not to make a terrible mistake, in having children when they didn't want them, or if they weren't ready. Her career was as important to her as his was to Steve, and in its own way, hers was equally demanding. Unless she wanted to cut back radically, or leave the firm, there was no way she could reconcile her business life with having babies. Even Steve understood that, and she couldn't imagine why Callan Dow didn't. Just because he had three kids didn't mean that everyone else was suited to it, or would even enjoy it. God knows his wife certainly hadn't, and what she had done seemed worse to Meredith, having them, and then giving them up and virtually abandoning them for a man, a career, and a life in another country. That was something Meredith would never consider doing, once she had them. She preferred not to put herself in the same bind Charlotte Dow obviously had, and then renege on her responsibilities as a mother. Meredith would have had her tubes tied before that, and had often thought about it, but she knew that Steve would be upset if she did that. He had in fact begged her not to.

But she couldn't understand why she couldn't convince Callan Dow that she was completely committed to her marriage, and the simple reality that she didn't want kids certainly didn't mean she didn't love Steve. On the contrary, she loved him so much, she didn't want to share him.

She was still upset by what he'd said when she got into bed that night, and after lying in the dark for half an hour, stewing over it, she decided to call Steve, just to tell him she loved him. The nurse answering the phones at the trauma unit said she didn't know where he'd gone, she'd seen him only ten minutes before, but she thought he was on another floor, picking up some X-rays, so Meredith paged him. She punched in her number at the hotel and waited for his call. But twenty minutes later, he hadn't called, and she wondered if he was back in surgery again. And as she waited for his call, she drifted off to sleep, thinking about him, but even as she did, she had a gnawing, uneasy feeling. She knew in her heart of hearts that she was entirely committed to him, in fact very much in love with him, and she didn't give a damn who believed it, as long as Steve did. And the fact that she didn't want kids was irrelevant, all it meant was that she had other priorities in her life, she assured herself. But once she slept, she tossed and turned all night, pursued by dreams where Steve was shouting at her, and as he did, he was surrounded by armies of children who howled and screamed and clawed at her like little demons.

Chapter 5

THE DUE DILIGENCE tour that Meredith put on for Callan Dow went brilliantly. Chicago was a huge success, his speech went over very well, and even the CFO performed admirably. The questions the audience asked were intelligent and to the point, and Cal's answers were exactly what they wanted to hear. And Minneapolis went even better.

By the time they got to L.A., Cal and Meredith were both on a high, and they were already nearly fully subscribed. There was almost certainly going to be a "green shoe" on this one. They were going to have far more investors than they needed.

She was in such good spirits, and had had such a good time with him, that Meredith had almost forgiven him for the ridiculous thing he'd said in Chicago about her marriage. She had decided by then that his point of view was based on his own bad experience with marriage. Neither of them had ever mentioned it again, and they had fallen into an easy camaraderie as they moved from city to city. And she had spoken to Steve twice since then. He had finally gotten home for a night, and things had calmed down considerably in the trauma unit. She could hardly wait to see him.

She put on another dinner in Los Angeles, and three more presentations the next day, and between breakfast and lunch they had had time to meet privately with two major investors. Things were looking great for their offering, and after the second dinner in L.A., on Thursday night, they flew to San Francisco. They landed at ten fifteen, and she had a car and driver waiting for him, and another to take her to the Fairmont Hotel. Cal was planning to go home to his children and would meet her for their breakfast presentation at the Fairmont. It had been a long three days for both of them, but it had been extremely fruitful.

"Will you be okay?" he asked solicitously. They were constantly exchanging roles. She took care of him during their meetings and presentations on the due diligence tour, and he acted like her older brother as they traveled, or chatted between meetings. "I feel guilty just leaving you here at the airport." After three days of being together night and day, they felt like old friends now.

"I think I can manage," she smiled at him. "Go home and enjoy your kids. I'm just going to go to the hotel, take a hot bath, and relax. I'll see you in the morning."

"I'll be there at seven thirty," he promised. The presentation was scheduled for eight. They were doing another one at lunch, they were seeing two more private investors after that, both of them universities, and then she was catching the red-eye. "Maybe you can come to dinner with the kids tomorrow night, after our meetings."

"See how you feel by then," she said sensibly. "You must be sick of me by now. I don't want to intrude on you with your kids. I have plenty of work to do." She was still carrying the ever-present briefcase.

"You need some time off too. And my kids would love to meet you."

"Let's play it by ear tomorrow," she said as they walked out of the airport together. "See you in the morning." She waved as they went their separate ways, and as soon as she got to her room in the hotel, Steve called her.

"When are you coming home? I miss you!"

"I miss you too, sweetheart. I'll be home by seven Saturday morning. Are you working?"

"I am now. But I'm off tomorrow night. Just climb into bed when you get home on Saturday and wake me."

"That's the best offer I've had all week," she smiled. The ugly things Cal had said about her marriage were all but forgotten. She knew they didn't apply to her. He was just a cynic.

"I should hope that's the best offer you've had all week. That guy's not hitting on you, is he?"

"Of course not. This is strictly business."

"How's it going?"

"Terrific. I can't wait till we get to New York. We're doing Boston on Monday, and then New York on Tuesday. I don't have to leave for Boston till Sunday night, by the way. We'll have almost two whole days together."

"Shit. I was afraid of that. I'm working on Sunday, for Lucas."

"That's all right, at least we'll have Saturday."

"I told you, it's like being married to a flight attendant. The only thing you don't do is serve me dinner."

"I'll bring home some of those little bottles of tequila from the flight tomorrow night if you want."

"Just bring you home. I can't wait to see you." It had been a long week for both of them, and she was equally anxious to see him. She had been following the aftermath of the Empire State bombing on the news, and they still hadn't caught the men who did it. More people had died since the initial blast. The death toll was up to more than three hundred, in spite of Steve and his colleagues' best efforts.

They chatted for a few more minutes then, and she took a bath. And as she was reading in bed, Callan called with a few casual questions.

"It seems odd not being in the same hotel with you, Merrie. This could become a habit." He sounded relaxed and friendly.

"You'll be happy to see the last of me after Europe, trust me. But first we go to New York. That's the biggie."

"I know it is. I'm still a little anxious about it."

"Don't be. It's gone great so far. And the word is out on the street now. The book is going to be oversold by New York. And the tombstone is going to read like a Who's Who of investment banking." She was referring to the ad that would appear in *The Wall Street Journal* the day following the offering that would announce the completion of the deal, listing all the underwriters in the syndicate. And in this case, they would be impressive.

"Thanks to you, Meredith," he said gratefully. "I could never have done this without you."

"Bullshit," she said irreverently, and he laughed. He had come to enjoy working with her, and he was sorry it was going to have to end soon. "How were your kids when you got home? Happy to see you, I'll bet." Especially with no mother around, she knew how important Callan must be to them.

"They were asleep actually. My housekeeper rules the roost with an iron fist. It's good for them. I'll see them tomorrow night when I get home. I thought I'd stop by the office first. Maybe you'd like to come with me."

"Sure. I can come by on the way to the airport." She had every intention of sitting in the first-class lounge with her reading material, having a sandwich quietly, and catching the red-eye.

"We'll talk about that later," he said discreetly, and then told her to get some sleep and he'd see her in the morning.

And after they hung up, she lay in bed thinking about him. He was a nice man, and had the makings of a good friend, but in a way she felt sorry for him. It was so obvious, even to her, that he had been badly wounded by his wife's betrayal, and eventual desertion. He loved his kids, but there obviously was no longer room in his heart to trust another woman. It was as though Charlotte had destroyed a part of him, and now, eight years later, there was a piece of him still missing. As a result, he couldn't understand the kind of bond she had with Steve, and he was suspicious of it. Thinking of it brought her mind back to Steve again, and she smiled to herself, thinking of how much she missed him, and how happy she would be to see him on Saturday morning. They were lucky, after fourteen years, they still had something very special. And Cal's theory that she didn't love or trust him enough to have children with him seemed like nonsense to her. She drifted off to sleep thinking of Steve, as usual, and her dreams that night were peaceful.

She met Cal the next morning in the lobby at seven thirty, as agreed. They took a short walk around Huntington Park to get some air, and then came back for a cup of coffee. Meredith was surprised at how chilly it was, there was a brisk breeze and a halo of fog still hung over the city. But it felt good to get out for a change, instead of sitting around in stuffy rooms, giving their presentation.

"Ready for the next round?" she asked him as they shared a blueberry muffin.

"All set. What about you? Tired of Dow Tech yet?" He looked energetic and refreshed after a night in his own bed, and he had been happy to see his kids as he left the house to meet Meredith for breakfast.

"Of course I'm not tired of Dow Tech," she smiled at him, as the waitress poured them each a second cup of coffee. "We still have new worlds to conquer." But they both knew that San Francisco was going to be easy for them. It was his hometown, and people in San Francisco were familiar with what he had already accomplished in Silicon Valley.

Their first presentation of the day went well, they got a brief break after that, and she got a chance to call her office. And then they went right into lunch, and their next presentation. They had the ritual rubber chicken, and by two thirty they were finished, and everything was packed up. Callan glanced at his watch, and said he thought he might go back to his office, and he invited Meredith to join him.

"I think I might try to catch an earlier flight," she explained. There was a five o'clock she said she could be on, which would get her home to New York by one o'clock in the morning. And she knew Steve would love it.

But when she called the airline from the hotel, they told her the flight was booked solid. She was stranded till the red-eye. She told Callan she'd wait at the hotel, and do some reading. But he was insistent. He wanted her to come to Palo Alto with him to see the people at his office again, before she left San Francisco. And he wanted her to come to the house, if she had the time, to meet his children.

"You've been gone all week, you'll have plenty to do without having me underfoot," she insisted.

"I like having you underfoot. Besides, I'm always open to free advice." He had enormous respect for her opinions, and she knew almost as much about Dow Tech now as he did. He was so proud of his company and family that he was anxious to share both with her. He was so insistent about it that, in the end, it seemed rude not to go with him. She went upstairs and got her bags, and joined him ten minutes later in the lobby. And by three thirty, they were in Palo Alto, everyone in his office seemed pleased to see him, and wanted to know about the road show.

"It's gone off without a hitch so far," he said with a broad smile, and a glance at Meredith. "Thanks to Mrs. Whitman," he told his colleagues. Charlie McIntosh had gone home after the lunch at the Fairmont. He wasn't a young man, and he was tired after a solid week of presentations. Meredith would have hated to admit it to Cal, but it was a relief not to have his cantankerous comments and negative opinions to deal with. It had been a strain working with him. And as they sat in Cal's office that afternoon, he commented on it. "I don't know what to do about him, Merrie. I thought he'd be on the bandwagon by now, but he's still mad as hell that I'm taking the company public. He's fundamentally opposed to it, for entirely sincere reasons. But it's counterproductive at this point. But because he feels so strongly about it, he resents the work it's going to represent for him, dealing with analysts, and the SEC, and shareholders. He just plain thinks we're wrong about all this. And he doesn't want anyone looking over his shoulder, not even me at times. He's going to make money on this, but I'm not even sure he cares. He just doesn't want me to do it."

"Let me talk to him," Meredith said. She still thought she could bring him around. Charlie hadn't said anything that had hurt them yet, but he hadn't helped them much either.

"I'm not sure that's the right tack," Cal said cautiously. Charlie's resentment of Meredith had not abated, and he didn't want to aggravate it any further. "Let's wait and see if he calms down, and can make the transition on his own. I really don't want to push him." Cal had a lot of respect for him, and Charlie had been a friend of Cal's father.

"If he doesn't adjust his attitude," Meredith warned, "your shareholders may not find him too charming." She was still worried about it, as Cal was.

"Poor old Charlie," Cal said, and they went on to other subjects. He showed her a number of reports, and they talked about some new ideas he was developing, and once again, she was impressed by how creative he was, and how far ahead in his thinking. It was an important part of why he was so successful. And at five thirty he looked up at her, as he sat back comfortably in his chair, and asked her a strange question. "Have you ever thought about leaving investment banking, Meredith?" She was extraordinarily good at it, he knew better than anyone, but she also had a profound interest in high-tech business. "You'd be good at the kind of thing I do, and you'd probably make a hell of a lot more money."

"I do all right," she said with a shy smile.

"You'd make more here," Callan Dow said gently. "If you ever decide to make a change, I'd love to hear from you, Merrie. I hope you know that."

"I'm very flattered. But I'm not going anywhere for the moment." She and Steve were too tied into New York to think of going anywhere. He had a good job in the trauma unit, and she was married to Wall Street.

"That could be truer than you know," Callan Dow said. "In an old-guard firm the size of yours, Meredith, how high can you go? You're already a partner, but there are a lot of very old, very solid, very well-entrenched senior partners. You're never going to run the place. They'd never let a woman do that, and you know it."

"They might someday," she said calmly. "Times are changing."

"Times have already changed just about everywhere else. Things are a lot slower moving in investment banking. It's the last bastion of the gentlemen who used to run the world, and still do in some places. I think you've already carved a remarkable spot for yourself, particularly in dealing with high-tech companies for them. But the reality is they're still sending guys like Paul Black out to see clients with you. Those guys still have more power than you do. You do the work, and they get all the glory." It was something she had thought herself for years, but she didn't want to admit it to him.

"You're a real rabble-rouser, aren't you, Mr. Dow?" She looked at him with a broad grin. "What do you want me to do? Go back and quit? They'd love that."

"No, I guess I'm just shit-disturbing a little bit. When I see a good thing, I hate not having a piece of the action. We work well together, Meredith. We think alike in a lot of ways. I hate to waste that."

She couldn't help agreeing with him, but they hadn't exactly wasted it either. "I wouldn't say we've been wasting time, would you?" They had put together a hell of a good IPO, working together.

"Of course not. I'm just already thinking about how much I'm going to hate it when our stint together is over. I may have to call you for advice every day. I'm already having withdrawals, thinking about it."

She laughed at what he said. "I told you, you'll be sick to death of me by the time the road show is over. But you can always call me."

"You'll probably be on the road with some other novice, whining and sniveling and needing you to hold his hand while you take his company public."

"Not for a while anyway. I'm going to take it easy for

a few weeks. Steve and I have hardly seen each other all summer."

"I don't know how you do that," he said admiringly. "Maybe that's how you've kept your marriage together for fourteen years. Maybe it works better if you don't see each other all the time," although that hadn't been true for him, and he knew that.

"Steve says it's like being married to a flight attendant."

"Not exactly," Cal smiled at her, and seemed to relax at the end of a long week. He was looking forward to spending the weekend with his children before he left for Boston on Sunday. "How about an early dinner with my little monsters? I'll take you to the airport myself in time for the red-eye. You won't have to leave the house till eight thirty."

Although she had agreed to meet them, she had resisted the offer of dinner earlier, but it seemed too awkward now to keep insisting she didn't want to impose on him, she enjoyed his company, and was curious about his children. "Are you sure they won't mind your dragging a stranger home from the office?"

"They'll survive it. They're used to businesswomen, like their mother. They don't pay much attention to what I do. At this point, all the girls are interested in is short skirts and makeup. And all Andy cares about is my Ferrari. I don't talk about work much with them."

"That's probably just as well. They've got plenty of time for that later."

"We just got back from Tahoe last weekend, and they started school yesterday. They were all complaining about it this morning."

They walked out of his office together, and almost everyone else had gone home by then. His Ferrari was in the parking lot. He had driven Meredith down from San Francisco in it, her bags were still in the trunk, and as she got back in now, he put the top down.

"We're only five minutes from my house. It's nice to get a little air," he said easily. It was at least fifteen degrees warmer in Palo Alto than it had been in the city. And Meredith enjoyed the brief ride with the top down.

They were chatting comfortably, as he pulled into a driveway with hedges on either side, and a gate opened automatically when he pressed a button on his visor. And once it opened, she saw a handsome stone house, with a large expanse of lawn to one side, several beautiful old trees, and a big swimming pool, with a bunch of children in it, and several others sitting on deck chairs wrapped in towels. And there was a nice-looking woman in her midthirties watching them, while a golden retriever stood next to a little boy and then ran after a ball he'd just thrown him. It was an idyllic scene, and in total contrast to his high-tech business life. This was the world he loved to come home to. Several of the kids waved as he drove in, and parked the car, and Meredith could see one of the girls watching her with interest.

"Hi, kids," he shouted in their general direction, and walked across the lawn toward them. There were at least ten children there, and Meredith realized that some of them had to be friends, but as soon as they approached, it was easy to see which ones were Callan's. The two girls he had described to her, Mary Ellen and Julie, looked exactly like him, so much so that it

was almost funny. And Andy looked like a miniature of
his father. All three of them stared at her as though she
had just arrived from another planet, as he introduced
her.

"We've just been on the due diligence tour together. In Chicago and Minneapolis and L.A. And next
week we're going to Europe," he explained as Andy
eyed her with suspicion.

"Are you my dad's new girlfriend?" Meredith smiled
at the question, and Cal was quick to reprimand him.

"Andy! That's a rude thing to say, and you know it."

"Well, is she?" he persisted, as the dog brought the
ball back and dropped it at the boy's feet, but Andy
ignored him. Interrogating Meredith was more interesting than playing fetch with the retriever. And his
sisters seemed to be listening with interest.

"Actually, I'm married. Your dad and I are just working together. My husband is a doctor," she said, hoping to gain safe passage from them. Their friends were
circling nearby, and the two girls seemed anxious to
rejoin them.

"What kind of doctor?" Andy asked her. "Does he
take care of kids?"

"Sometimes. He takes care of people who have terrible accidents, he's a trauma doctor."

"I fell off my bike and broke my arm once," he said,
smiling at her. He had decided that she was pretty, and
not necessarily after his father.

"That must have hurt," Meredith sympathized.

"It did. Do you have children?"

"No, I don't," she said, wondering if she should
apologize for it. The two girls were still watching her,
but neither of them had said more than hello when

their father introduced them. But they didn't make any move to step away either. They were listening to her answers to their brother's questions, and seemed satisfied by them. "I'm going back to New York in a few hours," she said, as though to reassure them. She somehow sensed that they thought she was a threat, even if she was married, and she wanted to assure them that she would be gone soon.

Cal offered her a glass of wine, and the children went back to their friends then. And half an hour later, as he and Meredith sat on the patio, drinking wine and chatting, the last of the friends left, and his kids went upstairs to change for dinner.

"Your children are beautiful," she said after they'd gone in, "and they all look just like you."

"Charlotte always said that Andy looked like my clone, even as a baby. And both of the girls look just like my mother. I think it was actually part of why Charlotte never bonded with them." But from everything else he had said to her by then, Meredith suspected that there were more severe reasons for her not bonding with them, mostly her long-term affair with another man, and the fact that she had never wanted children. "They're not used to seeing anyone come home with me. They've only met one or two of the women I've gone out with."

"Why is that?" She was startled by what he said, and it explained why they had seemed so suspicious of her.

"I don't think that part of my life is any of their business," he said bluntly. "There hasn't been anyone serious enough in my life to warrant introducing them to the children." It was hard to believe that in the eight years since his divorce he hadn't been seriously involved with a woman. It made her wonder about him, and come to the same conclusion she had come to before, that he was commitment-phobic ever since his wife's betrayal, although he claimed to have recovered.

They sat outside for a while, enjoying the balmy evening, and then he invited her to come inside to the large elegant living room, filled with English antiques and handsome works of art. And a few minutes later, the housekeeper told them dinner was ready. And like clockwork, the kids trooped downstairs, and then stood in the door of the living room, staring at her. She felt like an animal in the zoo, as the two girls glared at her, and she couldn't help wondering what they were thinking.

Callan got up, and walked slowly toward them. "So how was school, guys?" he asked easily, as Meredith followed behind him.

"I hate school," Andy announced, but without any particular fervor. It sounded like a standard response, and Julie said grudgingly that she liked her new teacher. Mary Ellen said nothing.

"Are you in high school?" Meredith asked her politely as they walked into the dining room, and Cal pulled out the chair next to his and Meredith sat down in it.

"I'm a freshman," Mary Ellen said tersely, and the word that sprang to Meredith's mind was *sullen*. She was totally unlike her easygoing father. She was a pretty girl, but her lack of enthusiasm and seeming lack of warmth made her appear somehow less attractive. From what Meredith could see, there was very little charm about her, and more than anything else, she seemed unhappy. Meredith couldn't help wondering if she was always that way, or if it was just due to the presence of an unexpected guest, and seeing her father with a woman.

Conversation during dinner was awkward and slow, with the children saying little, and Callan pretending he didn't notice. And Meredith eventually gave up trying to engage them in conversation. The one thing they made plain, without actually saying it, was that they had no interest in talking to her, or even in answering her questions. And she wasn't all that at ease with children. After a while, she had no idea what to say to them, and even Callan couldn't seem to draw them out much. They asked to be excused immediately after dessert, and ran upstairs so fast when he let them go, they almost knocked each other down in the doorway.

"I'm sorry, Meredith," he turned to her apologetically as the housekeeper served them coffee, and Meredith relaxed visibly. It had been a strain having dinner with his children. "I think they were worried about you. They're not usually like this. They're good kids. I think they just couldn't figure out who you were, or why you were here. I'll have to talk to them about it."

"Don't be silly," she said politely, "if you never bring women home, no wonder they were worried. Isn't that a little unreal, though? Don't your dates want to meet your kids?" It seemed an odd way to live, to her. And it obviously had disadvantages, if his children sat like stones when he finally did bring a woman home, even if she was a friend in business.

"What my dates want and what they get are two different stories," Cal said, smiling at her. "There's no point introducing them if they're not going to be around long."

"That's a hell of a statement, Cal. How do you know that right from the beginning?"

"Because that's the way it's been for a long time, and probably the way it will be for a lot longer. If I change my mind about it, I can always do something about it later. It's a lot easier to introduce someone to the kids down the road, than to explain to them why I'm not seeing her anymore. They don't need to know that."

"I think not dealing with it must make them very possessive of you." Which was a polite way of saying that they had looked like little ax murderers as they sat there. Their eyes had bored holes into Meredith all evening, and she hadn't enjoyed it. No one would have. But she was afraid to say too much. They were his children after all, and it was hardly her place to tell him that he wasn't bringing them up right. She suspected they probably were nice kids. They were healthy and good looking, and seemed intelligent, but they sure hadn't been friendly. In fact, given a bit of rope, she suspected they would have been hateful to her, especially Mary Ellen. Meredith couldn't help pitying the woman who would walk into that, because she was in love with Callan, and it might happen someday, in spite of his protests.

They talked about business again then, and at eight thirty, right on schedule, he drove her to the airport. He helped her check her bags in, and then walked her to the first-class lounge, and she thanked him for an interesting afternoon and a pleasant evening, and told him she had enjoyed meeting his children.

"I wish I believed that," he said apologetically. "They weren't exactly terrific, Merrie, and I know that. I guess I need to start introducing them to people, friends like you, if no one else."

"It might make it easier for them in the long run, if there's no threat involved. They have nothing to fear from me," she said candidly, and he frowned.

"I'm not sure they believed that. Maybe they thought I was lying, and that I am involved with you. Maybe they thought you made up the story about your husband."

"Why would I do a thing like that, Cal?" She looked shocked at the suggestion.

"Because it's the kind of thing their mother would do, if it suited her purpose. She lied to them about the man she eventually married. They suspected her involvement with him long before she admitted it to them. I've tried not to do the same thing to them, by telling them nothing."

"Maybe the right thing to do is somewhere in the middle."

"I'll have to try that," he smiled, and then wished her a good trip, and told her he'd see her on Sunday night at the Ritz Carlton in Boston.

"I probably won't be there till midnight," Meredith told him. "I wanted to spend a little time with my husband, but as it turns out he's working, as usual. At least we'll have tomorrow together. And I'm on a ten P.M. flight out of New York on Sunday."

"I should be at the hotel by seven," he explained. "If you're bored after he goes to work, come on up and have dinner with me."

"I'll call if I decide to do that. In the meantime, have a good weekend."

"I'm going to play tennis with the kids tomorrow, and spend the rest of the day lying around the pool. I can hardly wait," he admitted, and she laughed at the contrast.

"I'm planning to do my laundry."

"Somehow I can't envision you doing that, Meredith," he laughed. She seemed too beautiful and too glamorous to be spending time in a laundromat, or over a hot washing machine anywhere. He couldn't imagine her doing housework.

"Someone has to do it, and Steve draws the line at cooking. I'm not sure I blame him."

"I'll have to meet this guy one of these days. He sounds too virtuous to be true, saving lives, and doing the cooking. The perfect husband."

"Pretty damn close," she smiled at him.

He left her in the lounge with her briefcase, and half an hour later she boarded the plane. And shortly after takeoff, she took out her laptop. But she only worked for an hour, and then she finally put it away, and lay back against the seat and closed her eyes. She was thinking of Cal. She couldn't imagine the kind of woman he was drawn to. She wondered if they were just pretty faces, or great minds, bimbos, or soul mates. With his aversion to marriage and long-term relationships, it was hard to envision who he went out with. But she also realized, as she thought of it, that it was none of her business.

It had been a long week, and she was tired. And she could hardly wait to see Steven. As she thought of him, she drifted off to sleep, and the flight attendant woke her when they landed. She was one of the first to disembark, pick up her bags, and hail a taxi. And at ten minutes to seven on Saturday morning, she was letting herself into their apartment.

She set her bags down in the front hall, took off her shoes, and walked on tiptoe into their bedroom, so as not to wake him. He was sound asleep in their bed, naked as usual, and she peeled off her clothes, and slipped under the covers beside him. He stirred slightly and pulled her close to him, as though she had been there all night, next to him, and then he opened an eye and realized what had happened.

"You're back," he whispered, and she smiled as she nodded and then kissed him. "I missed you," he said, pulling her even closer, and she could feel the warmth of his flesh next to hers, as he kissed her.

"I missed you, too," she said, and meant it. He ran a hand slowly along the gentle curves of her body, and she realized with longing how long it had been since she'd last seen him. It had been more than a week, nearly eight days, much too long, and they were both starving for each other.

There were no words between them after that, only the passion that had burned between them like an eternal flame since the day they met. It was something they both cherished, and wanted, and desperately needed. And however little time they spent together, it made every moment more precious between them. It was a long time before they spoke again, and when they did, her blond hair lay tousled and silky on his pillow, and he looked down at her with a familiar smile, and she put her arms around him again, and kissed him.

Chapter 6

THEY SPENT AN easy, quiet weekend. They stayed in bed until noon on Saturday, and slept off and on, and when they got up, it was raining, and they decided to go to the movies.

They saw a film they'd both wanted to see for a long time, and then they walked home slowly in the rain, and stopped on the way for an ice cream. They talked about going out for a hamburger, but in the end, they opted to stay home, watch a video, and have Chinese food delivered. The hospital left them alone for once. He wasn't on call, and there were no fresh disasters that required calling him when he was off duty. And for the first time in months, she didn't even touch her briefcase.

By eleven o'clock that night, they were back in bed, curled up in each other's arms, and it made him hate the fact that he had to go back to work the next day, and she was leaving. She was coming back to New York on Monday night, with Cal, and they would be in town for two days, and leave Wednesday night for Europe. But he was going to be at the hospital until that morning, and she doubted if she'd even see him. She was going to be spending Thursday in Edinburgh, Friday in London, and she and Cal would be there over the weekend. Monday in Geneva after that. Tuesday in Paris, and then back to New York on Wednesday. So all in all, it meant she wouldn't see Steve for eleven days. They were used to it. But it suddenly seemed like an eternity to them.

"I'm not going anywhere after that for a while, I promise," she said, as she lay next to him, cuddled up against his back, with her arms around him.

"I'm going to hold you to that. I don't care how much money you make, you work too damn hard, and we're missing too much like this. Maybe it's time for you to slow down a little." But Meredith knew that her partners didn't think so. Steve wanted to talk to her about having a baby again, but there was no point until this deal was done and they had some time together to discuss it. He figured it was time now, before either of them got much older. He had always wanted to have three or four kids, but he would have been happy with one now. And he figured Meredith would at least concede that much. And they could afford a nurse or an au pair if she wanted to go back to work after she had the baby. He was thinking about it as he lay next to her, but he didn't say anything. He didn't want to get into a serious discussion with her, or worse yet, an argument, he just wanted to enjoy her. He thought she was scared of having kids, and once she took the leap, and actually decided to give in, he was sure she'd love it.

They slept soundly in each other's arms that night,

and he hated to pull away from her when his alarm went off at six o'clock the next morning. He had to be at the hospital by seven. She was still dozing when he left, and he shook her a little bit so he could say good-bye to her, and she opened her eyes with a look of surprise. She couldn't figure out where the night went. It all went by so quickly.

"I'll see you when you get back, Merrie. . . . I love you."

"I love you too. . . . I'll call you tonight from Boston."

He nodded, kissed her again, and a minute later he was gone, in his scrubs and his clogs, off to save the lives that others would attempt to destroy, tilting at windmills.

Meredith slept until eight o'clock, and then got up, made coffee, read the paper, and went to pack her suitcase. She packed for Europe as well, knowing she probably wouldn't have time when she came back to New York with Cal for his road show. They were going to be incredibly busy with all of the New York presentations. This was the most important city for them, and the last one before they headed for Europe. She wanted to have their book completely sold before they left for Europe, and she thought there was a good chance that would happen.

She was finished and packed shortly after noon, and after that she wasn't sure what to do. There wasn't anything she wanted to do alone. And she didn't really feel like going to a museum. In the end, she decided she might as well get to Boston. She could always have dinner with Cal once she got there. It was better than sitting alone in her empty apartment.

She took a cab to LaGuardia at three, caught the four o'clock shuttle, and at six o'clock she walked into the lobby of the Ritz Carlton. She was there even before Cal was. She left a note for him at the desk telling him she'd arrived, and the phone rang in her room promptly at seven.

"You beat me to it! How long have you been here?"

"For about an hour." She smiled when she heard his voice. He sounded so pleased to hear her. "How was your flight?"

"Boring. How was your weekend?"

"Relaxing. We just took it easy, and went to the movies."

"Did you do your laundry?"

"No, Steve did." She laughed. "He spoils me."

"I think you're making it all up. No guy in the world is this good . . . cooking . . . laundry . . . saving lives . . . the rest of us look like total slobs compared to him, Meredith. I think I'm beginning to hate him."

"I'm pretty lucky," she smiled. "How was your weekend with the kids?"

"Fun. We played tennis on Saturday, and after that, Andy and I played golf."

"I have the perfect husband, but you are the perfect father." Although she knew Steve would probably have been perfect at that, too, if she'd ever wanted to let him try it, which she still didn't.

"And you are the perfect woman," he said in a tone that made her blush, but she knew he was just kidding. Even on their travels, he had never attempted to be more than a friend to her, and she respected him for it.

"No. Just the perfect investment banker, I hope."

"Super Woman. How about having dinner with me?"

"That sounds good." It was actually why she had come up early. And they agreed to meet half an hour later in the lobby and find a place where they could eat pasta or pizza. Neither of them wanted to get dressed, or have an elaborate dinner.

"Do you mind if I wear jeans?" he asked, and she sounded relieved when she answered.

"I'd love that." She had traveled in a little cotton dress and sandals, and she figured that was good enough if they were just going out for pizza.

But when she met him in the lobby, he still looked like an ad in *GQ*. He was wearing jeans, and a clean white shirt, with the sleeves rolled up, his well-polished loafers, and he was carrying a blazer over his shoulder.

"That's cheating," she scolded him, as he looked her over admiringly. She looked fresh and young and pretty.

"What is?"

"You look much too good to just go out for pizza. Do you ever just wear a T-shirt or look a mess?" She couldn't imagine it, but he couldn't imagine her that way either.

"When was the last time you looked a mess, Meredith? In first grade maybe . . . or before that?" She laughed at the backhanded compliment, and they walked out of the hotel, laughing and talking, like the friends they were rapidly becoming.

They found a little Italian restaurant a few blocks away, and they spent the rest of the evening deeply engrossed in conversation about the investment banking business. He was fascinated by what she did, and intrigued to discover how much she liked it. But at the same time, she seemed to have a considerable grasp of the intricacies of his business. And they batted information and opinions back and forth all night like tennis pros at Wimbledon. They were the last people to leave the restaurant, and they hated to end their conversation, but they both needed to get some sleep before their presentation the next morning.

Meredith knew that Charlie McIntosh, Callan's CFO, had flown in from San Francisco that night too, but his flight hadn't been due in until midnight. They both hoped he would warm up in Boston and New York, and for the last leg of the trip in Europe.

"I had a long talk with him on the phone last night," Cal told her as they rode up in the elevator. "I told him he really has to put more life into his presentations. I hope he got it, and realizes that I mean it," Cal said, sounding unconvinced. He was beginning to see just how intractable Charlie was, and how unlikely to improve his attitude in the near future. Even on the phone the night before, he had criticized Callan for taking the company public. He was like a dog with a bone, and he just wasn't letting go of it, no matter how ardently Callan urged him to drop it. Callan was beginning to fear that his attitude was going to cause a permanent rift between them. And he said as much to Meredith as he walked her down the hall to her room, and she nodded as she listened.

"These things are hard to predict sometimes. Maybe once it's done, he'll do an about-face and surprise you.

Maybe he'll finally see that you've done a great thing
for your company, and not a bad one. You can use your
stock to acquire other companies eventually. I think
that might be something that could appeal to him."

"I think too much growth too rapidly is part of what
scares him," Cal said thoughtfully, and Meredith
looked pensive. Charlie was definitely a knotty problem.

They continued to talk about it, and a few minutes
later, he left her and promised to meet her for breakfast with Charlie McIntosh the next morning. Meredith
had promised to do everything but seduce him to win
him over.

She had two messages from Steve when she got back
to the room, and when she called him back, for once
the nurse who answered the phone was able to find
him. He said it had been a quiet night, it was still raining in New York, and everyone seemed to be staying
home and out of trouble.

"Maybe you can get some sleep for a change," she
said with a smile, still thinking of the night they had
spent together the night before, and their lovemaking
when she got back on Saturday morning. It already felt
like an eternity since she had seen him. Their days and
nights were so full that it seemed to create too much
time and space between them.

"You try and get some sleep too. These people keep
you out till all hours, and then expect you to be Dinah
Shore and sing your heart out for them the next morning."

"That's what I get paid for. I'll be home tomorrow
night, sweetheart." At least she could sleep in her own

bed for once, but unfortunately Steve wouldn't be there. He'd be sleeping on a rollaway bed in his office until they called him.

"I'll call you," he promised, thinking that in the old days, she had gone to see him at the hospital sometimes, but they both knew there was no point now. Whenever she tried to do it nowadays, he was always too busy to see her, and it ended up just being frustrating and annoying. It was easier just talking to her when he had a break, and he could find her.

She stayed up reading late that night, brushing up on their presentation again. There were a few things she wanted to change in her brief introduction of Cal, and she had some suggestions about Charlie McIntosh's presentation.

But when she shared her thoughts with Charlie at breakfast with him and Cal the next day, he got enraged the moment she made the suggestions to him. What she was offering wasn't criticism, but simple ways to improve the way he presented Dow Tech to their potential investors.

"I'm not sure you understand what I'm trying to say," she explained patiently, trying to turn it around another way, so he wouldn't resist as much and would get it. But he was incredibly defensive, and openly hostile to her.

"I understand perfectly. You think you're so goddamn smart, Miss Hot Shot Investment Banker from Wall Street. Well let me tell you, I don't agree with a damn thing you've said in the last ten minutes, or in the last ten weeks for that matter. This whole thing is a huge mistake, and you people have Cal's head so turned around, he's dazzled by the dollar signs, and he doesn't know his ass from his elbow." In spite of herself, Meredith looked shocked not only by what he said, but by the disrespectful way he had said it. He had managed to insult both of them in one breath, and she could see that Callan hadn't liked it either.

"Maybe if you stop fighting the fact that the company is going public, Mr. McIntosh, you could figure out the best way to help us do it. Because it's going to go public, whether you like it or not. That's what Callan wants, and what he's going to get from us. Now, you can be part of it, or you can sit there like a rock and refuse to cooperate, but if you do, I assure you that the river is still going to go around you. You're not going to stop it at this point."

He looked startled by what she said, and the force with which she said it to him. And Callan looked like a storm cloud as he paid the check and finished his coffee. All he said as they left the restaurant was that he wanted to meet with McIntosh after the presentation, and she could imagine what that meant. He was going to give him a dressing down second to none, and maybe even threaten his job if he had to. But this was no time for Charlie to be threatening mutiny, or insulting their investment bankers.

The three of them walked out of the dining room in silence. And when Meredith introduced him a little while later at the presentation, she thought that the CFO was slightly mollified and a little better behaved, but she could tell that Callan still didn't think so. He was raging about him after the potential investors left, and he and Meredith were alone for a few minutes before the next one.

"Who the hell does he think he is, talking to you

like that?'' He was more upset about what the CFO had said to Meredith than about the insults he had flung at Callan.

"He's just a crusty old man resisting change, Cal. And there isn't a hell of a lot you can do about it. You can try to win him over, and I know you have. But if he remains unconvinced, you'll have to decide what you want to do after the road show. But this isn't the time to rock the boat. We have to make a great showing in New York, and we still have to get through a week in Europe.''

"I know that,'' Callan said, still looking angry. He felt as though his hands were tied, and Charlie McIntosh knew that.

They got through their second presentation over lunch, and the three of them flew to New York together that afternoon, and Charlie McIntosh said very little to either of them. Meredith couldn't help wondering if he was sorry about what he'd said, and was just too embarrassed to admit it. But he never apologized to her, and Callan was barely speaking to him by the time they got to New York at six o'clock. Callan was so angry at him by then, that she almost felt sorry for the CFO and the situation he'd created. He had gotten himself way out on a limb, and Meredith had the feeling that Callan was about to saw the branch off.

She had hired a limousine to pick them up, and she rode with them to their hotel. They were staying at the Regency, and after that, she had the car drop her off at her apartment. She knew Steve wouldn't be home that night, but it felt good to be home anyway, and have some time to herself before they left for Europe.

On Tuesday their presentations went extremely well.

They were already oversubscribed at the end of the first day, and investors were clamoring for more stock than she was going to be able to give them. It was exactly the situation they had wanted. But even then, Charlie McIntosh didn't have the grace to back down, and he stormed off after the last presentation to go back to the hotel, and if only to calm him down, Meredith suggested that she and Cal have dinner.

She took Callan to "21," and they talked for a long time about the serious problem that the CFO presented for him.

"You don't need his support, Cal, but it would certainly be nice to have it," she said sensibly.

"I swear, if he goes crazy on me in Europe, and alienates anyone, I'm going to knock him out cold right in the middle of his presentation."

"That would certainly impress our investors," she said, laughing, because she knew from dealing with Cal that he wasn't likely to do it, but he was understandably furious at the CFO who was continuing to give him an enormous headache. But the success of the IPO far outweighed the aggravation of his personnel woes, and he was still in pretty good spirits.

"How would you handle him in my place?" Cal asked as they finished dinner. It was all they had talked about all evening. He respected her advice, her cool head, and her sensible decisions, and she seemed to think about it for a minute before speaking.

"I guess I'd probably have to kill him. Poison him maybe. He eats a lot of sweets, mints mostly, I think. It would probably be pretty easy to slip a little cyanide tablet in his candy." She had said it so seriously that for a minute Cal thought she meant it, and then he laughed at what she said. She had a way of adding a little levity at the right moment.

"All right, I guess I'll calm down about it until we get back from Europe."

"I don't think you have any other choice. You can deal with the whole situation once you get back to California."

"I think I'm going to have to."

"Meanwhile, you should be celebrating. You took New York by storm. I couldn't have asked for anything better."

"Neither could I." Callan Dow looked extremely pleased, and in light of that, his problems with the CFO seemed to fade momentarily into the distance. They were meeting with more private investors the next day, and that night, they were leaving for Europe.

"Will you get a chance to see your husband before you leave?" Cal asked, looking concerned. He was beginning to realize how much of her time he was taking up, and how dependent he was becoming on her. And he felt a little guilty.

"No. I'll be in a meeting downtown with you by the time he gets off duty. I might see him when I go home to pick up my bag on the way to the airport, unless he gets called back to the hospital before that."

"Hell of a life you lead, my friend. I don't know how you manage to stay married."

"We love each other," she said simply, and then decided to tweak him a little bit, "in spite of the fact that I don't want his children."

"You're beginning to make me think I should review my theories on that one. I'm beginning to think you do have the perfect marriage. Maybe because you don't have children. What do I know?''

"What do any of us know about relationships? Sometimes I think it's all blind luck, or luck of the draw or something. Who could have guessed fourteen years ago that Steven and I would be this crazy about each other, or lead a life where we practically never see each other? When we got married, he thought he wanted a rural family practice in Vermont, and I was thinking about going to law school. And the next thing I knew, he fell in love with the trauma unit and said he had to live in New York, and I fell in love with Wall Street. Things never work out exactly the way you expect them to. Maybe it's better like that, sometimes at least.'' Callan's life hadn't worked out the way he expected either. She wondered sometimes if anyone's did. "I'd probably have been bored to death in Vermont, and we might have broken up years ago. I don't know why, but this works for us.''

"You're damn lucky, Merrie.''

"Yeah, I know,'' she said softly. "One of these days you'll have to meet him.''

"Not professionally, I hope. Maybe we could have dinner when we get back from Europe.''

"He'd love that. He's familiar with what you do. Actually, he was the first one to tell me what your products do, and how good they are.''

"Obviously, a great guy,'' he said with a smile as he paid the check, and they left the restaurant, and then walked slowly back to his hotel. After she dropped him off, she took a cab back to her apartment.

And the next morning, they were back downtown,

meeting with investors, and making their pitch to them. After that, they had lunch with some of her partners, and yet another group of investors, and were finally finished for the day. When the partners congratulated him on the success of his venture, he tried to give Meredith as much credit for the IPO as he could, but they were more interested in talking to him, than in giving Meredith accolades. As far as they were concerned, she had only done what was expected of her, and there was no reason to celebrate her for it. It annoyed Cal to see the way they handled it, and he mentioned it to her in the car on the way back to the hotel to pick up his bags, en route to the airport.

"They sure don't throw you a lot of roses," he said, looking disgruntled for her.

"They would have done the same things I did. They know that. And as far as they're concerned, Paul Black brought you in as a client. I didn't."

"That's stretching it a bit, isn't it? He made the initial contact, but you've done everything since then."

"That's just the nature of the business. There are no heroes among investment bankers."

"And not much gratitude either."

"I don't expect that. I'll make plenty of money on this deal. We all will."

"It's not just about money, Merrie, and you know that. You can't tell me that's the only reason why you do this. You do it because you believe in the companies you take public for them, and you love what you're doing." He had more respect for her than that, and it bothered him that they didn't.

"That's all true. But there isn't a lot of romance in

this business. They figure I'll make plenty on it, and so will they. They don't feel they need to throw me a lot of kisses.''

"I think they're harder on you, and expect more, because you're a woman. It's almost as if you have to prove something to them, that you're as good or as smart or as capable as a man, and there's something wrong with that. You're a hell of a lot smarter than most of them, Paul Black certainly. He's nothing but an old windbag with good social connections. All he is is a rainmaker.'' She laughed at his description.

"Thank you for noticing, on both counts. But there are plenty of those in this business.''

"And not enough like you. I've had a great time working with you.'' And more than that, he had really come to like her, and admire what she stood for. She was honorable and decent and loyal and as far as he was concerned, brilliant. And a hell of a nice person. He was also impressed that she spoke so highly of her husband.

"I've had a great time working with you too. And that's a good thing, Cal, because you're stuck with me for another week.'' She laughed, and a few minutes later, they picked up Cal's bags and Charlie McIntosh at the hotel, and then went on to her apartment. Her bags were standing in the hall, and she ran upstairs alone to get them, and was back in less than five minutes. Steve had left her a note. He had gone back to the hospital, for a meeting, and was sorry that he'd missed her. She jotted down a few words at the bottom of the note, mostly just to tell him that she was sorry that she had missed him too, and that she loved him.

"Did you see Steve?" Cal asked with a look of concern as she came downstairs. He was beginning to worry about her, almost like a little sister.

"No, he had to go back to the hospital for a meeting. It's okay. I didn't really expect to see him." She seemed disappointed but not surprised by it. It was the nature of the life they led, and she was used to it, far more than Cal was.

"That's too bad. I'll bet he was disappointed."

"I'll see him in a week," she smiled. "I might even take some time off when we get back. We might go to Vermont for a few days, if he can get away. If not, maybe we'll take a long weekend somewhere."

"It's too bad he couldn't meet us in London for the weekend."

"I tried to get him to come to Paris," she smiled, "but he's covering for the head of the trauma unit next week, who has to go to Dallas."

"You two lead a disgusting life. I don't know how you stand it. Well, maybe we can go to the theater this weekend in London. Or Annabel's. Do you like to dance?" he asked, and Charlie McIntosh glanced out the window, looking disgusted. Mixing business with pleasure, for Cal at least, clearly did not meet with Charlie's approval, and most of all not with Merrie.

"I love to dance," she said, smiling, as much touched by the invitation, as she was amused by Charlie's obvious disapproval. It entertained her to shock him. "And I love the theater."

"Maybe we can do both then." He felt he owed her some fun for all her trouble. And they were both going to be alone in London, except for Charlie.

The three of them went over some papers together when they got to the airport, and by the time they boarded the plane to Edinburgh, they were all tired. The plane was making a stop on the way, in London. But as soon as they had eaten, Charlie and Cal turned off their lights and settled down under their blankets. Cal and Meredith were seated side by side, and Charlie was sitting right behind them. But as Cal put his seat back as far as he could, Meredith reached down for her briefcase.

"Merrie," he asked softly in the darkened plane, "what are you doing?"

"I thought I'd do some reading."

"Stop that!" he ordered her gently. "You need to get some sleep too. I order you to turn your light off."

"You 'order' me?" She looked amused. "That's a novelty."

"Maybe it's time someone said that to you more often. Come on, give it up for tonight. Turn your light off." She hesitated for a moment, and then decided that maybe he was right, and her work could wait till morning. And quietly, she reached up and turned her light off. "Good girl. It'll still be there in the morning." His tone was kind and fatherly, and she could suddenly imagine how he was with his children. She knew instinctively that he was a good father.

"That's what I'm always afraid of," she said gently, "that it'll all still be there in the morning. I keep hoping the work fairy will show up in the middle of the night and do it for me."

"You're the work fairy, Merrie. But even fairies need to rest sometimes." It made him more determined than ever to give her some fun in London. She deserved it. She had done more for him than anyone had in a long time, maybe ever.

She moved her seat back like his, put a pillow behind her head and pulled up her blanket, and lay there, quietly beside him.

"Can you sleep on planes?" he asked, whispering. They were like two kids at a slumber party.

"Sometimes. Depends on how much work I have in my briefcase," she said, smiling at him.

"Pretend you left it in New York. Pretend you're going on vacation." She smiled at the game, and whispered back at him.

"Where would I go on vacation?"

"How about the South of France? . . . Saint-Tropez . . . how does that sound?" He was still whispering and she was smiling.

"That sounds very good. I like it."

"Then close your eyes and think of Saint-Tropez," he whispered gently.

"Is that an order too?" she whispered back again.

"Yes . . . now, be quiet, and just think about it." And much to her surprise, she did. She lay there with her eyes closed, envisioning the South of France, the little port, the narrow winding streets, the Mediterranean, and the flower market. And the next time he looked at her, she was sound asleep, and he gently pulled up her blanket and tucked it around her.

Chapter 7

THE PLANE STOPPED in London, and then flew on to Edinburgh, and Meredith was surprised that she slept for most of the flight. It was morning in Scotland when they arrived, and they went directly to the location where they were to make their presentation to the officers of several of the Scottish trusts. It was part of the standard ritual of the due diligence tour, and one of the routines Meredith knew well.

As it had for nearly two weeks now, the tour was continuing to go very well, and Callan was ecstatic when they got a fax from her office in New York, telling them that the order book was oversubscribed ten to one now, which meant that they had ten times more demand for stock than they needed.

By evening they were ready to move on, and they flew back to London that night. And by the time they got to Claridge's, even the indefatigable Callan looked exhausted. It had been a long day, after flying all night before they arrived. And the next morning, they had to be fresh to make their presentation again in London. Callan was pleased with everything, the tour was going extremely well, better than he had ever dreamed, and he had Meredith to thank for it.

"What are you up to tonight, Meredith?" he asked as they checked in, and a liveried desk clerk showed them to their rooms. Charlie McIntosh was on another floor, but their rooms were side by side.

"What am I up to?" she asked. "Sleep, I hope. I don't know about you, but I'm beat. I thought I'd go to bed so I don't screw things up for you tomorrow."

"There's no risk of that. Do you want to go out for something to eat?" Even as tired as she knew he had to be, he wanted to go out. Callan Dow liked to work hard all day, and then go out to play at night.

"Not tonight, thanks. I'm going to order room service, and then hit the sack."

"Party pooper. What about dinner at Harry's Bar, and then Annabel's tomorrow night?"

"Where do you get your energy, Cal? Don't you ever get tired?"

"Look who's talking. You never stop," he said admiringly.

"I think I just have," she said, looking tired. The jet lag and the long day and long flight had finally caught up with her, and she could hardly keep her eyes open as the porter set down her briefcase and her bag, and then let Cal into his room. Hers was handsomely done in Art Deco style. His was all done in pale blue taffeta with pastel chintz covered in flowers. And they both looked like they'd been recently redone. But Meredith would have been happy to sleep in a haystack that

night, and she wanted to be fresh for the next day.
They were doing their first presentation at eight A.M.
But she didn't feel as pressured here as she had in New
York. The European market was of slightly less interest
to them. Traditionally, they tried to keep the size of the
European investments down. It was important to have
them participate for the long haul, but they preferred
to keep the bulk of hot IPOs for U.S.-based investors,
who would spin the stock more often, generating more
commissions.

Cal wandered back into her room after they had
brought him his bags. He tried to convince her to go
out again, but she said she was in for the night. And a
little while later, she heard his door open and close,
and knew he had gone out. She was in bed and sound
asleep by nine o'clock. And she was bright and cheery
the next day when they met for breakfast.

"What did you do last night?" she asked him over
scones and coffee in the dining room. His CFO hadn't
joined them yet.

"I caught up with some old friends. I know a lot of
people here, some of them through my ex-wife."

"I was dead to the world by nine." She smiled at
him.

"We'll do better than that tonight," he smiled, as
Charlie McIntosh arrived at their table. He was in a
fairly decent mood for once, and the three of them
chatted amiably as Charlie ordered sausages and eggs.
And by eight o'clock they were making their now familiar presentation. It was a huge hit, just as all the others
had been.

They met with private investors at noon, and at one

o'clock made their presentation again over lunch. And by four o'clock, all three of them were back at the hotel. Charlie had plans to spend the weekend in France with friends, and they were to meet up again in Geneva on Sunday night. In an uncharacteristically generous gesture, Charlie wished them a nice weekend before he left, and Meredith allowed herself to hope that it meant he was mellowing a little.

"Ready for a night on the town?" Cal asked as he walked her back to her room at five. They had reservations at Harry's Bar at eight o'clock, and were still planning to go to Annabel's to dance after dinner.

"Are you sure you don't mind wasting time with me?" Meredith asked comfortably. "You can probably have a lot more fun with a real date," she said honestly, they were like brother and sister by now, and they both seemed to enjoy it.

"I'd rather have dinner with a good friend anytime," he smiled, as they stood in the hall and chatted a little bit about their afternoon. The presentations had gone even better than expected.

"I thought Charlie did better here too," Meredith said charitably. Even at his warmest, Charlie McIntosh was no ball of fire. But at least he didn't seem as truculent as he had in Los Angeles and New York. Cal said he had noticed it too. "It's a shame it took him so long to warm up." Callan didn't comment on it, and after a few more minutes, they went back to their respective rooms. He said he'd come by to pick her up at a quarter to eight, which gave her plenty of time to unwind, relax, and take a bath. And as soon as she slipped into it, the phone rang in her room.

She was wrapped in a towel and had wet hair when she answered it, and she smiled the moment she heard the voice on the other end. It was Steve.

"How's it going, sweetheart?" He sounded in good spirits, it was early Friday afternoon for him.

"Everything is great," she answered with a broad smile, pulling the towel closer around her in the air-conditioned room. "We're almost through, and we're oversubscribed ten to one. It's a sure green shoe on this one." He knew that meant they'd be adding five to ten percent more shares. After a dozen years of her Wall Street career, the jargon was familiar to him. "Callan is really pleased."

"Is his CFO still being a pain in the ass?" he asked with interest.

"He's been a little better here. He actually smiled today, he left for the weekend with some friends in France. It's kind of nice to get him off our necks." Most of the time he was like having a crabby grandfather around. But Steve didn't sound pleased to hear it.

"Does that mean you and Dow are alone?"

"More or less. Along with about eight million people in London, I think it's pretty safe." She was amused by his concern.

"You know what I mean. He's not coming on to you, is he, Merrie?"

"Of course not. He's smarter than that. And by now, we're good friends. After these due diligence tours, you either end up best friends for life, or you never want to lay eyes on each other again. He's been a good sport, and I think he'll stay a good friend. I hope one of these days you'll meet him."

"All right. . . . I don't know why, but I don't trust him. I'd much rather be spending the weekend in London with you myself."

"Then come," she teased. "You can still meet me in Paris next week."

"Very funny. You know I'm stuck here. Just get your ass back here as fast as you can. What are you doing this weekend?"

"Just hanging around. I thought I'd do some shopping tomorrow, and Cal and I are going to have dinner tonight at Harry's Bar." Given what he had just said, she didn't tell him they were going dancing at Annabel's afterward. She knew there was nothing to it, but there was no point upsetting Steve. It was all harmless, and Cal was a perfect gentleman, just as she had said he would be.

"If he gets drunk, just take a cab home by yourself. Don't take a chance."

"Sweetheart, stop worrying. No one is going to get drunk. We're going to have dinner, and go home. That's all. It's better than room service, but it's no big deal."

"All right," he said, sounding mollified, but still slightly unsure. The guy was too young, too successful, too good looking, from everything he'd read and heard. He couldn't imagine any man being able to resist his wife. But even if he was suspicious of Callan, he trusted her completely.

"What about you? What are you up to tonight?" she asked him.

"Sleep. I'm back on call tomorrow. But I've got nothing else to do this weekend anyway. I'm off next weekend at least. I traded it so I could be with you."

"Why don't we go away somewhere?" She sounded happy at the prospect.

"We'll see."

They hung up a few minutes later, and she went back to her bath, which was cold by then. She ran some more hot water into it, and sat smiling in the bathtub, thinking of him. It seemed cute to her that he was still jealous after all these years. He had no reason to be, and he knew it. She had never even remotely for a single instant thought of being unfaithful to him. She was still very much in love with Steve, just as he was with her.

When Callan picked her up shortly before eight, she was wearing a short black cocktail dress, high-heeled evening sandals, and a string of pearls. She was wearing makeup and her hair shone like gold. She looked very striking and very pretty, and Cal took a step backward to look at her and seemed impressed. She was always fairly conservatively dressed when she worked, and was given to wearing navy or black suits. She usually looked very much the part of a banker, but tonight she looked young and sexy, and the back of the little black cocktail dress was fairly bare.

"Wow! If I may say so, Mrs. Whitman, you're a knockout. Maybe you should have been wearing that when you made your speech on the tour. If you had, we'd be oversold a hundred to one."

"Thank you, Callan," she said, blushing slightly. It was fun getting dressed up for a change, and going out with him.

And when they got to Harry's, all the trendy in-crowd, well-known names and faces, and aristocrats were there. It was still one of the most exclusive

restaurants in London, and because it was a club, it
looked more like a dinner party in someone's house,
than a public place.

They had drinks at the bar, and when they were
taken to their table, Meredith recognized the people at
the tables on either side. One was a group of important
international bankers, some English, some French, one
Saudi, and two from Bahrain. And at the table on their
right were two movie stars and a director and a well-
known Italian prince. It was a star-studded crowd, and
it was fun being there with him.

And for once, they didn't talk about business. They
were just two people out for dinner on a Friday night.
Except for the fact that she was married and he was a
client, it was almost like a date, but better in some ways.
Neither of them had to worry about the outcome, or
the impression they were making, the intentions or
agendas of the other, they were just friends enjoying a
fun evening.

"Steve must be pretty open-minded," Callan commented as the waiter poured them each a glass of Châ-
teau d'Yquem with their dessert. It was a sweet sauterne
that Meredith had always loved, and it tasted like liquid
gold as she sipped it.

"What makes you say that?"

"I'm not sure I'd have wanted my wife going out to
dinner and dancing, when I was married. I'm not sure I
ever trusted Charlotte that much," and they both knew
he hadn't been wrong to distrust her.

"Steve knows he has nothing to worry about. I'm a
sure thing," she said with a smile, as she noticed a very
stylish-looking dark-haired woman walk into the restaurant in a red dress. Several people seemed to know who

she was, and she was with a very attractive older man. Meredith thought she looked familiar, but she couldn't figure out who she was, and finally, watching her chat and laugh from table to table, Meredith asked Cal if he recognized her. And he looked at her for a long time. "Is she an actress?" She was too old to be a model, but not by very much. And she could have been, when she was younger.

"No, she's an attorney," he said with a last glance, and then turned around to face Meredith again with a somewhat pinched expression.

"Do you know her? I've seen her somewhere, but I can't place the face."

"You've seen her in *W,* and assorted magazines. She's very social, and fairly well known by association, most of her clients are very important. She moves in a very jet-set crowd," he said simply.

"Who is she?" Meredith looked puzzled, and Cal looked unconcerned, but there was suddenly something hard about his eyes as he answered.

"That's my ex-wife," he said, looking right across the table into Meredith's eyes. He did not look pleased about it.

"I'm sorry," she said. She could see that it was a reminder he didn't need. And it was unfortunate that she'd been there.

"Don't be. We're on good terms now. I see her whenever she comes to visit the kids." But Meredith could sense easily that no matter how he covered it, the encounter was painful for him. She wondered if they were going to say hello to each other, but as the thought crossed her mind, the woman in red was suddenly standing at their table, and holding a hand out to

Cal with a dazzling smile, which glittered almost as brilliantly as the diamonds on her ears and fingers. "Hello, Charlotte," he said simply, "how are you?"

"Fine. What are you doing in this part of the world?" She glanced at Meredith in her simple black dress and string of pearls, and the elegant young investment banker was instantly dismissed as unimportant.

"I'm here on business. And this is Meredith Whitman," he introduced her politely, and a minute later Charlotte moved on and joined her friends at a table in the rear, for a private party. It struck Meredith after she left that she had never bothered to inquire about their children. She said something about it to Callan, and he shrugged and looked at Meredith with a wry smile. "I told you, Meredith, children aren't her thing. She likes glamour and the jet set, and business, and glitz. All that interests her are the big stars she represents. She's very happy here." Meredith wondered how much it upset him to see her, but didn't press him about it.

"She's very striking," Meredith commented, and very beautiful. It said something about the kind of women he was attracted to. It was hard not to be somewhat dazzled by her looks, and from everything Cal had said, she was obviously smart too. It was the important things, like values, and compassion and integrity, which she seemed to lack, from what Cal had told her.

"She was a model as a kid. I think it kind of went to her head. She liked all the attention, and the money, but she knew it couldn't last. So she built something for herself that would. She's actually a very fine attorney, and she loves that whole entertainment world. She adores all her little movie stars, I think she lives vicariously through them. And they're all crazy about her.

Maybe that's why she's not as interested in her own kids. Her clients are her children, and she gets all her strokes from them.''

"Kind of like me," Meredith grinned. "My clients are my kids. Like you. I get everything all set up, and then I send you out into the world to make lots of money and be a big success." He laughed at the comparison and shook his head.

"I think it's a little more than that. But what do you get out of it, Meredith, other than the obvious?" They both knew she would make a lot of money on his deal, but he also knew she did it for more than that. She loved what she did. And she was brilliant at it. In the months he had worked with her, and particularly lately, he had been enormously impressed by her.

"I love what I do," she said in answer to his question. "And it's true in a way, my clients are my kids. I don't need children. I get everything I need from them and Steve."

"It's not the same thing, I promise. You're missing out on something important," he glanced across the room then at the table where Charlotte sat, "so is she. She never understood what she was missing. And in her case, it's a real crime. At least you haven't had children, you're not hurting anyone by your decision, except maybe yourself, or Steve. In her case, she's not only missing out, but she's cheating our children out of having a real mother."

"Maybe it's time for you to remarry," she said bravely, "not only for your sake, but for the kids' sake."

"Great. And then what? Let them live through a divorce again? At least last time most of them were too young to understand what was happening. Mary Ellen was six, and it was heartbreaking for her, but Julie and Andy were four and not quite two. It was a lot easier for them. Next time it wouldn't be. They're older now. Old enough to be hurt by it.''

"What makes you think you'd get divorced next time, Cal? Don't you think you learned something last time?''

"Yeah, not to get married," he laughed, but it wasn't a sound of humor, but of bitterness and remembered pain, "and not to trust, and not to be as stupid next time. Charlotte started her business in London on the settlement she got from me.''

"Lucky for her.''

"I thought so," he said, as he signaled for the check. "Besides," he said with a look of amusement, "my kids wouldn't let me marry again. I think they're pretty clear that they want me to themselves now.''

"That's not fair, and it's not good for them, or you.''

"It's very good for me. They're like three little guardian angels, who keep me from making a fool of myself, or doing something stupid.''

"You're too smart to be that cynical, Cal, or that cowardly." She was speaking to him as a friend, and he knew it.

"Why are you trying to sell me marriage?" He was intrigued by her persistence.

"Because I think it's a great thing. Best thing I ever did.''

"Then you're very lucky," he smiled warmly at her, and seemed to relax again, "and so is Steve. Come on, kiddo, let's go dance." He took her hand, and led her out of the restaurant, without a glance back in his ex-wife's direction. For him, it was a closed book, and

Meredith was relieved when they were back on the street. She had sensed his tension, and his pain over running into Charlotte. He clearly had no warm feelings about her, no matter how many children they'd had together.

They chatted easily on the way to Annabel's, in the chauffeured Daimler he'd hired at the hotel. And Meredith loved it when they got to Annabel's. He ordered champagne for both of them, and led her out to the dance floor, and it was an hour later when they came back to their table. She was having a great time with him. He was a wonderful dancer, and fun to be with. And she was sorry for him that in some ways he was still so bitter. He had been badly wounded, but in every other way, he was an immensely appealing man, and she thought he deserved more than he was willing to allow himself to have. Somehow, his work and children did not seem enough for a man like him, although she didn't know what else he had in his life. In all the time they'd been traveling together, he had never mentioned a girlfriend or a companion, or a woman in his life, and she couldn't help wondering what he did for fun, other than work, and go dancing with his investment banker.

They stayed at Annabel's until two o'clock in the morning, and then went back to Claridge's. They were laughing and happy and tired and relaxed. And without a thought of anything more than friendship, she could have easily danced with him all night. He held her comfortably in his arms, dancing slow or fast, moving perfectly with her, but still never out of line, and never too close. She wasn't uncomfortable with him for an instant. In fact, she felt even closer to him than before. And seeing Charlotte at Harry's Bar, and his reaction to her, had been an intriguing glimpse into his past for her.

"What's on the agenda for tomorrow?" he asked as he left her at the door to her hotel room.

"I thought I'd do some shopping. I love the antique shops here."

"So do I," he said easily. "Mind if I come with you?"

"Of course not." But she remembered the treasures she'd seen in his house. "You may want to go to some fancier places than I do. I was just going to browse a little."

"I can't think of anything I'd like better," he said comfortably, and then added, "I had a great time tonight. You're wonderful company, Meredith." Maybe, but she certainly wasn't as sophisticated or as striking as his ex-wife. Charlotte was a whole other breed, and she wondered if in comparison, Callan found her a little dull. She was far more conservative than his ex-wife. But also a great deal more real.

"I had a good time too. Thank you, Cal. Dinner was terrific, and I loved dancing. I never get to go dancing with Steve. He's always either too tired, or at work, and I've come to the conclusion over the years, that most surgeons just can't dance. This was fun. Thank you," she said warmly, and meant it.

"I'll come to New York and take you dancing anytime. We can be the new Ginger Rogers and Fred Astaire, dancing partners and good friends." She laughed at the comparison, and after she said good night to him, she closed the door to her room. She was tired, but she had had a great time, and when she glanced at the phone, she saw that the message light was on. And when she called in for her messages, they told her Steve had called three times, but she was tired and decided to call him in the morning.

She tossed her dress on a chair, kicked off her shoes, brushed her teeth, put on her nightgown, and went straight to bed.

And she was still asleep at eight o'clock the next morning when the phone rang. It was Steve.

"Where were you all night?" He sounded annoyed this time.

"I told you I was going out with Cal." She was half asleep, and she yawned.

"What time did you get in? Four A.M.?"

"No. Two. We went to Harry's for dinner, and then to Annabel's afterward for drinks." She had no secrets from him. She had always intended to tell him about Annabel's, she just didn't want to worry him beforehand.

"Did you dance with him?"

"No. But I danced with several waiters and the maître d'. Of course I danced with him, silly. It was no big deal."

"Maybe it is to me." He sounded like a petulant child and she was mildly amused. He knew better than to worry about her with another man. Even if they had gone dancing.

"Well, it shouldn't be. It was a perfectly respectable evening. We even ran into his ex-wife."

"That must have been fun. Anyway, I'm sorry if I'm being stupid. I just miss you, and I don't think I like you traveling around with another man."

"I'll only take female clients from now on, I promise. I'll be sure to let them know at the firm."

"All right, all right, so I'm a jerk. But I love you, and you're too goddamn beautiful to be traveling all over the world with handsome single guys."

"He's a perfect gentleman, baby, I promise." She was awake then, and sorry that he was upset about it. It was one thing to tease him a little, and another if he was genuinely worried. Making each other intentionally jealous was a game neither of them had ever played. "We won't go dancing again, I promise. It was just a one-time thing because we're both stuck here for the weekend, and we've been working so damn hard. I think we wanted to celebrate our success, but he really is harmless, and we're just good friends. You'll like him."

"All right, I'm sorry, Merrie. I trust you. Do whatever you want. What are you doing today?"

"Nothing much. Some shopping. I asked the concierge to get me theater tickets." The theater was so good in London, she always went when she was there. "I'm leaving for Geneva tomorrow night, and then we'll be back at work."

"I'm just glad you'll be home soon." He sounded antsy and worried, and she was sorry about it. She hadn't meant to upset him. He was far too decent to deserve that.

"He keeps trying to talk me into having kids."

"Hopefully not his." Steve sounded mildly worried again and she laughed.

"No, yours. He keeps telling me how lucky we are. I think he was pretty badly burned by his ex-wife. He's been divorced for eight years, and I think he's still one of the walking wounded. You should see his ex-wife, she's gorgeous, but a real piece of work. She lives here.

She left him with the kids, and took off with her partner."

"Nice woman. I'll have to take a look at this guy sometime."

"He's short, fat, ugly, and has warts."

"Yeah, and looks like Gary Cooper. I remember that part. I don't remember Gary Cooper having warts."

"Maybe you never looked that close."

"Well, don't you look that close either. Come home soon, baby, I miss you." It was odd but he seemed totally unnerved by Callan Dow, which was unusual for him. Most of the time, he was unconcerned about the men with whom she did business. But for some reason, this time seemed different. Maybe he had read too much about him. The newspapers always made Callan sound glamorous and dashing and like a financial wizard. He was all of those things, but like everyone else, he was human. And Meredith was very much in love with her husband.

"What are you up to today?"

"I don't know. I'm off as of nine this morning. It's three now. But it's so boring when you're not here to play with."

"I'll be home next week, and we can play all weekend."

"I can't wait to see you." He was lonelier than usual, and for some reason, he seemed restless to her. Maybe he really was jealous and unnerved by her traveling around with Callan. She was almost sorry she'd told him they'd gone dancing, but she never lied to him. And he knew that about her. "Have fun shopping today. Call me when you get back to the hotel."

"I will," she promised, and she meant it. But as it

turned out, she and Callan dragged around the shops until six o'clock, and then rushed back to change for dinner and the theater.

They went to Rule's, and sat upstairs in a private room, and then dashed off to see a new production of *Romeo and Juliet,* and thoroughly enjoyed it. They went to Mark's Club, which he was a member of, for drinks afterward, and by the time she got home, she was too tired to call him.

She called Steve on Sunday afternoon before she left for Heathrow, but he was out, and she tried again when she got to Geneva, but by then he was working. So she gave up and had dinner with Callan and Charlie McIntosh, went to bed early, and the next morning they made their presentation to the Swiss investors. Charlie was in a much better mood than he'd been, and was actually civil to Meredith after the meeting. And Callan was pleased to see it.

And at four o'clock, they were on a plane to Paris, and all three were surprisingly congenial on the trip, which led Meredith to hope that Charlie had finally begun to understand the wisdom of what they were doing. And his benevolence toward her had been considerably enhanced by two martinis on the flight to Paris.

They were at the Ritz by dinnertime, and before Meredith could say a word, Callan informed her that he had made reservations at the Tour d'Argent for them. Charlie had other plans, and she put on the only other dinner dress she'd brought, a pale green silk the color of her eyes, and when she appeared in the bar at the Ritz, a number of heads turned, and Callan beamed at her.

"You look smashing, Meredith!" he said, without hesitation.

"Thank you."

Dinner was predictably fabulous, and they spent most of the evening talking business, despite the sumptuous meal and the elegant surroundings. She wanted to prepare him for their presentation in the morning. The French weren't always easy, but news of their offering had already reached the important French investors, and they were as anxious to get on Callan's bandwagon as everyone else. Meredith didn't think they'd have any problems with the French.

The car brought them back to the hotel, and she and Callan walked slowly around the Place Vendôme, to get some air. It was mid-September by then, and a beautiful, balmy evening. And as they walked back to the hotel, she felt chilly in the thin dress, and Callan put his jacket over her shoulders. It smelled of his cologne, and they looked like a happy couple as they chatted and laughed and glanced into the jewelers' windows. It had been a very pleasant evening. And after their presentation the next day, they were spending one last night in Paris, and then flying back to New York early on Wednesday, in time for their final meeting with her partners, about the pricing of the stock. The stock would be traded the next day, the syndicate would dissolve as soon as all the stock was sold, and his work with Meredith would be over. He seemed to feel almost nostalgic about it as they walked slowly back to the hotel across the most elegant square in Paris.

"What am I going to do without you to talk to every day, Meredith? I'm going to have withdrawals."

"No, you won't, you'll be too busy worrying about

your shareholders and what they want to even think
about me."

"I feel like I'm being pushed out of the nest to fly
on my own now," he said, as they walked past
Boucheron and Meredith admired an enormous emer-
ald necklace.

"You did fine without me before you met me," she
said confidently, and then she laughed, pulling his
jacket a little tighter around her. "Besides, you have
Charlie to talk to."

"That's a frightening thought," Callan said, looking
more handsome than ever in a white shirt, and dark
blue tie. He always looked impeccable, and had an
enormous amount of style. He looked like more of a
clothes horse sometimes than the head of a successful
high-tech venture in Silicon Valley. It made her think
of Charlotte and what a handsome couple they must
have been years before. He seemed like the right kind
of man for a very beautiful, glamorous woman, and
there was something very pleasant about being seen
with him. People always looked at them when they were
out together. "Anyway, my dear, I'm going to miss
you."

"You can call me for free advice anytime you have a
problem."

"If I can even find you. If you're not away or too
busy to return my calls," he said wistfully. He actually
looked sad about it, as she smiled at him.

"My office always knows where to find me," she
reassured him, as they walked up the steps of the Ritz
and into the lobby.

They passed down the long corridor of vitrines full

of jewelry and gifts, and he left her at her room, with a look of regret, as she handed him back his jacket. It had been another lovely evening, and she had agreed to dine at Lucas Carton with him the next day, but she was charging that one to the firm. He had picked up the tab at the Tour d'Argent, as he had at Harry's Bar, and both had been pretty impressive. He liked dining in fashionable four-star restaurants, and he didn't mind paying for it himself, even when he didn't have to.

They met again the next day, with Charlie McIntosh, and made their final presentations. And the French were as anxious to invest in Dow Tech as everyone else had been, right from the beginning. Their results for Callan had been beyond what her wildest hopes for him had been, and far better than their analysts had predicted. They were going to make an impressive entry onto the scene when the stock was first traded on Thursday. And the tombstone in *The Wall Street Journal,* announcing who had underwritten the deal, was going to be full of impressive names. She had explained to Cal that there were going to be "majors out of order," which meant that some of the big firms had agreed to take less stock and were willing to appear beneath the names of the smaller firms specializing in high-tech issues. It was the sign of a very hot deal, and would be very prestigious for them. It was yet another goal she had accomplished for him.

By the time they got back to the hotel at five o'clock, it was clear that they were entitled to a victory celebration. At that precise moment, their due diligence tour was officially over. It had succeeded beyond everything she'd hoped for him, and even Charlie McIntosh was smiling. Although he still didn't agree with what Cal had done, officially, he had to concede a job well done and thoroughly accomplished. He even commented to Cal that Meredith was an extraordinarily competent woman. And Charlie shook hands with her and congratulated her on how well they had succeeded. He had to leave them a few minutes later, as he was catching an eight o'clock flight that night, back to California. Cal was flying to New York with her the next day, for the final meeting with her partners at her office. And they were hoping to hear that their prospectus had been approved by the SEC by then.

She wore a simple black suit to their dinner at Lucas Carton that night, and it was a leisurely evening, and an extraordinary meal. He said he had talked to his children, and they were fine, but anxious for him to come home.

"So is Steve," she said over coffee and brandy. "We've done a damn good job though." She looked pleased, and happy for him. She loved what she did, and it had been fun traveling with him. She had enjoyed him more than most of her clients. They worked well together, and seemed to have a lot in common. They shared a number of views about the financial world, and she had always been excited about the high-tech companies she worked with. She had pretty much specialized in them for the past five years, and she knew her stuff, which had vastly impressed Callan. He'd been warned that he might have to do a lot of educating with the investment banking firm he chose. But she had actually educated him about the entire

IPO process, and the investment banking world, and he admired her for it.

"So where to from here?" he asked her, as they sipped their brandy.

"The next public offering that comes my way. Same old game. And you? What are you going to do now for excitement?" she teased him. They had a great camaraderie between them. But she had a fairly good idea what he was going to do next. He had already talked to her about a whole new range of high-tech surgical products that he wanted to develop.

"Actually, I'm thinking about acquiring another company," he confessed. "Give me a couple of years, and Dow Tech will be ten times the size it is today." He was counting on it, and planning to work toward that.

"I'd love that," she smiled. They chatted about it for a while, he hadn't mentioned new acquisitions to her before. He was full of good ideas, and he wanted to strive for new horizons. He wasn't a man who rested on his laurels, and she liked that about him. She wasn't one to do that either. They were both ambitious in a very similar fashion.

They were still talking about his ideas when they went back to the hotel, and sat in the bar for a little while. He had another brandy, but she only sat with him. She didn't want to have a headache when they flew to New York the next day.

And he looked comfortable and relaxed as they sat side by side in a booth and chatted till long after midnight. There was always so much to talk about and share and discuss. They agreed about a lot of things, but she also challenged him, and dared to disagree with him, which he enjoyed about her. They shared a world that few people either enjoyed or understood, and he said that to her with a look of admiration.

"Do you talk to Steve about all this?" he asked, curious. There had never been another woman he could talk to as he did her. It was very rare, in his field, and he knew that.

"Some of it. Not the high-tech world. But he's gotten pretty knowledgeable about investment banking and how it works. He impresses the hell out of people when he talks about IPOs and red herrings and green shoes. Some people think he's a banker instead of a doctor." She smiled as she said it.

"I still think he's one hell of a lucky guy, and I hope he knows it."

"He does," she smiled again. "I'm lucky too. We're very different, but it works. Maybe because we've been together forever. Nearly half my life." She'd been married to him for fourteen of her thirty-seven years, and that was pretty impressive.

"I was only married half that long, and I felt like I'd been sent to Vietnam and was being held hostage by the Viet Cong. In fact, I enjoyed my two years in Da Nang a lot more than being married to Charlotte." Meredith could see why, but she still felt sorry for him.

"At least you got three wonderful children out of it."

"I did. I'm grateful to her for that. Sometimes, it's hard for me to believe they're hers. She seems so removed from them, but that's how she wants it to be." It didn't surprise Meredith, she hadn't looked like a very warm person when they'd run into her in Harry's Bar.

Beautiful, and charming, but ice cold. It made Meredith question what Callan had been looking for when he fell in love with her, if only appearances had been important to him then. And perhaps they still were now.

They sat for a long time talking in the bar that night, holding on to the last moments they were going to share. The next day they were going back to their own lives again, their offices, the people who were important to them, his children in his case, and in hers Steve. But for this one moment, this last evening, they were celebrating their joint victory, and the common world they had so briefly shared.

Knowing that, it didn't surprise her when he touched her hand, and looked at her very gently. "I want you to know how important all of this has been to me. You did an incredible job, Meredith, and you've been a wonderful friend."

"I've enjoyed working with you, Cal." And traveling, and laughing, and talking about everything from IPOs to having kids. She had also learned a lot from him.

"I hope we have a chance to work together again sometime," he said, looking wistful.

"Well, if you're serious about acquiring another company, I might be able to introduce you to some prospects. I'll keep an eye out for the right one for you."

"That's almost reason enough to do it, in spite of Charlie's objections," he said, with a smile, and a little while later, he walked her back to her room. He left her outside, as he always did, but this time, he lingered for just an instant, seemed about to say something, and then stopped as she opened her door with the heavy brass key. "Good night, Meredith," he said simply, watching her. And then, without word or explanation, she leaned toward him, kissed his cheek, turned away, and took a step into her room.

"Good night, Cal," she said softly, and then as he walked away, she quietly closed the door. She sat down in a chair for a long moment, looking out the window, and thinking about him. A lot had happened in the past few weeks. And she hoped that, whether or not they worked together again, he would always be her friend now.

Chapter 8

THE FLIGHT TO New York on Wednesday seemed to go too quickly. Cal slept, and Meredith worked. Her office had sent her a stack of faxes before they left Paris. And she was still working when they landed at JFK.

Cal woke up and looked at her with a sleepy smile, and then glanced out the window. The landing wheels had just hit the runway.

"What time is it?" he asked, stifling a yawn.

"Two o'clock local time. They're expecting us at four o'clock in my office." It would take them that long, she knew, to get through customs, claim their bags, and take a limo into the city. "Everyone wants to congratulate you."

"They should be congratulating you, Meredith. I hope they realize that." There were times when he worried about her. He had seen very clearly that Paul Black didn't appreciate her, and Cal wondered if her other partners were any smarter.

"They do realize it," she smiled, slipping her papers into her briefcase.

But when they met with the senior partners at four o'clock for the pricing meeting, everyone shook hands with Cal, and all the partners who had come congratulated him and each other. In the melee of people in the conference room, Meredith was all but forgotten. Paul Black made a point of telling her it had been a job well done, but most of the others were intent on talking to Callan and the other senior partners. She was used to it, and it didn't shock her. They were an old boys' society of sorts, a secret fraternity that still had trouble acknowledging women. Knowing that, it had meant a great deal to her when she made partner. But as Callan had said during one of their many talks while they were traveling, there was some question as to how far she would go in the firm, and whether or not she had already hit the glass ceiling. For the moment, she still refused to believe she had.

"Meredith is the one you should all be talking about," Callan made a point of saying to them. "She's the magician who put it all together. She was incredible," he said more than once, but no one seemed particularly interested in hearing what he was saying, and it annoyed him. And they were all interrupted by the phone conference with the salesmen of all the firms in the syndicate to handle the last aspects of due diligence. Meredith announced to everyone that the deal had been approved by the SEC, and would be effective in the morning when the market opened. They were all pleased to hear that there would in fact be a green shoe, and the only thing left to do was determine the size of the offering, and the price per share. And Callan agreed to stick with the number of shares indicated in the red herring, and to set the price at only a twenty percent premium over that in the prospectus, so that in the initial trading, given the tremendous oversubscription they had, the stock would rise sharply and quickly. Meredith explained it as "leaving something on the table," which she knew would make everyone feel good about the offering, and allow the syndicate to dissolve immediately. It was the perfect deal, and it had come to the ideal conclusion, and Callan had no doubt that she was responsible for its success from beginning to end.

He said something about it to her two hours later when he dropped her off at her apartment in a limo. He was on the way to the airport, and heading back to California. Their venture was done, the book was oversubscribed eleven to one, they would go effective the next day, and the tombstone would appear in *The Wall Street Journal* the day after, on Thursday. Mission accomplished. But Callan still didn't feel that Meredith had gotten her fair share of the glory.

"They practically ignored you at the meeting, Merrie," he said with a look of irritation. "What's wrong with those guys?"

"That's just the way they are. It doesn't mean anything. They know what I do. They're just not very vocal about their recognition."

"Bullshit. They take you for granted, and you know it. You could have screwed this up royally for them, or done a half-assed job of it, and you didn't do that. You did a first-rate job every step of the way, better than that. I don't believe for a minute that we'd have an eleven-to-one oversubscribed book on this if it weren't for you. The least they could do is say so."

"That's not important," she said simply.

"You're a better man than I then. I'd be mad as hell right now if I were you. You worked like a Trojan on this offering. They ought to be carrying you around on their shoulders." He was really angry, and she smiled as they reached her apartment building.

"I'm okay with it, Cal. Honest. I'm a big girl. All I'm interested in are the results. They don't need to make a fuss about me. This is my job."

He had made plenty of fuss over her, that was enough, and the stock had been well priced. Meredith was expecting the stock price to rise at least twenty percent above the offering price. Everything had gone exactly the way she wanted. And he felt they owed her more than just cursory thanks for it.

"Have a good flight home," she said with a smile, as the limo stopped at her front door, and the doorman took her bags from the driver.

"I'm going to miss you," he said, looking sad.

"I'm going to miss you too. We'll talk tomorrow when the stock starts trading. I'll keep you posted." She hesitated for a moment before leaving the car, and he held her hand for a minute.

"Meredith, thank you for everything." It was an emotional moment between them. She had helped him fulfill his greatest dream, and it meant a lot to him. "Take care of yourself. And tell that lucky guy of yours that you both have a friend in California."

"Thanks, Cal." She kissed his cheek and left the car, and then stood in the doorway and waved as the limo sped off to the airport. And it felt odd after that going upstairs to her apartment. It seemed so anticlimactic now to be home, and even more so when she found the apartment empty.

Steve had left her a note, he'd had to go back to the hospital that night, but he promised to be home the next day, by the time she got home from the office. "Welcome home . . . I love you," he'd said, and she smiled as she read it.

She wasn't upset that he wasn't there, she was used to it, and she could use the time to read her mail, get her papers in order, and do her laundry. And she was happy later that night when he called her. She was reading in bed, and she jumped when the phone rang.

"Welcome home, Merrie. Sorry I'm not there with you."

"That's okay. I'm tired anyway. I'm going to go to bed early." It was six hours later for her, by French time, roughly five o'clock in the morning. "How's work?"

"Crazy as usual. Two head-ons, the usual gang members shooting each other up just for the hell of it, and some lunatic who jumped in front of the subway."

"Sounds like an ordinary night in your part of the world," she smiled. By his standards, that was business as usual.

"Yeah. It shouldn't be too bad tonight. I'll be home tomorrow. Everything okay with you?"

"Fine. I'm just tired." And depressed for some reason. But that happened sometimes when she came home from a road show. It felt good to be home, but there was a kind of a letdown. Her baby had left the nest and flown, and her job with it was finished.

On to the next one. But there was an emptiness in the lull.

She slept fitfully that night, thinking of it, and when she got to the office the next day, she saw the proof for the tombstone for Friday's *Wall Street Journal.* It was just as she expected it to be, their name was on the left, which indicated that her firm had been the keeper of the book, and there were several majors out of order, which meant that some of the smaller firms were listed above them, a sign of how hot the deal was, as she had told Callan, when she explained it to him. And she had been in her office in time to make sure that the stock was trading well.

Everyone was talking about Dow Tech. The stock price was already rising, but not so fast or so much that it made her look foolish for not having priced it higher. It was a textbook offering, and what everyone wanted to happen when they took a company public. She was sitting at her desk, feeling pleased with all of it when Cal called her.

"So what's our next stop, Meredith? I'm ready for the next city." He was teasing and she laughed.

"Me too. I can't believe it's over. Looking back it all seems so easy." She smiled as she said it, but it had all gone very smoothly.

"Yeah, like childbirth. It only seems easy now because everything went so well, thanks to you. I don't know what to do with myself now that I'm back."

"You'll think of something." She knew he had plenty of new projects on the back burner, they had talked a lot about them.

"How was Steve when you got back?" he asked politely. They seemed like old friends now.

"I haven't seen him yet. He was working. He's taking the weekend off, and he said he was going to lock up my briefcase."

"I don't blame him. I would too. Tell him to take you dancing." She laughed at that. Steve was no Fred Astaire, like Callan. In fact, he hated dancing. He'd rather sit home and watch TV with a glass of wine.

"That's not his thing, I'm afraid. We'll probably go to a movie tomorrow. That's more his speed. What about you? How are the kids?"

"Great. I don't think they even missed me." Cal and Meredith were like two kids home from camp or boarding school, they didn't know what to do at home now. "They have endless plans to torture me all weekend. The girls want me to take them into town, and I have to take Andy to soccer practice. Pretty exciting." They both led fairly quiet lives, although Meredith suspected that wasn't always the case for Callan. Charlotte had been a good indication on that score.

"No big social doings this weekend?" She was still curious about him, even after the time they had spent together, or perhaps even more so.

"You mean like bingo at my church?" he teased. "I do that on Tuesdays."

"Yeah, me too," she laughed. "Actually I'm meeting a new client next week about an IPO, it sounds pretty interesting. They're a small high-tech firm in Boston."

"I've been gone for less than a day, and you're already being unfaithful to me. I thought you'd want to hang up your spurs after this one, and just live on our memories." He sounded poetic as he said it.

"How's Charlie doing, speaking of memories? Happy to be back in the fold?"

"I'm not sure," Cal said vaguely. "He scheduled a meeting with me this afternoon, and I get the feeling something's brewing. He's still ticked off that we went public, but that's no secret. You knew that."

"Charlie doesn't exactly keep his feelings secret, does he?" she laughed. She didn't miss him. He had remained ornery right up to the last few minutes, but he'd been momentarily gracious when he left them. And even he had to admit that the entire process had gone far better than anyone had expected.

"Well, have a good weekend, Meredith, and a good rest. You've earned it."

"So have you, Cal."

"I'll call you sometime next week and see how things are going," he promised.

She hung up, and got caught up in her office all afternoon, and when she got home at six o'clock, Steve was waiting for her. He swept her off her feet as soon as she walked into the living room, twirled her around, and kissed her.

"Boy, have I missed you."

"I've only been gone a week, you goof."

"It seemed a whole lot longer. To me at least." He smiled and kissed her again, poured them both a glass of wine, and an hour later, after they chatted for a while, he started dinner. He had been hungry to talk to her, and see her, and feel her next to him in bed at night.

He made pasta for them, salad, and garlic bread, and halfway through the meal, he got amorous with her, and the rest of the meal went untouched as he carried her into their bedroom. They never got up again that night, and when she got up the next morning, she threw the remains of their dinner away and put the dishes in the dishwasher. Steve was still asleep, and when she checked *The Wall Street Journal,* the tombstone she had proofed the day before looked exactly as it was meant to.

She left for the office quietly, and Steve called her at the office when he woke up at noon, and for once she managed to go home early. Steve was waiting for her in the living room, he already had dinner on, and as soon as they finished, they went to the movies.

In every possible way, it was an idyllic weekend. They talked and laughed and went for long walks in the park. The weather was still warm and balmy, it was that perfect time of year in New York that felt almost like spring, that happened nearly every year in the last weeks of September.

And on Saturday night, they went out to dinner at a neighborhood restaurant they both liked. It was a far cry from Harry's Bar where she'd spent the previous Saturday night with Callan, but this was just what she wanted. She and Steve managed to spend uninterrupted time with each other for the first time in months. He was off call all weekend, and she lived up to her promise to him not to touch her briefcase. Everything was perfect. And on Monday morning when she left for work, he put on his scrubs and left for the hospital. He was going to be gone for two days this time, some of it on call in the hospital, and the rest actively on duty. And they both had easy weeks ahead of them, or at least Meredith did. With him, he could never quite predict it.

She checked on the Dow Tech stock when she got in, and it was still going up at a good clip, which pleased her. She was thinking about calling Cal to congratulate him again on it, when her secretary buzzed her.

"Callan Dow on the line for you, Mrs. Whitman," she said briskly, and Meredith stopped what she was doing and took the call.

"Hi there. I was just about to call. The stock's still going up very nicely." She had bought a fair-sized chunk of it for herself right after the opening, as the SEC permitted, so she now had a personal interest in it as well. "What's new in California?"

"Well, Meredith," he said, sounding strange to her for a minute, "things have been moving and shaking out here." A lot had happened since Friday, and he hadn't had a chance to call her all weekend. He'd been busy with his kids.

"What does that mean?" Meredith sounded puzzled, but intrigued by the way he'd said it.

"Charlie handed in his resignation on Friday, which could be a problem, if it upsets the stockholders, or triggers a lawsuit, but I'm hoping that won't happen. We had a long serious talk, and he just can't make his peace with the fact that we're a public company. He doesn't want to answer to shareholders, and he's violently opposed to my acquiring another company eventually. Actually he was pretty decent about it, and he says I've outgrown him. He says he's too old to make the adjustment. And I honestly think he made the right decision, given how he feels."

Meredith nodded as she thought about it. "It may be for the best, Cal, although I know you have a lot of history with him. You need to find someone now who fits the direction you're taking and is willing to grow with you, and is even enthusiastic about it.''

''That's what I'm hoping,'' he said simply.

''Do you have anyone in mind yet? How much notice did he give you?''

''The answers to both those questions are 'yes,' and 'two weeks,' in that order.''

''That's hardly a generous notice.''

''To tell the truth, I think he made his mind up before the road show, and he was just waiting to tell me when we got back. He doesn't think he should stick around now that he's decided he's going.'' And it was hard for him to go too. Callan knew that, in his own way, Charlie loved Dow Tech and what it represented to him. Callan knew that better than Merrie.

''So who are you thinking of for the job? Someone on the outside, or within the company?'' she asked him, sounding pensive, trying to think if she knew anyone for him, but she didn't offhand.

''Outside actually.'' Sitting at his desk, he was smiling, but she couldn't see it. ''I wanted to see what you thought of my idea.''

''Do I know them?'' She sounded interested. She had a maternal interest in Dow Tech now, and was touched that he had called her to advise him.

''Intimately, actually. In fact, I think this person is the ideal replacement for Charlie.''

''I'm dying of curiosity, Cal,'' she said, smiling. ''Who is it?''

''Go look in the mirror, Merrie,'' he said softly, and there was a long pause as she absorbed what he was saying to her.

"What does that mean?" She sounded startled.

"I'd like you to be our new CFO, Meredith. You're exactly what this company needs . . . and what I need. You have the same kind of vision I do, the same goals for the company. You know everything there is to know about this business. And I've shared all my secrets and future plans with you. Merrie, you're perfect." At first, she thought he was kidding. At least she hoped so. It was very flattering, but there was no way she could do it. She already had a job, a home, and a husband, and there was no way she could leave New York now. What would Steve do?

"That's the nicest thing anyone's said to me in years, Cal." She hated to turn him down, but she knew she had to. "But you know I can't do it."

"Why not?" He didn't sound as though he were going to take no for an answer. "Of course you can do it, if you want to." And he sounded as though he was going to be insulted if she didn't.

"I'm an investment banker, Cal. And I really don't know enough about your business to be an effective CFO. As impossible as he is, Charlie knows a hell of a lot more about it than I do. What's more, I'm a partner in my firm, and I have a husband who works here. I can't just drop everything and move to California."

"People do it all the time, Meredith, and you know it. They change careers, jobs, fields, that's what life is all about, changing and growing. You'd be terrific at it. And what's more, you're heading for a dead end where you are, and you know that too. It's written all over the walls there. They don't appreciate you, they don't have any concept of how extraordinary you are, but I do. You would be invaluable to me here. And if you want me to be crass about it, you'd make a hell of a lot more money. This could be a great thing for you. And Steve could get a job here. We have trauma units here. SF General has one of the best in the country. Does that answer all your objections?'' She was overwhelmed for a moment as she listened.

"Some of them. But I can't just make a decision like that at the drop of a hat. I'd have to discuss it with Steve. He has a great job here.''

"As the number-two man. Maybe he could be the number-one guy here. Why don't you talk to him about it?''

"And say what? That I'm giving up a career I've spent twelve years on, and I want him to drop everything too, and follow me out there? Cal, this is an enormous decision.'' She sounded breathless as she answered. He had really stunned her.

"I know that, Meredith. I didn't expect you to do it lightly. But as your friend, I can tell you that I think it would be the best thing that ever happened to you. Why don't you come out this week and talk to me about it?''

"I can't,'' she said, sounding panicked. It was the first time he had ever heard her sound ruffled.

"Why not?'' He was relentless when there was something he wanted, and she felt as though there were an express train heading toward her. There were reasons why Callan Dow had been so successful. When he wanted something, he pursued it, until he got it.

"I have meetings this week,'' she said weakly.

"Then come next week, or this weekend. But let's at least discuss it.''

"I know the job, Cal. I know the company. I know

you. That's not the problem. You don't need to woo me. But I have a life here."

"You'd have a better life here. Do you want me to speak to Steve about it?"

"No, I'll talk to him myself. But he's going to think I'm crazy, or you are." She sounded worried, but he seemed euphoric, which scared her. He didn't want to listen to her very sensible objections.

"Maybe I am crazy, but it's the best idea I've had in years. I think Charlie McIntosh did me a great big favor."

"I think he turned my life upside down is what he did," she said, laughing, catching her breath finally. Cal was amazing.

"Will you consider it at least? Talk to Steve and see what he thinks. He's a smart guy, from what you tell me. It could just be he'll see this as a tremendous opportunity, which it is. Meredith, I'd be willing to give you options to acquire up to one percent of the company, and I could pay you a lot more than they do." There was no question about it, with the stock options he was talking about, the offer was very tempting. But they still had a life in New York, and Steve's job to consider. Palo Alto was a long way from Manhattan, and everything they had and knew there.

"Cal, your offer is incredible. But I just don't know. I don't think it would be easy for Steve to leave the trauma unit. I hate to even ask him to do it. It's just not fair to him."

"And if the shoe were on the other foot, and he were getting the fantastic offer, which involved moving, would you go?" He was putting her feet to the fire and she knew it.

"He wouldn't ask me to, Cal. He's too decent to do that."

"It's not a matter of decency, Merrie, this is business, big business, and a chance to make some real money for both of you, and have a good life here."

"I'll talk to Steve," she said finally, "but don't get your hopes up. I have to respect the fact that he has a good job here, and might not want to relocate. You probably need to find someone right there in California, maybe someone right in the company that you're not thinking of at the moment."

"No one in my outfit can hold a candle to you, Merrie. Even Charlie suggested that I talk to you. He was very impressed by you. Come on. . . . I need you. . . . You can't let me down now, not after everything we've just done together. This is my baby, Merrie, and a little bit yours too. Don't you want to help me make it even better than it is now?"

"Stop guilt-tripping me," she said laughing, "you're terrible!"

"I just want you to come out here to talk to me about this. The sooner the better. Will you come out this week, Merrie?"

"Let me talk to Steve about it. He's at the hospital but he'll be home on Wednesday. I don't want to talk to him about this on the phone."

"I don't want to wait that long. Go see him. You could come out on Wednesday."

"And what am I supposed to say to my partners?" She sounded flustered again at the prospect of dropping everything and running out to California to discuss a new job with Callan. This was beginning to sound scary. But intriguing.

"Tell them you need a vacation. You've earned it."

"I hate to lie to them, Cal."

"Oh for chrissake, then tell them the truth, that they don't appreciate you, and don't know their asses from a hole in the ground when it comes to treating you right, and they don't deserve to have you, I do. So you're coming out to California to see me."

"They'll really love that, Cal."

"It's the truth, you know, Merrie. And they know it too. Now go talk to your husband at the hospital, and call me tonight."

"Don't push me."

"I will push you till you agree to come out here, to talk to me at least. You owe yourself that much."

"I owe my husband a lot too, Cal. I can't just rip his career out by the roots and tell him to find a job in California, because it suits me. He may just tell me to forget it."

"Not if he's the guy you say he is. I think he may surprise you."

And as it so happened, he did, when Meredith met him that night in the cafeteria at nine o'clock to report the conversation to him. She felt half crazy telling him about it, but as she stumbled along, explaining what Cal had offered her, Steve looked at her intensely.

"Is that what you want, Merrie?" he asked her bluntly.

"I don't know what I want, sweetheart," she said honestly. "It's a hell of a good offer, and his company is very exciting. But we have a life here. I've been where I am for twelve years, and I love being a partner in an investment banking firm that's a major player on

Wall Street. And you have a great job here. I don't think it's fair to ask you to just walk out on all that, and move to California."

"Why not, if it's better for both of us in the long run? We might like it out there." The thought had crossed his mind almost immediately that if he could get her away from Wall Street, she might finally want to have children. And California would be a great place to raise a family.

"Would you really be willing to move out there?" She looked startled by what Steve was saying to her.

"Maybe. If I can find a job, and I don't see why I couldn't. People shoot each other in California too. They even have gangs there," he said, smiling. He had taken it a lot better than she'd expected him to. He even seemed enthusiastic about it, possibly even more than she was. She was still very nervous about it. It was a big change for her, into a whole new career, although Cal's offer was undeniably very tempting. "Why don't you go talk to him at least?"

"That's what he said." She still seemed hesitant, but Steve didn't. He was excited for her.

"I think you should do that. When did he want you to come out?"

"Maybe Wednesday. I have a meeting with a new client tomorrow."

"So go. And if you love it, I'll fly out to meet you on Friday. I'm off again this weekend."

"How'd you manage that?" She looked intrigued, and touched by how open he was to Cal's offer. It was obvious Steve wanted what was best for her, and he was willing to make sacrifices himself, even big ones, to help her achieve that.

"I sold my soul to get the weekend for us, Merrie. Sounds like it was lucky I did. Maybe we can talk to some hospitals while I'm out there. He must have some connections. And I know a couple of guys at Stanford. They trained here."

"You're incredible, baby," she said, reaching across the table to hold his hand. He was even more wonderful than she had told Cal he was.

"So are you. So go home and call him."

"I can call him tomorrow." But in the end, she didn't. She called him as soon as she walked into the apartment, and he was thrilled to hear her.

"So what did Steve say?"

"He wants me to come out and see you. He's incredible. He isn't even opposed to relocating."

"That's because he's smart and knows a good deal when he hears it. And besides, he loves you."

"I love him too. He has to be the most decent man alive to be willing to do this. He said that if I want him to, he'll fly out to meet me over the weekend, and take a look around. He knows some guys at Stanford."

"I can help you with that, Merrie. I know plenty of people in hospitals. He can have any job he wants here. And you can be my CFO, and we'll all live happily ever after."

"You make it sound so simple," but they both knew it wasn't. It wasn't easy to transplant two careers across a country, or maybe he was right, and it wasn't as complicated as she thought. She didn't know what to think now. The obstacles that had seemed so huge to her at first seemed to be dissolving one by one, and she really had to decide now if this was what she wanted. But before she could make that decision, she had to talk to Cal.

"It can be simple, if you want it to be, Meredith. If it's right, it will be," he said confidently. "So when are you coming out? What about tomorrow?"

"I have to meet a new client," she reminded him.

"With any luck at all, you could be wasting his time. At least I hope so."

"We don't know that yet, do we?" she said firmly. She still had responsibilities to her partners in New York, and she had to respect that. "What about Wednesday? I could spend three days out there with you, if you like. The rest of my week is pretty open."

"That sounds perfect." He sounded delighted about it, and she was too. Everything was happening so fast it was a little bit terrifying. "I'll pick you up at the airport, just let me know when you're coming."

"Are you sure you're not making a huge mistake, Cal? Just because we did a successful IPO together doesn't mean I'd make a good CFO for you." She had never done anything like it. But she knew a lot about Dow Tech and she loved it.

"Trust me, Meredith. I know what I'm doing. One thing I do know is talent when I see it, and I haven't been as impressed in years. If I'd known you'd even consider it, I'd have kissed Charlie when he resigned. This is the biggest favor anyone's ever done me."

"Well, don't get too excited. Let's talk first."

"We'll do lots of that, I promise. Ask me anything you want to know when you get here, Merrie. I have no secrets from you." She loved that about him. He was an honest man, with integrity and a brilliant mind. It was a terrific combination, and she already knew they worked well together. But still, it was an enormous decision, and she couldn't let Steve risk his career for her either. She had to look out for his best interests, even if he was inclined to be kind to her. She wanted him to be happy too, that was vital to her. "I can't wait to see you," Cal added.

"I didn't think I'd see you again this soon." She laughed. This was all so new and so unexpected. She had never dreamed anything like this would happen as a result of his public offering and their road show. It seemed almost providential to her. But she was still worried about it. She wanted to make the right decision for all of them, and it was an awesome responsibility to do that.

"I was afraid I'd have to start another company just so I could take it public and see you again. This is great news, Merrie. And you and I do such great work together."

"We do, don't we," she smiled. She was still so pleased with how his stock was doing. "Well, let's see what happens when I come out to California."

"I'm going to start burning candles, Meredith . . . or doing rain dances or something. I'm going to do my damnedest to talk you into this. I hope you know that."

"I kind of suspected you might," she laughed again. He wasn't the kind of man to take no for an answer. But she was also very grateful to her husband for letting her go out there, he was being incredibly generous to encourage her to do it, especially if it represented a sacrifice to him, which was entirely possible. But for her sake, he was willing to chance that, and she loved him all the more for it.

"See you on Wednesday," Cal said cheerily as they hung up, and after they did, Meredith sat silently in her living room, staring at the phone, and wondering what would happen in California.

Chapter 9

THE FLIGHT TO California on Wednesday went easily, and Cal was waiting for Meredith at the gate, as she came off the plane carrying the familiar briefcase. He was standing to one side, watching for her, and his face broke into a broad smile the moment he saw her.

"I had a moment of panic while I was standing here. I suddenly wondered if you had changed your mind, and were too chicken to call me."

"I wouldn't do a thing like that," she said with a look of surprise, as he took the heavy briefcase from her.

"I know. I used to feel like that when I was a kid too. I was always afraid my father would lose the tickets to the circus. He never did, but I always worried about it."

"Well, I'm here." She had done a lot of thinking on the way out, and she still didn't see how she could expect Steve to leave his job in the trauma unit. She was more concerned about him than about what Cal would offer. She knew how solid his company was, and he had already told her about the stock options he would give her. But Steve was still her principal worry. "I can't believe I did this," she said, still feeling stunned by his entire proposition, and Steve's willingness to let her explore it.

"I should have thought of it before. It just never occurred to me that Charlie would quit." He was still a little concerned that it would create problems with his shareholders, but there was nothing in Charlie's contract that said he couldn't do that. It would only have been a violation if he'd left during the road show, and Charlie knew that, which was why he had waited till they got back to California. "Meredith, if you do this, it could be the most important decision of your career. And I don't think you'd ever regret it. If I were just your friend, and not involved here, I would tell you you'd be very foolish if you didn't do it."

"I know. It's just such a big change. Not only a change in careers, but moving to California is a big decision."

"I know you're worried about Steve," he said, as they picked up her bag at the baggage claim, "but there are great hospitals out here. I've already made some contacts at SF General for him. And you told me he has friends at Stanford. And there's a UC hospital in the city, and a very good trauma hospital in Oakland. There are a lot of options out here for him. This could be very exciting for him." But the one who was most excited was Cal. On the way back to his office in Palo Alto, he talked endlessly about how important she would be to him. And Meredith was as enamored of the idea as he was. From a purely business standpoint, it was the opportunity of a lifetime.

At two o'clock that afternoon, they hadn't even stopped for lunch yet. They'd been talking for three hours, and his secretary finally brought them each a sandwich. Both he and Meredith had the same kind of work ethic, the same drive and passion about their work, their love for what they did was not only creative, it was almost obsessive. And they spent the rest of the afternoon talking about new diagnostic tools and new products.

"Meredith," he said, looking intensely at her late in the afternoon. "I can't do this without you."

"Yes, you can," she said quietly, but she had loved everything she had heard since eleven o'clock that morning.

"The point is, I don't want to. I want you here to share all this with me."

"And the truth is," she sighed, "I want to be here. But I don't know if I have a right to do it." She felt incredibly torn between an important career decision, and her personal life. She was still worried about Steve, no matter how good Cal said the local hospitals could be for him. He was already firmly entrenched where he was, as the number-two man in an internationally known trauma unit. And there was no question in either of their minds that he would be the number-one man someday, and probably sooner rather than later. Harvey Lucas had been talking about retiring from trauma work and going into research for years, and Steve had been convinced recently that Lucas was getting closer to it. He was tired, he'd had problems with his heart, and the trauma unit was getting to be too much for him. There was a high burnout rate in trauma, you just couldn't live with that kind of pressure forever. "I have to give Steve a chance to think about this seriously," she said to Cal. "He's a major factor in this decision."

"I'll find him a job if I have to, Meredith. I don't want to lose you."

"You don't have me yet," she said with a tired smile. She wanted this as badly as he did. She loved his company, and she knew that they worked well together, and she thought that she could do some important things for him, given the right opportunities. He had convinced her. The only real problem was Steve now. She didn't even feel as guilty about leaving her investment banking firm. Cal was right, she realized, they didn't really appreciate her. And if she hadn't hit the glass ceiling yet, she knew she was damn close to it. But at Dow Tech, as Cal said, the sky was the limit.

"What do you think, Merrie? Will you do it?" He had tried not to pressure her all afternoon, but it was hard to hold back. He just wanted her to take the job so badly.

They had also met with Charlie McIntosh that afternoon, and she was surprised that even he encouraged her to take the job. Given the direction the company was taking now, he thought she'd be very good for them. "You won't regret it, if you come out here," he said, sounding more like an old friend than the thorn in her side he'd been for the entire road show. "And you already know the company, Meredith. There won't be a lot of surprises here for you. Besides," he smiled at her benevolently, "Cal is a great guy, and a pleasure to work for." He treated him more like a son or a nephew than the CEO of the company that employed him.

"I've never worked for a publicly held company, and I just don't want to start now. I'm too old to start worrying about shareholders, and whether or not the stock market is going up or down and taking us with it. But you two are young enough to enjoy it." He seemed relieved by his decision. "I hope you take the job, Meredith," he urged, and she didn't feel so much pressured as wanted and appreciated. Here, she really was needed.

Cal invited her to dinner that night but she said she wanted some time to herself, to do some serious thinking. She had room service bring her scrambled eggs, and she called Steve at the hospital, and was lucky to find him.

"So how's it going?"

"Great, unfortunately." She sounded tormented. She had been weighing the pros and cons all night, and she felt more confused than ever. One part of her wanted to leap at the chance, and the other told her that she owed it to Steve to stay in New York and stick with what she was doing. She felt guilty even putting the possibility out there for discussion. But she had come this far, and now she had to. "It looks terrific. And I think I'd love it here, or the job at least. I have no idea what living in California would be like. The job is the real draw for me. But what about you, sweetheart? What do you really think about this?"

"I think it's something you really have to look at," he said fairly. "That's why I told you I thought you should go out there."

"But what about you? If I take this job, what will you do?"

"Find another trauma unit," he said simply. He didn't sound as emotionally invested in the decision as she did, which surprised her.

"But what if you don't like what's out here?" Where he was was state of the art, and in a far bigger city than San Francisco. In many ways certainly, San Francisco seemed very provincial. You really couldn't compare the two cities, although Cal said that the quality of life would be better in California. But both she and Steve had had a love affair with New York since they'd gone to college.

"Do you want me to come out and take a look?" Steve asked sensibly. "I think that's the only way we'll be able to make the decision, don't you? I'll catch a plane tomorrow after work, take a look around, and see who I can talk to in the trauma units out there. Maybe I can take Monday off too, and then at least we'll know what we're talking about."

"Baby, I love you," Meredith said with tears in her eyes. He was always committed to make things easier for her, not only in small ways, but in some very big ones. "It would mean a lot to me if you'd come, Steve."

"Good. Then I'll do it. Besides, I want to take a good look at this guy and make sure he's not too good looking before I let you take the job. I'm not sure about all this stuff about Gary Cooper." He was only half kidding and she knew it. But Steve knew he had nothing to worry about. They had a solid, happy life together, and nothing could jeopardize that, for either of them. She was certain of it.

"That's not what appeals to me about the job," she said easily. "It's just such a great company, and he's a good person to work with. He's got integrity, tremendous energy, and some fantastic ideas for the future. I think he's going to triple the size and impact of the company in the next two years, not to mention the profits.''

"Then you should give it some very serious thought, Merrie. I'll be there tomorrow night. Just tell me where to meet you."

"Let me know your flight, and I'll pick you up at the airport. And Steve . . .'' She hesitated for only a fraction of a second, loving him more than she ever had, because he wanted the best for her. He was astoundingly unselfish, and such a decent person, it was part of what she had always loved about him. That and the fact that he was smart, had a great sense of humor, worked like a dog, really cared about what he was doing, and had the best body she'd ever seen, and she still found him incredibly sexy. It was an unbeatable combination, no matter how different their jobs were. And besides, she liked that part. It stimulated both of them that their careers were so different. "Thank you, baby, you don't know what this means to me,'' she said gently.

"Listen, maybe this will be the best thing that ever happened to us. Maybe we'll even decide to have kids in California.'' She made no comment and he didn't push it. She felt she had enough to think about, just worrying about his job and Cal's company, without adding babies to it. And as she hung up the phone, she felt as though an irresistible force were propelling her forward, almost as though this had been meant to happen. It frightened her a little bit, but it was also incredibly stimulating.

She spent all of Thursday with Cal again, following him to meetings, and talking to key employees. She had a better sense of his organization and staff than she'd ever had before, and so far she still liked everything about it. She checked in with her office that afternoon, but nothing much was happening, and they had no idea what she was doing. She had told them that she had to go away to attend to family business.

"Would you like to come to dinner at the house tonight?" Cal asked as they wrapped up at six o'clock. Everyone else was gone, and she noticed that most people didn't work as late as they did in New York. It was never unusual to see people working till nine or ten o'clock in her office, and sometimes considerably later. But as Cal had pointed out to her from the first, the quality of life in California was considerably different. People seemed to care more about their health, their personal lives, their time off. And after work, they went home, or out to play tennis, or work out. It seemed a healthier, happier, more well-balanced existence. In New York, the people she met in the business world looked as though they existed under a flat rock, they were pale and tired and stressed, and most of the time looked frantic and unhealthy. This was certainly very different.

"I'd love to come to dinner, but I have to pick Steve up at nine," she explained. "I don't want to screw up your dinner." They exchanged a smile, they already had an easy, close, comfortable working relationship. After the time they'd spent on the road, and now here exploring the intricacies of his company, it was almost like being married.

"I was going to have dinner with the kids early anyway. Do you want me to drive you?"

"You don't have to do that. I'll take a cab, and we'll go back to the hotel and talk." Cal had made an appointment for him at SF General for the next day, and another at the hospital he'd mentioned in Oakland. And she knew that Steve had called his friends at Stanford. He was going to have a busy day on Friday, while she went out to meet some important clients with Cal, he said he wanted her to meet them. Meanwhile, they had heard that day that his stock had gone up further. It had skyrocketed in the week it had been on the market. Everything was coming up roses for him, particularly if he could get Meredith to join his company.

"Why don't you come home with me, and I'll barbecue some hamburgers and hot dogs?" It was the other side of his life that always intrigued her, it was so out of sync with the business genius she saw in him, and the young high-tech tycoon that the rest of the world saw. The thought of him barbecuing in his backyard amused her.

"Okay, I'll come," she agreed, "if you don't think your kids will mind." She still remembered the cool reception she'd gotten from them on her earlier visit.

"They'll be fine," he assured her. And they were, for the most part. Andy remembered her and shook her hand with a smile this time. He even remembered that her husband was a doctor. And Julie was cool to her, but politer this time, she even asked how their trip had gone, and told her that her father had brought her a really great sweater from Paris. Meredith didn't tell her that she had helped to pick it out, but she was secretly

pleased that the child had liked it. Mary Ellen was still
the only holdout. She looked irritated as soon as she
saw Meredith get out of the car with her father, and
disappeared upstairs to her room moments after. She
came back downstairs again for dinner, but only long
enough to pick at half a hamburger and then say that
she had to go back up to do her homework. But she
had looked startled, and not particularly pleased when
Meredith mentioned that she'd met her mom in London. If anything, it seemed to make Mary Ellen more
suspicious of her.

"She doesn't get along terribly well with her
mother," Cal explained after the kids left the table
they'd set in the backyard. He and Meredith were
drinking coffee by then, and the pleasant young housekeeper who took care of the kids as well had cleared
the table. Cal said he'd had her for years and she was a
godsend. "I think Charlotte feels some kind of rivalry
with Mary Ellen, now that she's getting older, and she's
hard on her. Mary Ellen just thinks she's mean. And
she took it the hardest when Charlotte left. She was six
then, and it wasn't easy for her." Meredith felt sorry
for the girl suddenly. Even though she wasn't particularly welcoming, or even polite at times, she had obviously suffered, and maybe as a result, she was
suspicious of women. Charlotte didn't look like anyone's dream mother.

They talked about business again then and the children never reappeared. When Cal went for a swim,
Meredith watched him. He had a long powerful body,
and said he'd been on the swimming team in college.
He looked a lot younger than his fifty-one years, and
there was no denying that he was very attractive. But

Meredith was anxious to see Steve, and when it was time for her to leave to pick him up, Cal called her a cab, and renewed his offer to take her. But Meredith insisted that she wanted to take a taxi, and Cal didn't want to force himself on them. They had a lot to talk about, and he didn't want to push it.

He invited them to dinner the following night, and Meredith accepted and told him that Steve was anxious to meet him. She didn't tell him why, that Steve was minimally nervous about him, because for the most part she thought Steve was teasing about it. But she did think it was important, for a variety of reasons, that Steve meet him. And she trusted Steve's insights and opinions. She suspected, and hoped, that the two men would like each other, and she respected each of them, though for different reasons.

When she met Steve at the gate, he came off in wrinkled khaki pants and a shirt that looked like it had never been ironed, and he was still wearing the clogs he wore at work. He had come straight from the hospital to the airport. And the old tweed jacket he'd brought had holes in both elbows. It was like watching a kid come home from boarding school, and wondering what he'd done with the decent clothes you'd sent with him.

"Why on earth did you bring that jacket?" she asked. She had hidden it, two years before, at the back of the hall closet. But no matter what she did with it, he always seemed to find it. And she'd never had the courage to just give it away. She'd done that with a favorite pair of pants of his once, and she'd never heard the end of it.

But she couldn't believe he had actually brought this relic to San Francisco.

"What's wrong with it?" He looked amazed by her question. "We're not going to a black tie dinner, are we?"

"No, but we're having dinner at Callan Dow's to-morrow night. I hope you brought another jacket." It was the kind of conversation married people have, which to others always sounds so stupid.

"Don't worry about it. Guys understand these things. It has personality, and history." He hated new clothes, and he could never understand why she thought his pants should be pressed. He spent so much of his life in wrinkled scrubs that to him, the rest was no different. He was immaculately clean, but every-thing he owned was always wrinkled.

"I think that little speech about personality and his-tory means you didn't bring another jacket, right?"

"Correcto." He grinned at her and leaned over to kiss her as they picked up his single bag, which felt like it had bricks in it.

"My God, what did you bring? A bowling ball?"

"No," he grinned, "some reading." He never went anywhere without a stack of new medical books he felt he had to read in order to stay current. In truth, it was all he cared about. Steve was a brilliant doctor, but no clothes horse. Unlike Cal, who was incomparable in his own field, but always looked impeccable and very ele-gant. The two men couldn't have been more different. "So how's it going? Anything new today?" Steve looked happy to be there, which pleased her.

"No, it's better than ever," she beamed at him, and talked animatedly about Cal's company all the way back to the hotel in the cab. And then they sat in their room and talked till long after midnight.

She left Steve at the hotel the next day. She was going to meet clients with Cal, and Steve had rented a car to go to his assorted appointments. She had suggested he use a car and driver, which wasn't his style. He had gotten a couple of maps from the place where he'd rented the car, and said he was sure he could find the hospitals where he was going. Meredith kissed him when she left, and promised to meet him at the hotel at the end of the day. She wished him luck and rushed off to Dow Tech to meet Callan.

It was another extraordinary day with him. They visited three of his most important customers, and had a tour of one of the hospitals where his diagnostic equipment was in greatest use. It was a fascinating afternoon for her, and Cal was pleased with her reaction. And when she left him at the end of the day, he reminded her to be at his house at seven thirty. "I can't wait to meet Steve, I feel like we're already old friends," he said warmly. She had talked about him so much during the due diligence tour that he honestly did feel as though he knew him.

And when Meredith met Steve back at the hotel, he looked relaxed and sounded surprisingly enthusiastic. He had been impressed with all three hospitals he'd seen, and had been given a referral to a fourth one that handled only the most extreme trauma cases. They had a helipad, and apparently ran a trauma unit very similar to the one where he worked, and he could hardly wait to visit it on Monday. He already had an appointment with the director. The hospitals where he'd been had been interesting, and very interested in him, but they had no openings that were suitable for him, although they'd been very impressed with his credentials, and they promised to keep him in mind if anything came up. But he was too senior and too experienced for them to offer him less than the top job and none of theirs was open. He said he could have been happy in any one of them, but he had his hopes pinned on the one in the East Bay that he was visiting on Monday.

"So what are you thinking?" She smiled at him, they had both had a good day, and she could see that he was very positive about it.

"I'm thinking that I love San Francisco," he beamed at her. "The city is a little jewel, and the people are so nice here. It's not like New York, they don't all look like they think you're about to mug them. Even in the trauma units, people seem pretty relaxed here. The one in Oakland was a little dicey, but they'd just gotten six guys in with gunshot wounds two minutes before I got there. To be honest with you, I love it, Merrie. I can see why it appeals to you." She suddenly felt as though a whole new life was opening up for them, and there was something very exciting about it. The one problem was that they had no job for him, yet, but there was still the hospital in the East Bay that he was going to see on Monday, and they had sounded hopeful, but they didn't want to commit to anything on the phone. He had faxed them his C.V., but they still had to meet him.

"Where would you want to live?" he asked her casually, as though the decision had already been made, or at least as though they were closer to it. "In the city or out here? I actually like it out here, and I wouldn't mind commuting."

"It would be easier for me out here, but that's up to

you. You have to go back and forth to work at crazier hours than I do, and a lot more often.''

"We'll see. I kind of like the idea of a house in the suburbs, and,'' he paused dramatically, searching her eyes cautiously for a reaction, "I think this would be a great place to bring up kids, a lot better than New York. And you wouldn't be under the gun the way you are there, you wouldn't have to do any more due diligence tours, or hopefully work till midnight. This might be the right time, and the right place, to do it.'' He almost held his breath as he waited for her to answer, and she paused for a long minute, seeming to weigh what he'd been saying.

"Maybe,'' was all she finally came up with. But she didn't want to get into that discussion with him. Not yet anyway. There were still a lot of other factors to think of.

"That's it?'' he said, looking mildly disappointed, "just 'maybe'? I think if we're ever going to do it, Merrie, it would be great here. What better life than to be a kid in California?''

"To be a kid with other parents,'' she smiled at him, and then seemed to relax a little bit. It always made her feel tense when they talked about having children. But she had to admit, it might not be so bad here.

They were both in good spirits when they set out for Cal's house at seven fifteen, and they arrived promptly at seven thirty. He was waiting for them in the garden, next to the pool, with margaritas and caviar. The kids had just gotten out of the pool, and he looked relaxed and as handsome as usual in a perfectly pressed blue shirt, and beige gabardine slacks, with his bare feet in

Gucci loafers. Steve was wearing an old striped shirt
and the threadbare tweed jacket that she hated, and
she wished she had had the forethought to pack his
bag for him before she left for California. Next time,
she vowed to herself as the two men shook hands, and
greeted each other. Cal was telling him how much he
had looked forward to meeting him, after everything
he'd heard about him from Meredith during their time
together.

"Your wife is a one-man band on your behalf, Steve.
I hope you know that. She never stopped talking about
you." It was the right thing to say, and Steve seemed
pleased, as he looked Cal over.

The conversation was relaxed and moved with ease
as they discussed a variety of subjects, and eventually
Cal asked him about the hospitals he'd seen, and they
wound up talking about Cal's high-tech diagnostic
equipment. Steve gave him a critical assessment of it,
praised two of Cal's machines inordinately, and gave
him some interesting insights and pointers from a physician's standpoint. And Cal looked pleased by what he
was hearing from him.

They moved inside to the dining room after an
hour, and Cal served a Mouton-Rothschild Bordeaux
that impressed Steve no end. And at eleven o'clock
they were still talking over brandy. It was nearly midnight when they left, and Meredith had the impression
that the evening had gone well. Both men seemed to
have liked each other.

"What did you think of him?" she asked in the car
on the way back to the hotel as Steve drove. She was
interested in Steve's assessment of him.

"He's a hell of a bright guy. And you're right, he's good looking of course, but you forget about it after a while. He's got so many innovative ideas, and there's so much he wants to do, you kind of get caught up in his head and forget the fancy clothes and the movie star looks. I can see why you like him." And then he smiled sheepishly at his wife. "I'm sorry about the jacket, Merrie. I'll bring a better one next time."

"Who cares?" She smiled at the man she loved. She was so proud of him and loved him so much, and she was glad he had liked Cal. And she was a little stunned by what he said next. "I think you ought to take the job. I don't think you'll ever forgive yourself if you don't. You'd always wonder what might have happened if you'd come out here. Baby, you've got to do it."

"You're amazing. What about you?"

"I'll find something. There's plenty of work. They just have to make room for me." And he felt sure they would, in time. "Right now, this job for you is the main thing. I want you to be happy." There were tears in her eyes as he said it. He was so good to her, and so kind, and so generous of spirit.

"I'm not making any decisions until we know where things stand for you. This involves both of us, not just me, no matter how altruistic you are about it."

"Let's see what happens on Monday. And in the meantime, let's have a good time this weekend." Cal had offered to tour them around the next day, but Steve had told him they wanted to discover the city on their own, and they had agreed to come over on Sunday afternoon to swim, and have dinner with him with his kids. And Cal had promised to do a barbecue for them. But Steve and Meredith were looking forward to spending time in the city before that.

On Saturday, they went to Marin, and crossed the Golden Gate Bridge with the top down on their rented convertible. They had lunch in Sausalito and wandered around in the shops, and they had dinner at Scoma's. The view was spectacular, and afterward they drove around San Francisco, and wound up at Fisherman's Wharf for an Irish coffee. He took her to the Top of the Mark at midnight just to see the view, and then they went back to the Peninsula, and talked about what they'd seen of the city. Cal had told them that Pacific Heights would be the place for them to live, and they had driven through it, with its neat rows of pretty Victorians and brick houses and colorful stuccos. Everything looked tidy and neat and clean, and the streets were immaculate. And Steve had fallen in love with the city.

On Sunday morning, they visited the Stanford campus, and then strolled through Palo Alto. They were both overwhelmed by what they'd seen and how much they'd liked it. They arrived at Cal's on Sunday afternoon and joined everyone at the pool. Steve was playing Marco Polo in the water with Cal's children, as Meredith chatted with Callan.

"I think you've made a convert," Meredith said softly as they watched him. "He loves San Francisco."

"And you, Merrie?"

"I love your company, and the work." She smiled at him. She would have been happy at the north pole with a job like the one he was offering, and they both knew it.

"You're a workaholic, like I am. We're hopeless."

He glanced at her husband playing with his children and smiled back at her. "He's a nice guy, Merrie. You were right. And I hear he's a damn good doctor." He had made some polite inquiries before recommending him at the hospitals where he'd sent him. "How's the job front looking?"

"Nothing yet. No one has an opening for him, but he doesn't seem too panicked about it. He's got an interview in the East Bay on Monday."

"I hope it works out," Cal said fervently, and meant every word of it. He was more desperate than ever to have her come out and join him. The past three days had confirmed to him everything he'd thought about her.

"So do I," she said quietly, as Steve threw the ball to Mary Ellen and she squealed with pleasure. As cautious as the children had been around Meredith, they seemed to have no trouble opening up to her husband. But she had never been very comfortable around children, and they sensed that.

It was an easy afternoon for them, and Steve and Cal and Meredith got into long, interesting discussions that night, mostly about politics and their effect on business. Steve had his own pet peeves in what related to medicine, and they exchanged points of view for hours, and when they left, Cal wished him luck the next day at his interview, and told Merrie he'd see her in the morning.

She was in Cal's office with him when Steve called at noon, and he sounded exhilarated.

"What's up?" she asked, sounding distracted. They'd been going over some projections for the next quarter.

"I thought you might like some news."

"What's that?" she asked, smiling, as Cal watched her intently.

"I have a job. And so do you, I suspect. They want me on January first. The head of trauma here is leaving, and if my references check out, which they should, if they call Lucas, I'll be their new head of trauma. How does that sound?"

"Wow!" Her eyes met Cal's as she said it. "Congratulations, sweetheart!" She was nearly speechless. It was all falling into place with so little effort. It was as though it was meant to be. It was obviously kismet.

"The same to you. Are you going to tell Cal you'll take it?"

"What do you think?" she asked cryptically. She wanted to be sure it was really all right with him if she did it. But now they both had great new jobs to come to, and it lifted a ten-ton weight off her shoulders. She was free now to take the job Cal was offering her and that she wanted so badly.

"I think if you don't tell him you'll take it, I will. Go for it, sweetheart. You deserve it."

"Thank you, Steve," she said, feeling grateful and happy and relieved all at once. She was still smiling when she hung up the phone a few minutes later. And Cal was watching her with a worried expression.

"That sounded hopeful."

"Better than that." She beamed at him. "He got the job." Cal's face broke into a broad smile, he was as relieved as she was.

"Where does that leave us, Merrie?"

"Where would you like it to leave us?" she asked

directly, her eyes never leaving his for an instant. It was like dancing with Fred Astaire again, they were perfectly synchronized, their minds always working together.

"I'd like it to leave you as the new CFO of Dow Tech. Will you do it?"

She nodded slowly. She was sure now. It was almost like getting married, a huge step, and an important commitment. "Yes, I will, if that's what you want."

"You know I do, Meredith." He held out his hand then and shook hers. "Is it a deal?"

"It is. I can't believe this has happened." And it had all happened so quickly. Two weeks before, they'd been on a road show together, and now she was his employee and moving to California.

"Neither can I." He went to the small wet bar in the anteroom to his office and took out a bottle of champagne and two glasses. And when he came back, he was smiling from ear to ear. "Let's celebrate. This is the best news I've had in years. Maybe ever."

They toasted each other, and sat drinking champagne and talking for a while, and then they started talking about the details.

"How soon do you want me, Cal?" She knew that Charlie McIntosh had given him two weeks, but she assumed that he'd be willing to stay on for a while, particularly knowing now that she'd be coming out and would need a little time to tie things up at her end. Two weeks, if he'd stuck to it, would have meant the eighth of October, and there was no way she could do that. If nothing else, she had to give her firm a decent notice. She was thinking about a month, and she had to sell their New York apartment. And Steve had said they wanted him in the East Bay on the first of January. That sounded about right to her.

"No later than October fifteenth," Cal answered calmly. And she laughed, thinking he was joking.

"Very funny. I'm serious. Steve has to be out here on January first. Maybe December fifteenth, or just after Christmas?"

"No way, Meredith." The shrewd businessman she had seen in operation before had risen to the fore. He had to think of his own needs now, and Dow Tech's. He wasn't going to wait three months for her to come to California. "Charlie has already told me that he won't stay a single extra day, which is lousy of him, but that's Charlie. He can't wait to get out of here. He and his wife have already planned a two-month tour of Asia."

"Cal, there's no way I can be here in three weeks. That's crazy." She was more than a little startled, and she didn't want to be out two and a half months before Steve, that wouldn't be fair to either one of them. But she also had to think of Dow Tech and Callan's needs.

"I can't function without a CFO. I'd really like you here two weeks from now when Charlie leaves. I could manage for a week without a CFO, but no longer. You've got to come out sooner. Steve can commute on weekends, or you can. I'm sorry, Merrie, I hate doing this to you. But I need you." She liked that part of it, but she hated to tell Steve they'd have a bicoastal marriage till the end of the year. But Cal didn't seem to be willing to give her an inch on it. "I want to give you a signing bonus, of course. I assume you know that. I thought two hundred and fifty thousand dollars might soften the blow." And how was she going to argue with that? Callan Dow knew what he was doing. "I'm going to give you an apartment here in Palo Alto for three months, at our expense of course, longer if you need it. That'll give you time to decide where you want to live, and to find a house you like." He was doing more than she could possibly have asked for.

"It's all very generous, Cal. I'm just a little stunned that you want me out here so soon. I wasn't expecting that." She still sounded worried about it, in spite of the on-signing bonus, which was more than generous, it was outstanding.

"I wasn't expecting Charlie to give me two weeks' notice. I'm sorry to put pressure on you, Meredith, but the heat is on all of us. Shall we say the fifteenth?"

"I guess we have to. I'll just have to fly back to New York on weekends, when Steve's not working. He can come out midweek when he's off. We'll work it out," but she was concerned about what Steve would say about it. She was meeting him at the hotel at four o'clock, and they were flying back to New York on a six o'clock flight.

Cal gave her a big hug when she left, and told her to call him if there was anything he could do to help, and she told him to call her if he needed any input from her before she got there, and he laughed at that.

"Are you kidding? I'll be following you around every ten minutes for the next three weeks, Meredith. I hope everything goes smoothly at your end." He knew her partners were going to be upset, but as far as he was concerned, they deserved it. The one she was really

worried about was her husband. It was going to be a
tough two and a half months not living with each other,
she wasn't looking forward to it, and she knew he
wouldn't either.

But as usual, he surprised her. "If that's what it takes
sweetheart, then so be it. You have to go for it now, it
won't wait, and I'll be there before you know it." Once
again, she told him he was amazing.

They talked about it again on the plane, and Steve
said he could take care of selling the apartment, and
he reassured her that he was willing to fly out to San
Francisco to see her whenever he had a few days' break
from the trauma unit.

"You know," Steve confessed to her somewhere over
the Rocky Mountains, with a glass of wine in his hand,
"I liked Cal a lot more than I thought I would. From
what you said," he confessed, looking a little sheepish,
"before that, I was a little jealous of him. But I think his
motives are pure. I think he has enormous respect for
you, but he's only interested in his business." Meredith
was happy to hear it, and she had always had the same
impression. They had gotten very close to each other
on the trip, but not in any way she had ever really
worried about. They were good friends and devoted
colleagues. "I like his kids too. They're nice. Too bad
about their mother." Meredith nodded, glancing out
the window, and then she saw that Steve was looking at
her with a gentle smile, and she suspected what was
coming.

"Speaking of which, what do you think if, after
you've been there for a while, a few months maybe,
maybe six . . . we start thinking about a baby." She'd

be thirty-eight by then, and there was no denying that it was getting to be time, if that was what they decided they wanted. She had always said that if they had children, she wanted them before she was forty. And if they started pursuing a pregnancy in the next six months, she'd be thirty-nine when the baby came. Medically, Steve had always been uneasy about her starting their family any later.

"Why don't we see how things are going then?" she said vaguely. It was an old refrain he knew only too well. And he was disappointed by her answer.

"If we keep waiting to 'see,' I'll be ninety and we'll still be talking about it. Meredith, one of these days, you're going to have to bite the bullet." He thought she was physically afraid of pregnancy and delivery and he wasn't entirely wrong, but she was far more afraid of the commitment a baby would require of her.

"Why do I have to bite the bullet?" she said, looking disturbed. She knew she owed him a lot after what he was willing to give up in New York, but she wasn't sure she wanted to make a baby part of the deal. In fact, she knew she didn't, and she didn't want to make false promises to him. All she wanted now was to help Cal expand his business. To her, that was a lot more exciting than having children.

"Cal seems to be able to manage a family on his own, and to run a business. I think you could do it too, Merrie. I'll help you."

"I know you would," she said, looking upset. "I just don't know what I want yet."

"Maybe you never will until you just do it."

"And then what? What if I hate it? What if it's just

too much for me, if it screws up my career, or we decide we can't handle it with both our jobs? You can't send it back if you don't like it.''

"I can't imagine you not loving a baby," he said gently.

"Kids scare me," she said honestly. "I'm not like you. You're some kind of pied piper with them. They always look at me like the witch in *Sleeping Beauty*." He laughed at the comparison and leaned over and kissed her.

"No kid of mine is going to think you're a witch. I promise."

"We'll talk about it again when we get settled." She dismissed the idea as summarily as she always had, for the past fourteen years, and turned her mind to other things. It always made her feel anxious to talk about having babies. "When are you going to give them notice at the hospital?" She asked him the question as much to distract him from an awkward topic as because she wanted to know the answer.

"As soon as we get back, I guess. I want to give them three months' notice. This way, I can be out West with you by Christmas." It sounded perfect, except for the time they'd be commuting before that, but Steve had assured her it would go quickly, and she would certainly be busy. "What about you?" he asked.

"I'm going to tell them tomorrow." She had stayed away an extra day, and she was beginning to wonder if they suspected something. "They're not going to like it."

"Cal is right on that score. They deserve it. They don't appreciate you."

But apparently, they appreciated her more than he

or Cal thought they did. They were devastated when she told her partners the next morning. They couldn't believe it. Particularly when she told them she was leaving in three weeks for California. But after the initial shock, they were gracious about it, and gave her a very pleasant dinner the week before she left. It was hard to believe that a twelve-year-long chapter in her career was ending.

And as she sat in their apartment with Steve the night before she left, with open suitcases all around, she looked at her husband in amazement.

"It's like going off to college or something, isn't it? I still can't believe it."

"Neither can I," he admitted with a grin, "but I love it." He had told the hospital he would be leaving and they were shocked, but happy for him. Lucas was particularly sorry about it, because he knew it meant that it would be at least another year before he could leave trauma for research. But they were already looking for someone to take Steve's place, although they had no prospects yet. And if they found someone soon enough, Steve had promised to train them. The one thing he had promised them was that he wouldn't leave until they had a replacement. And the hospital in California had agreed to go along with it, even if it delayed him slightly. They had been entirely reasonable about it.

Steve left for the hospital when she left for the airport the next day. It was a Sunday, and it had been an emotional week for her. She had left her office for the last time on Friday, and she was sorry to leave her friends there. There had been some tears, some warm good-byes, and a lot of good wishes. And as she turned

to leave the apartment, she glanced around as though
she was never coming back again, trying to remember
what she'd forgotten.

"Take it easy, babe," Steve said gently. "You'll be
back next weekend."

"I know. I guess I'm just a little nervous."

"Don't be," he reassured her. "Everything's going
to be fine. It's going to be terrific."

"I know," she smiled at him, and closed the door
behind them.

Chapter 10

THE JOB IN California was everything Meredith had hoped it would be. It was exciting, challenging, and working with Callan Dow was even better than she had expected. And professionally, it was the chance of a lifetime. They moved together in perfect harmony through meeting after meeting, and sat in each other's offices for hours, talking about new projects. Meredith finished every day exhilarated and excited.

And the furnished apartment he had rented for her was airy and spacious and pleasant. She called Steve as often as she could, to let him know what was happening in her life, but as always, it wasn't easy to get him. But when they did manage to speak, he was happy for her. He was even understanding when she told him she had too much work to get away and come back to New York over the first weekend. She was still trying to get through the stack of unfinished projects Charlie McIntosh had left her.

"I'm sorry, sweetheart," she told him late Thursday

night. She had been in California, and in the job, for four days, and she hadn't caught her breath yet.

"Don't worry about it. Maybe you can look at houses for us over the weekend." They had agreed that since he'd be working in the East Bay, they would look for houses in the city. They would both have to commute that way, but it was an easier commute for Steve than if they lived in Palo Alto. It would have taken him two hours to get to work that way, which was just too much for him. The city was a good compromise for them, and Meredith had agreed to it.

"I'll look on Sunday," she promised. And she had every intention of doing it, but by then, she was still buried in work, and sitting with stacks of it on the terrace of her apartment. Cal had invited her to come to dinner the night before, and she refused his offer and ate a sandwich while working. But when he called on Sunday afternoon, having gotten more work done by then, she relented.

She had an early dinner with him and the kids, and this time all of them were fairly pleasant to her. They were getting used to her, and after meeting Steve, even Mary Ellen finally believed that she wasn't their father's girlfriend.

Her second week at Dow Tech was even better than the first, and by midweek she was sure that she could get to New York for the weekend. But this time, it was Steve who called. Harvey Lucas was sick, and he had to cover for him. But Meredith wasn't as disappointed as he was. She had so much to do, she was grateful to be able to stay in Palo Alto again, and get more work done.

"We're not exactly winning gold stars on our

commuting, are we?'' Steve said, sounding mildly depressed about it. He was busy at work, but he missed her. It was sad coming home to the empty apartment at night, when he finally got off duty, and he felt like a kid who had no one to play with. It had been two weeks since he'd seen her.

But the real crunch came on her third weekend in California. They had promised each other that nothing would stand in their way this time. She had reservations on a flight to New York on Friday night, and on Wednesday Cal learned that customers they were going to entertain on Thursday would be delayed till Friday, and Cal asked her to stay. The customers were important to him.

''I know you were probably planning to go to New York this weekend,'' he said apologetically, ''but I'd really appreciate it if you'd stay here. Just this one time. I think it might make a big difference to the people and they haven't met you.''

''Of course, Cal,'' she said, without hesitating. She knew how important it was to him, and she could see his point, and she hoped Steve would understand. But she was still surprised and upset when he didn't.

''For chrissake, Merrie. It's been three weeks. Is this what it's going to be like for the next two months? When the hell am I going to see you?'' For once, he was furious with her, and she was upset that he wasn't more understanding. She also felt a little guilty about not going to New York and it made her defensive.

''I'm not staying out here for a tennis tournament, or my garden club. This is business, baby. I have to be here.''

''Bullshit. Cal can entertain them without you.''

"No, he can't. Or at least he doesn't want to. And I work for him. I can't just walk out when he's asked me to be here. We didn't plan it this way. TIQ is our biggest account."

"Great. So what am I supposed to do? I have to work Sunday so I can't come out. You knew that." He sounded angry and disappointed.

"I'll be home next weekend. I swear, scout's honor." But he was still annoyed when she hung up, and he called back and complained about it again later. He was upset that he hadn't seen her. But there was nothing she could do about it. Business was business.

Cal had hired a caterer to serve them dinner at his home on Friday night, he had invited three other couples, and it was a very pleasant evening. He asked Meredith to come before the other guests arrived, which she did, in a new black cocktail dress that was sleek and sophisticated and very chic, and he looked very pleased when he saw her.

"That's a knockout, Merrie! And so are you." He briefed her quickly about the other couples, and he knew she had already done extensive reading about the people from TIQ.

And when they arrived, she was a very gracious hostess for him. She moved easily among the guests, talked to the men about business issues, and then spent an appropriate amount of time with the women. But most of them were talking about their children, and Meredith eventually drifted back into the male-generated business conversations. And Cal beamed as he watched her, she was perfect.

When the guests finally left, they all agreed that it

had been a wonderful evening, great food, interesting people, and lively conversations. And the man from TIQ seemed to be in love with Merrie.

"You totally snowed him," Cal said with a look of admiration. "You were terrific. Thank you for staying. I know you were planning to go to New York, but this was important to me."

"I knew it was," she said simply.

"Was Steve upset?" he asked, looking concerned and she hesitated.

"A little. But I'll be home next weekend." But she had realized that it wasn't as easy getting back to New York on weekends as she had thought it would be. But they only had to do it for two more months. It wasn't forever. And Steve had to be understanding about it. She was establishing herself in a new business.

"I'm really sorry," Cal said sincerely. "Why don't you leave early Friday next weekend?"

"Thanks, I might. I'm going to use this weekend to house-hunt in the city," she said, as they walked slowly toward her car in his driveway. She was pleased that the evening had gone so well for him.

"Can I come?" he asked unexpectedly.

"It's pretty boring," she said, and she'd been planning to do some shopping. "You probably want to be with the kids," she said, as he opened her car door for her.

"As a matter of fact, they're all busy. My chauffeuring services aren't even needed. I'd really love to come with you. I like looking at houses."

"All right," she said with a smile, "if you really want to."

"What time shall I pick you up?"

"How about ten thirty? There's one I want to see at eleven."

"I'll come by at ten fifteen to be on the safe side. And thanks again for tonight . . . you were really great," he said with a warm smile, and a minute later she drove off with a wave, and he was at her apartment building at ten fifteen the next morning, wearing khaki pants, a navy turtleneck, and a blazer, and as usual, he looked very handsome. She was beginning to wonder if he ever looked disheveled. Knowing Cal, it was hard to imagine.

He drove her to the city, as they chatted comfortably, about business, as usual. And the first house they saw was a disappointment. But after that, they saw two others, both of them in Pacific Heights. One needed too much work, though it was a pretty, old house and had great views, and the other seemed a little small to her, although Cal liked it. But she thought it was a little claustrophobic.

"Depends how many kids you plan to have," he said, as they got back in his car. He had just suggested they have lunch at The Waterfront, they were both starving.

"Very funny. You know I don't want kids, Cal. I have Dow Tech now. That's my new baby."

"I'm not sure your husband is as clear on that as I am," he smiled. "He said something about it to me when you two came to dinner, after he'd been swimming with my children."

"I know," she said uncomfortably. It was a sore subject. "He keeps pushing, and I think that's part of why he wants to move out here. I just can't see it for me, now more than ever."

"I think you're just scared, and I still believe in my earlier theory."

"What? That I'm not committed to Steve? Now that you've met him, how can you say that?"

"I'm not saying you're not committed to him," he corrected her. "I think you are, as much as anyone ever is. Maybe you don't trust the relationship, or the future." It was an old theory with him. She had heard it that first week and here it was again.

"After nearly fifteen years, I don't know what's not to trust. He's not going anywhere, and neither am I. I just trust my own instincts. I know myself, and just as you said about Charlotte a long time ago, I'm not very maternal. I think it's a mistake to go against that."

"Is that what you always agreed on right from the beginning?" he asked, as they headed down Divisadero Street toward the water.

She hesitated before she answered. "Probably not. But I was twenty-three years old when we got married, I'm not sure I knew myself that well then, or understood how much my career would come to mean to me. It takes a while to figure that out," she said very clearly.

"I know. But there's usually more to it than careers, and I think you know that."

"I don't know what you mean when you say that, Cal."

"I've known people who were married to the same people for years, and never had kids, either because they didn't want to, or thought they couldn't, and the next thing you know, they've fallen for someone else, get remarried, and bang, they're pregnant. It's not a new theory. Just the nature of the beast," he said matter-of-factly.

"Are you saying you think Steve and I will get divorced?" She looked startled by the suggestion. It was something she never even thought of.

"God knows, I hope not. I guess I'm just saying that nothing is predictable in life, and if you look deep enough, I'll bet there are other reasons why you don't want children, not all of them work-related. Maybe you don't think you'd be good parents."

"I think he would, if he weren't working forty-eight-hour stretches. I'm not so sure about myself. Maybe you're right though. If we'd have wanted kids, we probably would have had them. People do seem to have them no matter what, no matter how wrong the circumstances are, or how bad the timing."

"Maybe he doesn't really want them either, and he uses you as the scapegoat." They were all new ideas to her, but some of them were worth a closer look, and she wondered if Cal was closer to the truth than she wanted to believe.

Lunch at The Waterfront was fun, and the view was spectacular. And afterward, they drove by the Palace of the Legion of Honor, and walked around for a little while, chatting, and admiring the paintings. And when they left, he invited her to join him and his children for dinner.

"You're going to get tired of me, if you eat three meals a day with me," she teased, but he insisted.

"Since I got you stuck alone here all weekend, the least I can do is feed you." But she was having such a nice time with him that she didn't resist him. He was so easy to be with, and they always had so much to talk about, mostly about his business.

The kids didn't seem surprised to see her that night.

Mary Ellen was at a friend's, and Andy and Julie were watching videos. But when they came down and saw her, they greeted her like an old friend. Andy was all excited about the football game they were going to on Sunday. The 'Niners were playing the Broncos.

"Are you coming with us?" Andy asked her with interest over dinner.

"No, I'm not," she said politely.

"Why not?" Cal asked, as he smiled at her. "That's a great idea. Do you like football?"

"Sometimes. I'm a big baseball fan. It's usually too cold in New York to go to football games without freezing to death."

"It's better here," Julie reassured her, and somehow Meredith got swept away by the tides of their enthusiasm, and the next thing she knew she had agreed to join them.

"Are you sure the children won't mind?" she asked Cal after they left the table.

"Of course not. Why would they? You're part of the family now, Meredith. They're perfectly comfortable with you."

"They just liked Steve because he played Marco Polo with them."

"Yes, they did. But they like you too. Julie thinks you're smart, and Andy thinks you're very pretty. He has good taste," he said proudly, "he takes after me."

"And Mary Ellen hates me," she said, laughing at the double compliment. "Maybe you should ask her."

"She likes you too. She just takes longer to warm up to people than the others. But the last time you were here, she loved what you were wearing. At her age, that's a major issue. She said you were 'cool,' which is a big deal to her. I'm not 'cool,' in case you want to know, because I'm her father. She thinks I'm two hundred years old, and really dumb most of the time. Last week she told me I was pathetic.''

"See what I mean," Meredith said, looking awed by him, he handled it all with such ease, from business to babies. "I wouldn't know how to deal with that. If my daughter told me I was pathetic, I'd be heartbroken.''

"You toughen up eventually. After they tell you they hate you a few million times, you begin to miss it when they don't say it. 'Pathetic' is high praise, coming from a fourteen-year-old. It's better than 'retarded.' I was 'retarded' last year, and 'evil' earlier this summer. And last week Julie told me I was really stupid, but that was because I said she can't wear lipstick. You have to learn the jargon.'' He was laughing and so was Meredith. He made it all seem so easy.

"I think business school was a lot easier than having children would be.''

"This is different," he said, and then touched her hand gently. "You're a hell of a nice woman, you know, Merrie. And good company. Thank you for being here this weekend.'' He knew it had been a sacrifice for her, and he wanted to make it up to her. And she was so pleasant to be with. He had even enjoyed house-hunting with her, and they had both laughed when the real estate agent thought he was her husband, but it had been a normal assumption. He had noticed that she hadn't been too anxious to find a house, and seemed to find fault with all of them. He wondered if she really wanted to live in the city. He knew it was a concession

she was making for Steve, but he was beginning to suspect she wanted to stay in Palo Alto. It would certainly
be easier for her. "How are you liking your apartment,
by the way? Are you comfortable there?"

"I love it," she admitted. "I'm going to have to give
it up and move into the city. Steve has his heart set on a
house there. Actually, I think I prefer an apartment."

"I'll bet I can guess why too. No room for a baby.
God, you're stubborn!"

"Look who's talking!" She teased him then about
some positions he'd taken that week that weren't entirely reasonable, but he had dug in his heels and refused to be swayed, no matter how much she argued
with him.

"So you've figured that out, have you?" He looked
vaguely embarrassed as he poured her another glass of
wine, and they sat in his comfortable living room for
hours, talking. It was after midnight when she finally
went home. And he was back at her front door at
eleven the next morning, to take her to the football
game, and his kids were with him. They swarmed over
her apartment like little bees. The girls both thought it
was "cool," and Andy said he liked it.

And they had a ball at the football game. The Broncos won, and Andy was outraged. But other than that,
they had a great time, eating hot dogs and peanuts and
ice cream. And when they left, without even thinking
about it, she went back to the house with them, and
helped Cal cook them dinner. It was nice being with
them, and being part of a family, and she was actually
sorry when Cal took her home that night, and she
thanked him for a wonderful weekend.

"I had the best time." She had seen him all three

days, for a variety of events, all of them enjoyable and none of them boring. "I hope your kids didn't mind my hanging around."

"Not at all. They loved it. You set a great example for the girls, it shows them that women can be smart and beautiful and successful *and* nice. That's important for them."

"Well, I enjoyed myself thoroughly. Please thank them for me. And thank you, Cal."

"You're the best thing that's happened to me in a long time, Meredith. And I hope you know that." It seemed a serious moment between them, and then he lightened it immediately. "Besides, Charlie McIntosh wasn't nearly as pretty as you are." They both laughed and he left her then, and told her he'd see her at the office, and a few minutes after she got in, Steve called.

"Where the hell have you been all weekend?"

She was surprised by his tone, it wasn't like him to be that angry. But their current living arrangement was putting a considerable strain on both of them, and she was willing to be understanding about it.

"I've been everywhere. The dinner with customers I told you about on Friday night. I looked for houses in the city on Saturday. I had dinner at Cal's last night. And they took me to a football game today. I just walked in the door five minutes ago, sweetheart." She thought it accounted perfectly for her whereabouts, but he was even more furious when she was finished.

"Are you telling me you spent the whole weekend with him? Why don't you just move in with him while you're at it?"

"Come on, Steve, don't be silly. I had nothing else to do this weekend."

"You were supposed to be here." He sounded petulant and childish.

"And you're working today, so I couldn't have been with you anyway. So why make a big deal about it?"

"Did you find a house?" he snapped at her. She didn't like the tone of the conversation, and wondered if he'd had a bad day, or was just tired. It wouldn't have been surprising.

"Not yet. But I'm looking."

"It can't be that hard. The paper was full of houses for sale when I was out there."

"I haven't liked anything I've seen, Steve. Relax. We have time, and the apartment is fine here."

"Then maybe you should try spending some time in it, and not spending all your time at Cal's house."

"Come on, Steve, for chrissake. I was there for a business dinner on Friday, and hanging out with his kids today. Don't make it a big deal when it isn't." She was startled to realize he was jealous.

"You hate kids. So tell me, what's the big attraction, or do we both know what it is? Is that what all this is about, Merrie? Are you falling for him? Is that why you haven't been home in three weeks? Am I just being a fool here?"

"Of course not. We're just friends, sweetheart. You know that. You met him. I don't know that many people here yet, and he felt badly that he got me stuck here this weekend."

"He should feel like shit about it," Steve was almost shouting at her, "he spent the weekend with my wife, and I didn't."

"Baby, calm down. I told you. I'll be home next

weekend. There is absolutely nothing between me and Callan Dow, except work and friendship.''

"I'm not so sure of that. I saw the guy. He's handsome, successful, charming, and he looks like he'd pounce on you, given half a chance. I know that type." He was being completely irrational, and she knew it.

"If he were going to do a stupid thing like that, he'd have done it when we were traveling together, and I wouldn't be working for him now. I have no interest whatsoever in getting 'pounced' on. And he is *not* that kind of guy. He's a perfect gentleman, and you know it."

"I don't know what I know anymore, but whatever this is, I don't like it. You're leading a completely independent life, like a single woman."

"That is absolute crap, Steve Whitman. I'm doing my job, and trying to find a house for us. This isn't easy for either of us, but if you're going to be stupid about it, and make insane accusations about Cal Dow, you're going to make it even harder. He's my boss. What do you expect me to do? Refuse to see him?'' She was making sense, but he still didn't like the situation.

"No . . . I guess not . . . I just hate having you so far away. It's harder than I thought. I thought you'd be home every weekend. I didn't realize I'd be seeing you once a month. This just isn't working." He suddenly sounded depressed more than angry.

"I know, baby. I'll be home next weekend, come hell or high water. I promise," she said gently.

"You'd better."

"I'll be there."

And when she started to get a cold on Thursday night, she didn't say a word. She just loaded up on pills the next day, and got on the flight. But by the time she got to New York, she was coughing, had a pounding headache, and an earache. And when she got to the apartment, she looked awful. She had gotten stuck at the office and missed the earlier flight. She didn't land at Kennedy till midnight.

Steve had dinner waiting for her, and a bottle of champagne, and it was one A.M. when she walked in the door, and all she wanted was her bed, but she sat at dinner with him, and drank champagne, and pretended to feel better than she did. But he could see she was feeling lousy. He was dying to make love to her, but she ached all over by the time she got into bed, even her skin hurt, and when he touched her, he could tell she had a fever.

"Poor baby," he said, feeling sorry for her. He took her temperature and she had 101.4. He gave her Tylenol, and tucked her in, but in the morning she felt worse instead of better.

"You probably shouldn't have flown," he said, feeling guilty.

"You'd have killed me if I hadn't come home," she said, coughing.

"You're right. I probably would have." He smiled at her.

She spent the whole weekend in bed. By Sunday the fever was down, and they went for a walk on Sunday afternoon, and he seemed depressed, although they had finally made love that morning. But neither of them was in great spirits. She was planning to take the last flight to San Francisco that night, and get in late, but she'd be at her office in the morning.

"It's only for another seven weeks," she reminded

him, as he cooked her dinner, but she wasn't hungry. She picked at it, in order to please him.

"It seems like forever," he said grimly. And it did, to both of them, but there was nothing they could do about it. They just had to grit their teeth and get through it.

She wasn't planning to come back until two weeks later, for Thanksgiving. They had promised to go to the Lucases' for dinner.

Steve took her to the airport that night, and gave her some decongestants before she got on the plane, and she kissed him good-bye, still looking miserable. And he looked even worse when he went back to the apartment. It was a lonely life for him now, and missing her was almost a physical ache. He lay in their bed and nearly cried when he smelled her perfume and shampoo on his pillow.

"How was the weekend?" Cal asked when she came into the office on Monday. She looked terrible, and she was coughing and sneezing. The flight had made her cold worse, and she felt awful.

"Pretty lousy," she said honestly, "I was sick, and Steve was unhappy. I wasn't much fun. It was just bad luck I got sick before I went," she said miserably.

"I'm sorry, Merrie. You'd better take care of yourself. This commuting is hard on you and we've got some big meetings coming up this week."

"I know. I'll be fine," she reassured him, but she felt rotten all week, and spent the next weekend in bed. The last thing she needed was to be too sick to fly over Thanksgiving. She knew Steve would never forgive her, and she didn't want to miss the holiday with him.

Cal had invited her to spend Thanksgiving with

them, in case she didn't plan to go home, but she assured him that she was spending it in New York with her husband.

"Just so you're not alone here," he said kindly, and she thanked him. He was very good to her. He had every interest in keeping her happy. He wanted her to stay at Dow Tech forever.

The next week flew by, what there was of it. No one did much work before the holiday, and on Wednesday afternoon she flew to New York as planned. She was over her cold, and looking forward to Thanksgiving. Steve had said he'd meet her at the airport, but he wasn't there, and she paged him when she got back to the apartment. He returned her call an hour later.

"You're not going to believe this," he said grimly. "There was a subway fire at rush hour this afternoon. And they sent everyone to us. No fatalities, but I'm dealing with some mighty sick people. I'm not going to get out of here till tomorrow."

"Don't worry about it," she said cheerfully, "I'm here. I'll be here whenever you can come home."

"I should be off by tomorrow morning. The chief resident is going to cover for me and Harvey, so we can at least have Thanksgiving. Poor bastard, I know what that's like."

But the chief resident's six-year-old son managed to get a ruptured appendix at midnight. And neither Harvey Lucas nor Steve had the heart to force him to come on duty. The kid was really sick, in another hospital naturally, and he wanted to be with him. And Lucas hadn't been well all week. There was no one to run the show except Steven.

Steve sounded near tears when he called her. "I'm

stuck here," he said bluntly. "I can't get out, Merrie."
She hesitated for a moment, these days it was such a big
deal when either of them couldn't get free. It was as
though they were walking on eggs now. But she recovered quickly, for his sake.

"Don't worry about it. I'll bring you turkey dinner."

"How are you going to manage that?" He sounded
startled.

"I'll figure out something," she promised. And true
to her word, she showed up with a roast chicken she'd
bought at a deli on Second Avenue, potato salad, stuff-
ing, and cranberry sauce, at two o'clock that afternoon, and they ate it on paper plates in his office. She
had even bought pumpkin pie, and he smiled as he
looked at their makeshift meal and then kissed her.

"You're pretty terrific," he said, holding her, as a
nurse walked by and smiled. They were cute together.

"You're not so bad yourself," Meredith smiled at
him. They managed to get a whole hour to themselves
before Steve had to go into surgery with a patient with
a gunshot wound in the groin. His patients managed to
shoot each other, even on Thanksgiving.

"I'll be home when I can," he promised. And he
finally made it on Friday morning. And for the rest of
the weekend, they had three uninterrupted days together.

They went to movies, and held hands, they made
love and slept late. They even went skating at Rockefel-
ler Center. It was just what they needed, and they both
felt renewed again when she got on the plane on Sunday night. He stood in the airport and kissed her, and
they looked like young lovers.

"I had a great weekend, Merrie. Thank you," he whispered.

"Me too," she said, and kissed him again. And she had to tear herself away to leave him. He had promised to fly out to see her the next weekend. They only had five weeks left before he moved out, four if he could leave before Christmas. Their apartment hadn't sold yet, but there were some people who were interested and hadn't made their mind up. But the Thanksgiving they'd shared had given each of them the strength they needed to get through the last stretch of their seemingly interminable separation. She had been living in California without him for six weeks now.

And the good feelings they'd shared over the holiday carried them through the next few days. Meredith was still floating on air when he called her on Thursday.

"Are you sitting down?" he asked. She couldn't imagine what he was going to say. Maybe that he'd sold their apartment for twice the asking. It had to be good news the way he said it.

"Sure. Why?" she asked with a smile.

"I just lost the job in California." She felt as though a bomb had hit her.

"*What?* Are you kidding? This is a joke, right?"

"This is no joke. The guy who was leaving, the number-one guy, isn't. He changed his mind. And they can't force him to leave. They're probably the only trauma unit in the world that's overstaffed. They can't make room for me." He sounded devastated, which was exactly how she was feeling. "I called all the other hospitals I saw, and all they have is a spot as low man on

the ER team at SF General.'' And Meredith couldn't
bear the thought of his doing something like that. The
job in the East Bay had been so perfect. "They were
very apologetic about it, when they called from the East
Bay. But they can't ask the guy to leave, and besides,
they don't want to. They love him.''

"Oh shit, Steve. What are we going to do now?''

"I don't know. Wait, I guess. There's nothing else we
can do. Something will come along eventually. And in
the meantime, I can stay here. Lucas was thrilled when
I told him.''

"He would be. I don't know what to say, sweetheart.
I never thought that would happen.'' If she had
thought it wasn't a sure thing, she wouldn't have taken
the job with Callan. Now they were stuck with a miserable situation.

She told Cal about it late that afternoon, when they
finished a meeting.

"That's terrible. Why don't you let me make some
calls and see what I can do?'' But his conclusion the
next day was what Steve's had been. There seemed to
be no opening for him anywhere at the moment, unless he wanted to take a far more junior position. And
Cal told Meredith he didn't think Steve should do that.
"He's just going to have to be patient.''

But it had been so difficult for them for the past
seven weeks. And now with no hope in sight, it was
going to add further stress to their situation. And commuting bicoastally hadn't been the easy deal they had
both thought it would be. Most of the time, one or the
other of them couldn't make it. Their lives were just
too busy where they were working.

Meredith was depressed about it for the rest of the week, and Steve sounded even worse whenever she spoke to him, and as usual, he was working that weekend. And she wasn't due back in New York until Christmas. She was planning to take the week off between Christmas and New Year, and then they were supposed to return to California together for good. But everything was up in the air now. All she could do was hope that a job would open up in a trauma unit somewhere quickly.

December was a grueling month for both of them, as it turned out. At work, Cal was trying to tie up a lot of loose ends before the end of the year that kept them working day and night. And with the ice and snow in New York, there was a constant stream of accidents, hit-and-runs, broken hips, and head-on collisions. Only the gang wars seemed to have diminished in the bad weather. And the week before Christmas, they were hit by yet another bolt of lightning. Harvey Lucas had a bad fall on the ice at his home in Connecticut, and broke a hip and his pelvis. He was going to be out of commission for eight weeks, and even if Steve had had a job to come to, he couldn't have left the trauma unit where he was working. Steve felt he owed it to Harvey to stick around until he had recovered. The only break for Steve was that they had hired a *locum tenens* trauma doc to work with him for the duration. Her name was Anna Gonzalez, and she made her career doing fill-ins, and Steve said she was smart, had trained at Yale, and she was the only thing making life bearable for him at the moment. She was acting as his assistant, while he took Harvey Lucas's place and ran the unit.

So all Meredith and Steve knew now was that, whatever happened, they had another ten weeks of separation ahead of them. And Meredith had already been alone in California for more than two months now.

"What on earth did we do to deserve this?" Meredith asked, near tears, when they talked about it.

"At least you'll be home in a week. I'm going to see if I can take some time off when you're here, Anna says she'll cover for me."

"Thank her for me," Meredith said, feeling as miserable as she had since she'd heard the news about Harvey Lucas.

For the next few days, Meredith did everything she had to do, and got ready to go home for Christmas. She was taking all her presents for Steve with her. And as she packed a few days before she was to leave, a blizzard hit the entire eastern seaboard. It only made things harder for Steve, there were more accidents and more broken bones, he never seemed to have a free moment.

Meredith was planning to fly east on Christmas Eve, and the night before, she had dinner at Callan's with him and his children. There was a pretty Christmas tree in the living room, and in contrast to New York, they were having unseasonably warm weather, which seemed ironic.

"Maybe you won't be able to leave tomorrow," Andy said ominously as they talked about the bad weather in the East, and the volley of snowstorms that had hit them. There were more than two feet of snow covering New York now, and Steve had said the city was at a standstill.

"I hope not, Andy," Meredith said fervently. She had just given them all their presents. A dress for Mary

Ellen that had elicited squeals from her, another for Julie with a funny pair of shoes that she said were the "coolest," and a robot for Andy that could play ball with him, and pour a can of soda. "Steve is going to be really upset if I don't get home tomorrow." That was a major understatement.

"You could have Christmas with us," Julie volunteered. They were spending Christmas with Cal, and their mother was coming in the day after to take them skiing in Sun Valley. She hadn't seen them since the previous summer, and they were only halfheartedly looking forward to it. Understandably, they seemed to have a lot of reservations about her.

"I'd love to have Christmas with you," Meredith said, "but I need to go home to my husband."

Cal was going to Mexico with friends, and she knew he had chartered a yacht there, while the kids were away with their mother. All she wanted was a week in New York with Steve. Their life at the moment seemed to be filled with nothing but problems and disappointments, and for the moment worrying about it was overshadowing her love for her job. Knowing they would be apart for several more months, she was beginning to worry about her marriage. And Cal could see she was troubled.

After dinner, he chatted with her and talked to her about it. "You two just have to tough it out till he finds something out here, Merrie. He'll find something. He's too good not to." He was worried that she would feel pressured into taking a leave of absence, or worse, going back to her husband.

"This is a lot harder than we thought," she admitted to him, looking depressed about it.

"Men go through it all the time. They take jobs in other cities, and sometimes it takes a year for their families to join them. Houses have to be sold, kids have to finish the school year where they are. People get through it. And you and Steve will too. Just try to be patient."

"I am . . . we are . . . but I feel as though I deserted him when I came out here. And I think that's what he feels. I'm not sure he understands it."

"Sure he does. He's a big boy. He knows this job was important to you. And in the end, it'll be good for him too. I'm sure he's willing to make some sacrifices for your career, Merrie. He loves you. Women do this kind of thing for their husbands all the time. They give up jobs they like, and friends, and homes, to follow their husbands when they're transferred. He just has to be patient. You did the right thing when you came out here, Meredith, and I'm sure Steve knows that." She wasn't sure what Steve knew anymore, except that he hated the way they were living. He was trapped in New York by force of circumstances, and he seemed to think she was having a grand old time in California. She loved her job certainly, but she missed not being with her husband.

"I hope he finds a job out here soon, a good one, not a big step down for him like the one at SF General," she said sadly, as Cal put a sympathetic arm around her shoulders. He wanted to do something to cheer her, and the only thing he could think of was to give her her Christmas present.

"I have a little something for you, Meredith. It's just a thought." He handed her a small box he'd had in his pocket, as he said it. And she had something for him too. She had left the orange box in the hall with her handbag, and she went to get it before she opened his present. As she handed it to him, he recognized the box and ribbon instantly. It was from Hermès, she had bought the gift for him the last time she'd been in the city.

They sat down side by side, and began opening their gifts. And as she opened hers, there was a sharp intake of breath. He had bought her a beautiful gold watch at Bulgari, it was exactly what she would have bought herself, if she had dared to spend that much money on a wristwatch.

"My God, Cal, you shouldn't have . . . it's so beautiful," she put it on and it fit perfectly, and he was pleased that she seemed to like it.

And then he opened the box she had given him, and was equally impressed. She had bought him a very handsome leather Hermès briefcase. The leather was rich and smooth, and it was every bit as elegant as he was. He loved the gift, and he gave her a big hug and kiss the minute he saw it.

"You spoiled me, Merrie! I love it!" He beamed as he looked at it, and she was excited about her watch, as she hugged him back.

"Look who's talking! I've never had a watch like this, Cal."

"Well, you should have." It was something she could wear every day with her well-tailored suits, and the pantsuits she wore to the office. It was businesslike and at the same time it looked chic and expensive.

They sat and talked for a while afterward, and at eleven o'clock, he flipped on the news, so they could see what the weather was doing in the East. There had been stories about people snowed in and stranded all week, and all the major cites and airports had been shut down one by one as the storms continued. And things had not improved while they were eating dinner. Another major front had moved in, and a fresh load of snow was being dumped on New York, New Jersey, Connecticut, and Massachusetts.

"You know, I hate to say it, but I'm not sure you're going to get out tomorrow, Meredith. You'd better check your flight before you leave for the airport."

"Steve will kill me if I don't make it home for Christmas," she said glumly. It would be the topper on an already terrible situation. She really missed him.

"It won't be your fault if you don't, he's got to understand that."

He drove her home after that, and she thanked him for the gift again. She was still wearing it, and she smiled as she pulled up her sleeve and admired it again. "Thank you, Cal. I really love it."

"I'm glad," he said with a look of pleasure. "I love my briefcase."

"We're going to be the two fanciest people in the office," she said, smiling.

"What are you going to do if you can't go home?" he asked, worried about her.

"Cry," she said, and then laughed ruefully. "What can I do? If they close the airport, or cancel my flight, there isn't a damn thing I can do about it."

"If that happens, I want you to spend Christmas Eve with us. I don't want you sitting alone here."

"Thank you, Cal, I appreciate it. But hopefully, I'll get out tomorrow."

"I hope so too. But just in case . . . I don't want

you sitting around feeling sorry for yourself all alone in your apartment."

"I won't. I promise. I'll feel sorry for myself at your house." They both laughed, but she was desperate to get out, and he knew it.

But no matter how desperate she was, the next day the snow was still falling in New York, and by nine A.M. on the West Coast, noon in New York, they had closed Kennedy Airport. She managed to reach Steve at the hospital, and he was disappointed, but philosophical about it.

"You'll get here sooner or later, sweetheart. We'll just have to postpone Christmas till you get here. What are you going to do tonight?"

"I don't know. The Dows said I could come over if this happened." She didn't have any other friends there. She hadn't had time to meet other people yet, she had been too busy at the office.

"At least you'll be with kids," he said, but she could tell by the tone of his voice that he wasn't overly pleased about it. But he could hardly expect her to spend Christmas Eve alone, and he didn't say anything to her. He was going to stay on at the hospital. He didn't want to be alone either. And most of the staff was working.

Cal had heard on the news that the airports were closed, and before he left at noon, he reminded her of his invitation. He was going to do some errands with the kids that afternoon, and he told her to come over around four o'clock, they'd be home then.

She arrived with a huge can of caramel popcorn for them, and candied apples, and the kids dove into them with glee. They sat around the tree in Cal's living room, and he put on a CD of Christmas music. She shared an early dinner with them that night, and afterward the kids went to their rooms, Cal lit a fire for them, and the two of them sat talking about Christmas and their youth and childhoods. He told her his mother had died when he was a child, and how hard the holidays had been for him after that, and she began to understand how loath he was to make a commitment to women. As far as he was concerned, although he didn't express it that way, women always deserted him, one way or another.

"Did your father ever remarry?" she asked with interest.

"Not until I was grown up. My stepmother and he died a long time ago. I have no family other than my children."

"I only have Steve. He has no family either. I think that's why he wants kids so much, to form a family of his own. I guess I'm unnatural because I don't want them."

"Not necessarily. Maybe you're right for you. But that's why I wanted children of my own. I wanted the perfect family, and I have it now . . . I just picked the wrong wife," he said, helping himself to a handful of her popcorn.

"Your kids are great," she said, eating some too, and he looked at her from where he sat, the room was warm, and the fire was crackling softly.

"You're pretty great, too," he said softly. He hadn't expected to spend Christmas with her. It was nice to have an adult to talk to, and she was grateful not to be alone in her apartment. She didn't know what to make of the compliment, and she just looked at him, and then stared into the fire, thinking of Steve. She really missed him. "I didn't mean to make you uncomfortable, Merrie . . . I'm sorry."

"You didn't," she said, looking back at him again. "I was just thinking . . . about you . . . and Steve . . . and how different you are. You're both very important to me, for very different reasons. I love the way you and I work together. I love a lot of things about you." It wasn't what she had meant to say to him, but it was true. She admired him a great deal, and enjoyed his company, they shared so many of the same views, and through their work and their styles, they had so much in common. In some ways, more than she had with Steve. One of the things she had always enjoyed with Steve was how opposite they were, they seemed to complement each other. But with Cal, it was more of a synchronicity, a similarity they shared, that made it so easy for them to be together. "I'm so comfortable with you."

"I've never been as comfortable with anyone in my life," he confessed, sharing her opinion. "It's what marriage should be, and usually isn't. At least mine wasn't."

"Steve and I have always been best friends. But now I feel that way with you too." She felt a little disloyal to Steve when she said it.

"Maybe that's not such a bad thing, since we spend so much time together. Most people spend more time with their business partners and secretaries than they do with their spouses." They both smiled at that, and she helped herself to more popcorn. "Will you come to church with us tonight, Meredith? We go to midnight mass at Saint Mark's."

"I'd like that." She had always been a churchgoer, and Steven had never been religious.

They sat and talked for a long time, and at a quarter to twelve he rounded up the children. Andy was half asleep, but he wanted to go anyway. And the five of them drove to Saint Mark's in Cal's car. Andy was asleep in the backseat when they got there. Cal picked him up and carried him in, and set him down gently on the pew next to his sisters, and never woke him. The girls were serious and sang the hymns, and she and Cal shared a prayerbook and a hymnal. It was a lovely service, and she glanced at him once or twice, and he smiled at her. He had a deep melodic voice, and their voices rose in unison as they sang "Silent Night" together. And afterward, they walked back to the car, and it was an odd feeling being with them. It was as though she belonged there, with his little family. It was a strange illusion, and she was quiet when he dropped her off that night. He took her upstairs, and walked her into the apartment, to make sure she was all right, and he said not a word to her, he simply pulled her gently into his arms and kissed her. And without hesitating, she kissed him back, and he held her in his arms for a long moment, and then looked at her, and was startled to see her crying.

"I'm sorry . . . I don't know what's happening to me, Cal . . . I feel like my whole world is starting to come apart, I'm part of a whole new life here, and I'm not even sure if I belong here."

"I shouldn't have done that, Merrie . . . I'm sorry. . . ." It had just felt so right, to both of them, for an instant. But one kiss could lead them into a world that they both knew they had no right to. "I'm really sorry. . . . It won't happen again. . . . I think I kind of lost it for a minute.''

"Me too," she said softly. There was so much about him that she liked, but she had no right to any of it, and she knew it. "I think the holidays make everyone a little nuts," she reassured him. "They make everyone think about what they don't have, and think they should. Being with your kids tonight almost made me feel like I want a baby."

"Maybe you do," he said gently. But she only shook her head. What she couldn't say to him was that the baby she had suddenly wanted was his, not Steven's. And she didn't understand the feeling. Suddenly everything in her life seemed topsy-turvy. And all she knew was that she had to get back to Steven before they lost each other. For the first time, she was afraid that they would, or might, or could, and feeling that was terrifying for her.

"Merry Christmas, Merrie," Cal said softly before he left.

"Merry Christmas to you, Cal," she answered, but they were both upset by what had happened. It was easy to explain in some ways, they were both feeling emotional because of the holiday, and she had been living apart from her husband for three months. Cal had no important woman in his life. And they were both lonely. But they both knew that it wasn't reason enough to risk her marriage or destroy their friendship.

And the next day, she called him and told him she couldn't come over.

"Because of what happened last night?" he asked softly.

"Yes. I think we both need a breather before we do something foolish. The airport will be open in a few hours, they said. It'll be fine when I come back from New York, let's forget about it, Cal."

He didn't want her to quit because he had been stupid. He didn't care what he had to do, or not do, but more than anything, he didn't want to lose her. "I'm sorry I was such a fool. I know how in love you are with Steve. I don't know what came over me suddenly." But he knew, and so did she, and they both knew it had to stop very quickly. She was sure that if nothing more was said about it, the moment would pass and they would both forget, and they could go back to the comfortable friendship they had shared for months. "I don't like to think of you alone in the apartment on Christmas."

"I'm fine. I promise."

"It was so nice being with you last night, and talking to you." It had been years since he had talked to anyone about his parents.

"We won't lose that, Cal. I promise. I'll be all right after I see Steve. And you'll be yourself again after your vacation in Mexico. I told you, it's just the holidays. I'll see you after New Year's."

"Will you really be all right, Merrie?" He was worried about her, he knew he had upset her.

"Yes, I will. We both will. Merry Christmas, Cal. Kiss the kids for me." And for some insane reason, after she hung up, she found she missed them.

It was a relief when they opened the airport in New York that night, and she got a seat on the red-eye. She sat awake, all the way to New York, thinking of Cal, and how foolish they had almost been. Enough so to wake her up. She knew that she and Steve had to do something. They couldn't live like this forever.

She took a cab to the apartment when she arrived, and the city looked like a fairyland, all covered in snow. Another light snow had already begun falling when she let herself into the apartment. It was the day after Christmas, but at least she was home. And when she walked into the bedroom, Steve was there, sound asleep in their bed. She took off her clothes, and slipped silently under the sheets beside him. And in his sleep, he pulled her close to him and held her.

Chapter 11

THE WEEK IN New York flew by too fast. Steve had taken the week off too, and the time they shared was idyllic. They played in the snow, and went sledding in the park. They went for long walks, and out for dinner. They made love more than they had in years, as though they were both desperate to cling to each other. And after the first few days, they finally talked seriously about their problem.

"What are we going to do?" Meredith was the first to ask. "We can't live like this forever."

"I hope we won't have to," he said sadly. With Meredith there, and so obviously in love with him, he was calmer than he had been in a while.

"Do you want me to quit my job? I will if it's what you want," she said honestly. They had been apart for almost three months, and with no job for him on the West Coast, there was no end of their separation in sight.

"Of course I don't want that. I want what's good for

you. Something will turn up sooner or later," Steve
said calmly.

"What if it's later? What if it takes six months? Or a
year?"

"Then we'll live with it. And if nothing great turns
up, I'll take a job in some ER and wait for the right
opportunity while I'm there. This is not a tragedy, it's
just a tough time. Other people seem to do it."

"Some of them don't make it," she said, looking
worried. The incident with Cal on Christmas Eve had
told her that no one was invulnerable, and no matter
how much they loved each other, living on opposite
coasts presented a real danger for them. For Meredith,
it had been a warning, but she had no intention of
saying that to him. She didn't want to hurt him.

"What does that mean?" Steve asked, looking confused.

"It means that some people's marriages fall apart,
living like this. It puts a hell of a lot of pressure on both
of us. Things haven't exactly been easy lately."

"I know that. But we can do it. It's worth it. I don't
want you giving up a job you love, or an opportunity
like the one Cal gave you. You love working with him,
it's the most exciting job you've ever had, and you're
making a goddamn fortune."

"It's not worth losing you for," she said clearly.
"Nothing is worth that to me, Steve. No job on the
planet would be worth that, and no amount of
money."

"I know that," he said, pulling her into his arms,
and kissing her. "I'll be out there in a couple of
months, and we'll look back on all this and laugh. We

can do it, Merrie. I promise.'' She felt as though she were being pulled away from him sometimes, by a force that was bigger than they were, as though the fates were conspiring against them. But she didn't want to say that to him. ''Let's just try and spend the weekends together more often.'' From that standpoint, the past few months had been a disaster for them. She seemed to get tied up in Palo Alto every weekend, and he was always on duty at the hospital, and between colds and meetings and blizzards and bad luck, they had hardly seen each other.

''I think that'll help,'' she said pensively, and he nodded.

''And I'll keep beating the bushes for work in San Francisco. I can't go anywhere right now anyway for the next two months, until Lucas recovers from his hip. So we know I'll be here for that long. And maybe by then a job will open up in the Bay Area.'' He sounded hopeful, more so than he had in a long time. Being with her had really boosted his spirits.

''Christ, I hope so,'' she said, and with that, they fell back into bed. They even managed to spend New Year's Eve together, without interference from the trauma unit, which was mostly thanks to Anna Gonzalez, who was covering for him. Steve said that she had absolutely forbidden anyone to call him. ''I owe her a giant thank you,'' Meredith said, as she packed her bags on New Year's Day, to go back to California. They were both sad she was going, but it had been a great week for them, and even Meredith felt more secure about the relationship than she had on Christmas morning. She felt as though they were safe again. And everything he had said made sense. A job would have to turn up for him sooner or later. And if not, he said he'd come out anyway, even if he had to be a paramedic, although she knew he didn't really mean that.

"I want you to meet Anna the next time you're here," Steve said over the dinner he cooked her before she left. "She's an amazing woman. She's from San Juan, and grew up dirt poor. She got a full scholarship to Yale, and then another one for med school. She was married to some rich kid at the law school, and I gather his family was none too pleased about it. They eventually forced him to ditch her, but not until after she had a baby. He left her high and dry during her residency with no money and a newborn baby. The kid is five now, and she's living in some miserable walk-up apartment on the West Side. She's an incredible physician. We were lucky to find her."

"What does she look like?" Meredith asked, and Steve laughed.

"You sound just like a woman," he teased her.

"I am a woman."

"So I noticed." They had just made love again an hour before. "One for the road," as he called it. "She's nice looking, not gorgeous. A little thin, a little nervous, a lot stressed out. She has a kid to support, and she seems to live hand to mouth, doing *locum tenens*. I'm trying to get them to hire her permanently. We could really use her in the unit. And when I leave, she could replace me. She'd love it."

"She sounds like a paragon of virtue." Something about the way he talked about her made Meredith uneasy. And somehow his vague physical description of her seemed just a bit too sketchy. "How old is she?"

"Thirty-three. She's no kid. And she's pretty bitter about her ex-husband." He sounded sympathetic.

"Doesn't he have to support the child?"

"He sends her two hundred bucks a month. Apparently, he won't even talk to her, won't see the child, and has since remarried some debutante, and just had twins."

"Nice guy," Meredith commented, and then realized that she was jealous, which was ridiculous. Steve wasn't the one who'd kissed Cal on Christmas Eve. She was still sorry that had happened, and feeling guilty about it, because she knew Steve would never have done that. He had always been faithful to her, and so had she. But she also knew it would never happen again. Cal knew how upset she had been, and she also knew she wouldn't let it happen.

Steve took Meredith to the airport when she left, and they looked like newlyweds as they hugged and kissed and held each other. She had promised to come back in two weeks, no matter how busy they both were. She knew now, more than ever, that their visits were vital to them. She left him with a last kiss, boarded the plane, and thought about him all the way to California. But she felt a lot better than she had a week before, when she'd arrived the day after Christmas.

She got back to her apartment in Palo Alto just after midnight, and she fell asleep dreaming of Steve. And she was up bright and early the next morning. She was at her desk, looking busy and pleased when Cal got in, and he stood in her office doorway for a moment. He was searching her face for signs of awkwardness with him, but there were none. She looked up and smiled at him. And he could see that things were different than they had been ever so briefly. She looked happier than she had in weeks, and he was pleased for her.

"How was New York?" But he didn't need to ask. He could see it.

"Terrific. How was Mexico?" She sounded at ease with him, and he was relieved.

"Hot and sunny. Lots of tequila and margaritas."

"No *turista*?" She laughed at him and he grinned. He was so happy that she wasn't angry or ill at ease with him, after his stupidity in kissing her on Christmas Eve. He had learned an important lesson. And he'd been lucky. This time. She might have quit, or been furious with him, but she obviously wasn't.

"I think the booze kills all the bugs. It was fine."

"I'm glad. How are the children?"

"A little jangled. They always are after being with Charlotte. She always seems to unnerve them."

"They'll settle down now that they're home."

"How was Steve?" he asked cautiously as he walked into her office carrying the briefcase she had given him for Christmas. He loved it. And she was wearing the Bulgari watch he'd given her. She had left it in San Francisco rather than upset Steve with it, when she went to New York. But all was well in the world for both of them now, and business was booming.

"Steve was off all week for once." She looked pleased as she said it. "And he's being very reasonable about the job situation. He's stuck there for the next two months anyway. I'm just going to have to make more of an effort to go home on weekends. I'm going back again in two weeks." And her saying that reminded him of something.

"I've organized a retreat, for top management, in Hawaii in three weeks. I was going to tell you. I think they can use it." He gave her the dates and she jotted them down on her calendar.

"Sounds good to me," she smiled at him, and then reminded him they had a finance committee meeting in ten minutes.

"Slave driver. Where's my margarita? Where's the beach?" She laughed and wagged a finger at him in answer.

"Never mind that. The vacation's over. We have a lot of work to do, Mr. Dow."

"Yes, ma'am," he saluted, and disappeared to his office to collect his papers.

They worked together after the finance meeting all afternoon, and he could detect only the faintest change in her attitude toward him. She was a little more businesslike, a little more cautious with him, but by the end of the day, everything seemed back to normal. And when she left, she waved cheerily and said she'd see him in the morning. It was as though she had shut him out just a little bit, but he couldn't say that she was wrong to do so. He had thought about her a lot when he was in Mexico, and worried about how things would be when they met again. But worse than that, he had missed talking to her every day, and he was surprised himself to realize that morning how glad he was to see her.

He invited her to dinner with the kids that weekend, but she said she had too much work to do. She spent the day in the office on Saturday, and on Sunday she went to look at more houses in the city, and this time he didn't offer to go with her. And when his kids asked where she was, he told them she was busy. They complained about not seeing her, but he realized it was just as well that he and Meredith backed off from each other a bit. They had ventured into dangerous waters for a little while, and luckily swam clear of them. It was better this way, he knew. But every time he looked at his briefcase over the weekend, he was startled to realize he missed her. He felt oddly close to her, closer than he had been to anyone in years.

Chapter 12

Anna Gonzalez had come to the trauma unit to work with Steve, but within two days of her arrival, Steve had realized that she was extremely independent. She knew what she had to do, and she had her own ideas. She took direction well from him, but she also had her own opinions. And by the time he came back from his week off with Meredith over the holidays, Anna had gained the respect of everyone she worked with. What's more, they liked her.

She filled him in on everything she'd done the morning he returned, and she had kept careful notes for him, and when he read them, he was astonished.

"You did all this?" he asked, with a look of wonder. She had had department meetings, reorganized a few things for the sake of efficiency. She had changed some schedules, and still managed to do surgery, and treat a staggering number of patients. "Don't you ever go home to your kid?" he teased.

"Not often," she said somewhat sternly. In spite of

the vague description he'd given Meredith, she was a pretty woman and looked younger than her age, but somehow when he was with her, he didn't notice. She didn't smile a lot, and she was intense about her work. There was something about her that said she was all business. But she was incredibly gentle and warm with their patients. She was clearly a woman of many facets.

She had started work before his holiday, but it was only as January droned on that he began to feel he knew her. She was tireless, and willing to work endless hours. She never seemed anxious to go home, although he knew she was devoted to her child, from things she said, and when he asked her why she was willing to work such long hours, and for so many days, she faced him squarely.

"Two reasons. I like what I do, and I need the money."

"What do you do with your daughter when you're here?" There was something about her that intrigued him. There was something hard about her, or protected perhaps, she had a tough outer shell, and yet at the same time she was very gentle in many ways.

"I leave her at my neighbor's. They have five kids, and she's happy with them."

"And what about you? Don't you need to go home once in a while? We all need to get out of here so we stay sane," he said with a tired smile. He had been on duty himself at that point for four days.

"You don't seem to go home much either," she answered. She had thick dark hair, and soft brown eyes that looked like chocolate.

"My wife lives in California," he said by way of explanation.

"Are you divorced?" He shook his head. "Separated?" She was curious about him too. There were a lot of rumors about him. People said that he was a good guy, and he had an odd relationship with his wife, and she wasn't sure what that meant. So she asked him. Anna Gonzalez was never afraid to ask questions, and something in her eyes said that she expected answers. And the best way Steve could have described her was that she was harder than Meredith outside, and softer inside. She had a blunt, gruff way in working with him sometimes, and then she would say something kind that genuinely touched him. More than anything, she seemed very guarded. She was a woman who'd been hurt, and she wasn't about to let it happen again. She was a fighter, and a survivor.

"My wife and I are bicoastal," he said, with a smile, and she laughed at his answer.

"Is that a sexual preference, doctor, or a diagnosis?"

"Both. It means I'm celibate ninety percent of the time, and I'm crazy about a woman who works in a city three thousand miles away from here, where I can't seem to find employment, but I'm looking. For a job. Not another woman."

"It sounds complicated," she commented, as they sat in his office, drinking coffee out of styrofoam cups. They had just finished a difficult abdominal surgery, and she had worked endlessly, and finally dislodged the bullet. Her nimble fingers, delicate techniques, and sheer stubbornness had saved the patient. Steve had been almost certain that he couldn't have done it himself.

"It is complicated," he admitted, referring to his living arrangement with his wife. "We've only been doing this for four months now. She took a job in California in October, and the job I had lined up fell through last month, and I'm stuck here anyway because of Lucas."

"That doesn't sound good." Her eyes bore into his, and were full of questions. She thought he was a good surgeon, and an interesting person, although perhaps marginally eccentric. Sometimes he liked voicing opinions that shocked the nurses.

"It's not good," he said. "She got a great job offer, and I encouraged her to take it. I got a job right away, for January, and then they flaked on me. Actually, it's the pits. But there's not much I can do about it for the moment. All I've been offered out there recently is a low man's slot in an ER that treats mostly hemorrhoids and sprained ankles, with the occasional case of hives, or asthma. Their log nearly put me to sleep."

"You're spoiled here," she said matter-of-factly. She was wearing the same scrubs he was, but even they couldn't conceal the fact that she had a great figure.

"Maybe. Maybe I don't need all these headaches anymore. Maybe I'm ready for something easy. It might be a relief."

"I doubt it. It sounds like you're trying to talk yourself into it. How can you go from this to something that won't challenge you?" She was practical about it. Anna Gonzalez was a no-nonsense kind of person. She'd had to be.

"Easy maybe. I don't want to lose my marriage."

"If it's yours, you won't. If it isn't, nothing you can do will save it."

"Do you charge extra for that kind of advice, doctor?" he teased, and she smiled.

"No, I give it for free, because I don't take that kind of advice myself."

"I hear you're divorced," he said simply and she nodded.

"Very."

"What does that mean?"

"It means we hate each other, and I hope I never see the sonofabitch again. He walked out on me when I was eight months pregnant, because his parents gave him a trust fund to do it."

"Oh that," Steve tried to make light of what she'd said, but the look in her eyes said that she was deeply wounded.

"He's never seen his daughter."

"From the sound of it, that could be lucky for her. No one needs a father like that, Anna," he said gently.

"No. But everyone needs a father. He's always going to be a mystery to her, a fantasy, some kind of lost hero, because she doesn't know him."

"Maybe she will someday. Maybe she'll find him."

"Maybe. I don't think he'd see her. He was embarrassed because of me." She still looked angry about it. He had given her a raw deal and she had never forgiven him for it.

"Then why did he marry you?"

"I was pregnant. He was noble. Then he was chicken."

"Ah, the human race, and its charming foibles."

"I guess." It was easy to talk about real life in the middle of the night when you were suspended between two worlds, saving lives and helping people. The world outside, the world beyond their walls, seemed at times like it was on another planet. And all they had was this, and each other. It formed strange bonds between people. Like being on a boat in the middle of the ocean. But Steve was sad for her, she sounded hurt, and angry, and bitter, and disappointed. The only time her eyes lit up and she looked young again was when she talked about her daughter. Steve knew from Anna that her name was Felicia.

They were called away to another emergency then, and two days later after some time off, they were back together, working. It was the weekend. And at midnight, they were both starving and ordered pizza. She seemed happier than the last time they'd talked, he made her laugh with some bad jokes, and old stories about assorted weirdos they'd had in the trauma unit over the years.

"Do you have a boyfriend?" he asked, as they wrestled with the mozzarella on the pizza, and she laughed at the question.

"Are you kidding? When? Does anyone who works here have a boyfriend? How do they manage that?"

"Some of the guys do," Steve said casually, and she smiled in response. "None of the women."

"What about you? Do you see other women?"

"Of course not." He looked shocked. "I told you, I'm married."

"Yeah, to a woman in another galaxy, far, far from here. I just wondered." But she had heard that he was faithful, and liked him for it. She was pleased with his answer. More than a lover, she needed a friend.

"When does she come here?"

"Not often enough. She's coming this weekend."

"That's nice. Do you have kids, Steve?"

"I'm not that lucky."

"Why?" She had seen him with children in the trauma unit, and it was obvious that he liked them.

"She's always been too busy. I guess we both have. I can't really blame her. She thinks she doesn't want them."

"If that's what she thinks, and that's what she says," Anna said matter-of-factly, "then she doesn't. Believe her. Guys always think they can talk women into it, but they can't. And if they do, it's a huge mistake."

"Is that what happened to you?" He sounded puzzled, and he didn't agree with what she said. He still thought he could talk Meredith into having a baby, she was just nervous about it. Anna didn't know her. But he had always thought Meredith would be a great mother, if she gave herself the chance.

"Nope," Anna answered him honestly. She was always honest with him. It was her style, and she liked him. "I got knocked up. Plain and simple. We'd been dating for about two months, and zap, bingo. He was panicked. And I wasn't too happy either."

"Why didn't you have an abortion? It would have been simpler."

"Lots. I'm Catholic. I didn't want to. I couldn't afford it. I always thought I could, if I had to. But I couldn't. My father went nuts. My mother cried. My sisters felt sorry for me. My brothers wanted to kill him. It wasn't my favorite time in my life. I was going to go back to Puerto Rico after my residency, you know, to help my own people, take care of the poor. I thought about specializing in tropical diseases for a while, but it's better for me here, working in the ER. Anyway, it's too complicated to go back to Puerto Rico now. It's easier for me here. Easier for them too. They don't have to apologize for me, or lie about Felicia. My father tells people I'm a widow." It was amazing sometimes the things families did to each other, but nothing surprised Steve anymore. He had heard too many stories. And hers didn't surprise him either. He just felt sorry for her. She was on her own, in tough circumstances, and somehow she managed. It was such a far cry from Meredith with her big job, and huge salary, the stock portfolio she had put together for them, and their comfortable apartment. It made him feel more than a little guilty as he listened. His life was so much easier than Anna's. It made him want to help her in some way, but there wasn't much he could do for her, except get her a real job in the trauma unit one day, instead of just a *locum tenens.* "What about you?" she asked him then. "Do you ever think of doing anything else? Private practice? Or maybe working in a clinic in a Third World country?"

"Only in my worst nightmares," he smiled at her and she laughed. "This is bad enough. I don't need snakes and parasites to make it any worse for me. Is that what you want to do when you grow up, Anna?"

"Yeah. One day. Maybe when Felicia's older. I can't do that with her now. That was my specialty as a resident, infectious diseases. But after Felicia was born, I switched to ER work and stayed in New York. It's safer."

"That's a depressing statement. If you don't get shot here, you never will. It's safer on the subway after dark than it is here, all those nuts who shoot each other eventually wind up here and could come after you."

"But at least Felicia has a normal life. I can't give her that working in the Third World."

It was a point, but Steve knew that life was also not easy for them here.

They worked together day after day, and Steve grew fonder and fonder of her. The brittle outer shell was only skin deep, and inside there was an extraordinary, sensitive woman. And the packaging wasn't bad either. He saw her leave in jeans and a T-shirt one night, and a ski jacket, with her hair down, and she was stunning. He couldn't even begin to imagine how great she would look in real clothes, with makeup. But she never wore either, she didn't have them, and didn't want them. She was a totally natural woman, with an incredible body, a fine mind, and a kind heart.

By mid-January they were fast friends, and he had come to rely on her. She was a person you could count on, and he did, often. She was hard on him at times, when she thought he was wrong about something, and she wasn't afraid to argue with him. But what surprised him most was that he liked that about her. She had her own opinions, and she voiced them with ease. Once in a while, she even shouted at him in Spanish, which amused him.

Once she called him "*hijo de putana,*" and he thanked her and said no one had ever said anything as beautiful to him, which incensed her.

"I called you the son of a whore, for chrissake."

"Shit, Anna, I thought you were telling me you loved me." It made her laugh, and the argument was over. Besides, as he reminded her frequently, he outranked her.

"That doesn't mean you can push me around," she pointed out to him and he was philosophical about it.

"That's right, unfortunately. But I can have a hell of a lot of fun trying," he said with a grin.

"You're hopeless." She loved to fume at him just to let off steam, but it was also obvious how much she liked and respected him.

She was happy for him when his wife came to town. But it was a difficult weekend for Meredith and Steve. They were trying desperately to make their lives mesh with the little time they had with each other, and it seemed to be getting more challenging from week to week. Steve was in surgery all night before Meredith arrived, and when he met her he was irritable from lack of sleep. She had gone out of her way to make the weekend nice for him. She'd brought the sourdough bread he loved, fresh crab, and two bottles of an excellent California wine. But he was too tired to eat or drink, and after they argued over petty irritations over lunch, he wound up sleeping all afternoon. Meredith hung around the house waiting for him to get up, but it was nine o'clock that night when he finally did.

They chatted for a couple of hours, and things were better than they had been earlier in the day, but there was no denying that the atmosphere between them was different than it had once been. They felt like strangers with each other now at times, and they were increasingly aware that they lived in separate worlds. It was no longer as easy falling into step with each other, and they seemed constantly out of sync.

By the time Meredith flew back to California on Sunday night, they were both depressed, and the treats

she'd brought him from San Francisco were still untouched in the fridge. And an hour after Meredith left,
Anna called and invited Steve to dinner at her place.
On an impulse, he brought the bread and wine and
fresh crab with him.

Her apartment was a tiny hole in the wall, with
barely enough heat, a cracked window the landlord
had refused to repair, and an army of cockroaches
scurrying everywhere, just above 102nd Street, but it
was the best she could do for herself and her daughter.
It shocked him to realize that this was how she lived.
Particularly knowing that the father of her child had a
trust fund.

"It's no big deal," she said to him, but it was, and
they both knew it. But something about her dignity and
pride and stubbornness touched him deeply. And the
little girl was adorable and was a blond version of her
mother. She looked just like her and when she didn't
like something her mother said, she stamped her foot
and told Anna she was naughty.

"She's got your personality. You're going to have
your hands full in a few years."

"I know," Anna smiled proudly. "Her father was a
real wuss, but cute though," she said and Steve laughed
at the description. But something about him must have
appealed to Anna, his looks or his brains, or his distin-
guished origins. Knowing Anna, it was unlikely that it
was his money. She didn't seem to care about that
much. Steve would have liked to invite them to his
place for dinner, but he was embarrassed by the extrav-
agance of his apartment. It was easier for him to come
here. Anna was embarrassed by the crab and the wine

he'd brought, but enjoyed them anyway, and they talked late that night about the stresses of living three thousand miles from his wife. Anna was sympathetic, and sorry for him. And when he went home that night, Steve realized he'd had a lot to drink, but in spite of that, they had both behaved. He and Anna were just good friends.

He missed Meredith when he went to bed, and wanted to call and tell her he was sorry the weekend hadn't been better than it was, but he realized, as he glanced at his watch, that she was still on the plane. He thought about leaving a message on her machine, but he was tired and a little drunk, and went to sleep instead.

He saw Anna and Felicia again for dinner later that week, after they had worked together all day. He took them to a deli near her place for sandwiches and ice cream. Felicia had a great time with both of them, and afterward he walked them home and read the newspaper while Anna put Felicia to bed. It was easy and relaxing just being with them.

"You're a good guy, you know," she said, when she walked back into the living room and sat on her broken couch next to him. "Your wife is a fool to leave you on the loose here." They were both tired, but comfortable in the tiny living room. It had been a nice evening after a long, hard day.

"She doesn't have any choice for the moment," he said honestly, "as long as I can't find a job in California. We have no choice, Anna," he said, looking glum, thinking about it again.

"There's got to be something for you out there, Steve," she said sympathetically, as he tried not to stare at the way she looked in a T-shirt and leggings. It was beside the point. The friendship they shared was important to both of them.

"That's what I keep telling myself, too, that there's got to be a job in San Francisco for me, but so far nothing." He had called all the hospitals in San Francisco to tell them he was available. "I'm almost getting used to it." But his words didn't convince either of them and it didn't help that the next week Meredith was off to Hawaii for her retreat, so it would be another two weeks before he could see her again.

"Doesn't that bother you?" Anna asked thoughtfully about Hawaii. "Do you worry about her getting involved with the guy she works for?" She asked him questions sometimes that probed too deep and made him uncomfortable, but forced him to think. And he always answered her honestly, no matter how much it hurt.

"I worry about it sometimes. He's a good-looking guy, and I like him actually. But I trust her. Merrie wouldn't do that."

Anna was polite enough not to tell him that she wasn't so sure. People were people, and if they got lonely enough, they did foolish things. "We've never cheated on each other."

"I admire that about you," she said honestly. She knew how lonely he was, and how unhappy, but he had never made a pass at her, or implied anything, or even given her the impression that he would have. Meredith was a lucky woman. Maybe they both were. She hoped so, for his sake.

"I just don't believe in fooling around. Besides, Meredith would know. I think being straight about it is the only way we can do this." It had been almost four months since she'd left New York, and living bicoastally was the greatest challenge they'd ever faced. It meant he never had anyone to do things with on weekends, when she was in California, or talk to at night when he got home, or complain to when things were difficult at work, or laugh with, or make love to in the morning. It was hard as hell, but it was only temporary, and they knew that. He didn't want to do anything stupid that would permanently screw up their marriage. And he had said as much to Anna.

"Well, you'd better get your ass out there one of these days, Steve, before one of you gets too lonely, or has too many drinks at a party one night, and blows it."

"I know," he nodded. He had actually been thinking about the ER job at San Francisco General ever since Meredith left the previous weekend. It was just getting too difficult to be apart. "She offered to give up her job a few weeks ago, and come back, but I don't want her to do that. It's a great job, and it wouldn't be fair to her," he said with a sigh.

"You're a nice guy, Steve Whitman. I just hope she deserves you."

"She does," he assured her. But when he went home that night, he found himself thinking of Anna and the hard life she led, in the cockroach-infested apartment she shared with her daughter. She deserved so much better. It was hard to accept how unfair life was at times. He and Meredith had so much, and people like Callan Dow and Anna's ex-husband had more, and she had so little, almost nothing. And yet she didn't seem to mind it. She believed in the integrity of what she was doing.

And as he went to bed alone that night, as usual now, he found himself thinking of what she had said, about Meredith going to Hawaii on her retreat, and whether or not he minded. And the fact that one of these days one of them would get too lonely, or have too many drinks, or maybe worse yet meet someone they cared about. The prospect of it was terrifying, if he really thought about it. But he also knew that for him or Meredith at least, that could never happen. But he lay awake for a long time that night, thinking about Meredith at first, and then about Anna and Felicia. And he was glad that they were friends. In a short time, they had come to mean a lot to him.

Chapter 13

THE RETREAT THAT Callan had planned for Dow Tech's senior management was scheduled to last four days, and was booked into the Mauna Lani, on the island of Hawaii. More than thirty of his staff had been invited to attend, and eighteen of them were bringing spouses. It was a large group, and managing the arrangements was like organizing the transport of an invading army. Meals had to be planned, activities for every night, luaus, dinner parties, hula displays, and of course meetings.

By the day before they left, Meredith was ready to throw them all out the window. And when she complained to Cal about it, he thought it was funny.

"People turn into children when they go somewhere," she moaned, as they went over the last details for the meetings. They had to be planned in the morning, so people could play tennis or golf, go to the beach, take island tours, or go shopping. The meetings weren't supposed to be too long, too demanding, or too boring. In truth, it was more of an excuse to get everyone acquainted, but suddenly there were requests for special rooms, special meals, and in two cases, massages.

"Just do the best you can," he told Meredith and the two women who were in charge of arrangements. Meredith was involved, because she had to keep track of expenses, and he trusted her judgment.

"Why don't we just send everyone a check, and tell them to go to Las Vegas for the weekend?" Meredith grumbled.

"We'll try that next year," Cal agreed, remaining good humored. He was looking forward to it, and only sorry he couldn't take his children. He knew the hotel well, had been there before with them, and knew they would have loved it. But this trip was strictly for adults, although they were behaving like high school kids going on tour with the school band. Before they even left, there were squabbles about room assignments. Several people were familiar with the hotel, and had preferences about floors, corners, heights, views, and air conditioning.

Meredith had told Steve about it, and asked if he wanted to come. But he was on call, and he knew she'd be busy. And with his schedule, he really couldn't get away.

"I'm going to miss you," she said to him on the phone the night before they left.

"You won't even know I'm not there. It sounds like you'll have your hands full keeping everyone happy." He was pleased for her. It sounded like a nice change, and in spite of the headaches, he was sure she'd enjoy it. Meredith was far less certain. Everyone had been real pains in the neck so far.

But on the day they left, as they congregated in the airport wearing everything from Hawaiian shirts to white linen suits, they were all in good spirits. It looked like a traveling cocktail party, and when she finally settled into her seat on the plane next to Cal, in first class, she was exhausted. Only a handful of them were traveling first class, the chief officers of the company. The others were in coach, in a large block of seats she had gotten for them at a healthy discount.

"Do I want to know what this is costing us?" Cal asked her with a look of amusement, as a flight attendant served them champagne, and Meredith declined it. At nine in the morning, it was just too early, and she asked for coffee instead.

"You only want to know, if they let me give you oxygen on takeoff," she said, sipping her coffee.

"That's what I thought. Don't tell me. It's good for morale. Or it's supposed to be anyway." And once they took off, she relaxed, and settled into her seat with a stack of reading. He scolded her for bringing her briefcase with her.

"I can't go anywhere without it, Cal," she smiled sheepishly. "It makes me feel too guilty."

"We'll have to sign you up for hula lessons to distract you. I don't want you working too hard on this trip, Meredith. You have to get a little fun out of it. Everyone else will."

"Not if they don't get their special diets, or their rooms are on the wrong floors, or they can't get into the luau."

"They'll survive it." They went over the schedule for
the meetings, and the groups, and the outlines he had
drawn up for discussions, and eventually, Meredith put
her papers away, and let Cal talk her into watching the
movie. They were on a direct flight to Kona, and the
flight was just long enough to allow for one meal, a
snack, the movie, and a short nap between takeoff and
landing. And halfway through the flight, she saw Cal
looking pensively out the window, and couldn't help
wondering what he was thinking.

"Are you okay?" she asked him gently.

"I'm fine." He looked at her. "I was just thinking.
We've brought this company so far in a short time. I
feel very lucky."

"It's not luck, Cal. You've worked hard for all of
this."

"So have you in the past four months." No one had
ever worked harder. He was grateful, every time he
thought about it, that Charlie had left, and Meredith
had joined them. She was one of his greatest assets. "I
hope you're as happy with us, as we are with you," he
said gratefully.

"I am. If we ever get Steve a job out here, my life will
be perfect." She looked sad as she said it. It was so hard
never having him part of her daily life anymore. He
seemed so far away now. And he was. He was someone
she visited once or twice a month, like an old friend, or
an old boyfriend. There were times when he no longer
seemed like her husband. He was no longer part of her
daily activities, never there to laugh with or talk to, or
share her problems with, except when she could reach
him on his pager. He seemed to be home less and less

often these days. Like her, he was always working. He had nothing else to do without her.

"I know it's hard on you, Merrie," Cal said quietly. "I wish there was something I could do about it."

"Maybe one day there will be. In the meantime, we just have to get through it." But it wasn't easy. He was one of the only spouses who hadn't come on the trip. And she hated the fact that he wouldn't be there.

"It's a damn shame his job fell through in the East Bay. That was rotten luck."

"Maybe it was fate," she said philosophically. "Maybe something better will turn up soon." She was still hopeful.

"I hope so." Cal sounded sincere as he said it. More than anything, he wanted her to be happy. Because if she wasn't happy, there was always the chance that she would leave the company, and the thought of that terrified him. Dow Tech needed her now, and so did he, to run the financial end of his business. More than that, he needed her personally. He told her everything, and shared all his fears and joys and confidences with her. They were almost like partners in the business. And there was more than that to it now too. He even confided in her about his children. They were confidants and coconspirators, and best friends.

"It's too bad he couldn't come on this trip. It would have done you both good," Cal said. He genuinely regretted it for her, and he knew she'd been disappointed when Steve said he couldn't come.

"It's probably just as well. I'll be too busy working." She was making three presentations with Cal, and another on her own in a separate meeting.

"You'd better make time for some fun too. I don't want you running yourself ragged to keep everyone else happy. Let them fend for themselves a little bit. You're not their tour guide."

"Tell them that," she laughed. "You'd never have known it, from the lists of requests I've been getting."

"Tear them up. And that's an order."

"Yes, sir," she said, and saluted smartly while he chuckled.

They talked about other things then, and he told her some funny stories about past retreats, and the crazy things people did when they were in an environment as totally different as this. Charlie McIntosh had gotten drunk and actually slept with one of the hula girls years before, and never lived it down. The story had circulated for years, and he always denied it, but everyone knew it was true, except his wife.

"I'll try to behave," she said, laughing over it with Cal, and then he looked at her pensively for a long moment, and she was suddenly reminded of Christmas.

"I hope not," he said softly. She didn't answer him, but they were so close sometimes that it frightened her. In some ways, Cal filled the role that Steve had, when they were living in the same city. There was nothing she didn't tell Cal. And whatever lack of ease had developed between them over the foolishness on Christmas Eve, had been dispelled when she came back after New Year. They were back to their comfortable friendship. But there were moments when the strength of his personality was like a magnet that drew her to him, not necessarily romantically, but she had a sense more often than not, that they were soul mates. It was as though they had been destined to meet and work together, and build an empire. They were like two halves of one entity that fit perfectly, and at times, she didn't understand it. It was hard to believe they hadn't known each other all their lives. It felt that way sometimes, even more so than with Steve. In some ways, she and Cal had more in common, they shared the same goals, the same needs, the same drive, the same passion for business. Steve lived in a different world, his motives seemed purer to her, he was a different kind of human being. And he cared absolutely not at all about money. He didn't understand the work she did, and he really didn't want to know about it. He just wanted to know that she was enjoying what she did. How she did it, and why, was of no importance to him. But Cal understood everything about it. In some ways, that was easier for her.

The plane landed shortly after noon, local time, and she and Cal herded their charges off the plane, and managed to get everyone on the bus to the hotel. The luggage would come later, and whatever was lost would eventually be found. They were all free that afternoon, and they didn't have to meet up until dinner. A luau had been arranged for them, and afterward there was to be dancing. The meetings weren't scheduled to start until the next morning. She and Cal were going to kick them off with a short speech, and after that, there was going to be a slide show. She had it all organized, and they had talked about it on the plane. There was nothing left to do except relax, go to the beach or the pool that afternoon, and then meet the others for dinner.

"Do you want to have lunch in my room?" Cal asked

as they checked into the hotel. His room was next to hers, and as it turned out, they shared a terrace.

"Sure," she said easily. "I want to go swimming afterward. Maybe we can escape the others until dinner."

"Sounds good to me," he said, and then carried her briefcase to her room for her. She was surprised to see she had a suite, and so did he, and then she realized he had personally reserved hers for her. It had a large, handsome living room, all done in sandy tones, and a beautifully done white bedroom. It looked like a spread in a magazine, and there were huge silver-dipped conch shells on the coffee table. She had a small kitchenette, a bar, and there was music playing when she walked into the room, with Cal just behind her. "This is spectacular," she said to him, as she looked out at the palm trees that framed the view of the ocean.

"I thought it would be pretty at sunset. And I wanted you next to me, so the others didn't bother you." They were all on other floors, which had been clever of him. It didn't even occur to her that they might think it was odd that their rooms were side by side. There had never been any gossip about them, and everyone knew she was married. She talked about Steve often.

Cal went to his own room then, and settled in, and their luggage arrived a few minutes later. Nothing had gotten lost apparently, which was nothing short of a miracle, with a group that size. Cal had ordered club sandwiches for them, and everything was set up on his terrace, when she joined him. He had even ordered her a mai-tai.

"I'm going to be following in Charlie's footsteps if I

don't watch out," she laughed, "and getting drunk at lunchtime."

"If you start chasing hula girls, Meredith, I'm going to send you home."

"I'll try not to," she said demurely.

The sandwiches were delicious, and the mai-tai was too strong, but she sipped a little of it, and they sat on his terrace for a long time, admiring the view, and relaxing. And then finally, she got up and told him she was going swimming.

"I'll keep you company," he offered, and they both went to change, and she came back a few minutes later in a bikini with a long shirt over it, and sandals, and she looked as impeccable as ever. So did he in a bathing suit with a matching shirt and a pair of driving shoes. They made a very handsome couple, and no one would ever have suspected they weren't married. They seemed so intimate and so comfortable with each other, it would have been hard to believe that they had never slept with each other. Cal commented on it as they went downstairs, and she looked surprised.

"Do you really think people would think we're married?" It seemed to amuse her. It seemed an odd assumption to make, to her at least.

"Yes, I do. We even look alike. We're both blond, and our eyes are almost the same color. We like the same things, we even dress alike sometimes." He had noticed it more than once, but she shook her head and laughed at what he was saying.

"That proves you're wrong. People never come in matched sets like us. They look like me and Steve, one dark, one fair, and he always looks like he dressed in the dark at Goodwill. I love him, but he looks a mess. I could have killed him when he came out the first time, to meet you, in his thousand-year-old jacket. I keep trying to throw it away, but he loves it. I've finally given up and accepted the fact that he'll keep it forever. And wear it.''

"He looked fine to me." Cal said charitably. But she was right, Steve looked odd with her. She was always beautifully dressed, and everything about her was neat and in order and perfect. Cal guessed correctly that Steve was more at ease in his hospital garb than in real clothes, or a proper suit. He wondered if he even owned one. He did, in fact he owned several, thanks to Meredith, who bought them for him, but he never wore them.

They went down to the beach, and one of the beach boys set them up on deck chairs with towels, and Meredith took off her shirt, and lay down in her bikini. And although he was tempted to, Cal made no comment. She looked incredible in her bathing suit. More so than he had ever dreamed. He picked up his book, but with Meredith in such close proximity, with her smooth flesh and gentle curves, he found it impossible to concentrate on his reading.

"Don't you like your book?" She had noticed him staring into space, and smiled at him. He had an odd expression as he looked out at the horizon. As though he had suddenly seen someone or something he hadn't expected to find there.

"No . . . no . . . I mean, yes . . . it's fine. . . . I was just thinking about something else."

"Is something wrong?" She wondered suddenly if she had done something to offend him, but he only shook his head, got up, and walked down the beach by himself. She was worried about him, and followed him slowly a few minutes later. She didn't want to intrude on him, but she had an odd sense that he was troubled. "Are you okay?" she asked as she caught up with him. She was reluctant to bother him, but he had looked so upset for a moment that it concerned her. And this time he hesitated before he answered. His head had been down as he walked down the sandy beach, with his feet in the water. He looked up at her then, and nodded.

"I'm okay, Merrie." But he wasn't convincing.

"What's up?"

"Oh, I don't know . . . life, I guess. Do you ever just stop and question yourself, and wonder if you've had your head up your ass for the past ten years, and didn't know where you were going?" She was surprised that he looked so unhappy. It was like a dark cloud that had suddenly passed in front of the bright sun, and everything was instantly in shadow, which seemed unlike him.

"What brought that on you? You seemed fine a minute ago."

"I was. I am. I just wonder about my life sometimes. I get so focused on some things, I forget others."

"We all do that," she said gently, as they neared the end of the beach, and sat down on the sand together, with the surf lapping near their feet, the ocean ahead, and the hotel behind them. There was no one around them. "You haven't lost track of the important things, Cal. You have great kids, a good life, an important business. You haven't been wasting your time."

"What makes you so sure of that? And how do any of us know what's really important? How do I know my kids won't hate me ten years from now for something I did, or didn't do, or failed to see or understand? I think I'm right so much of the time, and once in a while, I wonder if I'm headed in the right direction. Sometimes I think I've got it all ass backwards. In fifty years who is really going to give a damn about Dow Tech, and everything I think is so goddamn important? Maybe all that really matters are the people you care about," he hesitated and then finished his thought, which was what had upset him in the first place. "Or the lack of them. I've been so busy being pissed off at Charlotte for the last eight years, that there's never been room enough in my life for anyone else. All I had room for was my anger. All I cared about was how much she'd hurt me." It was the first time he had ever said that to her, or anyone, in just that way. "You know, for a long time I thought I hated her. Now I feel like I wasted all that time on feelings that got me nowhere. And now what?"

"What do you mean, 'now what'?" She was startled by what he was saying to her. They were serious thoughts to have while lying on a beach in Kona, getting a tan.

"Now what? I'm fifty-one years old. I've been pissed off at someone who's been gone for the last eight years. I've got three great kids who'll be grown up any minute. And my whole life is my business."

"It sounds like you're eating nails to me, Callan Dow." She was always honest and outspoken with him. "You're feeling sorry for yourself. You're fifty-one, not ninety. You've got a lot of time to do things differently, if you want to. No one says you have to stay alone for the rest of your life, if that's what's bothering you, and you don't have to stay pissed at Charlotte.''

"I don't think I am anymore actually. Maybe that's the problem. Other than what I feel for my kids, hating her has been the main emotion in my life for nearly ten years. Without that, what have I got? Maybe not enough, Merrie.''

"Maybe it's time to look in a new direction,'' she said simply. She had a way of cutting through complicated emotions and situations and getting right to the core of the issue. It was one of the things he liked about her in business. But there were a lot of things he liked about her. Too many. In some ways.

"What are you suggesting? Where am I supposed to look? To my kids to be my whole life until they leave and get their own lives? To some unimportant woman I don't care about who I can take to dinner half a dozen times before I figure out that she bores me, or someone else who is excited about what I have instead of who I am? Merrie, there's not much out there.''

"That's bullshit,'' she said, stretching her long legs across the sand toward the water, and letting her toes play in the wet sand as he watched her. "Not everyone is boring, and not everyone is after your money.''

"Don't bet on it. What about you?'' he asked, looking unhappy. "What are you going to do if it falls apart with Steve? Have you ever thought about that?''

"I try not to.'' But the truth was, she had lately. Living on separate coasts had put a tremendous strain on them, and at times now, she was frightened. She felt as though they were being pulled apart by fate, destiny, and a force greater than they were. She had never felt that before, and it was a terrifying feeling. "I don't know what I'd do," she said honestly. "Steve has been my life for so long, I'd be lost without him. He's good for me, and I love him. My life would be a huge dark hole without him." And she felt that way now, as though she would fall into an abyss of misery and terror if she lost him. She hated to even think about it. But she knew that if things didn't get better, and one of them didn't make a move soon, it could happen. She was just beginning to face that. After nearly four months of living apart, they seemed to be heading in different directions, and they had to do something about it soon.

"What would you do if you two got divorced?" She hated even hearing the question, much less thinking about it.

"Kill myself," she said too quickly to mean it, and then pondered the question. "I don't know. Pick up the pieces and start over, I guess. But it would take me a long time to do it. Just as it's taken you a long time, Cal. That's not surprising. You had a lot invested in that marriage, three kids, seven years, you obviously believed in her and trusted her, and she betrayed you. I think it must take a long time to recover from something like that, if you ever do completely."

"It has taken me a long time," he admitted quietly, lying on the warm sand next to her, and admiring the way she looked as she lay there. She was completely unaware of her effect on him, for which he was grateful. It was simpler that way. He wasn't about to make the same mistake he had at Christmas. "Maybe too long," he said. "I'm beginning to feel like I've wasted the last eight years. I just wanted to show everyone how hard and cynical I was, so they wouldn't know I was hurting. But I was. Too much, for too long," but he looked better as he said it.

"And now?" she pressed him. But he didn't mind. He was always open with her.

"I just want to move on and have a life again. Suddenly I miss everything I haven't had for all these years, and I'm sitting here wondering where the hell I've been and what I've been thinking."

"And you want it *now*," she laughed at him. As he was about everything, he was impatient and wanted instant results and immediate solutions.

"Of course," he beamed at her, feeling better than he had in years. He loved talking to her. Not only was she a brilliant addition to his business, but she was the best friend he'd ever had. He had been standing under a lucky star the day he found her. "Okay, so find me the perfect woman." He treated her like the friend she was, since he had no other options with her. For all their theoretical talk about what would happen if things didn't work out with Steve, he knew she was still very much in love with him, and deeply devoted to their marriage. The only man she wanted was Steve, and Cal as her best friend.

"Was pimping for you part of my job description?" she asked, looking amused.

"Of course. It was in the fine print."

"Great. And where am I supposed to find her?"

"Damned if I know," he said with a boyish grin. "I sure haven't. I don't think there are too many perfect ones out there. Lots of damaged goods, and boring stupid ones, as my kids say. The perfect ones seem to be hiding." He looked at her long and hard as they lay

there side by side. "Or they're married." She understood the compliment and was touched by it, but she
said nothing to him.

They lay there quietly for a while, and finally he got
up and pulled her to her feet, and they walked back
down the beach, hand in hand, like two kids. He felt
better after talking to her, and after they found their
way back to their chairs, they discovered that some of
the others had come down to the beach as well, and
were lying near them. But Cal looked like himself
again, and the cloud that seemed to have overshad-
owed him for a while had been dispelled. They ordered
drinks on the beach, and chatted with the others. And
after a couple of hours, Meredith and Cal went back
upstairs to change.

She took a shower and put on a white silk dress, and
some turquoise beads, her hair was clean and shining,
and she was wearing high-heeled white sandals when
he next saw her. She looked incredible, but he could
no longer forget how she had looked on the beach in
her bikini. Everything about her was unforgettable,
and when she smiled at him on the terrace they shared,
he could feel something go weak inside him. And she
knew him so well that he was worried that she'd see it.
But she gave no sign of it.

"Ready for the onslaught?" he asked her, handing
her a glass of white wine. They stood drinking together
for a moment, watching a glorious sunset. "It's beautiful here, isn't it?"

"Too much so." It made her sad seeing something
like that without Steve to share it with. There were so
many special moments they missed now. And she
hadn't been able to reach him since they got there.

The nurses had told her when she called that he'd been in surgery on and off since that morning. "I almost wish we didn't have to join the others, and we could just sit here on the terrace and have a quiet dinner tonight."

"No such luck, my dear," he laughed. They were going to be sharing dinner with fifty people, all of them hell bent on having a great time, and a noisy one, at the luau. But he shared Meredith's wish that they could have a peaceful evening.

As always, she was gracious with everyone, introduced people to others they hadn't met, kept an eye on what was happening, and seemed to dissipate problems before they occurred. Everyone was unaware of it except Cal, but he was well aware of everything that she did to ensure that the evening was a success for everyone who'd been there.

"You're amazing, you know, Merrie." He commented on it as they went back to their rooms at midnight. "You're like a magician passing through the crowd, you see everything and wave your magic wand and keep everyone happy. Even me." She knew he disliked Hawaiian food, he had confessed it to her once when they were planning the trip, and she had seen to it that they served him steak and french fries, and a salad. He had been startled when they set it down in front of him, and knew instantly how it had happened. "Is there anything you don't think of?"

"Hopefully, not much," she said, pleased that he noticed. It wasn't her job to take care of all the things she did, but she liked doing it, and it was obvious that no one else was going to.

"Thanks to you, it was a great evening. It couldn't

have been much fun for you though, you were always working."

"I actually enjoyed it too." The setting had been spectacular, and the atmosphere comfortable and festive.

"Do you want to sit on the terrace for a while?" he suggested, and she nodded. He had a bottle of champagne in his bar, and he poured a glass for each of them. She hadn't had anything to drink since the glass of wine they'd shared at the beginning of the evening. The others had all indulged themselves on scorpions and mai-tais, and she knew there'd be a few headaches in the morning. But she was clear and fresh and sober as she sat next to him in the warm, tropical night, and he was too. They just sat there quietly, at ease with each other. They didn't need to say anything, they were just enjoying a sense of harmony and fulfillment, and relaxing.

Meredith set down her glass after a while, and without saying anything, he reached out and took her hand, and they smiled at each other.

"Thank you for being such a good friend to me, Merrie."

"You've done an awful lot for me, Cal."

"This is just the beginning." They were going to take his company far, and he was even thinking of starting a new division with her. They had been talking about it for months, but he wasn't thinking of that now as he looked at her, and as he had six weeks before, he leaned over, unable to resist the pull he felt, and kissed her. He felt an electric current go through him as he did, and a sense of panic that he was doing the wrong thing, but he couldn't help himself, and neither could she. Her arms went around his neck, and she kissed him, and they sat that way for a long time, holding tightly to each other. He knew he should apologize to her again, but this time he couldn't bring himself to, because he knew the apology wouldn't have been honest. "I shouldn't say this to you," he whispered finally, "but I love you, Merrie." It was a cry from his heart, his soul. He had known it for a while. And she knew it too. She had known it without knowing, and she nodded. That was the force she had felt pulling her away from Steve. It was Callan.

"I love you too, Cal," she said softly. It wasn't just desire that raged between them. It was so much more. It was as though they were part of one body, one soul. And whatever happened next, she knew that for this one moment in time, she was his right now.

He took her in his arms again, and held her, and every inch of him hungered for her. He had longed for her for so long. She kissed him with a passion she had never felt before for anyone, not even her husband. Her hands slipped beneath his shirt, and felt his chest, and he gently slipped her white silk dress off her shoulders. And as she stood up, it fell to her feet, and she stood there in all her glory, in white satin bikini pants, and her high-heeled sandals. She took his breath away as she had on the beach, and a moment later, he picked her up and carried her into his bedroom. He laid her gently on the bed as she kicked off her shoes, and he took off his shirt and his trousers, and then he slipped off her underwear and admired her beauty.

"You're incredible," he whispered.

"I've never done this before," she said softly, sounding frightened.

"I know." She had told him long before that she'd been faithful to Steve. But this was different. This was a need so profound and so powerful that neither of them could resist it. "Don't be afraid, Merrie. . . ." His hands roamed all over her, and as their lips met, she moaned softly. "I love you so much. . . . I've never loved anyone like this before," he said, echoing everything she felt for him, and had known in some part of her since the beginning. She wanted to believe this was wrong, but in her heart of hearts she couldn't. And she knew in her very soul, that this was what, and who, she had been born for, and where she had to be.

Chapter 14

THE TIME CALLAN and Meredith spent in Hawaii was half fairy tale, half nightmare. Neither of them had been as happy in their lives, yet they both knew that the forbidden fruit they had tasted there would inexorably change their lives. Meredith had no idea how to resolve it. There was no question in her mind anymore, she was in love with Cal, and he with her, but the question was what, if anything, to do about it. They had no right to what they shared, yet neither of them could bear to think of ending it. The dream had just begun.

"What are we going to do about this?" she asked Cal, as they lay in bed late one night, having finally escaped the others. They were being completely circumspect in public and they were sure no one had guessed their secret. But all they wanted to do now was go back to their room and be alone, make love, and talk until all hours. They had talked one night until dawn, and then finally slept a few hours until their meeting.

They were working together as usual, but the new dimension they'd added to their relationship changed everything. And between the time difference, and his schedule, Meredith hadn't talked to Steve since she'd arrived in Hawaii.

"What do you want to do about this, Merrie?" Cal asked her seriously, as he lay on his side, looking at her, tracing a lazy finger down the gentle curves of her body. What they had shared so far were volcanoes of passion and islands of calm. But what waited for them beyond the shores where they stood was a storm of terrifying proportions and dangerously deep waters. It was no secret to either of them, and Cal looked happy and peaceful as he looked into her eyes. They knew they loved each other, but they knew nothing more than that yet. And he had no idea which way Meredith would choose to turn, toward the past or the future. Either was possible, and she herself was drifting slowly toward the unknown with no real sense of direction. She was like a ship that had gently slipped away from its mooring.

"I just don't know," Meredith said honestly, as she lay close to him, feeling his strength and his warmth enticingly near her. What she felt for him was so powerful it still took her breath away. "I can't do this to Steve, Cal. . . . I can't . . . I can't leave him." But she couldn't leave Cal either now, she knew that as well. She was trapped between two worlds, and she felt pulled in opposite directions.

"Let's not make any decisions right now," he said sensibly, trying to stay calm, and not frighten her. "We don't have to do anything now. Why don't we just enjoy this while we can?" She nodded silently in answer, he kissed her, and then slowly began to make love to her again.

They couldn't keep their hands off each other while they were in their rooms, but they were extremely circumspect when they were around other people from the firm, or in meetings. They gave the speeches they had prepared, led small groups, and joined the others for both lunch and dinner. Even the most observant of their colleagues would have been hard put to find anything out of the ordinary in their exchanges. But what Meredith felt when she was with him, more than anything, was a kind of unspoken intimacy and greater depth between them. It was intangible, but very real, and enhanced everything they had shared until that moment. And it was so obvious to her that it seemed incredible that no one else could see it.

"They must be blind," she said to Cal, as they sat wrapped in towels on their terrace before they went to dress for dinner. They had been swimming on the beach, and had just taken a long hot bath together, and had inevitably made love.

"People don't see what's right in front of them sometimes," he said comfortably, sipping a martini. He didn't drink during the day, but he enjoyed a cocktail before dinner, and occasionally Merrie joined him, but that evening she didn't. She wanted to be clearheaded for their gathering that night. What was happening to them seemed heady enough to her, and she didn't want to add to it. "Are you happy?" he asked, as she lay on a deck chair, watching the sunset with him.

"More so than I deserve." What they had discovered was very special to both of them, but she also knew that, for the moment at least, it was borrowed, if not stolen. And sooner or later they would have to pay their dues. But not yet. For the moment, it was still theirs for the taking, and neither of them could resist. The force that had pulled them toward each other was more powerful than they were.

"You deserve everything you want," Cal said lovingly, as he leaned down to kiss her.

"Sometimes that's not true," she said softly. "Things don't always work out the way you want them to. I wish we had met sooner."

"So do I," he said with a sigh, "but maybe neither of us would have been ready." But nor were they now. He may have been free, but she was married. "We do everything so well together, Meredith."

"Yeah, I know," she smiled, "like Fred Astaire and Ginger Rogers."

"No. Like Callan Dow and Meredith Whitman. We're special people, Merrie. We both are. We know what we want, and we're not afraid to work like dogs to make it happen. The same could be true for us now, if we want this. We could have a wonderful life together, if we decide to go for it. I don't want to push you into anything. The question is what do you want? And how badly do you want it? Getting from here to there might not be easy for you." It was something of an understatement, but it was the first time he had offered to share his life with her, although it was not yet clear on what basis. As mistress or wife or girlfriend? And she realized that maybe even he didn't know yet.

"I'm not willing to hurt Steve for us, Cal," she said quietly. "He doesn't deserve that." In spite of what she felt for Cal now, she couldn't imagine a life without her husband. He had been part of her life for too long now to give that up. He was part of her, body and soul. It was more complicated than Cal knew. She had never been unhappy with Steven. Circumstances had taken them from each other, not choice. The only choice she'd made was to move to California, and Steve had made it with her, but she still wasn't so certain that it was a good one.

They had dinner with the others that night, and stayed out later than usual with them, dancing beneath the stars, and then they went for a walk on the beach in the dark, just holding hands and talking softly. They never kissed when they were out of their room, for fear that someone would see them.

And finally, the next morning, Steve called her. Cal had just left her room, and she was startled when the phone rang and she heard him. And the moment she heard his voice, she felt incredibly guilty.

"How's it going, Merrie?" Steve asked cheerfully. "Having fun?"

"It's been great so far," she said, matching her tone to his, but she felt like a criminal when she did it. "We've been very busy."

"I'll bet you have. It must be like taking Boy Scouts to camp."

"More or less," she laughed, but it was a hollow sound, and she almost winced thinking of the pain she might cause him.

They talked for a short time, and she finally told him she had to go to a meeting. "I'll call you when I can," she promised, and he gave her dispensation, if not absolution.

"Don't worry about it, babe. I know you're busy. Just call when it's convenient." Everything he said made her feel worse by the minute, and when she saw Cal after their first meeting of the day, he sensed her tension.

"Is something wrong, Merrie?" he asked softly, as they walked to lunch with the others.

"I talked to Steve." She looked unhappy as she said it, and for an instant, he panicked. He was terrified of what she would say next. He didn't want their romance to end.

"Did you tell him about us?" He knew that it was an eventual possibility, but to him, it seemed early days to do that. They were still feeling their way along, trying to figure out where they were going. This was still very new to both of them, and he thought they needed some time to adjust, before she told her husband, although he hoped that she would eventually. The only thing he knew at the moment was that, if it was possible, he wanted a future with Merrie, one that did not include Steve.

"No, of course not," she answered. "But he was so nice on the phone, I felt terrible. Cal, he doesn't deserve this."

He nodded, not sure what to say to her, and then whispered, "No, but we do. Maybe we've earned it."

"Not at his expense," she countered. And there was no hiding from the fact that someone was going to get hurt. They had to. There couldn't be three winners in a situation like this. Someone was going to lose.

"What are you saying to me?" he said with a look of panic as they walked slowly behind the others. He wondered if she was already telling him that it was over, but she couldn't do that.

"I'm just saying that I feel badly for him. But at least he doesn't know anything about it."

"I understand," Cal said, relieved. And they walked into lunch side by side.

For the rest of the trip, they did what they had come to do, and the retreat went extremely well from everyone's point of view. And at night, they discovered new worlds in each other's arms, and cemented the bond that had been growing for months between them. By the time they left Hawaii, Meredith was so in love with him that in some ways, she wished the world could share their happiness with them. But there was no way for them to do that. More than ever, they had to be discreet.

Cal took her to her apartment when they got home, and spent hours there with her. And when the phone rang, she didn't answer it. She knew it would be Steve, and she just couldn't face it. This was rapidly becoming more than she could cope with.

Cal had to tear himself away when he left finally, and after he got home and saw his kids, he called her, and this time, hoping it would be him, she answered.

"I miss you," he said softly, and she laughed. They were like two high school kids, head over heels in love with each other.

"I miss you too. Do you want to come back later?" she whispered.

"I thought you'd never ask," he said, laughing at himself, and happy with her. He said good night to his children, left them with the housekeeper when they went to bed, and was back with her by eleven. And the next morning they went to work together. He had asked the housekeeper to tell the kids he had an early meeting, in case they didn't see him in the morning.

"How are we going to do this?" she asked, as she fixed him breakfast and handed him *The Wall Street Journal.*

"Carefully, I suspect. Wisely, sensibly. Slowly. We both have to give this a lot of thought, Meredith." They had talked about it a lot, and they both wanted to proceed slowly. They had a lot to think about. And she had told him from the first that she was not going to leave Steve. And he said he understood that. But what that meant, for both of them, was that this could be finite. It was only a question of how long it would last, how they could manage it with the least potential damage for everyone, and if it was worth it. For the moment, they were both convinced it would be, no matter how limited their future. And Cal knew he had to accept that, although he didn't like it. He wanted Merrie in his life now, as much more than just a friend and employee.

They spent the day together at work, as usual. And Steve called her before lunch. He was busy, dashing in and out of surgeries, and still covering for Harvey Lucas. Lucas was scheduled to be out for another month, or three weeks at least. But Anna was still helping keep all the balls in the air. The trauma unit was like a circus act, and he was on the high wire most of the time, riding a unicycle, and juggling flaming torches.

Steve barely had time to ask her about Hawaii, and inquired if she was still coming home that weekend. She said she was, and then the moment she hung up, she regretted it, when Cal walked in and asked her if she wanted to go to Carmel with him and his children.

"I'd love to," she said, looking disappointed, "but I

just told Steve I'd come home." She saw something flicker in Cal's eyes, but he said nothing. "Maybe I should call him and postpone it."

"That's up to you," he said quietly. He didn't want to put undue pressure on her. But as she thought about it, she hated leaving him, and she knew she wasn't ready to see Steve yet after everything that had happened in Hawaii.

She called Steve back that afternoon, and told him that something had come up at the office, and she had to see customers that weekend. He said he understood, but he didn't sound happy about it. And she felt like an ax murderer again when she hung up. She was doing something she had never done with him before. She was lying to him. And it also occurred to her that she was doing exactly what Cal's ex-wife had done, and he had hated her for it. She was sleeping with her boss, and lying to her husband. It wasn't a pretty picture, and she said as much to Cal that night, when they were at her apartment. He had come over after having dinner with his kids, and he was tired. But he didn't like what she said about Charlotte.

"This is *not* the same thing, Merrie," he said emphatically.

"How is it different? It's almost exactly the same situation."

"She was involved with him when I married her, and she never told me. She continued the affair after our marriage, and on and off while we were having children. We were married for seven years, and she was involved with him the entire time, and had been for several years before that. She never told me what was going on, and she left me for him. I'd say that's very different. I never knew any of it until I figured it out for myself afterward. And it's just a miracle that none of my children are his. If they didn't all look so much like me, I'd be worried."

"That must have been awful," Meredith sympathized with him, but she still didn't like the similarities in the two situations, and undeniably, there were some.

And that weekend they went to Carmel with his children. They stayed at the Lodge at Pebble Beach, and she had a separate room, but surprisingly, none of his children seemed to mind her being with them. They had accepted her as a friend. She shopped with the girls while Cal and Andy played golf. And they went to Platti in Carmel, and had pasta for dinner. And the conversation was lively. The children teased their father about a number of things, his hair, the way he dressed, the kind of women he liked, or didn't, even the way he played golf. But it was all in relatively good humor. It was obvious that despite whatever foibles they saw, they genuinely loved him. And they gave Meredith safe passage, because they knew she wasn't his girlfriend, and was married to Steve.

"It must be hard not having your husband live here," Mary Ellen said sympathetically, which startled Meredith. It was a surprisingly adult thing to say, and she nodded in agreement.

"It is. He's trying to find a job, but it's not easy, and right now he's stuck in New York anyway, because his boss had an accident," she explained.

"He fixes people who get shot, right?" Andy asked sensibly and she laughed.

"That and a few other things."

"People must shoot each other a lot in New York to need a special doctor for it," he added, and they all laughed. It was an interesting perception, and not entirely inaccurate, but it reminded her again that Steve was very much part of her life, and she couldn't avoid him forever.

She and Cal talked about it again that night, and she said she really had to go home the following weekend. But when Thursday came, she found she truly did have to see customers, coming in from Tokyo. And she didn't know what to tell Steve, since she had already used that excuse for the weekend she'd spent in Carmel with Cal and his kids.

"Again?" Steve said unhappily when she told him she couldn't come home that weekend. "Christ, Merrie, do you ever plan to get back here? You know how stuck I am, with Lucas gone."

"What about Anna? Can't she cover for you, so you can come out to California?"

"Not this week. She just worked six days straight on duty and on call. She hasn't seen her kid in days. I told her I'd at least be on call for her through Sunday."

"So if I'd come, then you might have been busy anyway. Maybe it's just as well I can't do it." She was making excuses that didn't quite fly with Steven.

"Look, Merrie. I don't care who goes where. I want to see you. The last bulletin I had was that we're still married. And if that's the case, I'd like to see you more than once a month, if that's okay with you." He was really irritated with her.

"I'll come back next week." She sounded apologetic as she said it.

"That's what you say every week, and then on Thursdays you call to tell me you have to see customers, or go to Hawaii, or fly a kite with Callan Dow. I don't know what the fuck you're doing out there, but all I know is that I never see you anymore." He sounded angry and tired and jealous, and she couldn't blame him.

"I'm sorry. I don't know what to say." She was feeling desperately guilty, and a little frightened by what she was doing. No matter what she felt for Cal, or how good it was, she was risking her marriage and she knew it. She couldn't expect Steve to put up with this forever.

"Never mind, Meredith. I'll see you when I see you. If you come to New York, call me. I have to get back to work now." He almost hung up on her, and she felt uncomfortable for the rest of the day, thinking about it. But she didn't say anything to Cal. Steve was her problem. And her husband.

She entertained at Fleur de Lys with Cal on Friday night, the Japanese loved French food, and they thought the restaurant was excellent. And on Saturday, they took them to Masa's. Their meetings with them went well, too, and they were enthusiastic about a new system Cal was putting together. Meredith spent all her time with them until they left on Sunday. And when she called Steve that night, he was out, and she drove over to have dinner with Cal and the children.

As it turned out, Steve worked all weekend in New York, and if Meredith had been there, he couldn't have seen her. They had another blizzard, and the temperature dropped dramatically. There were sheets of ice on the ground, and Steve said he had never seen as many fractures. He was assisting the orthopods in surgery day and night, and he had four head-ons, which involved children.

He had given Anna the weekend off, but he was thrilled to see her when she finally came in on Sunday evening, and he was still working.

"I hear you had a good time this weekend." She smiled at him. She had had fun sliding around on the snow on garbage can lids and plastic bags in Central Park with her daughter. "Thanks for the time off. We had a great time."

"Lucky you," he growled at her. "Every old lady in New York has been in here with a fractured ass since you left on Friday."

"I like that diagnosis. Did you tell them that?"

"Yeah. They loved it." He smiled grudgingly at her. He'd been in a bad mood since Thursday.

"Did Meredith fly in?" she asked casually, wondering if they'd had a fight, or if he'd even seen her. She'd had the feeling lately that things weren't going brilliantly between them.

"No. She had to see customers. Again," he snapped at her.

"You couldn't have seen her anyway if she had come," Anna said practically, judging from his work-load.

"That's what she said. She could have at least tried."

"Look, kid. You're both busy. You knew this wouldn't be easy when you let her move, but you thought you'd both have jobs. Now you don't and you're both trying to make the best of it. It's not her fault your job fell through." She was being reasonable, but it annoyed him that she wasn't as sorry for him as he thought she should be.

"Do you have to rub it in? Or do you just do that for the hell of it?" he snarled at her and shrugged, and then a minute later he apologized for it. "I'm sorry. I had a shit weekend. I haven't slept since Friday night. I'm sick and tired of the bullshit here. I miss my wife. And I get the feeling she never wants to come back here anymore, and it's driving me crazy."

"So go see her," Anna said sensibly. "Next Saturday is Valentine's Day. Why don't you surprise her?"

"What if she does the same thing and flies here and I miss her?" He was too tired to work it out in his head, but Anna wasn't. And at heart, despite her blunt words and bad breaks, she was still a romantic.

"So tell her you're on duty and can't see her, and she won't come. Then you fly out, and surprise her . . . you know, chocolates, roses, the whole Valentine thing. Very romantic. She'll love it." Anna smiled at him, wishing someone would do the same for her, but there was no one to do it. Hadn't been in years.

"Anna," he beamed at her happily, "you're a genius." He made his reservations on the phone that night, and was planning to fly out on Friday at noon when he got off work. With the time difference, he could be in Palo Alto before she left the office. "Thank you," he said to Anna before he went home to get some sleep, and promised her he'd be back in the morning.

"Just call me Cupid," she called after him, as she watched him go. He was so tired, he was weaving. She was glad he wasn't driving. She knew he'd take a cab home to the apartment he hadn't let her see yet. She had long since guessed that he didn't want her to feel bad when she saw how luxurious it was. But she knew his wife made a lot of money. He came to see her at her place instead sometimes for a glass of wine, or a burrito when she made them. He and Felicia were pals now, and they both enjoyed the visits.

It was quiet in trauma unit that night, and Anna didn't need to call him for anything. She handled the unit well by herself, and the residents and nurses all liked her. She was still hoping the job would become permanent eventually, but there was no sign of it yet. Steve didn't seem to be going anywhere. And when she thought about it, as she sat in his office that night, she was glad.

Chapter 15

"WHAT ARE YOU doing on Saturday?" Cal asked Meredith cryptically on Friday morning.

"Nothing much," she smiled at him. She knew what day it was, and what he probably had in mind. Saturday was Valentine's Day, and she was staying in California for yet another weekend. Steve had already told her days before that he was working and there was no point in her flying to New York. They had canceled yet another weekend, and it was worrying her that they seemed to be drifting apart so swiftly. It concerned her even more that the life that she was building with Cal was becoming more solid by the minute. They saw each other nearly every night, and he stayed over whenever he could get away with it. She had dinner with him and the kids, and went to basketball games and movies and other places with them, every weekend. She was becoming a fixture. And he was beginning to feel like her husband.

No one at work had spotted anything yet, and they

were supremely careful to see that that didn't happen. And his kids didn't seem to have any suspicions either. Everyone seemed to assume that they were the same friends they'd always been since she'd started working for him. But sooner or later she knew that someone might discover them, and then they would have a serious problem. It would hardly have been appropriate for people to know she was cheating on her husband.

"How about dinner at Fleur de Lys tomorrow night?" he suggested casually, and she smiled with pleasure.

"I'd love it." It seemed odd not to spend Valentine's Day with Steve, and she felt guilty about wanting to be with Cal in San Francisco. But the truth was, she wanted to be with Cal, not Steve, for the time being.

"Why don't you come over and hang out tonight? I'll rent some videos and we can make popcorn," he suggested.

"Do you want me to bring the videos?" she offered as she put her work into her briefcase. But she seemed to be taking less and less work home on the weekends. She was spending time with him instead, and not really in the mood to do "homework."

"Sure, you bring the videos. I'll make dinner for us after the kids eat," he volunteered. It sounded good to both of them, and Meredith tried not to think of what they were doing. They were living a fantasy that felt good now, but it couldn't go on forever, particularly once Steve found a job and moved to California. No matter how they avoided it now, eventually they knew they'd have to face it. But not yet, she told herself. Not yet. What she was sharing with Cal was too sweet to abandon. She knew it was selfish of her but she couldn't bring herself to break it off yet, no matter how guilty she felt about Steven.

"I'll come over in a couple of hours," she promised. She wanted to take a bath, and relax, and give him some time with his children before she joined him. She didn't want to wear out her welcome with them.

She drove home to the furnished apartment she was still living in. She still hadn't found a house she liked, and she was spending less time working on it. She'd been busy, and as long as Steve was still in New York, she couldn't see the point of living in the city. And she wanted to stay in Palo Alto to be near Cal now. He had told her she could keep the apartment she had for as long as she wanted.

She let herself into her apartment with her key, and as she walked in, she suddenly had an odd feeling. She sensed, more than saw anything different. There was just an eerie feeling as she walked into her living room, and set down her briefcase, and as she did, Steve walked out of her bedroom with a huge bouquet of flowers. She nearly jumped a foot when she saw him. The last thing she expected was to see Steve there.

"What are you doing here?" she said, as though he were an intruder, and he looked at her with an odd expression, as he walked toward her with the flowers.

"I thought you'd be happy to see me," he said, looking disappointed.

"I am." She covered her tracks immediately, and moved toward him. "I just . . . I didn't expect . . . you said you were working this weekend."

"I wanted to surprise you," he said, setting the flowers down on the coffee table. He put his arms around her then, and she prayed that he wouldn't sense any resistance. She hadn't seen him since things had changed with Cal, and she was desperately afraid that he might sense it. But she was sure he didn't when he kissed her. "Happy Valentine's Day, Merrie," he said happily, pleased with what he'd accomplished. It had been obvious from her expression that she didn't expect him, and her mind was racing.

"What a great surprise!" she said valiantly, and he didn't tell her it had been Anna's suggestion.

"I figured it was easier for me to come out than to get you away from your work here. You'd better be free this weekend. I want to take you out to dinner tomorrow." So did Cal, she thought almost the moment he said it. But that was impossible now. She had to spend Valentine's Day with her husband. As long as he had gone to the trouble to come out, she knew she had to spend every moment with him. And it seemed like something of a mixed blessing to her. "So what'll we do tonight?" he beamed at her. He knew what was at top of his list, but after that, he was thinking of taking her to dinner or a movie.

"I don't know. Why don't we just stay here?" She felt completely disoriented, and for some odd reason, she felt as though she were entertaining a stranger. Having slept with Cal, she felt as though her whole life was out of balance.

"I can cook if you want," Steve offered, "or we can order a pizza."

"Sure, sweetheart," she said amiably, "whatever you want. You must be exhausted." At least she hoped so, but he looked surprisingly refreshed, despite the time difference and the endless string of days he'd been working.

"I slept on the plane, I feel great actually." He put his arms around her again then, "I've really missed you." They hadn't seen each other in five weeks, and for three weeks she had allowed herself the delusion that he no longer existed. But he was all too real now.

"I've missed you too," she lied, feeling flustered and awkward as she moved his flowers to the dining room table, and thanked him. But as he watched her, he didn't know why, but he sensed that something was different between them. Maybe it was the surprise, and she hadn't had time to absorb it.

"How was your week?" he asked casually.

"Okay."

"It sounds like you've been working day and night since Hawaii." He'd called her, but she had hardly ever answered, and she'd only spoken to him from the office, because Cal had been there every evening.

"I've been pretty busy," she said vaguely.

"Why don't I take a shower, and we can relax for a while," he said with a smile. She knew what that meant. Sometimes when they'd been apart for a while, making love got them back on track and comfortable with each other again, but this time, at the thought of it, she felt panicked.

"I'd love that, but I've got one bit of bad news." She actually blushed as she said it, for a variety of reasons.

"What's that?" He looked momentarily worried.

"It's the wrong time of the month for hot romance. . . ." She tried to let him come to his own conclusions.

"You've got your period?" She nodded. It wasn't true, but she suddenly realized that she didn't want to deal with the physical aspects of her double life, and their complicated situation. She hadn't had time to prepare herself for what it would mean when she next saw him. "That's no big deal," he smiled at her. "It never used to bother us when we were in college, did it?" She looked stunned and felt trapped when he said it. "If we're going to live on separate coasts, we're going to have to take what comes, if you'll pardon the pun, when we do see each other."

"Thank you," she whispered, as he disappeared into the bedroom to undress and take a shower. And when she heard the water running, she reached for the phone and dialed Cal. He answered on the second ring, and was happy to hear her voice.

"When are you coming over? I bought a couple of steaks, and a nice bottle of wine."

"I can't come," she said quickly.

"Why not? Is something wrong?" He could hear the strain in her voice, and although she didn't need to, she was almost speaking in a whisper.

"Steve is here. He surprised me." There was a long pause, and a painful silence.

"I see . . . well, that's interesting. To what do we owe the pleasure . . . no, let me guess. He came out for Valentine's Day, for a little romance." Cal sounded cynical to cover his hurt as he said it. But it was the price he had to pay for having an affair with a married woman.

"I guess so. I don't know, Cal." Now she was lying to him too. The dream was slowly turning into a nightmare, but they had known it would. They had been kidding themselves for the past few weeks, but now the truth was staring them both in the face. The only one who didn't know what was happening was Steven. "I can't see you tomorrow," she said sadly.

"Obviously." And then he seemed to recover. "It's all right, Merrie. I understand." They had put off having any discussion about their future because they realized that until Steve appeared they could live the fantasy. But now he was here and they had to face the truth and all its implications. "We'll have dinner next week and talk about it. I'll see you on Monday. I assume he's going back Sunday night on the red-eye." In spite of himself, he sounded hopeful.

"He hasn't said yet." The water had stopped running and she knew she had to get off. The entire situation was making her extremely nervous. "I'll call you when I can."

"Don't worry about it. I'll spend a quiet weekend with the kids. Just remember one thing."

"What's that?" she whispered.

"I love you." As she listened, she realized that he was more than she deserved. They both were. She felt guilty about both of them. They were good men, and she loved them. But giving each of them half of her heart was less than either of them deserved and it was driving her crazy.

"Me too," she said as Steve wandered into the living room wrapped in a towel, still dripping water. "Have a nice weekend," she said and hung up, as Steve looked at her with a smile.

"Who was that?"

"My secretary . . . Joan . . . I needed her to do some work this weekend." The lies were endless, and Meredith hated herself for them. But there was no way

she could be honest with him. What was she supposed
to say? That it was Cal, and that she had just told him
she loved him?

"You all work too hard," Steve announced as he
walked into the kitchen and opened the refrigerator.
He liked beer, and she had none. All she had was some
white wine Cal had left there. "You're out of beer,"
Steve said, looked at the wine and raised an eyebrow.
"You're drinking mighty expensive stuff these days.
You never drink wine when you're alone," he said, but
it was more a question than an accusation.

"I had some people over. The Japanese people last
weekend."

"Too bad you didn't buy sake for them. I like that
better. We can go buy some beer later."

"I wasn't expecting you, so I didn't buy it."

"No prob," he said with a boyish grin. He seemed
like a big kid now, compared to Cal's sophistication. It
was odd to realize that she was more comfortable now
with her lover than her husband. The last four months
had not been kind to them. "Why don't we hop into
bed for a while?" he suggested with a look of mischief,
as he took her by the hand and pulled her into the
bedroom. She was still wearing the navy blue suit she'd
worn to work, with a gold necklace and a pair of pearl
earrings. She looked businesslike and cool, and the last
thing on her mind was sex or romance. But there was
absolutely no way she could refuse him. She had already tried time of the month, and he hadn't bought it.
And in the days before Cal, she would have been anxious to sleep with him after all the time they hadn't
seen each other. They had always had an active sex life.

She took off her suit, draped it over a chair, kicked

off her shoes, took off her jewelry, and pantyhose, and
a minute later, she slipped into bed in her underwear,
after a quick stop in the bathroom. She felt like one of
those legendary brides who lock themselves in the
bathroom and refuse to come out, but if she had done
that, he would have thought she was crazy.

And for a minute, he just lay there and held her, but
she could feel how much he wanted her, and suddenly
all her feelings for him came rushing back, not in the
form of passion, but of pity.

"What's wrong, sweetheart?" He knew her too well,
and he was shocked to feel that she was shaking.

There were tears in her eyes when she answered.
She had been so unfair to him. She had made a mess of
everything, and she couldn't even tell him about it. It
would only have hurt him. She wasn't sure what she
wanted to say to him. What could she say? That she was
having an affair and in love with another man? It would
have been so cruel to tell him. "I don't know," she
struggled to explain, without actually saying anything
too damning to him. "It's hard not seeing each other
for so long, and then coming together like this . . . it
feels strange, doesn't it?"

"Not to me," he said in a gentle tone, his voice
husky with desire for her, "but women are different."
Yes, she thought to herself, as Cal had once said of
Charlotte, they are fundamentally dishonest. She hated
herself for what she was doing to him. And she thought
she was no better than Charlotte.

"I'm sorry." She clung to him like a lost child as he
held her. He had been her friend, her comfort, her
mentor, and now he felt like a stranger to her.

"Don't be sorry, Merrie. Just let me hold you." He

did for a long time, and eventually she relaxed, but when he tried to make love to her, she was so stiff and miserable that she wondered if she was becoming frigid. With him, at least. It had been a different story with Cal since Hawaii. "Maybe surprising you like this wasn't such a great idea," he said finally. He didn't want to force her to make love with him, but he couldn't stand not having her either. He got out of bed and walked around the room, and then he saw the gold watch she had left on the table. "What's that?" he asked casually, as he picked it up. It was heavy and looked expensive.

"My watch," she said, watching him.

"I can see that. Where'd you get it?"

"Bulgari. It was a Christmas present from Cal." There was no point lying about that too. She had to be honest about something.

"That's quite a gift," he said, looking unhappy about it. "It must have cost him a pretty penny."

"He's very generous with his employees," she said coolly, as Steve turned to look at her, his eyes filled with pain and questions.

"Do I need to ask you if you're more than that to him?" he asked, and as their eyes met, she shook her head slowly. She didn't want him to know, and she wasn't going to tell him. She was sure now. It would have been easier to shoot him than to tell him. And she had neither the desire, nor the courage.

"No, you don't. The watch doesn't mean anything." He nodded, and set it back down on the table. And Cal's name never came up again for the rest of the weekend.

They went out for pizza that night, and hung around

the apartment the next day. He took her out for hamburgers on Saturday night, which was his idea of a Valentine's Day celebration. And finally, on Saturday night, she made love with him. It had none of their old spark and flame, and he knew something was wrong afterward when he held her.

"This lifestyle of ours isn't doing us any good," he said quietly. "We're going to have to do something about it one of these days. Things are going downhill fast, aren't they?" It was more a statement than a question.

"I know. We just have to be patient," she said softly.

"It's taking too big a toll on us," he said, as he went to help himself to a beer. They had bought a six-pack that morning. But what he didn't know was that the toll had already been taken. "I'll call around again, when I get home, and see what I can drum up. This can't go on forever." She nodded and said nothing in answer, and she lay awake for hours that night as he slept next to her. She was aching to call Cal, but she didn't dare. If Steve had woken up and heard her, it would have been a disaster.

They sat around and read the paper together the next day, and he looked at listings for houses in Pacific Heights. He was upset that she hadn't found one yet, but she told him she had been too busy.

"I guess we both have," he said, and told her that they had to fly back and forth more. The awkwardness they'd experienced this time had truly upset him.

He didn't attempt to make love to her again. The night before hadn't been much of a success for either of them. She had been in tears by the time it was over. They had a late dinner at the airport before he left, and she stood watching his plane after he got on the red-eye. He had kissed her before he boarded, and she had held him tightly as they stood there. She felt as though she would lose him forever if he left again, and she wanted to beg him to stay, but the words wouldn't come, and she knew he couldn't stay anyway. He had to go back to New York and his job there.

As the plane headed toward the runway, she turned and walked away, and she cried all the way back to her apartment. It had been a ghastly weekend. And when the phone rang, when she got home, she thought it was Cal, and picked it up. But it was Steve from the plane.

"Just remember one thing, Merrie," he said.

"What's that?" The words had a familiar echo to them.

"How much I love you." It was exactly what Cal had said the last time she talked to him on Friday.

"I love you too," she said in a choked voice. "I'm sorry it was such a lousy weekend." She owed him so much more than that, but it had all been too much for her, and she didn't know what she was going to do about Cal now.

"It wasn't that bad. It takes a little readjusting when we get back together. I'll try and come back in two weeks, if I can. And why don't you try and come home next weekend? We'll get back on track, sweetheart. And if I don't find a job soon, I'll come out and drive a cab if I have to."

"I wouldn't let you do that," she said sadly.

"Let's see what happens when Lucas gets back. That's only two more weeks. Maybe I'll just pack up and come out there." The words sounded like a death knell to her. She would either have to face the music with him, or end it with Cal, and the prospect of doing either was terrifying.

"I love you, Steve," she said, and meant it this time. She was utterly miserable, and more confused than she'd ever been. And what's more, she knew she deserved to be.

"I love you too, babe," he said before he hung up. And she sat crying for a while, not sure what to do now.

The next call, an hour later, was from Cal. He sounded a mess, and confessed that it had been a nightmarish weekend for him. He had been going insane thinking about her. He didn't want to tell her how jealous he had been, imagining her in bed with Steve. All he wanted now was to see her.

"Can I come over?" he asked, and she wanted to tell him he couldn't, but she felt the same pull toward him she always did. It was driven more by chemistry than by reason.

"I'm a mess," she warned. "This has been the worst weekend of my life."

"Mine too. Let's try and get over it together." She had no idea what she was going to do when she saw him again, or how she'd feel when she did. But the moment she opened the door to him, she knew. She fell into his arms and dissolved into sobs, clinging to him. And all he could do was kiss her and hold her, and within minutes they were in the bed she had shared with Steve the night before. But she couldn't even think of that now. All she wanted was Cal, as badly as he wanted her, and he took her with all the strength and power of the passion they shared, and they lay together in each other's arms, clinging to each other like two lost souls until morning.

Chapter 16

So how was it?" Anna asked Steve on Monday morning when he got in. He had taken a cab from the airport to the hospital, and he looked tired and drawn and, as usual, his clothes were wrinkled.

"How was it?" He looked at her blankly for an instant. "It stank, if you want me to be honest. I don't know what's wrong, but I'd say just about everything is. She acted as though I were a stranger. And when she wasn't refusing to make love with me, she was crying. I had a really fantastic weekend. Thanks for asking." He looked and sounded exhausted.

"Shit." Anna looked sorry for him, and wondered if she had made the wrong suggestion when she told him to go out there and surprise her. "What do you think is happening with her?" Anna was intrigued by what he was describing.

"Honestly? I don't know. I think she's working too hard. And maybe she's just getting weird living alone. What do I know?"

There was a question on the tip of Anna's tongue, but she was afraid to ask him. She liked him too much to want to hurt him. But he could see that she had something on her mind, as he poured himself a styrofoam cup full of black coffee.

"What are you not saying to me?" They had come to know each other well in the two months they'd worked together.

"It's probably a really dumb question. I was going to ask if you think she's seeing someone. Maybe she's freaked out about it, and feels guilty."

"Meredith?" He looked amused. "No way. We've never cheated on each other. I trust her completely. I think our being apart is turning her frigid and neurotic. It's a great combination."

"Maybe she needs therapy," Anna said practically.

"Maybe she needs me. And I'm stuck here, working my ass off, with no job to go to in California. It's a real shit situation."

"No one said it was going to be easy."

"Thank you, doctor, for the five-cent psychiatry. Now, tell me what happened here this weekend." He looked grim as they sat down in his office and got down to business.

"Two brain surgeries, a compound fracture of a femur, three head-ons involving a total of thirteen people, and four shootings, two fatalities as a result, the others all went home the next day. And that's about it. Oh, and two sprained ankles." She reeled them off like three BLTs and two salamis.

"Jesus, are you kidding?"

"Nope. We had a busy weekend. Sounds like more fun than yours though."

"You're right on that score." But he felt better that he was back at work now. In some ways, this was saner, and he understood it better. Here at least, he could make a difference.

Anna showed him the charts, and reviewed all her cases with him, and he was impressed by everything she'd done, and grateful for her shoulder to cry on about his lost weekend.

They worked together all afternoon, and did surgery together that night, and on Tuesday morning she went home to her daughter. He was going off duty that night, and the chief resident was taking over for him.

"Do you want to come by for macaroni and cheese and hot dogs?"

"Now there's a memorable combination. How about if I bring some steaks for you and Felicia?"

"We don't need charity, Steve," she said, looking insulted. "If you want what's on the menu, come. If you want something fancier, go to a restaurant." She had a lot of pride and a lot of heart, and more balls than most men he knew, and he liked that about her. She wasn't embarrassed about being poor, and she didn't want handouts from anyone.

"I didn't mean to insult your cooking. I love macaroni and cheese," he said with a look of admiration for her. "What time can I come by?"

"Come whenever you get off work. You can take a shower at my place, if you want, or you can just sit around looking a mess if that feels better. It's strictly come as you are." He also loved that about her. She didn't put on airs, or expect them from him. She was an honest, straightforward person.

"I'll see you around seven. Can I bring some beer,

or will you kick my ass over that too? I just don't happen to love orange juice," which was all she had had the last time.

"Okay, you can bring beer. But no wine or champagne." She knew how wealthy he was, because of his wife, and she didn't want to share the wealth with him. In fact, she was uptight about it.

"Do you mind if I come in my limo?"

"Whatever turns you on. Come in your jet plane, if you want." She was smiling at him, and he knew she had forgiven him for offering to bring steaks. She was a porcupine sometimes, but her inside was pure marshmallow.

"Can I land my helicopter on the roof?"

"Oh go fuck yourself, and go back to work," she growled at him, and went home to Felicia.

And that night, he showed up at her apartment on the West Side at six thirty. The resident had come early for a change, and Steve had used the opportunity to leave while he could, before any new patients came in and he'd wind up staying.

When Anna opened the door for him, she was wearing jeans and a white angora sweater. She looked pretty and soft, and the body that disappeared in scrubs was very much in evidence in the angora. Her jeans looked like they were wallpapered to her, and the sweater was molded to her breasts in a way that was very distracting. Her hair was down, and she was wearing a pair of comfortable old slippers. And Felicia was hopping around the room in a pair of clean pink flannel pajamas. And for once the cockroaches had disappeared. The landlord had "exterminated" them a few days before, which Anna claimed usually lasted about ten minutes.

But in spite of the simple fare, the dinner she made for him was delicious. The macaroni and cheese was good, the hot dogs were huge, and she had made cornbread. He had brought two six-packs of beer, so he could leave one for her, and a chocolate cake that had looked good to him at the deli.

"You don't have to eat it," he teased, "if you feel like I'm buying you."

"I will!" Felicia chimed in.

"I'll help you," Steve said, helping her to a big piece, as Anna grinned at him. He was always nice to her daughter, and she was sorry for him that he didn't have his own children. She wondered about Meredith sometimes, what kind of woman she really was. She had the feeling at times that Steve had a lot of illusions about her.

Steve gave Anna a piece of the chocolate cake, too, and they all agreed it was delicious.

At eight o'clock Anna put Felicia to bed, and Steve volunteered to read her a story, while Anna did the dishes. And by the time she was through, Felicia was sound asleep, and Steve had come back to the tiny kitchen.

"What did you read her?" Anna asked with curiosity. Felicia had a number of favorites.

"One of my medical textbooks. I figured you'd want me to influence her early."

"Very funny," she said, as she dried her hands on a clean towel. Everything in the apartment was threadbare, but spotless. She was immaculate, and had managed to turn the place into a cozy home for them, which had been a real challenge. The paint was peeling off the walls, and the rooms were small, and they looked out on another ugly building. It seemed light-years away from his apartment, but Anna had never seen it.

He handed her another beer, and they sat down on the couch, talking and drinking. They talked about the hospital, as they always did, and then they talked about Puerto Rico, and she admitted that she missed it.

"I miss my family, my friends. I miss a lot of things." And she talked about her dreams then. She still wanted to go to a Third World country one day, and help people who were in greater need than the kids in the gangs they saw constantly in the trauma unit. "Maybe some-day," she said, as she set the bottle of beer down on her coffee table.

"All I want to do is to get to California one of these days," he said, "that's about as Third World as it gets for me. You're a lot braver than I am."

"I'm just not as spoiled," she teased him. She always insisted that she didn't care about material things, but like everyone else, she did, to some extent, just not as much as some of the people they knew, or even him-self, or Merrie. Sometimes she tried to make him feel guilty, but he didn't.

"You're so damn politically correct, you make me sick sometimes," he said, with a grin. He felt relaxed with her, and very happy. The sting of the disastrous weekend in California had begun to dim for him. And he was beginning to think that maybe it hadn't been quite as awful as he first thought it. But for once, he didn't discuss Meredith with her. They just talked about themselves. She talked about Yale, and about her dreams for Felicia.

"I want her to be a lawyer. They make more money than we do."

"My garbage man makes more money than we do. And by the way, I thought you disapproved of making too much money."

"Not for my daughter," she smiled with good humor. She was a good mother, and a good person, and Steve liked her. Besides, she was beautiful and sexy and easy to be with.

"So how come you don't have a boyfriend?" he asked her after a while, and she smiled at him. They had a way of putting each other on the spot and asking tough questions. But they both gave each other honest answers.

"I don't have time. I work too hard. Besides, I haven't met anyone I cared about in years. All the guys I meet are gay, assholes, or married."

"That sounds appealing," he said, relaxing on her couch. "What's wrong with gay guys?" he teased her.

"I hate sharing my clothes with the guys I go out with. They usually look better in them than I do."

"That wouldn't be easy." He paid her a backhanded compliment and she smiled. She enjoyed being with him. "Well, that takes care of the gay guys. And I guess assholes are a little tough, but interesting sometimes. They have a certain charm, you'll have to admit. What about married?"

"I don't like the odds," she said simply. "I don't play games I can't win anymore. I learned that lesson early." The odds had been stacked against her with Felicia's father. His family had won on that one.

"That's sensible," Steve said matter-of-factly. "I've

never fooled around myself actually. It never seemed fair to Merrie. Besides, I've never found anyone I like better.''

"Even now that she's not here?" Anna's eyes bored into his with her pointed questions. And he tried not to look at her breasts in her sweater. "You're a pretty straight guy if you can be faithful to a woman you see once or twice a month, sometimes less. That's impressive.''

"Just stupid, I guess." He was a nice guy, and she knew it.

"What if you knew she weren't being faithful to you, Steve?''

"That couldn't happen. I know her. All she thinks about is her work anyway. She lives, sleeps, eats, breathes it.''

"That's not too sexy," Anna said bluntly.

"Not lately." He was honest with her. And there was something sad in his eyes as he said it. He didn't think Meredith was cheating on him, but he did think they were losing ground somehow, losing touch, and worse yet, losing each other. He had felt it clearly the previous weekend in California.

"You love her a lot, don't you?" He nodded, but there was more there, and feeling her probing eyes on him, he dug deeper.

"I love her. But I have to admit something has changed since she left. Sometimes it feels like we're not married anymore, and we're just dating . . . or just friends . . . or something. Living this far apart, when we see each other now, it's like I can't reach her. It's a lousy feeling.''

"It must be." Anna had her own theories about it,

but she didn't want to hurt him, so she didn't share them with him. But she knew women better than he did. She had also begun to think that he might never move to California. It just wasn't happening, and his wife didn't seem too anxious for him to be there. But she didn't say that to him either. Besides, he loved the trauma unit, and she couldn't see him leaving. "It's funny how people drift apart. I was in love with a guy once, and he moved away. I obsessed about him for a year. He was all I could think of. And when I saw him again, he was like a different person. I had this fantasy of him that had nothing to do with reality. He was actually kind of an asshole," she admitted and he smiled at her.

"At least he wasn't gay or married. There must be some other guys out there, Anna, single ones. Maybe you're just not trying."

"They're not out there, believe me. And it's too much trouble to find them."

"That's the real problem. You're lazy." She was anything but at the hospital. But he suspected she was too scared to get involved with anyone. She had old wounds and old scars to protect. She was hiding.

They sat and talked for a long time, and at ten o'clock she yawned, and he looked at his watch. "I should go," he said, but he hated going back to his empty apartment, and she was nice to talk to.

"You don't have to. I don't usually go to bed till midnight."

"What do you do all alone here?"

"Read mostly."

"That sounds lonely," he said softly. They were both lonely, in a city full of people.

"It is sometimes, but I don't mind it. Lonely is good sometimes. It makes you think, and know things you might not otherwise. I'm not afraid to be lonely," she said bravely.

"I am sometimes," he said honestly. "My life was so much better when my wife was here. Now I have nothing to go home to. You have Felicia."

"That's true," she nodded, as he looked at her, and almost instinctively he touched her cheek, and was surprised by how silky it felt. She was extraordinarily appealing, and very sexy. And she hadn't pulled away when he touched her, which surprised him. It made him feel bolder, and he pulled her gently toward him and kissed her. And she didn't stop him.

"Am I doing something stupid here?" he asked her in a whisper. "I'm not gay, but I am married, and I could turn out to be an asshole."

"I don't think so," she whispered back. "I know the deal here . . . and the ground rules."

"What are they?" He was startled at how open she was to him. They were two lonely, hungry people, and there was an almost irresistible meal on the table. It was hard for either of them to refuse it. And they felt safe with each other.

"The ground rules are that you love your wife, and you may wind up in California," she said simply.

"Not may, will." He didn't want to mislead her.

"I get it," she said simply, and slipped a hand under his sweater. He was wearing his scrub pants, and she gently untied them. "Do you want to stay here tonight?" she asked and he nodded, and then kissed her, harder this time. Everything about her made him want her. It was all so different than it had been for him over the weekend. This was sweet and pure and simple and honest, and as he touched her, he could feel her longing and her passion. She had no illusions about him, wanted no promises from him. Whatever she did want from him was there for the taking. "Let's go to my bedroom." Cheating on Meredith was something he had never done before, and yet with Anna, it seemed fair, and he wanted her very badly.

He followed her to a room the size of a closet. It was barely bigger than the bed, and there was a single light, next to the bed. She turned it on for a minute so they could get their bearings, and then turned it off and locked the door. He undressed her in the dark, and lay on the bed with her, and he could feel and sense her more than see her. But there was just enough light from the street lamp for him to see the silhouette of her beauty.

There were no words between them, no promises, no lies, only the sheer raw desire they had for each other, and as he took her, she moaned and moved and aroused him unbelievably. He felt completely overcome with passion. Being with her was like being exploded from a cannon, and when he lay spent in her arms afterward, they said nothing for a long time, and then she gently stroked his hair, like a child, and held him close to her. It was the happiest he had been in a long time, longer than he could remember.

"I don't want to hurt you, Anna," he said sadly. "This could have a lousy ending for us." It was almost sure to.

"So can life. It's good for now. If you can live with it, I can." She wanted so little from him, wanted to take nothing from him, and all she had to give him was in his arms at that moment, but it was a lot more than his wife was willing to give him. "Just tell me when it's over, or you want out. You don't have to slam the door. You can close it softly." But there were no doors he wanted to close now. He was still opening them, and as he explored her again with his hands and his tongue, she did the same to him, and what she gave him was a night he would long remember.

Chapter 17

MEREDITH DIDN'T SEE Steve for the next month, after the fiasco of the Valentine's Day weekend. She and Callan had to go to Tokyo and Singapore, and Steve could never seem to leave the hospital. They seemed to be drifting apart more each day, and they spoke on the phone less and less often.

She had been gone for five months, and romantically involved with Cal for nearly two, and she felt more a part of his life than Steve's now. They were with each other constantly, at work, at home, in her apartment at night, with his children on the weekend. And Andy finally looked at her curiously in mid-March, and asked her a question which shook her.

"Is your husband really going to move out here?" He wasn't being rude to her, but he wondered.

"I don't know, Andy," she said honestly. It didn't look like it, and she wasn't sure she wanted him to. And a week later, Andy asked his father if Merrie was his girlfriend.

"We're just friends," Cal explained, and Mary Ellen raised an eyebrow, but said nothing. They were fooling no one but themselves. But Steve was also no longer talking about the jobs he wasn't getting. In fact, he hadn't even complained about her not coming back to New York for weekends. It would have concerned her if she'd thought about it, but she was trying not to. And Cal asked her no questions. All he wanted was time with her, and he figured they would come to a decision later. He wasn't ready to make a commitment to her anyway. In some ways, this was perfect for both of them. And if Meredith had called Steve at home sometimes, she would have realized he was no longer sleeping in the apartment. She just assumed he was staying at the trauma unit. And she was relieved she didn't have to talk to him.

Harvey Lucas had been back at work for two weeks by then, but Steve had said nothing more about leaving. And he had asked Harvey to consider hiring Anna permanently. And after working with her for two weeks, Harvey agreed that she was terrific. They were trying to keep her for the moment, even on a temporary basis.

But when Meredith came back from Singapore, Steve said he wanted to see her. He had thought about it a lot lately and he was worried about what they were doing.

This time, he asked her before he came out. He didn't want to surprise her. She sounded hesitant at first, but she had no grounds to refuse him. She hadn't seen him in a month, and she knew that she couldn't avoid him forever.

"What are you going to say to him?" Cal asked this time. "Are you going to tell him?" He half wanted her to, and half didn't.

"Tell him what?" she asked honestly. "That I'm having an affair? That our marriage is over?" She didn't know what to say to him, or even what to think herself yet.

"That's up to you, Merrie."

"Where do we stand, Cal?"

"Does it make a difference?"

"It might," she answered.

"I think you have to make your own decision on this one. I don't want to be responsible for breaking up your marriage." That said a lot to her. It told her he was a decent person, but also that he was as confused as she was. The one thing he knew was that he didn't like the idea of her spending the weekend with Steve, though he said nothing about it when she told him. He didn't want to put any pressure on her, and make the situation harder for her.

And when Meredith saw Steve, she was more confused than ever. There was something so comfortable and familiar about him. But this time, when he said he wanted to make love to her, she said she wanted to talk first. They sat down on the couch, and she still had no idea what she would tell him. The one thing she knew was that she didn't want to hurt him.

"I've made a decision, Meredith," Steve said, and she braced herself for what was coming. She thought he was going to ask her for a divorce, and she didn't really blame him. She wasn't even sure what she would say when he said it. But he surprised her. "I don't think we have a lot of time left," he said carefully. "If we wait a few more months, living like this, I think it's going to be over between us. We've drifted apart, Merrie," he said gently. "I think we both know it." She nodded, and didn't deny it, and wondered if he would ask her why, but he didn't. It occurred to her that maybe he knew, and didn't want to hear the words from her. But she said nothing as she listened. "I'm going to leave the hospital in New York. I talked to a hospital here, in the city. It's small but respectable, and they have a decent ER. It's nothing much, but they have a part-time job available. They get pretty run-of-the-mill stuff, fractures, bellyaches, crying babies with earaches. I can live with it for a while, if I have to. If I wait for the perfect job, we'll be finished by the time I get it. So, I'm going to give notice when I go back, and get my ass out here." She was stunned by what he was saying, but she knew as well as he did, that if they were going to save their marriage, he had to do it.

"When would you come out?" she asked, without committing herself one way or the other. Her mind was racing as she asked him. Steve's announcement meant that she had to end the affair with Cal, and she didn't feel ready to do that, but knew she had to. "In two weeks," Steve explained. "Harvey is back, and they have Anna to replace me." He hadn't even told Anna yet. He wanted to talk to Meredith first, but he had a feeling Anna sensed it. It had gotten too good between them in the last month, and it was dangerous. He wanted to bail out now before he really hurt her. He had been more or less living with her for four weeks now, and he knew that if he wasn't prepared to make a commitment to her eventually, it would be bad for her, and Felicia. And he cared about them both too much to do that to them. According to her categories, he was married, and he was about to become an asshole.

Meredith was looking shocked by what he had just told her. "Two weeks?" Her voice cracked as she said it. But she also knew that it was now or never. They both did. And for the same reasons, although neither of them knew what the other was up to.

"There's no point waiting, Merrie. The hospital here will take me then. Harvey will be okay without me. I think if we're going to do it at all, we'd better do it now. We'll have been apart for nearly six months when I get here. That's a hell of a long time. Too long in my book."

"I know," she nodded. But all she could think of was Cal, and how she was going to tell him. And how much she would miss being with him.

"You don't look very happy, Merrie," Steve said sadly. They had reached a hell of a rough spot in their marriage, and they both knew it. But he wanted to give it a try, before they blew it completely, and Meredith wasn't ready to let go of him either. "Think we can still make it?"

"I want to," she said softly, and she did. She just didn't know if she could still do it. But she knew she had to try. Fifteen good years was too long to throw away, no matter how infatuated she was with Cal. She wondered if she'd have to quit when she told him. She had no way of gauging his reaction. And she realized she had to tell him now, before Steve gave notice. If she lost her job at Dow Tech, there was no point in Steve coming to California. She would go back to New York then.

"Let's do it, Merrie," Steve said, and she nodded. She couldn't think of anything to say. She was overwhelmed with her own emotions.

They spent a quiet evening after that, talking about it, and he sensed something very different about her. She seemed so sad, and he sensed her sorrow and her loss, without understanding what it came from. Anna had told him a while back that she thought Meredith was involved with someone else, but Steve had told her, and believed, that it was unlikely. And he still believed that.

They didn't make love to celebrate. It didn't feel like a celebration to either of them, but it was an important decision. He went to the hospital in the city on Saturday, and when he left, she called Cal.

"I have to see you," she said and wouldn't explain. She met him at his house ten minutes later.

"What's wrong?" He looked worried, with good reason. And she was quick and to the point when she told him.

"Steve's moving out in two weeks. He took a job at a small hospital, in an emergency room. He thinks that if he doesn't come now, it'll all be over between us, and he's right. I don't even feel married to him now. I feel married to you, Cal. But I don't think that's what you want. And I'm not sure I do either. I have to try this one last time. And if it doesn't work out, we can talk about us later, if you still want to. But right now, I owe it to him to see what we've still got. I don't think there's much left, but we have a lot of history between us. You and I have two months, and a very uncertain future.

We've always known that eventually this would happen," she said sadly. He had said not a word as she explained it all to him, but he looked devastated. Even though he had known this would come, he wasn't prepared for it. He didn't argue with her, or offer to marry her, or tell her he loved her. He didn't want to confuse or pressure her. He sat there stone-faced. But the problem was, after barely two months, he didn't know what he wanted either. He wanted her, but he didn't know under what conditions. And commitment was a big issue, and not one he was willing to undertake based on seven weeks of passion. He had been there. He should have been relieved that she was forcing him to make that decision. And yet as he listened to her he felt as though his world had ended. In fact, his world with her had.

"What I need to know from you," she went on, "is what happens to my job now. Do you want me to leave? I don't want him to quit and move out, and then find out I'm being fired. If you want me to go, I'll resign now, and I'll just tell him I've decided to go back to New York with him. Cal, what do you want?" She said it as gently as she could. Her job was the least of their problems at the moment, and not what really concerned them.

"I want you to stay here as my CFO," he said simply, in a voice that was raw with emotion. "I don't want to lose you." He didn't want to lose what he had with her either, but he knew he was in no position to say that, and she wasn't offering to stay with him. She had made her decision. She had told him right from the beginning that she wouldn't give up her marriage and however little he liked it, he knew he had to respect that.

"Are you sure, Cal?" she asked gently. "This is going to be hard for both of us. This isn't going to be easy if you want me to continue working for you."

"When is he coming out?"

"On April first, in two weeks."

"I want to spend most of the month in Europe anyway, looking into new products. That'll give us a chance to adjust, and you to figure out what you're doing. He may not last that long out here." He didn't mean to, but he sounded hopeful.

"He's tougher than that. I think he'll try to make it work here." What she didn't know was if they could still salvage their marriage. "It sounds awful to say it to you, but I love you, Cal. Maybe more than I love him right now. But I need to figure out what's real. My marriage, or whatever it is I have with you. I don't think either of us even knows what that is." He didn't argue with her, but as he listened to her, he looked angry. Callan Dow didn't like losing, and what he had said to her in the past two months was true. He loved her. But he had also known that she was married, and they couldn't avoid reality forever. And he was not prepared to offer her permanence or marriage.

"I'll leave for Europe before he gets here. And I don't want you to leave Dow Tech, Meredith. Please know that."

"Thank you," she said and stood up. There were tears in her eyes, but she didn't reach out to him, or cling to him. She looked at him for a long moment and walked to the door, and then his voice stopped her.

"When is he leaving this time?"

"Tomorrow morning," she said without turning around. She already had her hand on the door, and she felt a tug at her heart when he asked the question. She still wanted to be with him, but she knew she couldn't. Not now. Not anymore. Not until she knew what would happen with Steve. Maybe never.

"I'll call you," he said, and her heart leaped again, in spite of everything she had told him. She wanted to let go while they still could. If they could. But at least, they had to try it.

"I don't think you should," she said softly. And he said nothing, as she closed the door softly behind her.

Steve was waiting for her when she got home, and he looked strained, but he told her he had settled everything at the hospital in the city. And for the rest of the day, they made plans and talked. But they never made love during the entire weekend. This was more business than romance. And he left on Sunday morning. He had a lot to do in New York now. And when he was gone, Meredith sat grimly in the apartment. She had to find a place in the city for them to live now, and she didn't want to do that either. She didn't want to do any of it. She didn't want to leave Cal. Didn't want to live with Steve. Didn't want anything except what she'd had for the past two months, but she knew she had to give that up now. She was still sitting there, thinking about Cal, when the doorbell rang on Sunday afternoon.

It was Cal, and he just stood there and looked at her, and without a word, he pulled her into his arms and kissed her. He looked as unhappy as she did. He had wanted to hate her for what she'd said, and planned to do so, but he couldn't. He wanted her too badly. And without saying a word, he pulled her toward her bedroom, and she followed.

"We have two weeks, Merrie," was all he said. It was

a death knell for them, more than a promise. But they couldn't stop now. Not until they had to.

They spent the afternoon in bed, storing up what they would no longer have soon. Two weeks. And then it would be over.

Chapter 18

WHEN STEVE FLEW back to New York, he called the hospital to see if Anna was at work that day. The nurse in charge checked the schedule and said she was off till Tuesday. He didn't have to be at work himself until Monday at noon, so he went to her apartment on Monday morning to see her. Conveniently, Felicia was at school, and he found Anna alone when he rang her doorbell. He had called before to say he was coming over, and she sounded pleased to hear him.

But as soon as she saw his face that day, she knew that something was brewing. He looked more serious than usual, and he seemed quiet when he sat down on the couch, while she made him a cup of coffee.

"Should I ask how it was?" she asked quietly. "Or should I mind my own business?" She wasn't sure what had happened out there, but she could see in his eyes that something was different. And he hadn't called her all weekend. She also knew he was due back on Sunday night, and he hadn't come over.

"It was all right," he said, and took the mug of coffee from her and set it down on the table. "It wasn't as bad as last time. We did a lot of talking."

"Good talk or bad talk?" she asked, watching him, trying to read his face, but he looked guarded. Their affair had been going on for four weeks, and although she knew him well, she also knew that there were times when he was very private. Particularly about Meredith, and the situation in California. She didn't want to pry, but she wanted to help him.

"Good talk, I guess," he answered her, and then he took a breath, and dove into the deep water. He knew it would be hard to do, but there was no point stalling. More than anything, in spite of what he had to say, he didn't want to hurt her. "Anna." Just the way he said the word, made the hair on the back of her neck stand up. She sensed more than she knew what was coming. "I'm moving out there."

"That's not exactly news," she said calmly. She was stalling for time, in order to maintain her composure.

"I mean now. Soon. In two weeks. I'm going to give notice."

"Did you find a job?" In spite of herself, she looked startled. Her face had the look of an animal being hunted.

"More or less. I found something as low man in an ER. It's not great. But it'll do for now. You mean a lot to me," he said carefully, choosing his words like diamonds, but he knew that whatever he said, he would wound her. It was why he wanted to end it now, instead of later. He had realized he was falling in love with her, and because of that he had decided to press Meredith about his moving out there. He knew that if he waited,

the damage to Anna would be greater. And he wanted
to stop it before he hurt her too badly to recover. "I've
got to make the move now," he said. "If I wait any
longer, it'll be worse later when I do it. I don't want to
fuck up your life any more than I have in the last four
weeks. We're living a dream here. It's a dream I love. I
want to be here with you, working with you, sleeping
with you at night, playing with Felicia. But I can't. I'm
married to Meredith, and we have fifteen years behind
us. No matter how lousy the situation is for me right
now, I've got to go out there and try and put it back
together."

"Is that what she wants?" Anna asked. Her arms
were crossed and she seemed hunched over, as though
her stomach hurt, or her heart, and Steve hated what
he was doing to her.

"She agreed to it. I think she knows what I do, that if
we wait, it'll be all over. This is the eleventh hour for us.
We've either got to set it right, or give it up. And I don't
want you to wait for me. You have to assume that I'm
going to stay out there. You have to forget me." He said
it softly but firmly, and for an instant, she thought the
words would kill her.

"That's not so easy," she said as tears filled her eyes.
"Forgetting you is a tall order. You're kind of an asshole at times, but I love you."

"Just remember that I'm an asshole."

"That shouldn't be hard," she said, with her usual
bravado, but he could see that he was killing her. And
he didn't even want to think about Felicia. He had
fallen in love with her too, she was the little girl he'd
never had, and she deserved so much more than just
Anna could give her. She needed a father. But he

couldn't sign up for the job, he already had one, as Merrie's husband.

"I don't know what to say to you," he said, choking on his own words. "I love you. I want to be with you. If I were free, and you were dumb enough to have me, I'd marry you. But I can't offer you anything this way. I'm cheating you, and myself, by staying here. I have a responsibility to Merrie."

"She's a lucky woman," Anna said hoarsely. And then, "What if it doesn't work out? Will you come back?"

"No," he said, and the word sounded harsh even to him. He didn't want to leave her any hope. It wouldn't be fair. Because, with luck, he would stay with Merrie. And if he didn't, God only knew what would happen. "If it doesn't work out," he said, convincing himself as much as her, "I'm going to do something very different. Maybe what you suggested, I might spend a couple of years running a clinic in an underdeveloped country."

"You rich guys are lucky," she said bitterly. "You can do whatever the hell you want, and you don't have to worry about feeding anyone, or paying the bills, or supporting your kids. You just pick up your feet and pack your bags, and go wherever the hell you want to." He knew that she would have liked to do what he was talking about, probably more than he would. But he actually thought it would be a good idea for him, if his attempt to save his marriage failed. It was time for him to put something back into the world, instead of just patching up guys who shot each other.

"I'm not rich," he reminded her. "My wife is. That's very different. And what she has is hers. I don't want anything from her, except kids one day. I'm stealing something from you, Anna, I have been for a month now. The chance to meet the right guy, someone who can marry you and take care of you and Felicia, and give you more kids." He knew she wanted them, but could barely afford to support her daughter at the moment. "I don't have the right to take that from you. I'm giving that back to you now. I'm giving you back your life, and your freedom."

"How noble," she said sadly. "Do I get a voice in this?" she asked, slowly getting angry at him. What right did he have to make all the decisions, especially one that affected her so deeply? She loved him more than she had any man, and she had known the ground rules from the beginning. She just hadn't expected to fall in love with him to the extent she had, and so quickly. It made it harder to let go now.

"You don't have a choice here," Steve said firmly. "You can hate me if you want, or decide never to speak to me again. But you can't affect my decision to go out there."

"I wouldn't presume to," she said bluntly. "Nor would I want to. You were always free to do what you wanted, and so was I. I knew what the deal was from the beginning. I just didn't think you'd go so soon. I figured it would take you months to find a job, or maybe longer. I didn't realize you'd be willing to go without one, or with a job that isn't worthy of you." It made her realize again how desperate he was to save his marriage to Merrie, and Anna didn't think she was worth it. But the important thing was that Steve did. "Is there anything else you want to say to me?" she asked, standing up.

"Not really. Just that I love you, Anna. I want good things for you. I want you to have a happy life, without me."

"I get that. I always got it. You don't owe me anything. I want you to know that. I never wanted anything from you, except some time. You were a warm blanket in the winter."

"You were more than that to me. I want you to know that. I really love you."

"So what? You're still going." she said, as the tears swam in her eyes. "Felicia's father said he loved me too, but he didn't have the balls to stand up to his parents. Maybe you don't have the guts to face the fact that your marriage is already over."

"I don't know that. That's why I'm going out there. And if it is, I'll have to face it." She nodded and walked slowly to the door, and opened it. He wanted to hold her again, and kiss her, and make love to her one more time, but he loved her too much to do that to her, and he walked slowly to the door, watching her, as though to etch her in his memory forever. It would be tough working with her for the next two weeks, but at least he could see her.

He took a single step over the threshold, as she held the door, and with a last look at him, without saying another word to him, she closed it. He stood there for a long moment, wondering if she would open it again, and he could hear her crying softly just inside, but he didn't knock or ring the bell, or say anything, he just stood there. She never opened the door again, and after a few minutes, he walked slowly downstairs, thinking of what it had meant to him for four weeks to be there. It had been a home to him, a haven, and a refuge. And now he had cast her back into the world, and exiled himself to a life he was unsure of in California.

He went to the hospital from there, and he spent an hour with Harvey Lucas, and told him he was leaving. Harvey was disappointed, but he understood. He told Steve he was grateful that he had stayed after his accident. But he knew that Steve wanted to be with Merrie. He was sorry about the job Steve had taken in the ER, but he understood that too. If he wanted to stay married to her, he knew he had to be there.

"What did you do to Anna Gonzalez, by the way?" he asked Steve at the end of the meeting.

"Nothing. Why?" He felt awkward as he answered, and wondered if Harvey had heard about their affair. Steve and Anna had both been convinced that no one knew about it, and thought it was better that way.

"She called just before you came to work. She said that you'd been hard on her recently, over a difference of opinions, and she doesn't want to work on your shifts anymore. She asked me to change the schedule, and keep you away from each other. I get the feeling she doesn't even want to see you." Steve felt it like a physical blow, as he listened to Harvey Lucas. He had been counting on at least seeing her every day until he left, and working with her. But she was right. She wanted a clean break, and he had to let her have it, if that was what she wanted. He wondered what she was going to say to Felicia, and what the child would think, maybe that all men deserted her and her mother. It wasn't a pretty picture. But neither was his desertion of them, and he knew that.

"I guess I've had my head up my ass, as usual," he confessed to Harvey. "We had a couple of long days and rough nights, with no sleep, and I bitched at her. We had a disagreement about a diagnosis. She was right of course, and I apologized. But she's pretty tough herself. I guess she didn't forgive me. She's a hell of a good doctor, Harvey. You'll enjoy working with her."

"I already do. I'm sad to lose you, Steve. And of course you just blew my shot at research all to hell. I'm never going to get out of here now. It'll take us two years to replace you."

"That's bullshit, but I'm flattered. And I'm sorry about your research project."

"So am I. If it doesn't work out in California, come back. I'll take you back in five minutes, and get my own ass out of here in five more. I'm burnt out here."

"You love it, and you know it," and then he said pensively, "I'm going to miss it."

"No, you won't, unless you're bored to death putting ice packs on bruises. That could wear a little thin pretty quick. But you'll find something else. Keep me posted."

"I promise." And then, in as even a tone as he could produce, "Take good care of Anna. You'll be nicer to her than I was." He wanted to cry as he said it.

"Godzilla would be nicer to her than you are when you've been on for four days and haven't slept in three. Christ, when you get like that, I even hate you." They laughed and walked off to the operating room together. They both had surgeries scheduled that afternoon, and Steve wondered if he would ever see Anna again. He didn't think so. And he didn't.

For the next two weeks, he was at the hospital on a different schedule from hers, alternating days, and taking more time off than usual, so he could get organized, pack, and show their apartment. The realtor had a buyer for them at the end of the first week, at a lower price than they had wanted for it, but it was in the ballpark, and he and Meredith discussed it. In the end, she decided it was easier to sell it than to keep it empty or try to rent it. It was in escrow before he moved to California. And he had everything packed up and shipped to Palo Alto. He stayed at a hotel for the last three days, and on his last day at work, the nurses gave him a party. Anna wasn't there, as usual, and most of the nurses cried when he left. No one could imagine the trauma unit without him.

It was raining the day he left New York. He carried his medical bag, and one small suitcase. He had sent the rest with the movers. And as he boarded the plane, he realized that it was April Fool's. But all he could think about was seeing Merrie. He had missed Anna terribly the past two weeks, but he knew he had done the right thing, for her, as much as for him. If he had stayed, and continued the affair with her, it would have been worse for both of them in the end, and he knew that what he had said to her was true. She had a right to more than he could give her. He wanted her to find a great guy, neither married, nor an asshole. She deserved the best, he thought, as they circled slowly and flew west, and New York disappeared behind them.

Chapter 19

UNLIKE ANNA AND Steve in New York, Meredith and Cal spent every last moment they could together. There was a greater intensity than there had ever been between them before, and they spent their last weekend together at a small hotel in the Carmel Valley. They spent two days in bed, and went on long walks, held hands and kissed, and lay awake for hours, talking at night, after they made love, but there was no talk of the future. There was no future for them. There were only these final moments.

And on the day Steve was to arrive, Cal would be flying to London. The night before he left, he stayed at her apartment until after midnight. Even that would be gone soon. She had rented an apartment in the city, and was going to start commuting.

"I want to say I hope everything works out with Steve," he said as he left her, "but I'd be lying to you. I don't want it to work, Merrie. I want you to come back to me. Call me in Europe and tell me what happens."

But the worst of it was, she could no longer imagine a life without him. The most confusing part of it for her was that she felt almost as though she and Cal were married, and she would be cheating on him with Steven. But the relationship she and Cal had shared was a fantasy, a delusion, a time warp. They were in love, but had no real commitment to each other. Her commitment was to Steve, and Cal knew it. And although Cal said he understood that, he was angry at her for letting Steve come out, and wanting to continue their marriage, and angry at himself for not having made a commitment to her. And they both knew it was too late now for him to do it. She had to see things through with Steven.

"I can't throw away fifteen years without giving him one last chance, Cal. I can't do that. I'd always wonder what would have happened." Cal knew she was right, but in a way, he hated her for being so fair to her husband. But her sense of fair play was one of the things he had always liked about her.

"It's not going to work, and you know that," Cal said bitterly. "It's over with him, Merrie. Face it." But they were both having trouble facing the fact that she was going back to him, and for now at least, the affair with Cal was over. She was having withdrawal thinking about it. And Cal was distraught. And what's more, he didn't think Steve was right for her. "You two have nothing in common."

"We had enough to keep us married for all these years," she argued with him, but she was no longer convinced either.

"That was blind luck, and you know it. You've been

on separate career paths for years. I'm not even sure he understands what you do, or cares, or knows how good you are at it. You're wasting yourself on him." It was a plea for himself, but she knew she had to try anyway. She owed it to Steve as much as to herself, but rather than respect her for it, Cal was furious, and felt rejected. He looked like a wounded buck when he finally left her in the apartment. "Take care of yourself, Merrie," he said sadly, and kissed her one last time before he left. She cried for hours after he was gone, and when Steve arrived the next day, she was still so upset she looked sick. She was deathly pale and her eyes were swollen.

"Are you sick?" Steve asked when he arrived, worried about her.

"It's a cold, or allergies or something."

"You look awful, sweetheart." He gave her some antihistamines, but she wouldn't take them. And within two hours, he had made a mess of everything, his clothes were all over the bedroom floor, his shaving gear was all over her sink, and he was cooking her dinner.

But nothing about his arrival felt like a celebration, and he was disappointed to hear she had rented an apartment for them in the city. He had wanted her to buy a house, or at least rent one. And the night he arrived, he started in on her about having children. It was part of his reunification plan. He thought it would strengthen the bond between them.

"This is no time to even think about that," she snapped at him, wondering where Cal was then. By her calculation, he had just arrived in London. But they had promised not to call each other, and she was trying to stick by it, at least for the moment. Steve hadn't even been home for one night yet.

"This would be a perfect time to have a baby," Steve insisted. "You're happy at work, I'm not going to be too busy for a while. If you don't feel great for the first few months, I'll be around to give you a hand. And if I stay in the ER, I could even help take care of the baby."

"I don't *want* a baby. *Ever.* Can't you understand that?" she said miserably. She wasn't even sure she still wanted him, let alone a baby. "A baby will screw up my life, complicate everything. I don't want to feel sick for 'a few months.' I just don't want it."

"When did you decide that? Permanently, I mean."

"I don't know," she said, looking tired. Her nerves were stretched beyond the breaking point. They were moving, he was home, and the affair with Cal was over. The last thing she wanted to add to her misery was a baby. "I don't think I ever wanted one. You just didn't want to listen."

"That's nice to know now. When do we move?" he asked, changing the subject.

"Next weekend," she answered, and jumped when the phone rang. It was some kid trying to sell them the newspaper they already subscribed to.

"Our things should be out from New York in a couple of weeks." And he was starting the job in the ER the following Monday. Meredith felt as though there was chaos all around her.

It was a relief to go to work, and at least she didn't have to commute for the moment. She got faxes from Cal all week, about potential customers and research labs he was visiting in Europe. But all of the faxes were impersonal, and she was simply part of a distribution list. And he never called her.

By the end of the week, she was a wreck, and looked it. She looked less impeccable than usual, her nerves were frayed, and she felt as though Steve's mess had spread like a swamp through their apartment. She had forgotten what it was like living with him. It was like living in a college dorm, and she was constantly picking up socks and shirts and trousers strewn all over the living room, and his idea of dress shoes was a new pair of Nikes. And suddenly it all mattered to her. In her head, she compared everything to Cal, who looked immaculate and well dressed and perfectly pressed from the moment he got up in the morning. And everything he did and touched was as orderly as she was.

And predictably, their move that weekend was a nightmare. The new bed she had bought didn't arrive. And half of the plates she'd bought at Gump's were dropped by the movers and instantly broken. They had nowhere to sleep, nothing to sit on, and not enough to eat on.

"Come on, babe, take it easy. We'll manage till the stuff from New York comes. We'll eat on paper plates, and I'll buy a futon." It was not the way she wanted to start her days before undertaking a commute to Palo Alto. She was already depressed at the prospect of spending an hour and a half in traffic before she got there. And on Sunday night, as they sat on the floor, eating pizza with their hands, she found herself missing Cal's children. But she said none of it to Steve. There was no way she could explain to him what she was feeling.

And tensions only got worse when he started his new

job. As it turned out, they had lied to him. He was the lowest man in the ER and they were using him like a paramedic. Even the nurses had more responsibility than he did. They were having him do intakes, and all he did for the first two weeks was shuffle papers. He hated it more than he said, and when she came home at night, exhausted from work and the commute, he was sitting in front of the TV he'd bought, with an empty six-pack. And he was too depressed to even offer to cook dinner. They were living on Chinese takeout, burritos, and pizza.

"This is the shits," she finally said one night, after he'd had a particularly bad day at work, with absolutely nothing to do except baby-sit a four-year-old whose mother was having a baby. "You hate your job. I hate the commute."

"And we're starting to hate each other," he finished for her.

"I didn't say that."

"No, but it's written all over you. You're pissed off when you come home every night, and you take it out on me. What's happened to you?" But she couldn't tell him what had happened. The truth was that she was missing Cal, and the adjustment to living with Steve again had been harder than she'd ever dreamed it could be. Five and a half months of living alone, and two and a half of it with Cal had somehow changed her. She didn't feel like the same person she had been when they lived in New York together. And now everything about Steve grated on her.

"I just hate camping out and sleeping on the floor," she admitted, "and the commute to Palo Alto every morning."

"And I hate my job and this apartment," he added. "The question is, what do we like about each other? There used to be a lot of things I liked about you, Merrie. Your brains, your looks, your patience, your sense of humor. You're so damned unhappy these days, you just ooze poison." It was true, and she felt guilty as soon as he said it.

"I'm sorry, Steve. It'll get better, i promise."

But the problem was, it didn't. And when Cal got back from Europe after four weeks, it got worse again. He treated her like an enemy and a stranger. It was as though in the past four weeks, he had closed the door on her forever. She had hoped they could be friends, the way they had been in the beginning. But she realized now that too much had happened between them. Too much love and hope and loss and disappointment. And Cal was obviously angry at her for the way it had ended. For him, disappointment had turned to fury. And he had spent the four weeks in Europe seething about it. It was almost a relief to him to take it out on her every day. He seemed to enjoy it. He picked on her constantly, asked for reports and projections ten times a day, and quarreled with all of her conclusions and opinions. They almost had an open fight in one of the board meetings, which had never happened to them before, and she gave him hell about it later, and felt like a shrew when she said it.

"I don't give a damn if you disagree with me, Cal. You can discuss it with me privately, you don't have to humiliate me in public."

"You're overreacting, Meredith," he said curtly, and stormed out of her office. But so was he. That much was obvious to everyone. Their colleagues didn't know why, but they were beginning to wonder if he was going to fire her, and so was she. He seemed to have a vendetta against her. The real vendetta he had was with himself for not asking her to marry him earlier, but he had been too afraid of commitment to do that, and so grateful to just let the affair roll along. He doubted now if it would have changed anything for her because of her loyalty to Steve, but he wondered if he would have felt better. And more than anything, he hated losing.

"You look like you're in a great mood," Steve commented to her sarcastically when she got home that night, and it was just one straw too many on the proverbial camel's back, and the dam broke before she put down her briefcase.

"Actually, I'm not," she said nastily. "I had a fucking awful day today. I hate my life. And I had a flat tire on the goddamn freeway. How was your day?"

"Better than that. But not much. I treated hemorrhoids today, took a wad of gum out of a kid's ear, and put a splint on a broken finger. I figure I might get the Nobel Prize for it." He was on his fifth beer, and their furniture had been delayed for the last two weeks by flash floods in Oklahoma.

"Why don't we move to a hotel till it arrives?" she suggested when Steve told her.

"Because that makes us spoiled brats, if we can't sleep on the floor for a few weeks. You know, there was life before beds and couches."

"I'm tired of camping out here." She just wasn't in the mood to do it. Not with him, or anyone else for that matter. And she was furious with Cal for the way he was behaving. He was being petulant and childish, and he was making life miserable for her at the office. There was no place in her life that was going smoothly at the moment.

"I'm tired of your attitude," Steve looked back at her, and she looked at him with total frustration.

"I'm sorry, Steve. I just can't do better than this right now. I'm trying. But it's tough. That damned commute is going to kill me. Why don't we look at houses in Palo Alto?"

"Because the whole fucking world does not revolve around your job, Meredith. If I ever get a decent job here, I need to be close to the hospital. I can't travel an hour in traffic to get to my patients."

"I'd say a kid with a wad of gum in his ear could wait a day or two for you to get there." It was a put-down that was uncharacteristic of her, and a few minutes later, Steve stormed out of the apartment, and when he came back he was drunk, on more than just beer. He had had three tequilas, and a brandy chaser. But she didn't say a word to him. She was lying on the futon he'd bought, and pretended to be sleeping. But she'd been crying since he left the apartment. This wasn't the way she wanted to live. There was no camaraderie, no compassion, and no friendship left between them. They hardly made love anymore, and when they did, it was like making love to a stranger. They'd both had better more recently, but fortunately, neither of them said it. They just lay in lonely misery, as the walls between them grew higher and higher. The only thing worse than April was May. Despite good weather, their lives seemed to be filled with storm clouds. And they spent most of their time avoiding each other.

And when their furniture finally arrived, it was small

comfort. It was like a relic of a lost world, and none of it seemed to fit right in the apartment. And as far as Meredith was concerned, the place looked dismal.

By late May, they were ready to kill each other, and she was thinking of quitting her job. It was becoming more and more impossible for her to work with Callan.

"What do you want from me?" Steve asked one night. "I came out here to save our marriage. I took a job I hated, because I wanted to be with you. I gave up everything I cared about in New York. And you've been pissed off at me since the day I got here. What is it that you hate so much about me, Merrie?" The tragedy was that what she hated about him was the fact that he wasn't Callan. And the truth was that she didn't hate him. She just didn't love him anymore, and she couldn't bear to face it. She was angry at everyone, and mostly herself, for what had happened. But time had swept them away down a raging river, and she could no longer find him. All she could find when she looked around was the debris of their marriage.

"I don't hate you, Steve," she said quietly for once. "I'm just unhappy."

"So am I," he said sadly. The next day, he was waiting for her when she came home from work. And just like the old days, he had cooked her dinner. And as he poured her a glass of wine at the end of the meal, he told her what he had decided. "I'm leaving, Merrie," he said gently, and sounded more like the man she remembered. She hadn't seen him like this in two months. They had been savages to each other. But there was just too much distance and disappointment.

"Leaving for where?" She looked confused. But he

no longer did. He had finally come to a decision, and he wasn't happy about it, but he felt better.

"I'm going back to New York."

"When?"

"Tomorrow."

"Tomorrow? Why?" She looked dumbstruck.

"Because it's over. We both know it, and neither of us had the guts to do anything about it. This doesn't work, for either of us. I don't know what you're going to do about your job. That's up to you, if it's not working out. But I can't stay here anymore. And we can't stay married."

"Are you serious?" She was stunned. She had been beating on him like a punching bag, but it actually hadn't occurred to her that he would leave her.

"I'm very serious."

"What about your job?"

"I quit this morning. I'd be more useful rolling bandages for the Red Cross. Believe me, they won't miss me."

"Are you going back to the trauma unit?"

"I don't think so. I called some people in New York today. I want to look into doing some pro bono stuff for a while, maybe in underdeveloped countries, or in this country somewhere, like Appalachia. I don't know yet. I'll talk to them when I get back, and see where they could use me."

"You hate that kind of stuff," she reminded him, and he smiled sadly at her. She was still so beautiful, but she wasn't his any longer. He had lost her when she left New York, and he never knew it. But he knew it now. And he was finally willing to face it. He had to.

"I think I've grown up," he said quietly. "I think I'd like to do that kind of work for a while, and feel like I'm putting something back into the human race, and not just patching up broken bodies."

"But what about us?"

"I don't think there is an 'us' anymore. In fact, I'm sure of it. That's why I'm going."

"I don't want you to go," she said, as tears started to roll down her cheeks, and she reached out to him with a look of panic. He was all she had in the world, she had no family, and no friends here. And she didn't have Cal anymore. She had no one. She had Steve, and he was telling her it was over. It was a terrifying feeling.

"I can't stay here, Merrie. It's not good for either of us."

"Do you want me to quit my job and come with you?" she asked and he shook his head.

"No, I don't. You have a life here. I don't. I'll always be there for you. Wherever I am, if you need me, I'll come running. You don't forget fifteen years, Merrie. But I can't do this anymore. It's over." He sounded calm and relieved and he knew that when she adjusted to it, she'd be relieved too. "I'm sorry, babe," he said softly.

"Don't leave me," she whispered.

"Don't say that." He walked around the table and put his arms around her, but he could not be swayed by anything she did or said or offered.

"When are you going?" she asked him again.

"Tomorrow morning."

"What about our investments, and your share of the apartment money? You can't just disappear. We have to figure all that out. Have you called a lawyer?'' She was in shock over what he was saying.

"No, I haven't called a lawyer. You can do that whenever you want to. And I don't want to figure out anything, on our investments or the apartment. You made that money, I didn't. It's yours. I don't want anything, Merrie. I wanted you. But that's all over.''

"I can't believe this," she said, horrified by what he was saying. "Do you really mean it?''

"I do. We should have done this months ago when you were finding excuses not to come to New York. I didn't want to see what had happened, and I don't think you did either.'' He didn't ask her if there was someone else, although he was beginning to suspect there might have been. But there wasn't now. She seemed as lonely and unhappy as he did. And he didn't tell her about Anna. It was no longer important, and he didn't want to hurt her. For him, the marriage was over, and Anna was a thing of the past, and had never impacted on their marriage. If anything, she had inspired him to save it. But he knew now that nothing could have done that. It was a relief to finally know it.

Meredith lay in his arms and sobbed that night and she called in sick to work the next morning. She stayed with him until he left, and it was a terrible moment when he walked out of the apartment. She was crying piteously, and he held her for a long time, and then finally said he had to go. He didn't want to miss his flight, and there was a cab downstairs, waiting to take him to the airport.

"I love you, Steve," she cried. "I'm so sorry." She was almost incoherent.

"So am I." He kissed her one last time, picked up his bag, and hurried down the stairs to the cab. And as she watched from the window, he waved, and then was gone, as she stood staring in disbelief. Fifteen years of her life were over. And she had no one now. Not Steve. Not Cal. No one. Just herself to rely on. Steve had walked off to a new life. And as she stood there, looking out the window, she felt as though she had nothing.

Chapter 20

MEREDITH STAYED HOME from work for two days, and when she finally went back, she was unusually quiet. Callan was as disagreeable to her as he always was now, and she said nothing to him. Her personal life was no longer his problem. And she had nothing to say to him, except about what concerned his business.

As the shock of Steve's departure settled a little bit, she began to realize he had been right. They had been carrying a dead body around for seven months, and it needed to be buried.

And as she calmed down, she felt better able to deal with business. Steve had called from New York, to make sure she was all right, and he said he was staying with friends, and left her the number. But as lonely as she felt at night, she didn't call him. He had a right to his new life, and she knew she needed to recover.

She was thinking of quitting her job at Dow Tech and going back to New York. But she had decided to wait a month, and see if things got any better with

Callan. He still seemed angry with her, but she was firmer with him now, and when he was unreasonable with her, she pushed back, and he was slowly backing off and getting the message. The respect that they had once shared seemed to be returning, if not the friendship.

And three weeks after Steve left, he asked her to help him entertain some analysts from London. She wasn't anxious to go out with him at night, but he said he was taking them to dinner in the city, and it was easy for her to join them. He told her he'd made a reservation at Fleur de Lys, and he'd pick her up on the way. She said she'd rather meet him there, but he insisted.

The dinner went very well, and he seemed to relax. She wore a new dress, and had her hair cut that morning, and she was finally beginning to feel like her old self, not the one who'd been in love with Cal, but the person she'd been even before she'd met him. And he seemed to sense it. He was respectful of her at dinner that night, and almost pleasant, but not quite. And after dinner, he drove her back to her apartment.

"How's Steve?" he asked politely as he pulled up in front of her building. "Does he like his new job?"

"Very much," she answered, and thanked him for dinner.

"How are the kids?" she asked, and he said they were leaving in a few days to spend a month with their mother. It was late June and school was out. She didn't tell him how much she had missed them, or ask if they'd inquired about her. His children were no longer any of her business, just as her life wasn't his. They were simply employer and employee now.

"Are you enjoying living in the city?" he asked her as she started to get out.

"The commute is a little rough, but I like the apartment." It was a lie too. But he had no right to the truth now. There were a lot of new things she had to get used to. Being alone. Being divorced. She had called a lawyer and started divorce proceedings. It was all very simple. Steve wanted nothing from her. He had walked away empty-handed, and preferred it that way.

"I'd like to see your apartment sometime," he said, as he walked her to the door of the building, and she wanted to ask him why, but didn't.

"You'll have to come by for a drink the next time you're in the city." But it was only idle conversation. She had no intention of inviting him anytime in the future.

"Which one is it?" he asked, looking up. It was a fairly pleasant building in Pacific Heights, but nothing special.

"The top floor," she said, and then realized it was dark.

"Is Steve at work?"

"No, he's in New York," she said honestly, and then decided that it didn't matter if he knew the truth now. It was over between them. "Actually," she hesitated for a fraction of an instant, "he doesn't live here anymore. We're getting divorced. He left last month. He's in New York right now. He's going to do pro bono work in an underdeveloped country." Callan looked as though she'd slapped him.

"Why didn't you tell me, Meredith?"

"I didn't think it was important."

"It would have been once," he reproached her. He looked hurt that she hadn't told him, but it told him something. It told him that she expected nothing from him, and she didn't.

"That was three months ago, Cal. And we had an agreement. Whenever Steve came back, the affair was over. You never said you wanted more than that. I didn't want to press myself on you when he left." And she had realized since Steve was gone that she didn't want just an affair again, she wanted more than that, a real life, with a man who wanted to make a commitment. "I didn't think it was right to call you when Steve left. And you've been pretty angry at me since it ended."

"I was hurt. And I was mad at myself for being so stupid. I was afraid to commit, Meredith. And maybe it was easier to let you go back to him, no matter how much I loved you. Besides, you needed to do that."

She nodded. She couldn't deny that.

"And if I hadn't? What would have been different? You don't believe in commitment, Cal. You said so yourself. I respect that."

"It must have been a rough three months," he said gently, without challenging what she'd said about his feelings about commitment. But what he had said about loving her brought tears to her eyes, and she didn't want him to see them.

"It was rough. But I learned a lot. Not only about Steve, but about myself, who I am, and what I want." Something about her had softened in the past three months, and he could sense that.

"What do you want, Merrie?" he asked, watching

her carefully. She seemed different to him, and he liked it.

"I want a lot of things. Honesty, somebody, and something real. What I did was wrong. And I paid a price for it. A big price. But I know that I'm willing to be there for someone, and I want someone to be there for me. Not just for the good times." She smiled at him, but from a great distance. "I might even want kids one day. You were probably right about that. I don't think it was ever right with Steve, or not for a long time anyway. We were too different, and I think I knew that." And then she surprised him further. "I'm thinking of going back to New York. I was going to talk to you about it in a few weeks. I don't really belong here."

"I thought you loved it here." He looked personally wounded as they stood talking on the sidewalk.

"I thought so too. But I think it was a bad decision to come out here." It had cost her her marriage. They might still have been married if she'd stayed in New York, but it was too late for that now. She had felt compelled to come out, and she and Steve had been pulled apart by irresistible forces.

"I think you'd be wrong to go back there," he said firmly.

"Don't worry, I'll give you plenty of notice, Cal. Not like Charlie."

"I know you would. I was thinking of you when I said it."

"I'll let you know what I decide."

"I want to be part of that decision. Let's talk about it."

"Let's not," she said quietly. "We don't have a lot to talk about, do we?"

"I thought we were friends." He looked hurt by what she had said to him, and confused by everything she had told him. It was a lot to digest at one sitting.

"I thought so too," she said quietly. "Maybe we weren't."

"You did some wonderful things for me, Merrie. Not just for my business, for me. I was very upset when you went back to Steve. You know that."

"I know," she said sadly. "You had a right to be. I'm sorry I put you through that."

"I knew what I was doing. I just didn't know how it would turn out. Neither did you. I actually thought it would work with you two. I'm surprised it didn't."

"I missed you too much," she smiled at him, honest with him. "I changed too much once I left New York. I did a lot of growing up here. Some of it thanks to you."

"So I gather. Would it be inappropriate if I asked you what you're doing tomorrow night for dinner?"

"Not inappropriate," she smiled, "but probably foolish. We've already been there. We've given it up. We've gotten over it. Why do it?"

"Because I want to talk to you." He looked intense as he said it.

"Let's not do that. What would we talk about, Cal? Your hatred of commitment? The reasons why two people shouldn't trust each other, and can't count on each other? I don't want to talk about that. I've heard it. I got it. We've had our time. We've done it. We've both moved on. Let's leave it at that." She looked determined as she said it.

"You're not giving me a chance here."

She laughed softly. "I'm trying hard not to. I don't want you to confuse me." She didn't want to start an affair with him again, and take the risk of hurting each other. She felt older, wiser, and far more cautious.

"Let me try at least," he smiled at her, and she saw the man she had once fallen in love with. But she no longer wanted to see him. Steve was gone. And Cal was gone too. All she wanted to see in him was her CEO now. "I'll call you tomorrow," he said firmly. And she told herself she wouldn't answer the phone, thanked him for dinner again, and left him on the sidewalk, while she walked upstairs to her apartment. He was still standing there when he saw her turn on the lights, and then got in his car and drove away, and she stood at her window, thinking about him. She wasn't going to dinner with him. There was no point. For her at least, it was over.

He called her the next day, as he said he would, and she told him she was busy that night, and had forgotten. And when the phone rang late that night, she didn't answer. She had nothing to say to him. And there was nothing she wanted to hear from him. She felt strangely peaceful as she let the phone ring.

And on Sunday morning, when she went out for a walk, she found him waiting outside, and she was startled.

"What are you doing here, Cal?" she asked, looking confused, and he laughed, looking somewhat sheepish.

"Waiting for you. Since you won't answer your phone or have dinner with me, you leave me no choice but to hang around like a juvenile delinquent."

"You could have seen me at the office."

"I don't want to discuss business with you, Merrie."

"Why not? I'm good at it."

"I know. We both are. But we're lousy at this other

stuff. At least I am. I think you've gotten a little better
at it, but you've had more practice. And I'm not as
brave as you are. In fact, I've been scared to death for
the last nine years . . . scared of everything you represented. Love, caring, sharing a life with someone, trust-
ing, believing in them, being vulnerable. . . . I love
you, Merrie. Come back to me. Teach me to do this.''
He looked every bit as vulnerable as he said he wanted
to be, and she wanted to reach out and hug him, but
she didn't.

"How can I teach you anything, when I've made
such a mess of my own life?'' There were tears in her
eyes as she said it.

"You haven't made a mess of it. You've done the
right things. I think we were both scared. I thought I'd
go crazy when you went back to Steve. I was like a
madman in Europe.''

"I wasn't so terrific here,'' she admitted. "I was
pretty awful. Poor Steve. I made his life a living hell
while he was here.''

"Is that why he left you?'' Cal asked with interest.

"He left me because he was smart enough to figure
out that we didn't love each other anymore. Not
enough. And he was brave enough to do something
about it. I wasn't. He did the right thing. It just took me
a while to see it.''

"It's taken me a while to see how much you meant
to me, Merrie . . . how much you still mean to
me. . . . I still love you.''

"And then what? We hang around together for
years, too afraid to hold a hand out to each other. I
want more than that, Cal. I need it.''

"So do I. I'm holding a hand out to you now. Give

me a chance . . . let's try it. We'll make it work this time. It wasn't so bad last time.''

"And then what? What if it does work?"

"Then we get married," he said, and she stared at him, trying to absorb what he was saying to her. But he wasn't finished. "In fact," he said, looking terrified but determined, "I want to marry you now."

"Why?" She stood on the sidewalk, looking at him, wondering if he meant it.

"Because I love you, that's why. Isn't that how it's supposed to work?"

"I don't know, Cal. Is it?" There were tears in her eyes as he pulled her toward him and held her.

"I never stopped loving you. I tried hating you for a while, but it didn't work. I missed you so much I thought it would kill me."

"Me too," she said softly, wanting to believe in him, and afraid to do it.

"Marry me, Merrie . . . please. . . ."

"What if it doesn't work?" she whispered. She had just watched fifteen years of her life go down the drain. It was hard to trust anything else now. But somewhere in her heart, she knew she had to. She had no choice, just as she hadn't from the beginning. She had been drawn to him by something so powerful, so real, so deep within them both, that neither of them could resist it.

"It will work, you know," he said as he held her. "This is right for both of us, and we know it." She nodded, and he pulled away just enough to smile at her and then kiss her. And as they walked away hand in hand, he was talking animatedly about their plans, and she was smiling.

Chapter 21

WHEN STEVE GOT off the plane in New York, he went to the agency to find the kind of work he was looking for. He had heard about it from a doctor he knew from med school. It was a small dingy place with a battered sign outside. And it looked as bad as the places where they sent their clients. They gave Steve a brochure, a long list of countries that they served, and a description of the kind of jobs they offered. It seemed like the right thing to him, and they told him it would take them several weeks to process his application. But he had nothing but time on his hands, and no pressure to go anywhere in a hurry. He thought of calling Harvey Lucas to say hello, but he wasn't ready to talk about Merrie yet, or the fiasco in California, so he decided not to.

He stayed with an old med school friend, and spent most of his time walking, and going to museums. It was the first time in years that he had some leisure time. He went to the beach, and saw all the latest movies. And he thought constantly about calling Anna. But he thought it best to leave that a closed chapter.

And at the end of June, the agency finally called him. They had processed his application, and had several jobs for him. They offered him Peru, Chile, Kentucky, and Botswana. And the jobs they described sounded uncomfortable, but intriguing. In the end, he opted for Kentucky. He no longer felt the need to flee from Meredith. And they told him to come back in four days to sign the papers. It would be a two-year commitment.

Knowing that he was going to leave again, he decided to call Harvey Lucas. And after he did, he decided to drop in on Anna. He wanted to say goodbye to her, and to tell her that he was sorry he had been so hard on her when he left for California. He had no intention of trying to start something up with her again, he knew he had no right to do that. He just wanted to make sure she was all right, and maybe see Felicia. He had missed her. He had missed them both, and he hated the fact that he had never said good-bye to Felicia. It was the wrong way to leave a child, he knew, to simply disappear out of her life without farewell or explanation. And he felt even worse about the way he'd left her mother.

It was a warm, sunny day in June. The first big heat wave hadn't hit the city yet, and people looked happier than usual, and still in good humor. He called to see if she was in, and a baby-sitter said she'd be home from work by three. So he waited until five to drop in on her. He had decided by then that if he called her, she probably wouldn't agree to see him.

He took the bus up Broadway, and walked west on 102nd, until he reached the familiar building. And it looked slightly better in the summer sunshine, but not much. It was still an abysmal place, and he hated that she had to live there. But not nearly as much as she did.

He was about to ring the bell on the panel downstairs, when two young men in T-shirts and jeans approached him. They looked as though they were going to ask him a question. One of them said something to Steve, and he turned without hesitation toward them.

"Sorry, what did you say?" He was thinking about Anna, and had been away from New York just long enough to forget being cautious.

"I said, give me your wallet, asshole." Steve stared at them for an instant, not sure whether to give it to them, or try and talk them out of it, and as he hesitated, the second man pulled a gun on him. And he saw that the first one had a switchblade.

"Take it easy, guys, I'll give you my wallet, but there's not much in it." And as he reached for it, his hands were shaking. He started to hand it to the man with the knife, and the younger one with the gun looked nervous.

"Hurry up, man . . . we don't have all day. . . ." The one with the knife grabbed the wallet, as Steve looked at him, and without a word of warning or a sound, the other one shot him, at close range, somewhere in the middle of his rib cage. Steve made a sudden choking sound, and instinctively touched the bell he had been about to ring, and fell slowly down the stairs of Anna's building toward the sidewalk.

He lay there facedown, unable to move, and one by

one windows began to open, and he could hear people far above him, shouting, but by then the men had run away and there was no one to stop them.

He could hear voices far away, and after a while, there was someone pulling at him, but as they turned him slowly to survey the damage, he slid slowly into blackness.

He was unconscious as the people in the building ran down, and he never knew that they had gone to get Anna. Everyone in the building knew she was a doctor. She found him in the midst of a small crowd, and she was carrying her medical bag. They had told her someone had been wounded. She had heard the shot, but at first thought nothing of it. She thought maybe a truck had backfired. But as she looked at him, she heard sirens. Someone had called for an ambulance, and as she saw the wound, and then his face, and knew who it was, she realized with horror that he had come to see her.

She was holding a bandage to his gut when the paramedics arrived, and she told them what she needed. They got him on a gurney as quickly as they could, and she told one of her neighbors to watch Felicia.

"Are you going with him?" The paramedics looked startled, as she gave them the name of the trauma unit where she worked, and they agreed to take him there. Steve was still unconscious and bleeding profusely. And as they ran an IV into him, and she kept pressure on the gaping wound, she wondered why he had been there. She had heard nothing from him in three months, and hadn't expected to see him.

His blood pressure was dropping as they reached the hospital, and luckily, Lucas was on duty. Anna explained what had happened to him, or what she knew of it, and Harvey ran to surgery to get ready. Anna was still with Steve, and the trauma team had taken over from the paramedics.

"Does anyone know his name?" a nurse shouted at them, and Anna answered for him.

"It's Steve Whitman." Her face was gray as she watched him.

"What the hell's he doing here? I thought he was in California," one of the nurses said as she cut his clothes off with a scissor.

"Well, he's here apparently," Anna said tersely, fighting to put on scrubs as she followed the team to surgery, "and he has a hole in his gut the size of Texas. Jesus, can't you guys move any faster?"

"We are moving . . . we're moving. . . ." But they were losing him and Anna could see it. They were at the door to surgery by then, and Lucas was waiting for them. He already had a mask, a cap, and gloves on.

"He's going, Harvey," Anna whispered, as she went to scrub. She wanted to stay with Steve, but she also wanted to assist Harvey and she had to scrub to do it.

His blood pressure was still dropping by the time she got back to him, and they had already intubated him. Steve knew nothing of what had happened. He was deeply unconscious as the people who had been his friends fought to save him.

"What the hell happened?" Harvey asked, as they dug for the bullet.

"I think he was coming to see me," Anna said through clenched teeth as she watched, "and someone shot him."

"You're a dangerous woman," Harvey said, still unable to find or dislodge the bullet, and they were pumping blood into him as fast as they could get it.

"And he's an asshole," Anna added as tears rolled into her mask, and she finally begged Lucas to let her try it. "I'm good at this," she said.

"So they tell me."

She took over from Harvey then, and dug deep for the bullet. And with a small grunting noise, she found it. But it took her another twenty minutes to dislodge it. His blood pressure was stable by then, but he was still hemorrhaging badly. It took them another hour to stop it. But three hours after they took him into surgery, Harvey let Anna do the sutures. And Steve was finally in stable condition.

"I think he'll make it," Harvey said, as they wheeled Steve into Recovery and he took a good look at Anna. "You look like shit, Dr. Gonzalez."

"Thank you, Dr. Lucas."

She still looked gray, and her knees were shaking now that it was over. And then she went to sit next to Steve. It was another two hours before he stirred, and when he did, he was still groggy, but he saw her sitting there next to him, and he smiled when he saw her.

"Anna? I was coming to see you," he whispered.

"You never made it." She smiled down at him as tears filled her eyes again. She thought she would never see him again, and then she thought he would die before they could save him.

"What happened?" he whispered again.

"Someone shot you."

"Nice neighborhood," he said, and she smiled through her tears at him.

"What were you doing there?" But she knew before he answered.

"I came to say good-bye to you."

"You did that three months ago," she said gently, as he drifted off to sleep again, and then opened his eyes and continued the conversation.

"I wanted to see Felicia. I miss her."

"She misses you too," and then she decided to throw caution to the winds and tell him the truth. "So do I, even if you are an asshole."

He smiled at her then. "I'm getting divorced and going to Kentucky."

Anna frowned as she listened to him. "I think he's hallucinating," she said to one of the nurses.

"I heard that. It's true . . . divorced . . . Kentucky . . ." Steve insisted weakly.

"Don't talk so much . . . you can explain later. Why don't you sleep for a while?" she said gently. She was still worried about him.

"My chest hurts."

"Stop complaining. You had a great surgeon." Anna looked down at him with a grin, as he watched her.

"Who did it?"

"I did. You had a bullet the size of an egg in your chest. Now shut up and go to sleep before I hit you."

"I love you, Anna," he whispered softly but she heard him.

She leaned down close to his face so he could hear her better and the others wouldn't. "I love you too."

"Marry me." He was groggy but she knew he meant it.

"Never," she answered. "I'm allergic to it."

". . . good thing to do . . . good for Felicia . . . good for me . . . good for you . . . have more kids . . . a baby. . . ."

"I don't need a baby, if I have you to take care of. You'd be more trouble than ten children. . . ."

"Will you marry me?"

"No. Besides, you're on drugs. You do not know what you're saying."

"Yes, I do . . . and I'm not married. . . ." He sounded stronger as he said it. "And I'm not gay."

"What's he talking about?" Harvey Lucas came to check on him, and caught the tail end of the conversation. "Who said he was gay? He's not gay."

"No, but he's an asshole," Anna said firmly with a glance at Steve. He was coming out of the anesthetic nicely and Lucas was pleased, and left them to continue the conversation. "I thought you were gone forever," she said gently.

"I thought so too . . . I'm back. . . ."

"So I see. Why don't you stay here? You'll have to explain later about Kentucky." But even in his drugged state, he remembered that he hadn't signed the papers. He remembered a lot of things, leaving Merrie, leaving California . . . going to see Anna . . . and then he didn't remember much after that . . . until he saw her in the Recovery room and his chest hurt.

"I love you," he said again, determined to convince her.

"I love you too, now rest for a while. I'll be here. I'm not going anywhere, Steve." She had never been as happy to see a face as she had been to see his, especially once she knew he'd make it. She had cried over him every night for three months. But now he had come to see her, for whatever reason.

"Why won't you marry me?"

"I don't need to. Besides, I told you, I hate rich guys."

"I gave it all back to her . . . I'm poor now. . . ."

"You're crazy," she said, smiling at him.

"You too," he said, smiling at her, and then he drifted off to sleep as she watched him.

"How's he doing? Is he okay?" Harvey came by to check his vital signs and was satisfied with what he was seeing.

"He will be," Anna answered him, as he left them alone again. Steve was in good hands. He had been a lucky guy that afternoon. But no luckier than he deserved. Harvey glanced over his shoulder as he walked out of the Recovery room, and saw Anna holding Steve's hand and smiling at him.

"Is that Steve Whitman in there?" one of the nurses asked him. The word was out in the trauma unit.

"It sure is."

"What's he doing here?" Everyone was confused. They thought he was still in California.

"Recuperating, I hope," Harvey Lucas answered, "so he can take his old job back and I can get the hell out of here, and finally do some research."

"Is he coming back?" the nurses at the desk asked Harvey.

"Could be," Harvey smiled at her. "Could be. Who knows? Stranger things have happened."

And as she sat next to him and watched him sleep, Anna held his hand and watched him. Just being there with him was all she'd ever wanted or needed. She didn't need promises or wedding rings, or money. She just wanted to be with him. And he was back now. For both of them, the nightmare and the loneliness were over.

WATCH FOR THE NEW NOVEL
FROM

DANIELLE STEEL

On Sale in Hardcover
June 27, 2006

COMING OUT

Olympia Crawford Rubinstein has a way of managing her thriving family with grace and humor. With twin daughters finishing high school, a son at Dartmouth, and a kindergartener from her second marriage, there seems to be nothing Olympia can't handle . . . until one sunny day in May, when she opens an invitation for her daughters to attend the most exclusive coming out ball in New York—and chaos erupts all around her. . . .

From a son's crisis to a daughter's heartbreak, from a case of the chickenpox to a political debate raging in her household, Olympia is on the verge of surrender . . . until a series of startling choices and changes of heart, family and friends turn a night of calamity into an evening of magic. As old wounds are healed, barriers are shattered and new traditions are born, and a debutante ball becomes a catalyst for change, revelation, acceptance, and love.

Please turn the page for a special advance preview.

COMING OUT

on sale June 27, 2006

Chapter 1

Olympia Crawford Rubinstein was whizzing around her kitchen on a sunny May morning, in the brownstone she shared with her family on Jane Street in New York, near the old meat-packing district of the West Village. It had long since become a fashionable neighborhood of mostly modern apartment buildings with doormen, and old renovated brownstones. Olympia was fixing lunch for her five-year-old son, Max. The school bus was due to drop him off in a few minutes. He was in kindergarten at Dalton, and Friday was a half day for him. She always took Fridays off to spend them with him. Although Olympia had three older children from her first marriage, Max was Olympia and Harry's only child.

Olympia and Harry had restored the house six

years before, when she was pregnant with Max. Before that, they had lived in her Park Avenue apartment, which she had previously shared with her three children after her divorce. And then Harry joined them. She had met Harry Rubinstein a year after her divorce. And now, she and Harry had been married for thirteen years. They had waited eight years to have Max, and his parents and siblings adored him. He was a loving, funny, happy child.

Olympia was a partner in a booming law practice, specializing in civil rights issues and class action lawsuits. Her favorite cases, and what she specialized in, were those that involved discrimination against or some form of abuse of children. She had made a name for herself in her field. She had gone to law school after her divorce, fifteen years before, and married Harry two years later. He had been one of her law professors at Columbia Law School, and was now a judge on the federal court of appeals. He had recently been considered for a seat on the Supreme Court. In the end, they hadn't appointed him, but he'd come close, and she and Harry both hoped that the next time a vacancy came up, he would get it.

She and Harry shared all the same beliefs, values, and passions—even though they came from very different backgrounds. He came from an Orthodox Jewish home, and both his parents had been Holocaust survivors as children. His mother had gone to Dachau from Munich at ten, and lost her entire family. His father had been one of the few survivors of Auschwitz, and they met in Israel later. They had married as teenagers, moved to London, and from there to the States. Both had lost their entire families, and their only son had become the focus of all their energies, dreams, and hopes. They had worked like slaves all their lives to give him an education, his father as a tailor and his mother as a seamstress, working in the sweatshops of the Lower East Side, and eventually on Seventh Avenue in what was later referred to as the garment district. His father had died just after Harry and Olympia married. Harry's greatest regret was that his father hadn't known Max. Harry's mother, Frieda, was a strong, intelligent, loving woman of seventy-six, who thought her son was a genius, and her grandson a prodigy.

Olympia had converted from her staunch Episcopalian background to Judaism when she married Harry. They attended a Reform synagogue, and Olympia said the prayers for Shabbat every Friday night, and lit the candles, which never failed to touch Harry. There was no doubt in Harry's mind, or even his mother's, that Olympia was a fantastic woman, a great mother to all her children, a terrific attorney, and a wonderful wife. Like Olympia, Harry had been married before, but he had no other children. Olympia was turning forty-five in July, and Harry was fifty-three. They were well matched in all ways, though their backgrounds couldn't have been more different. Even physically, they were an interesting and complementary combination. Her hair was blond, her eyes were blue; he was dark, with dark brown eyes; she was tiny; he was a huge teddy bear of a man, with a quick smile and an easygoing disposition. Olympia was shy and serious, though prone to easy laughter, especially when it was provoked by Harry or her children. She was a remarkably dutiful and loving daughter-in-law to Harry's mother, Frieda.

Olympia's background was entirely different from Harry's. The Crawfords were an illustrious and extremely social New York family, whose blue-blooded ancestors had intermarried with Astors and Vanderbilts for generations. Buildings and academic institutions were named after them, and theirs had been one of the largest "cottages" in

Newport, Rhode Island, where they spent the summers. The family fortune had dwindled to next to nothing by the time her parents died when she was in college, and she had been forced to sell the "cottage" and surrounding estate to pay their debts and taxes. Her father had never really worked, and as one of her distant relatives had said after he died, "he had a small fortune, he had made it from a large one." By the time she cleaned up all their debts and sold their property, there was simply no money, just rivers of blue blood and aristocratic connections. She had just enough left to pay for her education, and put a small nest egg away, which later paid for law school.

She married her college sweetheart, Chauncey Bedham Walker IV, six months after she graduated from Vassar, and he from Princeton. He had been charming, handsome, and fun-loving, the captain of the crew team, an expert horseman, played polo, and when they met, Olympia was understandably dazzled by him. Olympia was head over heels in love with him, and didn't give a damn about his family's enormous fortune. She was totally in love with Chauncey, enough so as not to notice that he drank too much, played constantly, had a roving eye, and spent far too much money. He went to work in his family's investment bank, and did anything he wanted, which eventually included going to work as seldom as possible, spending literally no time with her, and having random affairs with a multitude of women. By the time she knew what was happening, she and Chauncey had three children. Charlie came along two years after they were married, and his identical twin sisters, Virginia and Veronica, three years later. When she and Chauncey split up seven years after they married, Charlie was five, the twins two, and Olympia was twenty-nine years old. As soon as they separated, he quit his job at the bank, and went to live in Newport with his grandmother, the doyenne of Newport and Palm Beach society, and devoted himself to playing polo and chasing women.

A year later Chauncey married Felicia Weatherton, who was the perfect mate for him. They built a house on his grandmother's estate, which he ultimately inherited, filled her stables with new horses, and had three daughters in four years. A year after Chauncey married Felicia, Olympia married Harry Rubinstein, which Chauncey found not only ridiculous but appalling. He was rendered speechless when their son, Charlie, told him his mother had converted to the

Jewish faith. He had been equally shocked earlier when Olympia enrolled in law school, all of which proved to him, as Olympia had figured out long before, that despite the similarity of their ancestry, she and Chauncey had absolutely nothing in common, and never would. As she grew older, the ideas that had seemed normal to her in her youth appalled her. Almost all of Chauncey's values, or lack of them, were anathema to her.

The fifteen years since their divorce had been years of erratic truce, and occasional minor warfare, usually over money. He supported their three children decently, though not generously. Despite what he had inherited from his family, Chauncey was stingy with his first family, and far more generous with his second wife and their children. To add insult to injury, he had forced Olympia to agree that she would never urge their children to become Jewish. It wasn't an issue anyway. She had no intention of doing so. Olympia's conversion was a private, personal decision between her and Harry. Chauncey was unabashedly anti-Semitic. Harry thought Olympia's first husband was pompous, arrogant, and useless. Other than the fact that he was her children's father and she had loved him when she married him, for the past fifteen years, Olympia found it impossible to defend him. Prejudice was Chauncey's middle name. There was absolutely nothing politically correct about him or Felicia, and Harry loathed him. They represented everything he detested, and he could never understand how Olympia had tolerated him for ten minutes, let alone seven years of marriage. People like Chauncey and Felicia, and the whole hierarchy of Newport society, and all it stood for, were a mystery to Harry. He wanted to know nothing about it, and Olympia's occasional explanations were wasted on him.

Harry adored Olympia, her three children, and their son, Max. And in some ways, her daughter Veronica seemed more like Harry's daughter than Chauncey's. They shared all of the same extremely liberal, socially responsible ideas. Virginia, her twin, was much more of a throwback to their Newport ancestry, and was far more frivolous than her twin sister. Charlie, their older brother, was at Dartmouth, studying theology and threatening to become a minister. Max was a being unto himself, a wise old soul, who his grandmother swore was just like her own father, who had been a rabbi in Germany before being sent to Dachau, where he had helped as many people as he could before he was exterminated along with the rest of her family.

The stories of Frieda's childhood and lost loved ones always made Olympia weep. Frieda Rubinstein had a number tattooed on the inside of her left wrist, which was a sobering reminder of the childhood the Nazis had stolen from her. Because of it, she had worn long sleeves all her life, and still did. Olympia frequently bought beautiful silk blouses and long-sleeved sweaters for her. There was a powerful bond of love and respect between the two women, which continued to deepen over the years.

Olympia heard the mail being pushed through the slot in the front door, went to get it, and tossed it on the kitchen table as she finished making Max's lunch. With perfect timing, she heard the doorbell ring at almost precisely the same instant. Max was home from school, and she was looking forward to spending the afternoon with him. Their Fridays together were always special. Olympia knew she had the best of both worlds, a career she loved and that satisfied her, and a family that was the hub and core of her emotional existence. Each seemed to enhance and complement the other.

COMING THIS FALL

H.R.H.

BY

DANIELLE STEEL

On Sale in Hardcover
October 31, 2006

In a novel where ancient traditions conflict with
reality and the pressures of modern life, a young
European princess proves that simplicity,
courage, and dignity win the day and forever
alter her world.

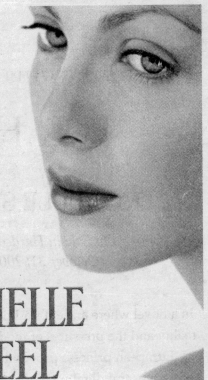

DANIELLE STEEL

H.R.H.

Everyone reads
DANIELLE STEEL

Accident
Answered Prayers
Bittersweet
Changes
The Cottage
Crossings
Daddy
Dating Game
Echoes
Family Album
Fine Things
Five Days in Paris
Full Circle
The Ghost
The Gift
Granny Dan
Heartbeat
His Bright Light
The House
The House on Hope Street
Impossible
Irresistible Forces
Jewels
Johnny Angel
Journey
Kaleidoscope
The Kiss
The Klone & I
Leap of Faith
Lightning
Lone Eagle
The Long Road Home
Love: Poems
Loving

SEE THE NEXT PAGE FOR MORE DANIELLE STEEL TITLES

DS FICa 3/06